Praise for the King's Curse

The King's Curse is a captivating adventure tale of one girl's quest to heal a kingdom through the power of God's love. It's got all the ingredients you could ask for in a fantasy novel: fantastical creatures (including a shape-shifting dragon), nail-biting action, sweet romance, and a colorful cast of characters that turn out to be not what you expected. I love that Rogers is unafraid to bring a Christian worldview into her wonderfully complex and multi-layered fantasy world. *The King's Curse* will transport you to a realm of wonder and mystery, and you might never want to go home again.

Gina Detwiler, author of The *Forlorn* Series

THE
KING'S
CURSE

THE CURSED LANDS BOOK I

J. F. ROGERS

NOBLEBRIGHT
PUBLISHING

www.noblebrightpublishing.com

The King's Curse - The Cursed Lands Book I

Edited by Brilliant Cut Editing
Cover design by 100 Covers

ISBN: 978-1-955169-15-8

Published by Noblebright Publishing
Sanford, Maine
www.noblebrightpublishing.com

"Thou shalt have no other gods before Me."
- Exodus 20:3

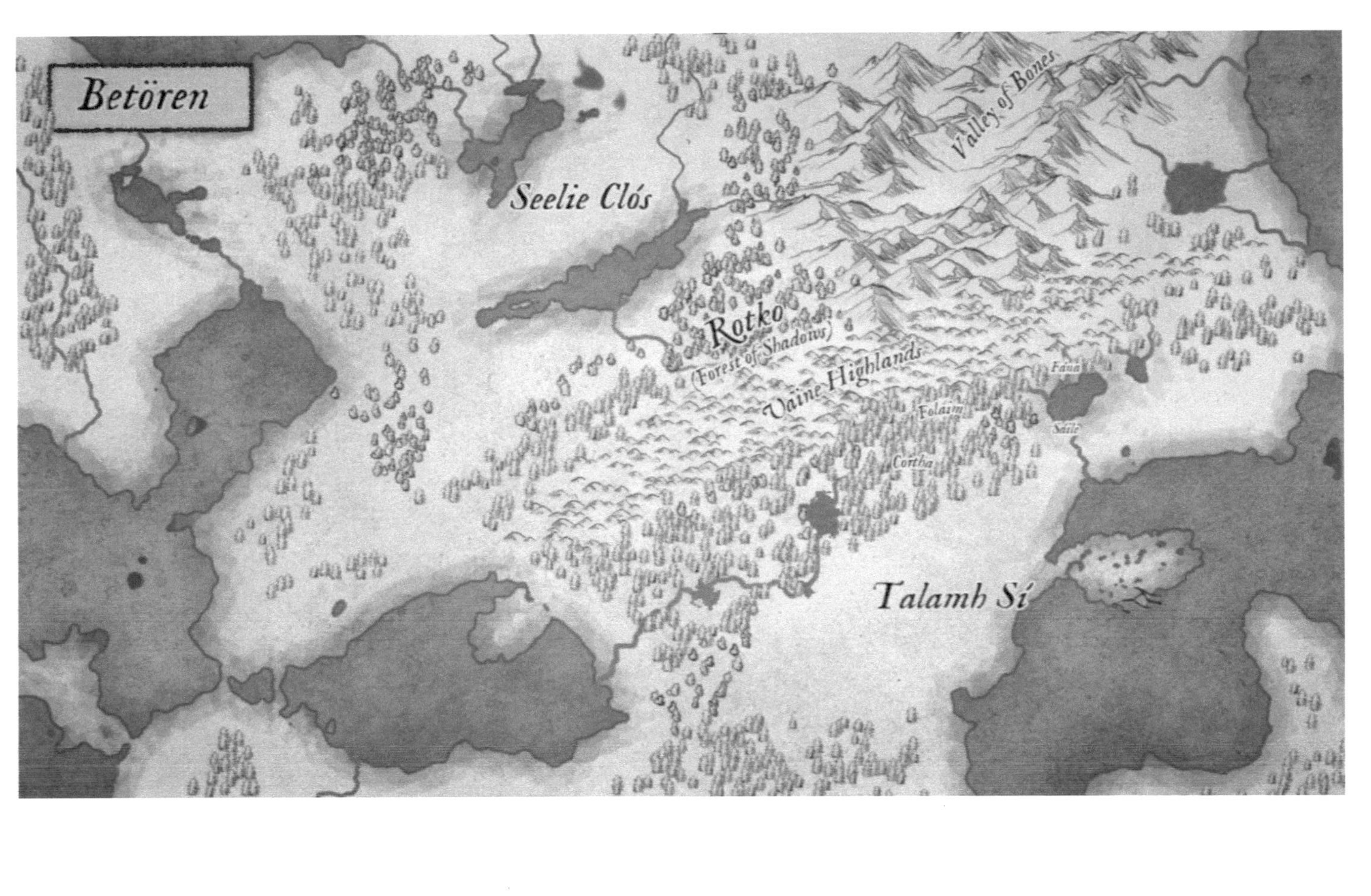

Betören
Seelie Clós
Valley of Bones
Rotko
(Forest of Shadows)
Väine Highlands
Fáua
Folaim
Sáile
Cortha
Talamh Sí

PRONUNCIATION GUIDE

PEOPLE

Auberon \ O-bər-ahn \ King of Talamh Sí

Balder \ BAHL-dər \ a strange man

Beagan \ BEE-gun \ Colleen's adopted brother

Corwin \ KAWR-win \ Colleen's adopted brother

Eerika* \ AIR-ee-kah \ the princess

Eerikki* \ AIR-ee-key \ King Auberon's father

Fallon \ FA-lən \ Colleen's adopted mother

Iida \ EE-dah \ Colleen's maid

Iisakki \ EE-sah-ki \ the dragon

Jaakko \ YAH-ko \ the pooka

Liam \ LEE-əm \ the Defender

Martta \ MAHR-tah \ the school administrator

Nialla \ NEE-ahl-ah \ Colleen's adopted sister

Noita \ Noy-tah \ the witch

Pepin \ PEP-ən \ a pech

Pirkko* \ PEER-koh \ a member of the Saoirse Trodaí

Reko \ REE-koh \ a member of the Saoirse Trodaí

Rhiannon \ ree-AN-ən \ Queen of Seelie Clós

Ruuta \ ROO-tah \ Collen's lady-in-waiting

Ryan \ REYE-ən \ Colleen's adopted brother

Rhys \ REES \ a boy who joins Colleen in her quest

Soini \ SOY-nee \ crew member

Taneli \ TAHN-ay-lay \ a member of the Saoirse Trodaí

Valtteri \ VAHL-teh-ree* \ leader of the Saoirse Trodaí

Vilppu \ VIHL-poo \ a driver

GROUPS

Fasgadair \ fahs-geh-deer \ Ariboslia vampires

Gachen \ GAH-chen \ an Ariboslian race of shapeshifters

Pech \ peck \ an Ariboslian race of small, strong people

Saors \ SEE-ores \ those who have been freed
Saoirse Trodaí* \ SEE-er-shay TRAH-day \ freedom fighters
Petturi* \ PEH-toor-ee \ a rebel group
Treasach \ treh-zack \ an Ariboslian race

PLACES

Ariboslia \ air-eh-BOWS-lee-ah \ Colleen's realm
Betören \ beh-TUHR-ən \ the new realm
Folaím \ FALL-eem \ the veiled forest city
Gnuatthara \ nu-aht-air-ah \ an Ariboslia city
Notirr* \ no-tear \ the village where Colleen grew up
Seelie Clós \ SEE-lee clohs \ the seelie court across the Divide
Rotko* / roht-goh \ the Divide, aka the forest of shadows
Talamh Sí \ tall-um she\ King Auberon's kingdom

THINGS

Aivopestä \ EYE-voh-pest-ah \ Auberon's curse
Ateria \ ah-tehr-ee-ah \ a traditional elfin dish
Bian \ bee-ahn \ the first time a gachen shape-shifts
Croí \ kree \ a spelled tree in Folaím
Drochaid* \ dro-hach \ the amulet Pepin created
Keino \ GAY-no \ a synthetic version of aether
Lustag \ loos-dag \ a flowering plant
Milis \ mill-ish \ a sweet berry
Neas \ nees \ weasels
Socrú \ suh-CRU \ dragon bond mark
Unohtaa \ oon-off-tah \ a potion that erases memory
Värikäs \ VAH-ree-kahs \ the color of aether smoke
Vastalääke \ VAHS-tah-lah-geh \ antidote

*trill the r

PROLOGUE

BANDIA - DURING THE FASGADAIR WARS

I waved the blanket, signaling the children to hide, fighting the urge to run and save myself—or scream. Fearful black surrounded Corwin and Nialla as they scurried under the table and disappeared in its shadow.

Little Beagan crawled our way. The baby boy's ever-changing aura settled into a deep purple, illustrating his confusion. I scooped him into my arms, thrusting out my hip to support his bulk. He clung on as I blew out the candle, and complete darkness bathed us. Corwin's and Nialla's groping hands guided me to the corner. I nestled into the awaiting pillow and arranged Beagan on my lap. They pulled the blanket over themselves and curved into me, clutching my side with one arm and holding Beagan with the other.

The electric scent of the fasgadair strengthened along with my thudding heart. Would today be the day the unholy beast discovered us? Part of me wanted it to... just to end this nightmare. I fought back tears. I wanted to sit on my mother's lap as she soothed me, assured me everything would be okay.

But that would never happen. I had no mother. Or any other adult to protect me. *I* had to be the mother to these three children barely younger than myself.

It wasn't fair.

What happened to all the adults? Where was everyone? Would we need to hide in this little house forever, constantly sniffing the air, wondering when the vampires would end our misery?

Silent tears slipped down my cheeks.

Be strong, Colleen.

Soft breaths escaped Beagan as he fell into a merciful sleep. His warm body rose and fell against my chest, dulling the sharp fearful edges threatening to overwhelm me.

The front door creaked, stilling my tears. Corwin and Nialla stiffened at my side. None of us dared breathe.

Please don't let them smell us. Please don't let them hear Beagan.

I squeezed my eyes shut, imagined us under the shelter of God's wings, and willed the fasgadair to pass us by.

Please hide us. Please hide us. Please hide us.

ONE

TWELVE YEARS LATER

I glanced over my shoulder to ensure I was alone, then placed my hands on the dirt covering the tiny seeds. My aura retracted into my skin as I summoned the energy within me to my core, warming my heart. I then pressed it down through my arms to my hands. Tingles ran up and down my arms as if they were covered with racing centipedes. My hands brightened as all the light within me converged there. I shoved tendrils of energy from my hands through the dirt where I sensed the seeds and sought the potential life within.

The seeds consumed the life force I fed them. Sprouts broke from their shell and cut through the soil. I fed them more until their first leaves appeared and dropped their shell. Then I broke contact.

My life force rushed back to where it belonged, and my aura returned. I sat back on my knees to admire my work. Ten seeds at the same time. Not bad. And I barcly noticed the lost energy.

Something rustled behind me.

"Colleen, there you are." My mom carried a bucket to the

compost pile. She peered over my shoulder. "Those are coming up nicely."

"Aye." I suppressed the urge to cringe like I was lying since they were supposed to be planted weeks ago. But I wasn't lying really. And I'd done my job. The plants sprouted on time.

I squirmed. Why did I keep my ability hidden from her of all people? Fallon was the most understanding person I knew. And she could keep a secret. But so many things about me made me so different from my family. I hadn't changed into my totem animal form as happens with all gachen around age fifteen. I could see auras. And I had pointed ears. My family knew about my ears, but that was all. I didn't want to feel like any more of a freak than I already was.

My mom dumped the bucket's contents and headed back toward the house.

"Mom? Is it okay if I'm done for the day?"

She studied the garden as if she had any idea what anything should look like. But she mostly left the gardening up to me. My dad helped some.

"My chores are done." My voice rose with my hopes.

"I was going to head into the village...."

I deflated. She'd want me to watch Ryan and ensure the others didn't cause too much mischief. She must need something else for whatever she was planning for my so-called graduation, or she'd never leave for the village at this hour. It was an hour ride on horseback. "I hope you're not going on my account."

She sighed. "Today is your special day. Nialla can look after Ryan while I'm gone. She's old enough now." Fallon skewered me with her perfected mom glare and jabbed a finger at me. "But don't be home late."

"Thank you, thank you, thank you!" I jumped up, snatched my satchel leaning against the fence, and scrambled away before she changed her mind.

"I mean it, Colleen! Don't be late."

"I won't!" I ran down the path into the woods, soaking up the freedom as the distance between me and my house grew.

I loved my family and the gardens. But it was all I did. I rarely went into the village. And pretending the crops took so long to grow while keeping my ability hidden was getting unbearable. I could cut hours of work down to mere minutes.

I needed to get away.

If only Fallon allowed me to travel to America with Stacy. But she wouldn't. Not if Turas was the only way. She'd never risk me passing through the spiritual realm.

There was no escape.

Well, there was one—books. I reached my favorite reading spot. A tree with stripping bark and an inviting crook nestled in a bed of green grass beckoned me. The trees opened up on this spot, and sunlight beamed down on me as I settled in to read of adventures in the human realm. My heart skittered as I fingered *The Secret Garden*'s cover, eager to rejoin my new companions and savor each moment like a bite of Aunt Stacy's monkey bread.

The irony of wanting to escape my garden for words on a page about another wasn't lost on me. But these were people I'd never met in an unfamiliar world and felt less stifling.

Crinkle, crinkle, crackle.

Something rustled in the weeds. A weasel, a neas to be exact, burst from its hiding spot and scampered across the green, its curved back undulating through the grass like a dolphin. It must've gotten separated from its pod. Should I rescue the poor creature? Its chances of survival were slim on its own. I laid the book down in the grass beside me and inched into a crouch.

The neas stood on its hind legs. Two brown stripes ran down its side. A male. His dark eyes trained on me while his whiskers twitched as if to smell my intentions. The lights emanating from him flickered between orange and black. Animals' emotions were much more basic and always had some level of black. Or had my presence caused their fear?

The creature's sniffing intensified, and its little black eyes found me. Black overtook all other colors as the neas let out a squeak, then bounded off the path past a megalith partially shielded by shrubs.

Wait... A *megalith?*

Could it be? A portal to another world? To America? It looked as Fallon had described with two large parallel stones and another balancing over their tops. But where had it come from? I'd walked these woods countless times over the years, and I'd never seen it.

I'd never seen *any* megalith. Other than Turas. But that was different. Very different. Turas was an enormous structure with many rocks that towered far above me, standing on end, forming a circle. It tapped into the spiritual realm to send travelers between realms and through time. This one was tiny, forming a tunnel to another realm in the current time. I'd have to drop to my hands and knees and crawl through.

Did it even work? If only I had an amulet to test it. Did anyone have one I could borrow? Mom didn't have hers anymore. She'd given it to Aunt Stacy as a language translator since she couldn't speak Ariboslian. No one else had an amulet... other than Pepin. But he wouldn't let me use Turas. He wasn't likely to let me use this megalith either. The pech had strict rules about megalith use and construction.

Which begged the question—Why was this here? Who built it? Pepin wouldn't have. Not without permission from the pechish council. But *someone* did. A rogue pech? A pech from another realm?

Had someone—or *something* else—come through?

The blood drained from my face. I stepped away from the entrance as if a swarm of demons might burst from the opening.

Don't be silly, Colleen. It probably doesn't even work.

I laughed at myself and closed in on the mysterious structure, stretching out a tentative hand as if to pet a wild creature, half-expecting it to bite. But my fingers met cool stone. No magical surge of power. Just the cold, lifeless feel of a normal rock. I explored the stones, seeking an indentation for an amulet like the one in Turas, but found nothing.

Cruunch. Cruuunnch. Craaack!

That was no small animal. Heavy footfalls tromped through the woods. My lurching heart urged me to hide. I dashed to my reading spot, rescued my satchel, darted behind the tree, and clung to its rough surface.

I searched for the sound's source and spotted my book on the ground. Creeping crabs! I surveyed the area. All was quiet but for normal woodsy sounds. No footsteps. Perhaps whoever it was had gone another way. I eyed the book and considered grabbing it before fleeing. I inched around the tree....

Cruunch. Cruuunnch. Snap! *Cruuunnch.*

Footsteps headed my way.

Squirming squids! I snapped back to my hiding place and dared peer around the trunk.

A strange man dressed unlike anyone I'd ever met in all of Ariboslia tramped past the trees. The color surrounding him was like none I'd ever seen. He resembled a circus ringleader in a picture book I'd read. Perhaps his hat brought that character to mind. Tall and round, like a cylinder. What was it called? A top hat?

Whoever he was, he wasn't from around here.

My heart thundered as he sniffed the air like the neas. But unlike the neas who searched for predators, this man was surely searching for prey. His gaze followed his nose, then fell on me.

I turned and, like the neas, ran for my life through the woods.

Two

My adopted dad sat in his usual seat on the veranda, plucking the strings on the torman-ciùil on his lap, the joyful tune contrasting with my mood. The lowering sun cast a wavering orange reflection on the shimmering lake beyond the balcony. Streaks of reds and orange surrounded the sun as if it, too, had emotions and was writhing with discomfort and ire. The strong winds had lessened to a mild breeze, but the stirred waters, like my soul, showed no signs of calming. Even the fruity-floral scents of the surrounding tropical plants failed to soothe me.

My siblings sat on the floor around the low table, playing cards. Light colors danced about them. If only I could be as content.

I should tell my parents about the strange man. And the megalith. But if I did, they'd tell Pepin, and the pech would tear it down. Then any chance of escaping this place, finding somewhere truly safe, would be lost.

But there was more to it than that. Something parasitic wriggled under my skin... an unshakable feeling. Like the hours before a storm when all was calm. An unseen force permeated the air. Animals quieted. Plants stilled. Everything awaited the disturbance fated to change their lives.

Like when the fasgadair neared.

Stop it, Colleen. The fasgadair are no more.

The gray mist surrounding me darkened, intermingling with a deep blue. The dismal color overtook the scene of my family before me. Nialla, Corwin, and Beagan morphed into the children I'd protected when I was only five or six. Their glimmering auras faded to black as I recalled their fearful faces looking to me for help. For protection. The room contorted to the home in Bandia where we huddled under the table as the electric fasgadair scent closed in.

Breathe, Colleen. Just breathe.

Light in. Dark out.

Light in. Dark out.

Brightness returned as the flashback waned. I blinked the memories away. My kids weren't frightened babies anymore. They were safe. And it seemed they didn't remember their time of hiding at all. How long had it been since Nialla's last nightmare? Seven years? Now sixteen and a striking beauty, she flung her strawberry hair back as she laughed, unconcerned about showing her rounded ears, unlike me. Corwin had grown into a handsome lad, though he didn't care to run a brush through his unruly locks. Beagan, on the other hand, was a stickler for his appearance, keeping his hair perfectly unkempt, as though it arranged itself just so by accident. These kids. *My* kids. Now my parents' kids.

It was better for them that they'd forgotten such a grim time. If only I could forget. I'd survived. But it hadn't made me stronger as Fallon had promised. I was beginning to suspect it had merely left me damaged. I had been rescued. Adopted. Given a good, loving home. And yet, I felt trapped. Stuck. As if I was still the little girl with impossible responsibilities.

I was broken.

Was that why I couldn't speak up about the megalith? If any healing was to be had, it lay beyond the portal. I was certain.

I watched my mom reading a book, her feet tucked underneath her on the couch, her black hair falling down her back. Her purple eyes scanned the page. She must be reading an intense scene. Her pink aura pulsed with orange and black. Soon she'd start biting her nails. I hated to interrupt, but I had to know. "Do all megaliths tap into the spiritual realm? Is there always a risk of coming in contact with demons?"

The music and banter stopped.

My mom put down her book. "Turas is the only one I know of. Why do you ask?"

"Can't Pepin make another one that isn't dangerous? It's simple enough to make, right? Just a few rocks piled just so? Then Aunt Stacy could visit us more."

Fallon quirked her lips. "The pech have rules. They can't just build megaliths anywhere. They have to be approved by the council. And the council is hesitant to build any without good reason. Portals are too dangerous. What if an amulet were to get in the wrong hands? My world could have been infected with fasgadair!"

I shuddered at the heinous beasts' name being spoken out loud. Then shame settled onto my shoulders. I'd only been thinking of the harm that could come to us... not to any other realms. But that was another reason to visit another realm—no fasgadair.

"It's best to keep the realms separate," she said. "Besides, only Turas can go anywhere in another realm. Normal megaliths are in the same place geographically in both worlds. Since the one I came through brought me from Maine to Notirr and we're now very far southeast, any portal near us would land us somewhere in Africa or in the middle of the Atlantic Ocean."

"Is that far from America?" I chose to ignore the ocean part. Was it possible to crawl through a portal into the bottom of an ocean? That would be terrible.

"Yes." Mom laid down her book and grasped my hand. "Very far from Aunt Stacy."

Her words broke something inside. Some deep need. A longing I didn't understand. It's not that I needed to see Aunt Stacy, but I'd hoped, now that I was done with school, they'd let me go back to America with her. But if Turas was the only way...

I wanted to crumple—to cry at some intangible injustice that hurt to my core. The colors surrounding me darkened. But I held it in. I would not cry. No matter what.

"Oh, honey." Mom hugged me. "I miss Aunt Stacy too."

I clung to her, inhaling the lavender from her freshly shampooed hair, letting her believe I missed my aunt, which was true. Her tight embrace both soothed me and threatened to squeeze out the tears I fought so hard to contain.

Light in. Dark out.

Light in. Dark out.

She gripped my arms and eased back to peer into my eyes. "Would some cake make you feel better?"

"Cake! Cake! Cake!" Ryan jumped off the floor.

Why was food Fallon's every solution? It wouldn't help. But she rarely made cake, and I couldn't disappoint her. I forced a smile. "Can't hurt to try."

Fallon pinched my sleeve and tugged. "Come on. Help me in the kitchen." Though she directed her request toward me, Corwin, Nialla, and Ryan followed us. Beagan took up his lute and played along with my dad.

While I pulled plates from the cupboard, Fallon retrieved the knife. "I'm sorry Aunt Stacy couldn't be here for your special day. I'm sure she's praying for you as we speak."

"It's only special to you and Aunt Stacy. Gachen don't celebrate ending their formal education." I clanked the ceramic plates on the stone counter.

"Well, humans do." Fallon stuck her tongue out at me.

"But you're not a human," Corwin interrupted.

"I'm half. And I grew up as one, so I know more about them than you all." She made a face at Corwin.

Ryan giggled as he leaned over the counter to sniff the cake.

"Get your snotty nose out of the cake." She tickled his armpit, and he laughed, revealing a gap where his front teeth belonged as he squirmed out of reach. Then she wagged the knife at me. "Even if gachen don't celebrate graduations, which is a shame, by the way. Being the first of my children to graduate, you will celebrate."

She plunged the knife into the soft cake. "Are you feeling uncertain? Your future awaits, and you haven't figured out what you want to do with your life yet. Is that what's troubling you?"

I shrugged.

"God has a plan for you, Colleen. Never forget. He will work everything out."

If only I had her faith.

"She hasn't even reached her bian yet." Corwin hung over the counter.

Nialla elbowed him. "Why are you here?"

"Many people are late. I was." Fallon threw me what she probably intended to be a sympathetic smile, but it made her look like she smelled something bad. And the deep blue engulfing her betrayed her true feelings.

I didn't want her pity. I didn't want anyone's pity. Nor did I care if I never shifted into an animal. The idea disgusted me.

"She's almost eighteen. You weren't *that* old," Corwin said.

"What is the matter with ye?" Nialla shoved his shoulder.

"I was seventeen. The same age as Colleen." Fallon cut through the words on the cake.

"What's that say?" Ryan asked.

Fallon smiled at her son. "It says 'Congratulations, Colleen' in English. I can speak Ariboslian, but I can't write it."

"Are you going to teach him English?" I asked to change the subject to something more interesting.

"If he wants to learn." She plated a slice. "Do you want to learn English, bud?"

Ryan scrunched up half his face. "Do I need to?"

"Nay, no one else speaks it but Mom, Colleen, and Aunt Stacy."

Corwin reached a finger toward the cake, and Nialla smacked it away.

"And Pepin," Fallon added.

"Aye, but Pepin also speaks Ariboslian, and Aunt Stacy has an amulet to translate. So, nay... you don't need to." Corwin snatched a plate of cake and left the kitchen.

"It's fun to speak another language." I ruffled Ryan's black hair, and he retracted his head as if he could pull it inside his body like a turtle. "It's like speaking in code. You can say things other people don't understand."

Mom handed him a plate. His eyes widened, and he smiled his toothless smile, then wandered away, sniffing the frosting as he went.

Once we were all seated on the veranda, the chatter lessened as forks scraped plates.

Was Fallon right? Did I fear the void of my unknown future lurking before me?

Or was Corwin right? I hadn't reached my bian yet. What if I wasn't even a gachen? I was adopted. I didn't know my real parents. No one else could see auras. Or revive plants. And no one else had pointed ears.

Or was I too stuck in the past to move forward? I still felt like that overburdened child fearful of both living and dying.

The answers—hope—lay beyond the megalith. They had to. One way or another, I would find a way through.

THREE

As soon as my chores were done, I tore off away from the house before Mom could change her mind. I patted the empty satchel as I trekked through the woods back to my reading spot. Surely, the strange man hadn't stolen my book. A flock of ducks quacked overhead. A cool breeze rustled the bright green leaves, shimmering from the passing afternoon shower. Gliding down the path, I held my arms out, and the foliage tickled and wet my fingers along the way. I sighed and soaked in the ambiance, inhaling the damp floral scents.

The path darkened as I neared the megalith. The light couldn't penetrate the thick foliage. But it helped me stay hidden as I darted from tree to tree. At each thick trunk, I stopped, watching, listening for the strange man before ducking behind the next sizable tree. I'd almost reached the megalith when I spotted a wilting lustag in the middle of the path. One of my favorite plants. Its sole purple flower drooped with fallen petals caught in its browning leaves.

"Poor thing!" I crouched beside the plant. "How'd ye get here? I don't recall passing ye yesterday. But then, I was a bit distracted." The soil was loose as if the lustag had been planted recently. But who would plant a dying lustag? And here of all places? In the middle of the path without sufficient sunlight?

I glanced about and listened. Satisfied we were alone, I returned to the plant. "Ye need a much sunnier spot." I pinched a dry leaf between my fingers. "Sometime, I'll transplant ye. But until then—"

I balanced on a knee and cupped my hands over the plant. My aura sucked into my skin as I siphoned the life force within me. A soft glow illuminated from the spot as if I held a lit light bulb, sending a tingle up and down my arms. The energy ventured forth like vines of light, winding through the plant's leaves to the roots, feeling for the waning life within. Dim energy met my reach. It wasn't too late.

A warming sensation surged from my heart through my arms to my hands as I pushed more of my life force through my palms to meet the plant's need. The lustag drank my energy and soon was satisfied. It swelled and straightened, returning to a healthy green, sprouting new growth.

"Looks like ye took a tad more than needed?" I laughed. Fortunately, the greedy little thing couldn't take enough to tire me if it tried. Already my aura had reemerged, looking brighter and healthier. I stood and pressed my hands together, casting an admiring gaze on the tender blossom. "That should hold ye till I return to move ye to a more fitting spot."

"Hello, elf."

I fell back onto my butt.

The strange man with the top hat and the odd-colored aura now blocked the path.

My breath caught in my throat as I scrambled to my feet. "Wh– who are ye?"

The man removed his hat, flipped it around with a flourish, and brought it to his chest with a bow, extending his other arm like a wing ready for flight. "Pleased to meet you, elf. The name's Balder."

"Eh–eh–elf?" With my breath clogging my throat, I coughed and stepped back, then peeked over my shoulder to ensure nothing blocked the path. And no one else overheard his preposterous accusation.

"You *are* an elf, are you not?" Balder pointed to the flower I'd revived. "Who but an elf could revive a flower in such a state? Are there more of you?" He squinted and surveyed the area as if an army of elves might come crashing through the woods.

"I'm no elf." I took a wide step back. I'd read about elves in human stories and wondered about my pointed ears, but I'd never spoken of it. Not even to Fallon. There was no need. The elves in the stories were nothing like me. And they were fiction.

I was most assuredly *not* an elf.

He neared, his finger making a circular motion toward my face. "To be sure, to be sure. None but an elf could possess such features. Hair like spun gold, cerulean eyes almost too big for such a narrow face"—he closed the gap, arm extended—"and elongated ears made to hear better from heaven."

My heart lurched, and I swatted his hand away. "Don't touch me." I felt the curls to ensure my ears hadn't somehow peeked through. Nay, my curls were far too thick. So, how did he know? My aura turned black.

He rubbed his hand, gave it an accusatory look as if it had acted on its own accord, then brought it down by his side. "Please accept my most sincere apology." With a flick of his wrist, a giant multicolored orb appeared in his hand. "And a small token."

"Wh–what is that?" I stepped on something, faltered, and checked to ensure my escape route was still clear.

"A gift."

"But what is it?" I shuffled backward.

"Open it, and you'll see." He held the proffered gift in both hands.

Warnings from Fallon about talking to strangers blared in my mind. "N–nay thank ye." I stumbled on a root, then ran back down the path home.

"Wait! Elf!"

Darting from the path, hoping to lose him, I raced through the woods in a zigzag should he wield a weapon. I dashed through shrubs, leapt over rocks and debris. Gratitude swelled for the speed and agility I rarely used.

When I'd gained enough distance, I scaled a tall tree, disappeared into the foliage, and rested on a thick branch. I fought to catch my breath as quietly as possible as I searched the forest floor. Leaves obscured my view, so I listened.

Insects buzzed, birds twittered, frogs yelped, rodents scuttled, and leaves swayed. But no heavy footfalls or any other sounds evidenced a man's presence. I released a pent-up breath, relaxed against the tree, and allowed the soothing sounds to envelop me as I focused on my breathing.

Light in. Dark out.

Light in. Dark out.

An urge to check my ears overcame me, something I hadn't felt compelled to do whilst alone since I was little and my hair wasn't quite as thick. My heart calmed some when my fingers met tufts of curls. My ears had no chance of escaping my mass of hair. Even after my mad dash through the woods. He couldn't have seen them.

Then why had the man been so sure I was an elf... going as far as to assume I had pointed ears?

But what was that he said...? Elves could heal plants? I'd never known anyone else with that ability. And what about my ability to see emotions? Was that an elf thing too? The strange man hadn't mentioned it.

I shook my head and laughed. I mustn't let some ridiculous man with a circus hat get to me. Elves didn't exist except in stories. It was a silly idea.

But then, when my mom wrote of her adventures in Ariboslia, which were quite real, she published them in her world under a fake name and passed them off as fiction. Could other authors have done the same?

Could I be an elf?

That would also explain why I haven't shifted into my totem animal form.

But what of this strange man? Who was he? Where was he from? Circuses didn't exist here. Neither did top hats. How then did a man wearing a top hat appear to call me an elf?

Unless he came through the megalith.

FOUR

I woke cradled between two branches. My back ached. Creeping crabs, how long had I slept? I descended the tree and slipped through the woods back home, listening for anyone following me, throwing suspicious glances over my shoulder the whole way. It was after dark when I arrived.

"Where've you been?" Cloth in hand, Fallon dried a dinner plate. She motioned toward a meal saver on the table. "Your dinner is cold."

"Thanks." My stomach growled. I sat at the table and removed the screened dome. Shrimp. Yuck. Cockroaches of the sea. I pushed the nasty little shell-less lobsters out of my way and scooped some salad.

Mom wiped her hands and sat down. She was a firm believer in eating meals together. Placing her chin in both hands, she leaned toward me. "You didn't answer my question, Coll. Where have you been?" She spoke the last words in English, then motioned toward Corwin and Beagan lounging on the carpet. Her signal I had her complete confidence.

I held up a finger as I chewed so as not to speak with my mouth full, then swallowed. "Don't freak out."

My use of one of her favorite very un-Ariboslian sayings brought a smile. "Okay." She narrowed her eyes. "Did something happen?"

"I always thought yer warnings about never taking candy from strangers silly. But... I saw a strange man wearing a top hat."

"A top hat... in Ariboslia?" She squared her shoulders. "Where?"

"In the woods. Along the southeastern path toward the village."

"And he offered you candy?" I'd never seen her look so thoroughly confused.

"Nay, not candy. I don't know what it was. He said it was a gift."

"What was it?"

"I have no idea." I thought back to the shimmering orb. "Something I'd never seen before."

Dark blues and purples radiated from Fallon's skin. But there was no black. She wasn't afraid, just worried. That eased my discomfort. "That—telling you not to take candy from strangers—was a joke. I never expected it to happen. Everyone knows everyone here. It's a village. There's not a bus station nearby. Or any white vans."

White vans? What in Ariboslia was she talking about?

Mom twisted her mouth as if that might help her think. "Did he say anything else?"

Should I tell her about the elf thing? Fallon knew about my ears. But she didn't know about my abilities to grow plants or see emotions. I'd learned not to speak of such things before leaving Notirr. People didn't understand. I checked to ensure the kids weren't listening.

"Keep speaking in English."

Fallon understood me like no one else. I should trust her. But would the kids know the word *elf*? There was no translation I was aware of. Then again, the kids wouldn't likely be familiar with it— only Fallon and I read the books Aunt Stacy brought. But just in case, I leaned in and whispered, "He called me an elf."

"An elf?" One eyebrow winging up, she waved a hand as if batting away the most preposterous thing she'd ever heard.

"Aye. He said I resembled an elf and wanted to see my ears."

"An elf?" Now she sounded thoughtful. Surely, she wasn't wondering if that were a possibility?

"You think it's true?"

Fallon took a deep breath, her eyes wide, her aura almost orange. Dark orange.

"You *do* think it's true."

"Ever since I was dragged through the megalith when I was only a little younger than you, I've come to expect the unexpected. You were one of the many babies rescued from Gnuatthara. And not all of those babies were Treasach... or from Gnuatthara. It would explain a lot." She rubbed her face, then rested her chin on laced fingers. "But an elf?"

"Shhh!" I observed the boys, who seemed intent on whatever they were reading.

"Do they even exist in Ariboslia?" She tipped her head to one side, her eyes glazing.

Sometimes I forgot she wasn't from here. I shrugged. "I've only ever read about them in books from your realm. Do they exist there?"

"No, they're fictional creatures in my realm."

"So are your books."

"True." Her glazed eyes narrowed into her thinking, distrustful face. Her aura darkened. "That makes me want to find this guy all the more. I'll talk to your dad and your uncles tomorrow. You can show us where you met him."

"Nay, you can't! If I am what he says, I don't want everyone to know."

"Not to worry, Collie. I won't mention that part. Your family needs little reason to hunt someone who accosted you in the forest." She huffed. "But I'll wait until morning. If I say something to your father now, there'd be no stopping him from scouring the woods tonight."

I laughed as my aura lightened. Knowing so many people would fight for me made me feel better. But it saddened me as well. If that didn't make me feel like I belonged, could anything?

She stood and patted my shoulder. "You are loved, sweet girl."

She shuffled about the kitchen performing her nightly cleanup ritual as I scarfed down the last of my meal, minus the revolting crustaceans with slimy translucent skin. My mind returned to the strange man and the wrath he'd face should my family find him. But he was only part of my concern. What if, when I showed them the lustag, they continued and found the megalith? With the top-hat man skulking about, they'd destroy it, no question.

About so, so many things in my life I was uncertain. But a desire —no, an inexplicable *need*—to protect the megalith ignited within.

I could only do one thing—hide it. First thing in the morning before anyone woke, I'd cover it in shrubs. Whatever it took to keep anyone from learning of its existence until I could figure out how to use it.

FIVE

I slipped away while the others slept. The cool stone chilled my toes as I tiptoed down the hall. A cry came from Ryan's room, and his bedding rustled as he stirred. I stopped and held my breath, listening for signs of him getting out of bed or Mom checking on him.

Please go back to sleep.

After a moment of quiet, I darted through the kitchen, eased the front door open, and crossed the lanai. My bare feet stuck to the tile, making a slight sucking sound with each step. Not something to rouse even a light sleeper from this distance, yet my teeth gritted with each step. I climbed the stairs up the hillside toward my parents' open window.

Fallon was a light sleeper, so I crept as silently as possible, then dropped to my knees to crawl under their window. The soft grass cushioned any sound, though my knees kept getting caught on my dress.

Once out of earshot, I donned my sandals and dashed down the path. Dawn's dim light lit my way. The plants glistened with moisture from a passing rain. But, being made from impenetrable selkie material, my sea-green dress repelled the water, and it beaded up and rolled off. Birds, the early risers, sang and flitted about as if this was their time and the world belonged to them. Their calls varied from solo chirps and staccato tweets to complex warbles.

An image of the man in the top hat dampened my mood and slowed my pace. What if I ran into him again? He'd been so close to the portal. And something about his strange aura iced my veins. Had he come from another realm? Perhaps America? That would explain the hat. And his knowledge of elves.

I listened for any suspicious sounds, watched for anything unusual. But nothing resembling a human appeared. Yet.

When I passed the healthy lustag, a whisper caught my attention. I strained to listen, but it wasn't audible. More of a tugging in my soul, beckoning me toward the megalith. My feet moved without awaiting my approval, drawing me to the clearing. The man was nowhere to be seen, but barely aware of my surroundings, I continued toward something shimmering on the ground.

Nestled in the grass at the megalith's opening was the gift the strange man had offered. Dread and intrigue intertwined, pooling in my heart and pumping through my body, clogging my veins. To leave the gift... Here? He must've come through the portal.

The orb, whatever the unearthly thing was, reeled me in as if it had snagged me on a hook. The sphere's aura throbbed like a heartbeat, strengthened with each step, in colors both familiar and unknown—including the one that had surrounded him.

I fought the pull, and the pulsing intensified as if it refused to be denied. What was this thing? If it had an aura, then it must be... alive? Or it was a thin shell, and something lived inside. Was it an egg? Why was my desire to touch it so strong? The inaudible voice called without words, and my feet gave up the fight.

Fallon would kill me if I neared this thing. She was freaked out enough to send the family to investigate. I should be cautious too. And yet, there was no stopping it. We were charged magnets overwhelmed by forces beyond our control.

A shadow moved within, jostling the orb.

Though my heart leaped, my body continued without hesitation. I knelt and reached. My fingers closed in, hovering over its surface. Heat emanated from the object, warming my hand.

My finger came closer and closer and—

Zap!

My hand snapped back, and the orb cracked. Light broke through, and I shielded my eyes. Something long with a sharp tooth-like thing poked through.

It *was* an egg.

I scooted back on my knees. If it was an egg, it wasn't of this world. Or any other I knew of.

What was about to hatch?

Six

The oscillating lights flared once more, bleaching my eyes. One big white blob took over my vision, then separated into multiple spots. I blinked them away. With each blink, an outline solidified amongst the eggshell and dulling light—a cat.

But that was impossible. Cats didn't *hatch.*

Then again, eggs didn't pulsate and glow or call to people and hatch upon contact.

Despite what reasoning deemed possible or impossible, a furry gray kitten sat before me, licking its paw and swiping its bent ear. A white streak began at its forehead, overtook its muzzle, then ran down its neck, chest, and belly.

The kitten's eyes widened as it licked. Its dilated pupils nearly overtook green irises, then scrunched into slits as it took a few more swipes at its ear.

"Aw. You're adorable." My heart melted at the mere sight of the sweet thing. I should've been concerned. Very concerned. But the power of cuteness bubbled up within, rendering any cautionary voices mute. I extended a finger toward the furry little face.

The kitten's gaze followed my finger, its large pupils crossing as I closed in. Then it inched forward, bridging the gap. Whiskers twitching, eyes crossed, it sniffed my finger. We made contact, and the cat jumped back, then returned for another sniff.

"Ye are the cutest thing I've ever seen." I flattened my hand and reached to pet the kitten's head. The moment my hand connected with the softest fur imaginable, the pulsing lights returned. A warm sensation accompanied the light as it snaked up my arm. I pulled up my sleeve, gaping, as the glow continued its path. The light dissipated, solidifying into an intricate tattoo encircling my upper arm.

"What in Ariboslia?"

I touched the mark encircling me—thick, interwoven bands with three leafy offshoots outlined a broken line within. It looked like a tattoo. Ink. But it didn't hurt and felt like nothing more than skin.

Had this kitten marked me? Was it permanent?

The kitten purred, rubbed against my leg, then darted toward the megalith, and disappeared through the opening.

I stared after the cat, refusing to blink lest I miss its return through the other side. But, as the seconds ticked by, I knew. The feline wasn't going to reappear. It had traveled through the portal.

Without an amulet.

Had I lost all sense? I ground my eyes with my fists, then cradled my face in my palms as if my hands might somehow keep my head together. Had I imagined the whole thing? A cat didn't just hatch from an egg some stranger in a top hat wanted to give me, then travel through a portal to another realm. How preposterous!

And yet, discarded bits of broken eggshell littered the ground. I picked up a piece and crushed it. A sharp edge nicked my finger as eggshell dust sifted through my hand. I peeked under my sleeve at the tattoo. More tangible proof. If my eyes didn't deceive me and my head was still on straight, the cat had gone through the megalith an entire minute or so ago.

If it had somehow opened the portal, was it still open? If so, how long would it remain open?

Should I follow it?

Could I follow it?

I had tried to crawl through the opening just yesterday. What made me think something different would happen now?

The cat just went through.

Assuming the cat that hatched from an egg existed and I wasn't off my head.

And yet, whatever had happened, whatever that cat was, an ache settled into my heart. Somehow, a piece of my heart had dislodged and was now running around outside my body. In a cat form. In another realm.

I needed to find it. We couldn't be worlds apart from one another.

I was losing precious time. If I was going to go after the cat, I had to go.

Now.

Desperate loneliness surged, igniting every sense, urging me to act. For whatever reason, I needed to be with that cat. We were connected. Losing it was not an option.

I gathered my skirt above my knees and crawled through the megalith. But I felt nothing. It was as if nothing miraculous had happened.

But it had.

I stood and dusted off my knees as I gawked. The surrounding trees had grown and sprouted so many flowers their branches could no longer contain them and bowed under their weight like over-loaded apple trees. Blossoms in varying shades of red shimmered as if dusted with glitter. Such flowers didn't exist in Ariboslia. Not that I'd ever seen.

I inhaled the effervescent air... like strawberries and peppermint. Wait. I knew that smell. Something about it tugged at the recesses of my mind. But the harder I reached for the associated memories, the more they eluded me.

Where was I?

My gaze darted about as I swiveled.

Where was the cat?

Finding nothing near the megalith, I pushed through the thick branches to the most fantastic sight I'd ever beheld. My heart beat like a drummer with no rhythm. The hill where I stood sloped downward, offering a view of the valley and the forests and the hills far, far beyond. The deepest shades of green rolled downward in patches of jagged hills. Brown paths disappeared under the foliage where grasses and shrubs gave way to trees. Colorful inverted teardrops with dangling baskets swarmed the sky like cherry blossoms in a soft wind.

Wait. I'd seen those in books. What were they called?

Balloons. Hot-air balloons.

People traveled by hot-air balloons in this realm? Or was it some kind of festival? Was I in America?

Was that a ship?

It looked like a ship. A massive wooden ship. It even appeared to have a rudder. But ships belonged in the sea, not the sky. Several orbs surrounded the vessels' sails. Balloons? But why put a marine vessel to the sky? I'd never seen such a thing. Not even in books. Was it both aquatic and avian, like a duck?

My overwrought mind could take no more. My legs gave out beneath me. Was all of this an elaborate hallucination I'd concocted? Had I read too many stories? Dreamed so much I'd confused my mind over what was reality? Was I in another world? Or was I somewhere else, perhaps tucked away in bed, trapped in a dreamworld of my imaginings?

"Purrrrrow."

My head snapped toward the unusual sound. The kitten brushed against a tree trunk. I pressed a palm to my heart and released my breath. It was the kitten. Only the kitten. I let out a nervous laugh.

"What was that? A half-purr, half-meow?" I asked. "What are you? You're no ordinary cat. That's for certain. And how did you open the megalith?" I reached to pet the feline.

The kitten pushed its head into my hand, then ran its whiskers along my fingers, its eyes forming contented slits as its purr deepened.

Peace settled into my heart at the kitten's touch, and I felt whole again. The missing piece of my heart had returned.

All we needed now was to get back to Ariboslia.

But my gaze returned to the valley. Something called to me, beckoning me to explore. Wasn't this what I wanted? To get through the megalith? And now, I'd gotten through, and I could think of nothing other than going home?

But what if I couldn't get back again? What if I got lost? Or what if I got hurt? My family needed me. Who would tend the garden? They would struggle without me. And I hated the thought of worrying them.

And I knew nothing of this place. What if evil creatures lurked here? Something worse than fasgadair? I shuddered.

"Come. Let's go home." I scooped up the kitten and hurried back toward the portal.

The kitten squirmed and leaped. It thudded to the dusty path, then sneezed. Puffs of smoke curled from its nostrils. Dust must've been embedded in its nose, appearing as smoke from the sneeze's force.

As I bent to retrieve the cat, it scooted away and darted downhill.

Seven

Dumbfounded, I froze as the cat disappeared into the greenery. My stomach lurched. Should I follow? I tried to peer through the branches to the megalith, but the foliage was too thick. I surveyed the hill. The place was green as far as the eye could see. It should be easy to find this place again. The blossoms stood out like red shells on white sands.

If I was going to find the cat, I'd better do it now. The kitten had run. At my pace, I might lose it forever. As I descended the hill, the window to my world closing behind me made each step more laborious than the last. Something squeezed my heart.

Wasn't this what I'd longed for? An adventure in America? I'd gotten through the megalith. It didn't matter how. But this cat was the key. Somehow. I needed to find it—especially if I had any hopes of returning home.

I jogged through the green grass to a path where I'd lost the kitten. It had to be around here somewhere. But then, it was so small and fast. It could be anywhere. "Here, kitty, kitty."

Green shrubs made way to trees blotting out the sky. Unsure if I should continue, I peered back from where I'd come once more to ensure I could easily return. Someone sauntered down the trail around the bend.

A boy.

I ducked behind the tree. Had he seen me? My breath came quickly. But I fought through it, trying not to make a sound.

"You there!" the boy called.

Squirming squids, he saw me. Should I run for it?

"Hello!" The boy's face appeared beside me. The aura surrounding him matched the strange man's color.

"Oh!" I jumped away from the tree, placing a splayed hand over my thudding heart as if to keep it from popping out of my chest.

"Are you hiding from me?" He stuck his face in mine. Brilliant blue eyes invaded my soul. Darker than the deepest parts of our lake with ripples of light, just like when you're submerged underwater and watch the dancing light filtering through. Transfixed, I stared. The unearthly eyes somehow seemed familiar.

He shot out a hand. "The name's Rhys."

Rhys. What an unusual name. Was it American? I pulled my gaze from his and gawked at his hand.

"Would you deny my hand?" He cocked his head.

I didn't know this boy or where he came from, and he expected me to touch him? What if he carried one of those diseases I'd read about?

"Or not." He dropped his hand. "Might you have a name?"

"Colleen."

"Colleen, pray tell, what realm is this?"

"You d–don't know?"

He shook his head, sending short black strands flying. They settled back into place as if they'd never moved. Twin rocks of shining lapis lazuli waited for me to respond.

"How is it you don't know? Aren't you from here?"

"Betören be my home, which this well may be." He shrugged. "Too many trips through the megalith render the mind a whirlwind blending the worlds. Upside right or downside left. Who can tell?"

My breath caught. "You came through the megalith?"

But how? And how could he speak so casually about it? Was it a normal mode of transportation wherever he was from?

"As I've confessed, I'm a foreigner in these lands. Please put my confusion to rest and inform me on what soil I stand."

Where were we indeed! How could I answer this strange-sounding boy with the bizarre aura? *I needed answers. I needed help.* Each breath drew in more questions and emitted dead air. Rhys's awaiting gaze threatened to break something within me as realization set in—I was lost.

"Perchance... might you be a mere visitor to these lands as well?"

How should I answer? Should I trust him? He'd been through the megalith several times. Maybe he could help me get home. "I'm from Ariboslia—the selkie lands. Do you know it?"

"Ariboslia, yes. I know not how many times as one can't be sure without a tour guide."

"Can you help me get back there?"

"That I can! To be sure. To be sure." He tugged at a chain under his collar, freeing a pendent. "But not with this, I fear. This amulet is spelled for one thing and one thing alone. I'll need another to get you home."

"Spelled? Like magic?" I shuddered. Magic was witchcraft. Witchcraft was evil.

"Magic? Hmm..." He scratched his ear. This kid didn't act like any boy I'd ever met before. Nor did he sound like one. "Magic involves summoning spirits, does it not?" He gave his head a vehement shake. "By no means. Perhaps manipulated is a better word? To be sure. To be sure. Let's say manipulate as all fae, both seelie and unseelie have natural abilities to manipulate elements... though the unseelie motives are questionable to be sure. But all that aside, this one"—he jostled the amulet in his hand—"has been manipulated to lead me to an elf."

EIGHT

"Y-y-you're looking for an eh–eh–elf?" Was he from the same place as that strange top-hat man? Did they know each other? It couldn't be a coincidence. The same aura surrounded them both. And they spoke with the same inflection. How many more would come looking for me, convinced I'm an elf? I glanced about as if more strange people with unusual auras hid behind rocks and trees, ready to throw me into a bag and deliver me to their superior. My gut clenched in a vain attempt to squeeze me free of this peculiar predicament.

"The fae that manipulated this amulet was seelie. The seelie's desire to free Betören is noble, to be sure. And their amulet was true." His smile widened to impossible new lengths as he motioned toward me. "For behold, an elf stands before me."

"I'm n–not an elf." I cast my gaze to my shuffling feet. Why did I feel like I was lying? Or would it take more strangers telling me I was an elf to convince me? And *what* was an elf? Certainly not those tiny busybodies who break into cobblers' shops uninvited to complete their work. By no means. If that were so, no one would mistake me for one. What then? Was I something from the imaginings of the likes of Tolkien?

No. Elves weren't real. Else their descriptions wouldn't vary so.

"I'm sure that's not true." Rhys pinched his black eyebrows together. "If asked what an elf looked like, I'd point to you."

Was he *trying* to rhyme? His speech was getting annoying. "I'm not." But the strange man and now this boy... They couldn't know me better than I knew myself, could they? "What do you want with an elf, anyway?"

"Betören be under a great curse. Dark magic, to be sure. Though its victims are blissfully ignorant. For their sake, we must break the curse. But alas, only an elf can complete the task."

"Are there no elves in Betören?"

"It is rumored the king who cast the curse murdered the elves to eliminate their threat to his rule." He spoke as if genocidal kings were as common as butterflies.

I swallowed hard. "And you expect an elf to volunteer to face him?"

"One will, to be sure." His confident smile waned. "Or all is lost."

"Well..." I started back the way I'd come. "Peace to you and your elf, should you find one. May God bless you in your quest." I picked up speed, but something nagged at me, stilling my feet. The cat. Creeping crabs, I'd forgotten the cat. "Have you seen a little gray-and-white kitten?"

"Alas, I have not." His lips settled into a mischievous grin. "Perhaps you will allow me to assist you in your quest."

I wouldn't call it a quest. But I could use the help. Suspicion prickled my neck. "You will?"

"To be sure. To be sure." He nodded with much enthusiasm.

"In return for...?" I steeled myself.

"An elf."

Though no surprise, his response still churned my gut.

"Mrrrrow!" The cat leaped from the thicket and snaked around my feet.

"There you are!" I knelt and petted its head. The cat's touch relaxed my tense muscles on contact.

"Ah, the lost feline returns." Rhys crouched, and the cat wove between us. "The powers that be have smiled upon us and our quest, to be sure."

I eyed him. Did he have the audacity to consider this the fulfill-ment of his side of the bargain? As I studied the odd boy, something in the cat's calmness and seeming affection for him eased my shoul-ders down to their rightful place.

"Pray tell, what do you call him?"

"Him? How do you know it's a boy?"

"There is only one way to discern an animal's gender. Unless we're referring to creatures, such as birds, with specific markings for females or males. Felines, neither big nor small, have no such mark-ings of which I'm aware."

"Oh." My face warmed. I should've guessed. But how could he tell without picking him up and looking? Not that I was going to ask.

He aimed those unearthly blue spheres at me as the kitten rolled at his feet. "Does the feline have a name?" The blues disappeared behind slits. "But then, you were ignorant of his gender. Perhaps the tom doesn't belong to you?"

"He's mine. He just hatc—" I coughed. *You brainless jellyfish! Don't tell strangers this cat hatched from an egg.* "We just adopted him."

"We? Who encompasses this we of which you speak?"

"My family."

"Where might they be?" He searched about as if they were hiding amongst the trees. "Perhaps *they* will assist my quest for an elf."

"They're not here. They're—" How much could, or *should*, I trust this strange, strange child? But he was no fasgadair or any other evil creature that I could see. He was just a boy. How much damage could a boy do? "They're home."

"In Ariboslia?"

I nodded.

"If I'm to understand, you do not hail from these lands nor are you the feline's master."

"Pah! You sure ask a lot of questions."

"Observations of no real consequence, yet you hesitate to respond. What holds your tongue?"

Time to turn this around. "Look, my cat has returned. So if you don't mind, would you help me find the megalith to return home?"

"But what of our deal?"

"What deal?"

"An elf for a feline." He motioned to the kitten. "You have yours."

Was he off his head? "You didn't help me. The cat returned on his own." My inability to read his foreign aura made it difficult to trust him. What if this was a ploy to stall me? What if he was in league with that other man? What if they refused to believe I'm not an elf and kidnaped me? Nay. I'd be foolish to trust him. "I'm sorry." I reached down and scooped the wriggling cat in my hands. I tripped over my ankle, shuffling away from him. "I have to go."

"Go? Go where?"

The cat nestled into my neck. I held him in place and darted away.

"But you found what you sought, have you not?" His voice grew at my retreating back.

Something was seriously wrong with this boy. He couldn't be trusted.

Please, God. Don't let him follow.

NINE

I clutched the kitten close to my heart and hurried down the path, then darted down smaller walkways, checking over my shoulder as I went. My heart slowed as minutes passed with no sign of him, but everything around me looked the same. Each tree... Each faint footpath in the grass... It all looked the same. I raced down one, then another. I stopped and spun.

Why did every tree look the same? No identifying marks. Even the branches seemed to grow in the same places. Almost as if this place was designed to make visitors...

... lost.

Squirming squids, I was lost. I should have risked it and trusted the odd boy. Now I was alone in a foreign world. Stuck in an endless maze. Nay, a real maze would show an end to a path. This was worse. Much worse.

If I could climb a tree, I might find my way back to the patch of flowers guarding the megalith. I studied the closest tree. Some branches were low enough to climb.

"Stay here." I lowered the kitten onto the ground and gathered my skirt.

The kitten sprinted down the path.

Curses!

I chased the cat. Was the thing worth all this trouble? I spotted the pain in the neck around the bend, diving through the boy's legs.

I sighed, slumping my shoulders as I plodded toward him.

He scooped the kitten into his arms. "T'would appear I've assisted you twice."

Was the little creep taking credit for having helped me—again? "You haven't helped me at all. The cat came to you both times."

The kitten nuzzled Rhys's neck and settled in to stay for a while.

Rhys trained his unnaturally blue eyes on me. "Why did you run? Have I offended you?"

"I just—" I steeled myself to tell the truth. "I'm not an elf. Your insistence makes me uncomfortable. I just want to get my cat and go home."

Rhys relaxed and threw me a lopsided grin. He turned back the way he'd come and tipped his head that way. "Come. You wish to return to your homeland, do you not?"

I fell in step beside him. "You're not going to hold me to our deal?"

He shook his head. "To be sure. As you so eloquently stated, I did nothing to aid your quest, so why should you reciprocate? And if you speak the truth, you know nothing of elves rendering you of little use to me."

The little-use comment stung, but I breathed easier. "I thought you said your amulet wouldn't work."

"If no elves live in your homeland, the amulet won't bring us there. To be sure. But I don't see any elves here, either. What have we to lose to see where it leads? To where did you wish to return? Somewhere in Ariboslia?"

"Right. The selkie lands. Have you ever been?"

"Perhaps yes. Perhaps no."

"How many worlds have you visited?" Though I knew of the human realm, it hadn't occurred to me there might be many more.

"As I stated earlier, I've traversed many a nameless land. Perhaps they were all one and the same." He waved it off as if the answer were of little consequence.

"How many times have you traveled through the megalith?"

"I have no record."

I blew a tuft of runaway curls and eyed him askance. Did this kid know anything? About a foot shorter than me, he didn't look like a short man. Nay, he looked far too young. Like a boy. "How old are you?"

"I know not."

"How is that possible?" The moment my words escaped, I regretted them. If anyone understood being uncertain of one's age, it was me.

"How old are *you*?"

"Seventeen."

Rhys stopped and studied me, tipping his head as far as he could without squishing the cat. "Are you?"

My breath caught, and my hand fluttered to my chest as if to remind myself to breathe. "Why would you ask?" My birth date, therefore my age, was uncertain. But I'd always answered with confidence, and no one questioned my response.

He resumed walking. "You look... old."

"Old?" I touched my face as if wrinkles might've sprouted since my last visit with a mirror. Had traveling through the megalith aged me?

"*Old* perhaps is the wrong word." He stressed *old* with a flamboyant sweep of his hand. "But seventeen? I find that hard to believe."

He found *my* age hard to believe? Did age differ from Ariboslia and the human realm in his world? But why wouldn't he know his age? Or at least an estimate. "If you had to guess how old you are... how old do you think you'd be?"

"Hmm... about twenty perchance?"

"Pah!" I laughed. "Twenty? You look like you're twelve."

His face twisted in unreadable ways. Then he continued, offering no further explanation.

If only I could read his aura.

Perhaps people aged slower where he's from. But I'd never met another person ignorant of their exact date of birth... with the exception of the other orphans in Notirr. Was he an orphan too?

We walked through the paths in silence. The trees cleared, and the grassy slope came into view, leading to the most welcome sight in this world—red and pink blossoms.

Thank You, God!

Was the air physically lighter up here, or was it only me? Joy replaced the trepidation with each step. We forced our way through the blossoms to the hidden megalith. Rhys placed the kitten in the grass and crawled through.

TEN

Rhys's body didn't disappear, yet he glanced about as if expecting to find himself somewhere else. His gaze fell on me, and his face crinkled. If only his aura would confirm or deny his confused expression. But the unnamed color refused to comply. "The amulet insists an elf resides in these parts. But it should allow me to return home. Allow me to test it."

"But—" I reached forward as if I could pull him back. But he was back on his knees and crawling through before I could stop him. What if he made it home and couldn't find his way back? The cat and I would be left here—alone.

But I needn't have worried. Rhys scrabbled through the other side.

"My sincerest of apologies, fair maiden." He brushed his trousers at the knees, then scratched behind his ear. "I fail to understand the amulet's change in rules at present." He held up his amulet. "The fae spelled this trinket to find an elf, to be sure. But never has it failed to return me home when that is where I wished to go."

"But we're trying to get to my home. What would going to your home accomplish?"

"It was a test. Nothing more. The destination is the amulet's choice alone. Had it delivered me home, I could have assisted you from there. But alas, it did not. I fear there's no going back that way until I find the elf the seelie seek. So, this is where we part ways—unless you care to join me in my quest."

The elf? I thought any elf would do. Was it a slip? Or was I misunderstanding his strange speech? Regardless, I couldn't be stuck here. With one last hope, I aimed the kitten at the megalith and gave him a gentle shove. He dodged the opening.

Curses!

"Pray tell, what are you hoping to accomplish?"

"This is how I got through before without an amulet. I followed him." I rerouted the cat, guiding him in the right direction.

He tiptoed, shaking each paw as though the ground was wet.

I clutched my hands to my mouth and held my breath as he neared the entrance.

Please, please, please open the portal to home as you somehow did here.

I inhaled as the kitten traipsed into the opening, held my breath as he sniffed the stones, and—deflated when he reappeared on the other side. "Creeping crabs! We can't be trapped here."

"The megalith has made itself clear. There's no going back that way." Rhys pushed through the blossoms back to where we'd come.

I scooped the cat into my arms and hurried after him.

Out in the open air, a cool breeze swept over my arms, covering me with gooseflesh. This time, the wondrous view sent foreboding shivers along my spine. The valley lay before us like a Venus flytrap—so beautiful, so enticing to its unsuspecting prey. But the balloons and ships had long since abandoned the sky, and the sun hovering over the distant hills prepared to do the same. Their retreat suggested I do likewise, if only I could. But where would I go?

Darkness invited evil creatures. What beasts prowled these lands at night?

"Should we venture this way, we must camp in the woods—

perhaps for several nights as I see no end. Perhaps this way..." Rhys ducked back through the brush toward the megalith.

Please let there be a better option than spending the night outside.

I gazed upon the megalith as we passed. As if it might feel sorry for failing in my time of need, repent of its wrongdoing, and offer us passage. But the portal could feel no remorse. It was nothing more than a pile of rocks bent to do the pech's bidding. And the fae's, apparently. Sadly, their wills didn't align with mine. And I had no such power over the ignorant stones.

I gave the portal one last glance before plunging through the bushes after Rhys in the opposite direction.

We hadn't gone far before the way cleared before us. The land-scape presented itself much like the green hills had, but this sight was something from a horror novel.

Blackened trees looked like death. Not charred from fire but decayed from disease. Their angry arms twisted at odd angles, ready to strangle prey in spindly fingers. Withered leaves clung to jagged branches, refusing to join their fallen comrades.

Though the lowering sun still reached this unholy place, it appeared as night, as if the light refused to touch such darkness lest it becomes tainted too. The place emanated wickedness like evil steam. I wanted to run—to recant my earlier thoughts and apologize to the valley for my unfair assessment. But as I stood staring into the depths of this unhallowed ground, memories of the valley faded from a real place upon which I'd stood moments ago, to a picture in a book, to a mere vapor of a thought that now eluded me.

What had I been thinking? Where was I?

I breathed in the permeating hopelessness. It ventured throughout my being, draining the life from my bones. I was alone. So utterly and unbearably alone.

A rancid, sulfuric odor wafted my way. Tears scorched my eyes. I covered my nose and mouth with the back of my free hand.

"I know this place."

My head snapped toward Rhys. The ungodly forest's dire loneliness was so thick, so all-consuming even from this distance, I'd thought myself alone. Rhys and the cat were forgotten under its unholy spell, though the kitten squirmed in my arms.

I coughed and backed away to untainted air.

Light in. Dark out.

Light in. Dark out.

A thick helping of unease slogged in my gut, and I gaped at Rhys. *This* he recognized? "How do you know it?"

"We're in Betören." He peeled his gaze from the nightmare and trained it on me. "Home."

Eleven

Rhys spun on his heel and backtracked to the way we'd come. Though I had so many questions, that act brought me comfort. At least he wasn't running *to* the vile, soul-stealing forest.

Clinging to the kitten, I raced after him. "This is Betören?"

"To be sure. To be sure."

We dove back into the thicket of red flowers. My eyes cleared as sweet-smelling strawberry-and-peppermint air purged the foul stench from my lungs, restored my mind. Branches smacked me in his hasty retreat. I protected the kitten as best I could while attempting to keep up.

"That was Rotko, the Divide," he said. "Also known as the Forest of Shadows."

We passed the unnatural rock structure that refused to play nice. I threw it a scathing look this time, then chased Rhys through the brush to the valley. He didn't offer me time to take in the view, but my previous dread had been vanquished. This place was heaven compared to Rotko. I'd rather sleep here for one hundred nights than spend one minute in those dreary woods.

"How did you recognize it? Have you been there before?" I asked.

"You might say that." Free of the shrubs, he sauntered down into the valley to the maze of trees.

"On purpose?" I called to his back. How could anyone make it through there and live to tell about it? From my brief experience on the outskirts, I couldn't imagine entering and ever coming out again. I'd lose the will to do anything. "Didn't it make you—make you—I don't know... want to give up on living?"

Either he didn't hear me or he didn't care to respond.

I raced to catch up. "So you know where you are now?"

As if we'd put enough distance between us and the Rotko, Rhys slowed.

I stroked the kitten's back. He relaxed his muckle hold and settled into the crook of my neck. I itched where his claws had broken skin, but I had no way to scratch it.

"Not here, per se. But if Rotko lay behind us, we're standing on the Uaine Highlands. The highlands lay between the Rotko and Talamh Sí. So this is the right direction."

I picked up my pace. "Talamh Sí? What's that?"

"The elfin kingdom."

"Elfin? You mean elves? Wait." I tugged his sleeve to stop him. "The amulet was supposed to lead to another realm to find an elf to save Betören, right? It brought you back to your homeland because there are already elves here?"

He looked over his shoulder as if questioning whether a brain existed in my head. It was the first I'd seen him appear impatient. "Have you heard my words? The king murdered the elves."

"Right."

He resumed his trek.

I didn't follow. "Why go to Tal—Talum?"

"Talamh Sí." Rhys took a double take when he saw I was no longer beside him and bridged the gap between us. "We aren't. We're going to find the Saoirse Trodaí. They will help."

"Who are they?" I asked.

"Rebels freed from the king's curse who seek freedom for the rest of Betören."

I glanced back at the way up to the megalith. The flowers were still in sight. "Why are you bringing me to them?" Was he tricking me into doing what he'd wanted me to do all along? "Are you bringing me to them because you still think I'm an elf?"

If his exaggerated sigh left any doubts as to his growing impatience, his foot tapping did not. "Perhaps you'd prefer to try the megalith once more?"

"That would be a waste of time."

"Perhaps you'd rather try your luck in Rotko then?"

I shuddered. "Definitely not."

"Then what choice have you? If anyone can help you get back to your realm, they can."

My face surely revealed my skepticism. "How? And why would they help me?"

Rhys blew out a breath and wagged his forearms. "Perhaps they will. Perhaps they won't. But as we've reasoned, there's no other choice. So, follow me." He waved me onward, spun, and continued at his hurried pace.

No other choice that he offered. This was his realm. His world. There had to be another option, but this was what he'd wanted all along. I watched his retreating back. What if this was all some kind of elaborate scheme to catch an elf?

But with the darkening sky, what choice did I have but to trust the only one who knew the terrain and what might lurk about at night? I rushed to catch up. The kitty bounced in my arms. He gripped me with his claws once more. "But we'll never make it through these trees before nightfall."

"Our feet won't get us there, to be sure. But if this be the Uaine Highlands, there may be another way."

"Another way? What other way? Like a horse?"

"Perhaps. Or better yet... a train."

Twelve

A train? Hot-air balloons and now trains… I'd only read of such things in books from Fallon's world. Was it possible? Could Betören be a territory she'd never had reason to mention? But I hadn't heard of Rotko or Talamh Sí either. This had to be a different realm.

Just how many realms were there?

We walked along the unnaturally pristine path through an endless maze of clone trees until the sun disappeared behind the tree line and the remaining colorful glow dimmed. Despite the cat's small stature, my arms grew heavy carrying him.

Rhys whistled as he trekked along the path. Every once in a while, he added a slight skip to his step. Did he not tire? Perhaps his day hadn't begun as early as mine. Should I ask him to carry the kitten?

No, he hatched this morning. Protecting him was my responsibility. I peeled him off my shoulder to switch sides, but he didn't seem to appreciate being manhandled. He leaped away and threw me a look to make it clear how much I'd irritated him, stretched, then strolled down the path.

At least he hadn't darted away.

I rubbed my cramped arms. "If you're going to walk for yourself, please stay with us. I don't need you getting me into any more trouble, thank you very much." I wagged my finger at the cat as if he understood my words.

"Have you plans to name the poor beast? Or do you intend to refer to him as 'the cat' indefinitely?"

"I've never named anything before." Somehow, it seemed so... ownery. Was that a word? Either way, it was a tremendous responsibility. The poor creature would be stuck with the name for life.

The kitten skimmed the path as if barely coming in contact with the dirt. He was gray and white, like clouds on an otherwise sunny day. "How about Stormy?"

"Stormy?" Rhys wrinkled his nose.

That was a nay, not that I understood why he had a say. But maybe he was right. And although I'd yet to see the feline do anything uncatlike, he was anything but. Cats didn't hatch from eggs or tattoo your arm with magical lights when you petted them. Regardless, Rhys best think of him as nothing more than a cat.

The creature bounded down the hill. He jumped into the air where his legs and torso elongated before my eyes. By the time he returned to earth, he looked like a puppy.

"What in Ariboslia?" I nearly tripped as I gawked. "Did he—"

"—transfigure into canine form? To be sure." Rhys bent and petted the dog's head. "But need I remind you you're no longer in Ariboslia? Where did you say you adopted him?"

The puppy pounced twice as if inviting me to play, then pranced his new canine body like a show horse along the path to flaunt his figure.

"It's an expression. And I didn't say." Creeping crabs, there was no keeping his identity hidden now. And why did Rhys seem undisturbed by a cat morphing into a dog? Was shape-shifting common here too? The gachen could shift into their totem animal form, but nothing else.... Just the human form of their birth and one animal totem when they reached their bian around fifteen. I'd never heard tell of an animal, a young one at that, transfiguring into another beast. But then, this so-called cat hatched from an egg... and branded me. What was it really? And what else might it do?

"You're aware this is no ordinary cat."

My heart thrummed. Should I tell him what I knew? I'd already trusted him enough to follow him from the highlands through the endless one-tree maze to find a train. "I found him. As—an egg."

"To be sure. To be sure."

"Why is this not a surprise to you?"

"The nameless beast is no cat, to be sure. The beast is a dragon."

I stumbled. "A dragon?"

"Dragons appropriate many forms, though they favor one or two."

A dragon... That made the most logical sense if logical sense was to be made. It explained the egg. And what about the smoke when he sneezed? Was that actual smoke? Not dust? Could this creature breathe fire?

The puppy ran to me and gnawed on my hand. A needlelike puppy tooth pricked me.

"Ouch!" I jerked my hand away and gave him a stern look. "No bite." I inspected the spot. No broken skin. "You mean he might shift into *anything*? Isn't that kind of dangerous?"

"For whom?"

"For anyone."

"To be sure—but only if he transfigures before the wrong sort."

"What *sort*?"

"Those loyal to the king—most everyone in Talamh Sí. The elfin king eliminated the dragons. His subjects would report a dragon sighting, to be sure."

Horrified, I covered the puppy's ears in case he understood English. "What if he shifts in front of others? How can we keep anyone from finding out?"

"According to the book *Mystical Creatures of the Past and Present*, dragons mature quickly. If one can rely upon the author's accuracy as some statements are audacious fabrications." He spoke the last sentence through gritted teeth. Then his snarl relaxed, and he continued in a calmer tone. "As they mature, their ability to communicate with their bondmate develops. Has the beast bonded to you, perchance?"

"I–I think so." I grasped my sleeve, then hesitated. How much should I trust this boy? But I needed the advice. I rolled up my sleeve to reveal the mark around my upper arm. "This appeared when I touched him after he hatched."

Rhys's lips formed a tight line. "The book contained similar drawings. So, there's *some* legitimacy to the author's words." He added the last words under his breath. The smile and calm demeanor returned once again. "You have bonded, to be sure. When circumstances warrant, advise him it's unsafe to transfigure. Use any means imaginable—words, thoughts, images—until you communicate reliably. With any luck, he'll understand. Until then..." He scratched his ear. "We must take care."

So, I had bonded to a dragon who preferred cat form, could shift into who knew what at will, and would soon communicate with me. What would *that* be like?

"The beast must be named."

The puppy rolled around on his back, then hopped up, and chased his tail. He snapped, caught the tip of his tail between clenched baby teeth, and continued circling. When he noticed us from the corner of his eye, he somehow appeared embarrassed but unable to stop himself.

"How about Iisakki?" Rhys asked.

"Ee–sah–key?"

"EE–sah–ki." He put added emphasis on the *E* sound. "It means 'one who brings laughter.' He is rather waggish."

"Waggish?"

"Amusing."

"Oh." I laughed at Iisakki's antics. "That seems to fit. Iisakki it is."

Iisakki released his tail and snorted. Twin pillars of smoke escaped his nostrils.

What little I knew of dragons came from books. They were destructive beasts that needed to die for the safety of those who lived nearby. But those were works of fiction.

Again, I shivered, reminded of how Fallon wrote her Ariboslia experiences and made everyone believe they were fictional stories. Her truth wasn't real to her readers, but that didn't make it any less real. With truth and fiction so intermingled, how was I to know what was real and what was make-believe? Trains, hot-air balloons, flying ships, elves, fae, and now dragons? Evidently, they were all real. But that didn't help me discern what aspects of their character were real.

But, of all I've read about dragons, his hatching from an egg made sense. They also tended to be scaly lizardy creatures. Would he ever turn into that? Did he have a true form he'd yet to show me?

One other thing about dragons all accounts seemed to agree upon —they breathe fire. That explained the smoke.

An overwhelming wave of reality hit me. I was bonded to a shape-shifting dragon. An illegal pet in an unfamiliar world. What would happen if someone caught him? How could I protect him *here*? I might as well be a child back in Bandia with an impossible responsibility. The familiar rush of emotions squeezed in on me, blocking my air. The horizon wavered. I braced myself to keep from falling as my vision doubled.

Light in. Dark out.

Light in. Dark out.

"Mrrreow." Iisakki stood on his hind legs and braced against my knee.

I picked him up and held him close. A strength I didn't know I possessed welled up within along with the determination that no harm would come to him. I'd do whatever it took to protect him. Come what may.

THIRTEEN

Night fell, and we made camp. The air grew cool. I wrapped my legs into the length of my skirt like a blanket. The selkie fabric kept me warm. Still, I huddled closer to the fire, holding out my hands to draw in the heat. Light danced in the sporadic breezes, making it appear as if monsters darted behind the trees, spying on us. Each pop from the fire made me jump.

"Are there any"—I braced myself to say the word—"f–fasgadair here?"

"Pray tell, what are fasgadair?"

He didn't know? That was comforting. "They're evil. They drink blood."

He jerked away from me. "Goodness, no. What would you want with such a creature?"

"I don't *want* one. I want to make sure there aren't any." I scanned the woods for anything that wasn't just a shadow. "Or any other scary creatures."

"Nothing like that exists here. To be sure, to be sure. So long as you stay out of Rotko."

"Does whatever lives in Rotko come here?"

"Whatever enters the Divide never comes out."

Every muscle within me relaxed. Maybe this wouldn't be a terrible place to visit until I found a way home. My stomach complained about the piddly bread and cheese Rhys had shared. There might be edible plants nearby, but I needed light to inspect them. And no way was I walking through these woods in the dark. With or without Rhys.

How many stories had I heard Fallon tell of her making camp on her countless adventures? It sounded so exciting—sitting around a fire, eating rabbit, listening to tales of Ariboslia. I spent hours imagining myself there, among them, joining in the camaraderie.

But reality—*my* reality—wasn't so glamorous. The only similarity was the fire that offered warmth, but no comfort. We had no meat. No bedding. And rather than consorting with friends, I distrusted my only companion—other than my bonded dragon.

Though I'd yet to behold Iisakki's true form and knew next to nothing about him, I trusted him without question—as if he were an extension of myself.

But Rhys and his unchanging and unreadable aura was a different story. What was he playing at? Was he trying to help me? Or trap me? He was searching for an elf. And he was certain I was either ignorant or lying. What if he could have brought me home and chose not to? What if he showed me the Forest of Shadows to frighten me? What if these woods weren't as identical as they seemed? What if he had us circling all day to get me here? Asleep. Vulnerable.

That was it. No sleep for me.

"I'll take first watch." Rhys sat beside the fire, rubbing his hands before the flames. "You rest."

Could he read minds? I stifled a scoff and attempted to think about anything else, just in case. I searched the patchy grass for a decent place to pretend to sleep. Iisakki, in his puppy form, had curled up on a comfy spot a suitable distance from the flames. I tried settling in beside him, but the ground left much to be desired. A rock poked my side. I turned to avoid the rock and a new one dug into my thigh. That wouldn't do.

On my hands and knees, I rooted around for every pebble that might interfere with my comfort and tossed it away.

"Everything okay?" Rhys eyeballed me over his shoulder.

"Just trying to get comfortable." I waited for him to look away, then swiveled to block my hands from him should he turn around again.

Once I was certain he wasn't interested in what I was doing, I placed my hands on the grass and reached for the life of each blade within my touch. My hands illuminated. Strands of my life force traveled down my arms, along with the familiar tickle, and escaped through my fingers. But the fibers never disconnected. Rather, they connected me to the plant as they coursed down through the plant to its roots. I tugged at its life force with care, offering some of my own, encouraging the grass to grow and thicken.

I checked to ensure I hadn't attracted Rhys's attention before moving on to plump up more grass. The thin blades required little energy. And I hadn't relinquished much. Not enough to exhaust me. I lay down on my plush bedding. It wasn't a down mattress, but it was an improvement.

I tucked my feet into my skirt and wrapped an arm over Iisakki. His steady breathing calmed my nerves.

What had I done?

I made myself comfortable when I was already exhausted. How was I going to stay awake to protect Iisakki and myself should Rhys prove untrustworthy? And without any weapons...

My heavy eyelids drooped. I snapped them open and worked my jaw as if that might help keep me awake. But I should have peeled myself away from Iisakki's warm body. I should have stood and moved about or splashed water on my face. Sang at the top of my lungs. Anything but lay in the lush grass snuggled with Iisakki. But my weary flesh refused to budge, content where it lay. And sleep was a cunning thing—a slippery slope down which I began my descent.

SOMETHING NUDGED ME. "Colleen, it's your turn."

I jerked awake. Where was I? Why wasn't I at home in bed? With Rhys prodding my arm with a stick, the events from the prior day rushed back like a tsunami.

Well done, Colleen. Good job not falling asleep.

Rhys settled down in the grass on the dwindling fire's opposite side. He hadn't tried to kill us. Or done anything else underhanded. There was something to be said for that.

My wrist ached. I must've slept on it wrong. I massaged it, only to aggravate it further.

Beyond the fire glow, shadows lunged and retreated, tricking my eyes into seeing things that weren't there.

I hoped nothing was there.

A thousand ants scampered along my spine and down my arms.

"You said there were no monsters here, right?" I hugged myself and faced Rhys. "So, w–what am I looking out for?" I worked to steady my words. "And w–what should I do if it arrives?"

"I don't know. But if you see anything—anything at all—wake me." He yawned and rolled over.

"Okaaay." I imitated Fallon's annoyed response and covered a yawn with the back of my hand.

Soft snores escaped him. Who fell asleep that quick? Was he faking? Nay, he must've struggled to stay awake. This darkness and quiet, punctuated by the fire's soft crackles, would lull anyone to sleep if you didn't let the shadow monsters get to you.

And why would he pretend? He hadn't tried anything, and I'd handed him the perfect opportunity. Now he was putting himself in the same vulnerable position.

Maybe he wasn't untrustworthy.

Iisakki stretched his legs in front of him, let out a high-pitched puppy yawn, then stretched his hind legs behind him before sitting beside me.

"You going to keep watch with me?" His ears flapped as I petted him. "You're only a puppy, but I suppose even a young dog would be a better companion in a fight than a cat of any age. Unless you were a big cat, like a lion. Can you shift into a lion?"

Iisakki slid forward and rested his head on his paws. He breathed a heavy sigh and deflated—loudly.

"But your dragon form—I'd like to see that. Can you fly? Can you breathe fire? That might come in handy."

He rolled onto his back, four long limbs floundered in the air.

I chuckled and gave him the belly rub he requested. "You know, I'm not much of a fighter. Not at all to be more precise—despite my uncles' attempts."

Iisakki rolled back onto his stomach. He yawned and placed his chin on my leg. I cupped his ear and stroked his temple with my thumb.

"Do you think I'm an elf too? I'm beginning to believe I am."

He blinked as if fighting to stay awake.

"It's okay to sleep, pup. Or kitty. Dragon. Whatever you are, you're still a baby. You need your rest." He hatched yesterday, for Pete's sake. I struggled to wrap my head around that. Normal puppies would be icky little fluff balls that still needed their mother.

His eyes gave up the battle. Soft, steady puffs of air escaped his nose, and his eyebrows twitched.

This strange creature was making a home in my heart. Nay, he already had. What would I do with that? I didn't know how to care for a dragon. How quickly did they age? How much rest did they require?

And what did they eat?

Iisakki had gobbled up his rations and part of mine. He seemed okay, so bread and cheese must be safe for dragons to eat. And he might've helped himself to snacks he'd happened upon when out of view. But we all needed a proper meal soon.

A low murmur sounded in the distance. Voices? Who would be walking through the woods at this hour? Bandits? Murderers?

Fasgadair?

My heart slammed into my throat and stilled as my eyes hyperfocused toward the voices. I held my breath and shimmied with as little sound as possible to Rhys and prodded his arm. He didn't stir, so I pushed him again, knocking his arm off his side.

"Uh?" He picked his head up and squinted as if the little light hurt his eyes.

"I heard voices." I fought to keep my voice steady. But panic was threatening to overtake me. I wanted to cry. Or run.

Hide. We needed to hide. Now.

Rhys bolted upright. "Where?"

I pointed away from where we'd come. He motioned for me to stay back as he crept forward, disappearing into the shadow-monster-infested woods.

FOURTEEN

My heart hammered, then seemed to stop. A heavy beat slammed my chest as if I'd been punched. The air rushed from my lungs. I covered my mouth, trying to catch my breath—quietly. I strained to listen for footfalls, voices, anything. But my thudding heart drowned everything out.

I bounced in place, conjuring every ounce of willpower not to run.

What happened to the voices? Had I imagined them? And where was Rhys? What was taking him so long?

Fasgadair faces flashed in my mind. What evil beings came out at night in this realm?

I should have gone with Rhys.

What if... What if...

I backed away from the fire, opposite the way he had disappeared, into the safety of the wood's shadow.

Something touched my leg, and I jumped, nearly stepping on Iisakki in his cat form. I wanted to admonish him for frightening me, but I didn't dare speak. He rubbed against my leg and meowed. Loudly.

"Shhh!" I picked him up. At least I *could* hear something outside my pounding heart. I'd take that relief. While he gripped my shoulder with his claws and purred, I stroked his fur.

Light in. Dark out.

Light in. Dark out.

What was taking Rhys so long?

Something rustled in the trees.

My feet tingled, urging me to act as my breath escaped and my heart stilled once more.

Rhys emerged from the tree line.

Relief rushed through me. "Wha—"

Figures appeared behind him.

One. Two. Three.

We were outnumbered. Three men to a boy and me... unarmed. As each figure emerged, I took a step back, clutching Iisakki tight, searching for the best escape route.

"Colleen, I've brought help." Rhys must've sensed my flight plan.

If the obscured figures had auras, there was no reading them in this darkness. Or from this distance. Would they be Rhys's unusual, never-changing, unreadable color? I'd never realized what an advantage it was to understand people's emotions. It was a great survival tool. And now, when I most needed it, my ability was impaired, like a bird with clipped wings.

The moon's dim glow didn't penetrate the trees at my back. Still, my feet itched to run. Should I take my chances alone in the woods? At night?

"Colleen?" Rhys asked.

The three men shuffled behind Rhys. One cleared his throat. Another scratched his head, displacing his hat, then returned it to its rightful place. Two of the men wore coats, one with his trousers tucked into tall boots. The other wore a loose shirt with suspenders. All wore similar flat caps that overlapped a brim in front, covering their foreheads, further obscuring their eyes.

They didn't seem like fasgadair. They didn't have pasty skin or the telltale electrical smell. But what other unholy creatures might prowl this realm, masquerading as men? And even if they were human—were they safe?

"Colleen!" Rhys rounded the fire. "Where are you?"

I backed away, deeper into the woods.

"These are the people I sought!" He yelled as if I were a considerable distance away, not mere cubits. "They can help us!"

Iisakki meowed and bounded from my arms. He ran straight to Rhys.

My empty arms groped for him as if I might be able to suck him back to me. Betrayer. I couldn't run now.

"Iisakki?" Rhys bent down to pet the cat, then searched the darkness as if he still couldn't see me.

Light in. Dark out.

Light in. Dark out.

I sucked in one last deep breath and stepped forward. "You know them?"

"Ah!" Rhys fell backward onto his rump. The others stepped back, sharing confused expressions. "There you are."

He searched about as if uncertain where I'd come from, then held a palm up as if to keep me in place. But he needn't have worried. I wouldn't leave without Iisakki.

"These men are part of the Saoirse Trodaí."

Their attire looked like something from books depicting historical America, England, or elsewhere in the human realm. But Rhys hadn't mentioned any places I recognized. Still, more and more evidence pointed to Fallon's home. Perhaps I could find my way to Aunt Stacy. She'd help me.

"They each bear the mark," Rhys said as if that somehow should assure me.

It did not. I crossed my arms. "What mark?"

"The mark of the Saors." The man speaking stepped into the firelight, but the color of his aura still wasn't clear. He clutched his hat, yanked it off his head, and gave a bow. "The name's Taneli." His broad smile revealed uneven teeth. Though he seemed kind enough and nothing struck me as insincere, something in the similarity to the top-hat man's greeting made my insides squeeze. He tugged his coat from his broad shoulders and pulled up a stained shirtsleeve to reveal a tattoo on his veiny upper forearm—three leaves. Nay, three half circles connected with another circle running through their center. "Means freedom."

His accent sounded similar to the Ariboslian brogue but lighter. Was he human? Gachen? Or something else? Whatever he was, his accent sounded nothing like Fallon's though he spoke English.

As if dismissing himself from the presence of royalty, Taneli bowed as he stepped back to rejoin his friends.

The other man with a coat closed in on me. Shorter than Taneli he gripped his hat but didn't remove it as I fought to stay put. Rather, he tipped his head forward, then thrust out a hand. "I'm Pirkko."

Fear of offending those who outnumbered me outweighed my concern of foreign diseases, and I raised a tentative hand. Pirkko gave it a firm shake, then flung it away. His hand was small and soft for a man. Perhaps he was young. The dim lighting didn't allow me to draw any conclusions, and his hat didn't help. He removed his right boot, then peeled away his pant leg and droopy sock. The same symbol appeared on his smooth ankle.

The last man with no coat stepped forward. "The name's Reko." His gruff voice and bulging muscles didn't soothe my distress. Nor did his narrow eyes. They were tough to see below his hat's brim, but his intense gaze pierced me as if it were a tangible thing.

I stepped back, bile rising in my chest. I was in the woods in a foreign world at night and now with three—no, four—strange men. My family must be off their heads with worry. If anything happened to me here, they'd never know.

How could I have been such a fool?

"Miss." The man seemed to soften. He tilted his head toward me, then loosened the cords tying his shirt. He pulled the collar down to show the same mark on his shoulder.

So, these men were part of the same group. Should that bring me comfort? This proved they were banded together. But for what purpose? For freedom? Freedom from what or who? Why should I trust them? What if they were terrorists?

Rhys held up both hands as if sending forth an unseen force that could subdue the panic welling within. "Fear not, fair maiden. They only wish to help."

Iisakki seemed to sense my unease. He scrambled into my arms. A soft purr whirred within his body, sending subtle calming vibrations.

"Help us do what?"

"Why, get you home, of course. That is your desire, is it not?"

What? Just when had they discussed this? Is that what took Rhys so long? And why did I doubt his intentions to help me get home? "They want to help me get home?"

The first man, Taneli, cleared his throat. "Ah, shure! Our leader, Valtteri, has means to return ya to your realm. He possesses an amulet spelled to take ya wherever ya wish."

"And he'll just give it to me?" I eyed them as though one might betray a lie. Oh, if only I could see the colors of their auras! Night blindness was terrible. "What do you expect from me in return?"

"Accompany us to speak with Valtteri for yourself." Taneli looked around. "Unless ya prefer takin' your chances in these woods—alone. It's well for some."

What did that mean? I scowled at Rhys. "This was where you intended to go?"

He gave a solemn nod. "They will aid our quest."

"Quest? What quest?" I held up a hand as if to hold him back. "No disrespect, but I don't know you either. You expect me to travel through dark woods with four men? To God only knows where?"

Rhys grinned and straightened. Was it because I'd called him a man?

Pirkko yanked his hat and shook his head. Long locks tumbled down past his shoulders.

Wait.

Pirkko wasn't a man? "You're a–a—"

"Lass, ya. Look." She reached out and grasped my hand in both of hers. "We're strangers. But we're harmless. We will do all we can to get ya home." She released me with a reassuring smile. "Willya join us."

The words seemed like a question, but she didn't phrase it like one. Something in her and Iisakki's calm demeanors lulled me.

What choice did I have?

Fifteen

The sun rose as we walked, and the auras surrounding my traveling companions revealed themselves. But they were dim from either lack of emotion or exhaustion assuming they worked the same for gachen as they did for whatever these people were. Either way, dull colors were better than strong emotions. Perhaps I could trust them.

Since their auras didn't tell me much, I stole glances to learn what I could about them without being obvious.

Reko appeared to be the oldest. Mid-twenties maybe? Stubble covered his jaw, but nothing else about him gave away that he'd been traversing the woods all night. He walked as though his back was strapped to a steel rod. Only the reddening of his brown eyes betrayed his weariness. Despite his stern countenance, something friendly lingered about him.

Taneli looked friendly-ish too. He smiled more than Reko. But something more dangerous lurked within him. A fiery glint in his green eyes. Even as everything else about him expressed his fatigue from his slouching shoulders to his stumbling feet.

Many strands of Pirkko's reddish brown hair had escaped her hat, and a smudge dirtied her cheek. I considered telling her, but I wasn't sure how it would be received. Girls could be funny about such things. So which would embarrass her more—being told or finding out later and wondering how long it had been there? She seemed the most amiable, and her easygoing nature made me most comfortable with her. But I didn't know her. I didn't know any of them. Until I did, I'd remain quiet.

Though my aching feet begged for rest, the rising sun renewed my spirits and awakened me enough to press on. Dew clung to the trees, and leaves glistened in the morning rays. The maze of trees morphed to some variety. I still didn't know where I was going, but I no longer felt I was walking in circles. And I had guides. All these things blunted the sharp edges of my thoughts.

My gaze continued to drift to Iisakki, expecting him to transition to his dog form or who knew what else.

Stay in cat form, Iisakki. Don't change in front of these people. It's best if they don't know you're a dragon.

I tried sending him a mental picture of himself as a cat with a strong sense that he needed to remain that way.

If anything got through, Iisakki gave no indication. But he hadn't changed. Yet.

Only Rhys seemed unaffected by the lack of rest. He carried on as if one side of his brain slept while the other soldiered on, like a shark. He even broke out in a whistle.

"Shhh!" Reko hushed him.

Pirkko threw Rhys a withering look.

"Eejit." Taneli huffed. "Ya tryin' to attract soldiers?"

Rhys shrunk as if he could retract into himself. "It was no louder than your speech to my ears."

"Do ya hear us chatterin' on like a canary?" Taneli asked.

Rhys fell back a few steps and maintained his shortened posture, but soon returned to his happy self.

We came to a path with two metal parallel rows. Evenly spaced wooden planks filled the gap. "Are these train tracks?"

"Ya say that as if ya never seen 'em." Taneli glanced over his shoulder. Something about him reminded me of Aunt Stacy. Freckles covered both their faces. Red hair peeked out from beneath his cap, and when he smiled, he had her friendly green eyes. He was much younger though, perhaps only slightly older than me.

"Nay, I've never seen a train."

"How'd ya know they were train tracks?" Reko aimed his narrowed brown eyes at me. Orange and blue hues brightening in flashes.

With my distrust of them, it hadn't occurred to me that they might be wary of me. I reached for a logical explanation, but nothing made sense, even to me. The last thing I needed to do was arouse more suspicion. Honesty was always best. "I–I read some books from the human realm."

"Which one?" Reko asked.

Taken aback by that question, I gawked at him. "Are there many?"

He grunted. "I only know of Betören and our ancestors' home in Ireland."

"Ireland! I've heard of that! It's a country in the same realm as America." Wait. If their ancestors were from Ireland and that was in a different realm, then that meant...

My worst fears had come true.

Everything else faded as a weight planted itself in my heart and took root—I was in another foreign realm. Not mine. Not Aunt Stacy's. Unventured foreign territory.

Without an amulet.

No hope of finding Aunt Stacy.

No way to get back to my family.

My surroundings wavered, and I faltered. Taneli put an arm around my shoulder to steady me. My vision blurred. I pulled at my collar, which was nowhere close to choking me. So why couldn't I breathe?

I doubled over, sucking in breaths that never seemed to reach my burning lungs.

God, what is happening? Please help!

Something rubbed against my leg. Iisakki. He twisted himself around my ankles, taking swipes with his face with each approach. I picked him up and held him close. His soothing rumble helped my breath come easier. Sweet air filled my lungs.

Light in. Dark out.

Light in. Dark out.

My mind returned as my eyesight cleared.

Pirkko squeezed my Iisakki-free shoulder. "Is all well with you? We still have a bit of a jaunt to go."

"I just realized how far from home I am."

"Not to worry. You'll get home." She smiled and patted my back.

If only that were true! In the meantime, I was in a foreign realm—with no knowledge of its inhabitants other than these emigrants from a somewhat familiar realm. If I were to survive this and find my way home, I needed to learn as much as possible... and trust these people who claimed to want to help.

"Now..." Taneli sidled up beside me as we walked along the tracks. "Ya read of trains from books, eh? From which realm? How did ya happen upon books from Ireland?"

"The entire realm isn't Ireland. That's just one country, like America. I don't know what it's called. Earth? Though we're all on earth, just different realms on the same planet..." Their confused expressions and auras made me stop rambling. "Anyway, my adopted mother is from America. Her best friend, Stacy, visits us from there. When she can. She brings us all kinds of things—food, household goods, books."

"But you're from a different realm?" Pirkko kept pace alongside me. "What's its name?"

"Ariboslia."

"Savage." Reko pinched his lips. "Is inter-realm travel common in Ariboslia?"

Savage? Ariboslia didn't have trains, but I wouldn't call it savage. "Uh. No. The pech build the megaliths and create amulets to operate them. They have guidelines as to where megaliths can be built and how they're to be used. Access is limited."

My gaze darted among them. Was I saying too much? I still didn't know if I could trust them. Their confusion hadn't lessened, but Rhys's infuriatingly foreign aura never changed. At. All. Why did they have normal auras, but not Rhys? If their ancestors were all from Ireland, they were human. What made Rhys different? He even spoke differently.

The leafy canopy thickened, yet bright light filtered through, making the leaves appear to give off their own light. Up ahead, the leaves formed a perfect rectangle, like a tunnel. A train-sized tunnel. The tracks ran straight into it.

"You say your ancestors are from Ireland? How did they come to be here?"

"Eerikki rescued them, to be sure." Rhys fidgeted with a pebble, passing it through his fingers.

"That's fair to say," Taneli said. "They would've starved in Ireland. Our great-grandparents depended on potatoes for food. Milk and potatoes."

"Crime." Reko shook his head.

"And sometimes herring." Pirkko shoved a hunk of hair under her hat.

Unsure that made sense, I threw my arms up. "I don't understand. Will people die if all they have to eat is potatoes and milk?"

"Hmph. If they don't have enough." Red flashed about Taneli's otherwise calm aura.

Pirkko eyed him, seeming to understand something about his bitterness that I didn't. "A blight destroyed the potato crops. Those who didn't flee the country died from starvation."

"And yet"—Rhys poised a finger in the air as if it held all the answers—"you live today because Eerikki rescued your ancestors."

"Who's Eerikki?" And why did Rhys mention him twice?

Pirkko weaved her arm through Reko's as they entered the tunnel. Were they a couple? "The first elven king. King Auberon's father. He brought our grandparents through the megalith. The first humans in Betören."

I ran my fingers along the tunnel's leafy wall and tried to imagine bringing inhabitants of another realm home. Even Aunt Stacy hadn't moved to Ariboslia. She just visited. Fallon was the only one from their realm who had made Ariboslia their permanent home... that I was aware of.

"If the legends are true"—Taneli waved his hands about as if he needed them to speak—"Eerikki happened upon a pooka caught in a net, dangling over rapids. Whether he helped the pooka out of the goodness of his heart or if he knew helping a pooka would make him Eerikki's slave for life, we don't—"

"Wait." I scooted closer. "What's a pooka?"

"An aetherian creature created by a witch. Its true form is a black rabbit." Pirkko wagged two fingers, making bunny ears. "I never seen one."

"That ya know of." Taneli kicked a pebble, sending it pinging against the rail. "They can shape-shift, so who really knows?"

Pirkko tipped her head toward him, wordlessly giving him the point.

"The slave debt is a mere ten years." Rhys raised a finger to inter-ject again. "The pooka may continue in service to their rescuer *if* they so desire."

Taneli snatched a pebble and copied Rhys's fidgeting. "Which-ever ways it were, the pooka led Eerikki to a megalith and explained what it was. Eerikki commanded the pooka to find an amulet to travel the realms, and so he did. In his travels, he came to the human realm —Ireland, to be precise. He saw their technology and weapons—"

"And extreme poverty."

At Rhys's interruption, Taneli threw him a threatening look. " and used our grandparents to kill the elves and make himself king. The peaceful elves were no match for their guns."

Rhys cleared his throat. "Do not confuse your history. The elves didn't fall under Eerikki's rule, but Auberon's. And that was after many years. King Eerikki gave the elves chance after chance to be hospitable. The Irish needed homes, farmland, food. But the elves would have none of it. Someone had to fight for them." He clicked his tongue. "Right or wrong, it also should be noted that the pooka had no part in such plans."

The others pinned him with questioning looks.

"How would you know that?" Reko crossed his arms.

Rhys squirmed. Did he actually shrink? How did he appear smaller? "I read. I believe it was in either *Talamh Sí: The Rise of Betören's Greatest Kingdom* or *The Role of Aetherian Creatures in Modern Society.*" He scratched his ear. "Or perhaps it was *Ireland's Great Potato Blight: The Inhabitants of a Starving Country Flee Their Homeland,* or perhaps it was—"

Pirkko rolled her eyes. "Does it matter?"

"I should say so." Rhys left his ear alone. "Eerikki was a good man, to be sure, willing to help people no one else would. *Your* people. The same people who killed the elves."

"Under Auberon's command!" Red blazed from Taneli as he thrust his chest out, towering over Rhys with unspoken threats.

Rhys held a bent arm before him as if to deflect a blow. "Then we agree. It was Auberon, not Eerikki."

Taneli sneered.

"Wait." This was getting out of control, and my head was spinning. Why was everyone so emotional? "If I understand this, Eerikki saved your grandparents from Ireland by bringing them here so they didn't starve. Then his son, Auberon, used your people to kill the elves, though he was an elf himself?"

"That's about the sum of it." Reko dragged a hand down his face.

Taneli huffed.

The humans survived and the elves died. So, apparently, Auberon rose to power and placed some kind of curse on his people that angered Taneli. But with my brain overloaded, I didn't want to risk angering him further by asking.

Rhys glowered at Taneli. "Eerikki was not to blame. And pookas are helpful, benevolent creatures." Was he growing again? "I'd hate for one questionable king to spoil the whole lot of them."

Taneli shrugged. "I wouldn't know."

The others murmured their lack of pooka knowledge.

"However it happened"—Reko sighed—"Auberon is on the throne. The elves are gone. And our people are under a curse."

"Wouldn't hurt to read a book or two," Rhys spoke under his breath. The others either hadn't heard him or chose to ignore him.

The ground rumbled beneath me, sending a shock of fear from my feet throughout my body. "What is that?"

The others smiled.

"Time to catch a train!" Taneli waved us forward.

"Catch? How do you catch a train?" Were they hoping the capture the metallic beast? Was that even possible?

"Jump on board," Taneli hollered over the growing roar.

"Jump? As in, while it's still moving?" My stomach dropped to my feet.

"Follow me. I'll help ya. But ya better run if you value your life. Get out of this tunnel before the train flattens ya." Taneli turned and ran.

My entire body shook with the ground. Then, as if the vibration reminded my limbs what to do, I dashed after him. But I felt slow. I could run fast, much faster than this. Still, I passed Pirkko and Taneli. Were they slow? Or did everything seem to be in slow motion? And how long was this tunnel? The thick wall seemed impenetrable, despite being made of foliage.

Someone yelled. I dared a glance back.

A massive mechanical monster roared behind me. It filled every bit of space, leaving no room to let it pass. Rhys had fallen behind. I ran back and snatched his arm. He stumbled in my grip.

"Hurry!" I yelled.

Where was Iisakki?

I slowed to allow Rhys to keep his footing. A whistle blasted, igniting everything within me, urging me to move faster. I eyed the walls on either side. At this speed, they seemed even more solid. I yanked Rhys and focused on my escape.

SIXTEEN

Another sharp whistle blared over the train's thunderous roar at my back. The blast struck as if it were a tangible force, pushing me forward. Faster. Gripping Rhys's hand tight, heart in my throat, I dashed for the exit. We were almost there. Just a little more.

Rhys tripped. His hand slipped from mine.

The others passed. Waving frantically, they screamed at us to hurry.

I stared over Rhys's shoulder at the machine bearing down on us. My heart stilled.

Move, Colleen!

Now!

My mind returned. I grasped Rhys's outstretched hand and tugged. We raced for the opening where the others exited. Rushing blood thudded in my ear. My upper body reached for the exit as my legs slogged behind as if trudging through mud. Something seized my shoulder, tore into my flesh, and yanked me into the air. I clung to Rhys as his feet, too, left the ground. Branches scraped my arm. Once free of the tunnel, I was released. I fell in the dirt beside Rhys and crab-walked away from the tracks as the metallic beast rumbled past. The sharp wind tossed my hair, whipping my face.

Rhys brushed away grass and dirt from his clothes and said something that sounded like "I'm indebted to you," but I couldn't hear well over the train.

What had yanked me away? Something strong. And big. I jerked about, searching in every direction. But I saw nothing capable of such a feat—only my rumpled traveling companions in their own state of bewilderment.

I reached for the wound in my shoulder and winced as I made contact. My fingers came away bloody.

Iisakki licked my face.

I released a pent-up breath. "Where were you? You could've gotten killed!"

He licked his paw and commenced washing his face, unconcerned.

Taneli righted himself and yelled over the unholy wind from the never-ending line of cars. "Let's go!"

The others followed.

So, he still intended to jump on board. While it was moving? Didn't people board trains at stations? I lugged Rhys to his feet and hurried to catch up. The train had slowed, but the idea of jumping into the belly of the mechanical beast while in motion made my legs wobble like jelly.

Taneli waved his hands in some kind of fit as he ushered us to hurry. "We need to get on the train before it reaches the station! Quick! This one!"

He grasped the ledge of an open car and heaved himself on board. His legs kicked as though swimming in midair. Then he tumbled inside. He reappeared in a crouch, grasping the train with one hand and reaching to Pirkko with the other.

Reko gave Pirkko a shove, and she latched onto Taneli's forearm. She seemed to fly into the train.

Taneli helped Reko next. Rhys squeezed my hand. "You're next!"

Taneli, Pirkko, and Reko yelled, urging us to board.

"Nay. I can catch up." I pushed Rhys, and his fingers batted Taneli's hand before they fumbled into a secure grip. Legs windmilling, Rhys fell into the car.

The train's horn blared. I faltered but caught my fall. My stomach felt as though it had already boarded the train and chugged away without me. I ran with all I had, my long skirt catching my legs, threatening to take me down. But I could almost reach Taneli's outstretched hand. He caught me and yanked with surprising force. Legs flailing, I swung inside the train car, thudded onto the floor, and rolled into a stack of crates. A shock jolted up my arm from the impact.

I threw Taneli a disgusted look as I rubbed my arm. "If the train is approaching a station, why couldn't we have boarded while it was stopped?"

He brushed his hair into place before replacing his cap and fiddled with his coat. "Sentries. Patrolling the ground and in towers. No way we could board without being spotted."

Reko attended to a scrape on Pirkko's knee while Rhys brushed the wrinkles from his clothes.

Panic rose anew before my thudding heart had a chance to settle. "Where's Iisakki?" Why did the little creep keep disappearing? I ventured as close to the opening as I dared. I couldn't have come all this way, following the cat-dog, just to lose him now.

"He's already on board." Pirkko motioned toward a pile of crates. Sure enough, there he sat on one of the higher crates, licking a paw, calm as could be.

"But how?"

"He flew." Reko narrowed his eyes. "It would appear your *cat* is, in fact, a dragon." He sat on a crate beside Pirkko, his back erect. "Is there something ya'd like to share?"

"Uh." My chest squeezed as though it would spew out the truth on its own if I failed to comply. I threw him and the other skeptical eyes a weak smile. "He's a dragon?"

"As I said." Reko crossed his arms. "Question is—Why did ya lie?"

"Did I lie?" I searched my mind. What had I told them? "I don't think I said anything one way or another."

Taneli rushed toward me. "You don't think—"

Reko stepped between us, pressing a splayed hand on Taneli's chest. Once Taneli stepped back, Reko returned to me. "You're not from our realm, so I'll trust ya didn't realize the position ya put upon us by traveling with a dragon."

Bright purple surrounded Pirkko. Taneli flashed red and black. At least Reko's aura was more purple than red and black. I could deal with confusion better than anger and fear. "I honestly didn't know. I still don't. Why is traveling with a dragon a problem?"

"Pah!" Taneli laughed without a smile or any colors that accompanied genuine laughter.

Reko pointed at Rhys. "Did ya know about this?"

"I—" Rhys blew out a breath that seemed to deflate his entire being. "Yes, I knew."

When Taneli steered his angry aura and threatening posture toward Rhys and closed in fast, Reko grasped Taneli's shoulders. "Leave it. He's not worth it."

Taneli snarled over Reko's shoulder, his accusatory finger jabbing the air toward Rhys. "Ya claim to be from Betören. Ya even knew to seek help from the Saors. Why hide the dragon?"

Throbbing pain settled into my shoulder. In all the commotion, I'd forgotten my injury. I inspected the damage once more. Yet again, my fingertips came back with blood. "Um. Can someone take a look at this?"

Pirkko appeared by my side and inspected the area. "Something scratched ya. Something with talons."

The others came to investigate.

"What did this to ya?" Reko asked.

"I–I don't know. Something carried me away from the train."

"Pro'bly your dragon." Taneli huffed.

The train's rocking slowed.

"We're almost at the station." Reko spread his feet, widening his stance. "Taneli, be on the lookout for sentries."

Taneli snarled but turned to keep watch.

"The wounds are superficial." Pirkko rummaged around a satchel at her waist and removed a tin. She rubbed a finger around the salve. "This will help."

I flinched at the sting of whatever she smeared on my injury.

"Only stings for a second." She placed a bandage on my shoulder and tied it there. "That should hold for now."

"What's the problem with dragons?" I eyed the innocent cat washing his face as though he might change into his dragon form and set the train car on fire.

Blue and orange overtook Pirkko's purple aura. What was making her sad? "Elves and dragons existed in this realm... even in our great-grandfather's days. But by killing off the elves, the king eliminated the dragons too."

"How's that?" My breath felt hollow.

"Dragons exist to serve elves. When their bonded elf dies, the dragon dies too."

I gaped at her. "You make it sound like dragons are extinct. But that's impossible if Iisakki is a dragon."

Reko threw his arms up. "We thought they were. Regardless, they only hatch for an elf."

"But that makes no sense. He hatched for *me*. I'm no elf."

While Pirkko and Taneli exchanged confused glances, their auras erupted in dark purple. Reko skewered me with a pointed stare. "There's only one explanation—*you* are an elf."

SEVENTEEN

I sucked in my breath and backed away. *Was* I an elf? It all made sense—pesky foreigners insisting I was an elf, my abilities, my ears, my never having reached my bian and shifted into animal form. I wasn't late. I wasn't gachen. I was... something else, like the Ugly Duckling.

All this time, I'd been comparing myself to ducks when I was no duck.

I was an elf.

But what did that mean? And how? There were no elves in Ariboslia. And they were extinct here, save the king, and I wasn't likely to get an audience with royalty. So, if I wanted to learn more about elves—real elves, not the ever-so-varying examples from human imaginations in scribblings on a page—how would I learn?

My heel connected with a crate, and I fell backward onto my rear. All eyes aimed at me. Why was it so quiet? And when had we stopped moving?

Shouts came from outside the open door.

"Sentries!" Taneli yelled in a hushed voice. "Hide!"

Everyone's auras blackened as they darted to hiding places

behind the crates. I called to Iisakki, who crawled into my arms as Rhys ushered me to hide beside him. I slid to sit, clutching the dragon-cat as a memory overtook my vision, transporting me to the past, hiding from the fasgadair in Bandia.

The youngest, Beagan, barely able to walk on his own sat on my lap while Nialla and Corwin each clung to an arm. We crowded together under the table in the corner. The fasgadair's electric stench penetrated the air, strengthening as the demon neared. I winced, not daring to look. At any moment, the monster's pallid face would appear and suck us out from under the table.

Please don't let them find us. Please don't let them find us.

"Twelve, all clear!" The voice pulled me from my memory. Shuffling sounded like someone jumping from the car.

In the distance, another voice called out, "Thirteen, all clear!"

We didn't move, barely daring to breathe, while we waited for the voices and pebbly footsteps to disappear.

Please help me!

A rumble began from deep within Iisakki, warming my chest.

Light in. Dark out.

Light in. Dark out.

Though we hadn't heard the sentries in some time, we remained hidden and silent until the whistles blew and the train chugged to life, lurching our creaky car forward. One by one, we emerged from our hiding places.

"Got the time?" Reko asked Pirkko.

She checked a gadget on her wrist. "Got it."

A watch? I'd never seen a watch before.

"How'd he not see me?" Taneli asked.

"I thought he looked right at ya," Reko responded.

"As did I." Taneli held a hand over his heart. "Thought for sure I was off to the clink."

"It was as if a veil protected us," Pirkko said. "But only the fae have that kind of power, right?"

"Far as I know." Reko plucked the hat from his head to run a hand through his brown hair. "But then, there are strangers among us." He eyed me, Rhys, and the cat as his aura flashed in oranges and purples, but no black. At least he wasn't afraid.

"She's an elf." Taneli pointed at me. "So, it weren't her."

Reko closed in on Rhys. "But what are you? If you're human, you're not from Talamh Sí. No human from Talamh Sí looks anythin' like you at all. And no humans reside elsewhere in Betören."

"Unless..." Pirkko claimed a crate seat behind Reko. "He's fae."

Rhys slumped and raised his hands. "I'm from Seelie Clós."

I gasped and swiveled to face him. He wasn't human. That explained the strange aura. But why lie to me? I searched my memory of our meeting. Had he claimed to be human? Or did I assume? I'd been so concerned with him thinking I was an elf, it never occurred to me to ask what *he* was.

Then again... did it matter?

"If you're seelie, why not be honest?" Reko's crossed arms tightened, bunching the cords on his shirt. "We've no quarrels with the seelie."

"C'mere. I'd like to know how he got through Rotko." The spark in Taneli's green eyes flamed.

Rhys held his arms up as if to ward off the attack. "I traveled by way of the megalith, thus bypassing Rotko."

"Why'd ya lie?" Pirkko asked.

"Either you're unseelie. Or"—Taneli's burning eyes narrowed as his aura blazed red—"you're workin' for Auberon."

Rhys's mouth fell open. "Were that true, I'd have brought her to him straightaway, would I not? You needed an elf, and I brought you an elf."

My breath caught in my chest. "You *knew* they were looking for an elf?" I had no idea what that meant, but my legs threatened to give out. My mind worked out the details aloud. "You tricked me. You could've returned me to my realm. You didn't want to." I picked up Iisakki and clutched him close to my chest as I backed into a corner. "Are you all tricking me now?"

The humans' auras erupted in oranges and blues. But not the nonhuman. The fae—seelie or unseelie—whatever that meant. Another reason not to trust him. He was a liar. But the others confused me. I could understand why they might be uncomfortable, but sad? Why sad?

Rhys approached me with his hands clasped behind his back, looking like Beagan after he was caught painting Nialla's face while she slept. Because I knew the kid so well, I knew he was sorry for what he'd done. He wasn't just upset he'd gotten in trouble. And his aura confirmed this. But Rhys—was he sorry for deceiving me? Or for getting caught?

"Many apologies, Colleen. I—"

"Stay away from me." I waved from Rhys to the others. "All of you."

Pirkko cast a beseeching glance to her cohorts, then crouched to sit as close as she dared. "We didn't trick ya."

"You said you'd help me get home. That's all." I remembered that much.

"That may be." Her gaze darted back and forth as if reading her memory. "Rhys knew we were Saors and in sore need of an elf. We thought ya knew of our need and followed him willingly—to help." She inched closer. Her aura matched her apologetic expression. She splayed a hand over her heart. "That was our fault. We should'a been clear with ya, not Rhys alone."

I couldn't fault her. Rhys was the one who sought them out. He was the one to blame.

"Valtteri can help ya get home. He's a good man." She reached out a tentative hand and squeezed my good shoulder.

"I'm sure he'd like ya to hear him out as to why we're in need of an elf first," Reko added.

Taneli huffed. "If we make it back to camp without getting caught with a dragon."

"Who says I'm planning to go anywhere with you?" I brushed Pirkko's hand from my shoulder.

"Colleen." Pirkko sat beside me but kept her hands to herself. "Where else will ya go?"

She had a point. I'd never find my way back to the megalith. Iisakki hadn't made it work last time anyway. And I'd have to follow the train tracks and risk going too close to the station. What if we were caught? If all the elves and dragons before me had been killed, wouldn't we be killed too?

Even if I were willing to risk myself, I could never risk Iisakki.

Creeping crabs, I was trapped. I had no choice now but to follow these people to their leader and hope he helped me return home.

I glared at Rhys. He withered under my stare. Why should I care? He'd gotten me into this mess. It was all his fault.

NESTLED in the corner with Iisakki napping in my arms, I fought sleep as the train car rocked along the tracks.

Pirkko tugged at her sleeve and consulted her watch—again. "One minute!"

"Right." Reko stood and looked at me. "We're approaching our landing. We'll go the rest of the way on foot." He pointed at Rhys. "But not him."

Flashes of color revealed their mixed emotions. I swallowed a lump forming in my throat. I didn't trust Rhys. Downright mad at him, I ground my teeth. But he'd been with me this far, and I hated to see him like this. So dejected.

Confusion racked my overwrought brain. I wanted Rhys to continue with us and remain behind with equal measure.

Taneli stood in the doorway. He took a couple of starts like someone preparing to plunge into the water from a great height. Then he jumped and tumbled away from the train.

Pirkko followed.

Reko wagged his finger at me. "You're next."

But Rhys... I shuffled in place. Should I fight for him?

Nay. He lied. He couldn't be trusted.

Better to focus on getting home with Iisakki. I turned toward the opening and neared the ledge. The ground swept by so fast. "Is that safe?"

"Tuck your legs and roll. The ground is soft here."

That wasn't an answer, nor did it make me feel better. I twitched a finger to Iisakki. "You coming?"

He hopped from the crates, transitioned from a cat midair, and landed on the floor in dragon form. I'd never seen him as a dragon. He looked rather... cute. A scaly version of his cat and dog self with similar markings, but his furry white muzzle trailing up between his eyes to his forehead was now yellow scales. Sharp teeth protruded from his snout. His dark fur—gray in cat form and black in dog form—was now green scales. Funny how his markings didn't vary much. How much control did he have over his appearance? He squawked out a baby roar and flew over my shoulder out of the train.

When would he stop taking off without me?

EIGHTEEN

This was going to hurt. Badly. I held my breath as if
diving underwater, jumped, and tried not to absorb
the shock with my feet. I failed. My right foot
connected with the ground, and pain shot up through my toes.
Then I tumbled into a ditch. I peeled my bruised body from
the dirt where I'd embedded myself. The moment I put weight
on my right foot, a renewed shock wave surged from my toes,
and I fell back onto the dirt mound. White dots crossed my
vision, and I winced as if my pinched face might stop the
onslaught. I clutched my leg until the surging pain dulled to a
pulsing thud.

I tried to stand without using my right foot. A tricky feat, but I
met success. I brushed the grass and soil from my dress. Green
stained it in spots, revealing the impact points, the worst being on my
formerly uninjured shoulder now sore to my light touch. I didn't feel
any broken skin, but it would leave a nasty bruise. I rolled it in its
socket. Nothing was out of joint or broken.

Other than my toes.

I tried pulling myself out of the ditch. Pain gripped my toes no matter how I angled them. I was about to walk along the ditch to a shallower incline when a hand appeared in my face.

Taneli.

I grasped his hand and allowed him to help me out.

Reko ran to us, panting with Pirkko at his heels. "We must leave this place." He waved us forward. "We're too close to the station."

Where was Iisakki? As if on cue, he came running in his little cat form—with Rhys.

Taneli stepped toward him. "Weren't we clear enough for ya? You're not to join us."

Right. I was to continue delving deeper and deeper into this world. Without Rhys.

Why did my palms itch? I scratched my hands. Did I dare go on to wherever these people were taking me—alone?

But then, did I want to continue on with a known liar?

Perhaps it was for the best to go without him. I reached for Iisakki who dodged my grasp, then darted behind Rhys's legs.

An inexplicable panic rose within me. "What are ye doing, Iisakki? Come here." I didn't know anything about Iisakki or being bonded to a dragon. But he was part of me somehow. I trusted him as I'd never trusted anyone, and I couldn't go anywhere without him.

I wouldn't.

Iisakki peeked out from between Rhys's legs. I blew out a frustrated breath, the obstinate little beast popped up onto his hind legs to rub his face on Rhys's knee with a loud purr. For whatever reason, he had no intention of going anywhere without Rhys.

Would he allow us to part ways if I left?

That was *not* going to happen. If Iisakki wanted Rhys to join us, so be it. "If you want me to go anywhere with ye, Rhys comes too."

Taneli's face morphed through almost as many colors as his aura. His arms waved as if they didn't know what else to do. He bit his lips, then wagged an accusatory hand at Rhys. "Your lad put us all at risk. He *knew* ya traveled with a dragon." He huffed out a series of scoffing breaths. "And he handed ya over to us. Ya know that, right?"

Pirkko closed in on Taneli. "That's enough."

Taneli recoiled from her rebuke. His red aura shifted to frustration.

He was right. Rhys had delivered me to them. Iisakki too. I didn't know his reasoning or Iisakki's for refusing to move on without him. But I stood beside Iisakki. "I'm not going without him."

Everyone stared at me as if *I'd* turned into a dragon, even Rhys. Though his eyes widened, a smile tugged at his lips. If only I could interpret that unreadable aura. Nevertheless, something felt right about this, even if I didn't trust him. "I mean it. If you don't allow Rhys to accompany me, we're parting ways right here, right now."

Iisakki sauntered over to me, holding his head high as if proud of me.

The three conversed in infuriating silent communication, speaking with their eyes and shrugs.

"As you wish." Reko waved us forward. Then disappeared into the woods.

I TRIED KEEPING up with the others, but pain shot up my leg with every step despite my care not to put weight on my toes. The uneven terrain didn't simplify the task. Only Iisakki seemed to notice. He circled me, running back to rub his head against my leg as if his facial glands had the powers of healing, then darted ahead. And repeat.

Pirkko and Taneli walked ahead with Reko in front. With Rhys trailing them, seeming lost in his own world.

I fell farther and farther behind until I rounded a corner and didn't see anyone. I hurried as fast as my injured foot would allow through the heavy brush to a clearing with two paths.

Two empty paths.

Dread bubbled up, thick like sludge.

Where had they gone? How could they not notice I was no longer behind them?

I wavered between the two directions. Fear of making the wrong choice stayed me.

My chest tightened, and my breath failed me. I sucked in, but it didn't reach my lungs. I fell to the ground and fought to breathe. But unlike the last times this happened to me when my heart was full of fear, it was almost as if what was happening to my body wasn't happening to me. Like I was somehow detached. Either way, I'd lost all control of myself.

Iisakki brushed against me.

"Colleen?" someone said.

Taneli.

"I found her! She's here!"

Rushing feet and cracking brush barely reached my ears past my thudding heart and attempts to suck in air.

Pirkko dropped beside me. "What's happening?"

With a whoosh, my body returned to itself, and I struggled to talk. "Can't." I gulped in a shaky breath. "Breathe."

I continued heaving. What was wrong with me? Why did this keep happening?

Iisakki climbed onto my lap and purred, loudly.

"She's having a panic attack." Reko knelt beside me. He patted my back. "You're all right. Close your eyes and focus on your breathing."

Light in. Dark out.

Light in. Dark out.

I blinked at Reko as my breathing normalized.

"Smashing." He smiled. "Feelin' better?"

My face warmed. My overwrought body needed a year's rest. Yet gratitude for his kindness and lack of judgment put me at ease.

"What happened?" Pirkko dropped to her knees.

I focused on keeping my breaths steady. "I fell behind and thought I'd lost ye."

"Forgive us, Colleen. We should've noticed you weren't keeping up." Reko removed his cap to rake fingers through his hair, bunching it to an odd angle. "Are you too tired?"

"I did something to my toes when I jumped." I moved my foot toward him. "They might be broken."

"Ya walked all this way on broken toes?" he asked. "Why didn't ya say somethin'?"

I shrugged.

He scrunched up his forehead and glanced about as if searching for a cart to haul me. He eyed Iisakki in my lap. "Too bad Iisakki can't carry ya. He's a bit young yet." Hands on his hips, he let out a sharp breath, then swiveled to his knees, his back to me. "Hop on."

"What?" Did he want to carry me on his back?

"What other choice is there? We need to get to Folaím before dark." He jabbed a thumb at his back. "And ya need a healer to tend to your foot."

I climbed onto his back. He grunted and slumped as if he hadn't been expecting me to weigh so much. How humiliating. Why did this remind me of the rescue from Bandia? But then, I'd had to walk. There weren't enough arms for me and the little ones. That was okay. I was able to walk. Even then.

Why was I so weak now?

We traveled for hours. My legs were sore. I couldn't imagine how Reko must be feeling. Guilt poked at me like an annoying little brother for doing this to him and slowing everyone down. "I can walk."

"You're not walkin'."

"How much further?"

Reko jostled me as he readjusted his load. "Not much."

Taneli glared at me over his shoulder. "Be sure to keep our location a secret."

"I couldn't give away your location if I wanted to. I have no idea where we are."

"Even if she could"—Pirkko shook her wild hair down her back, chin high and proud—"the king's men can't get through the veil."

"It's not her I'm worried about." Taneli jerked his head back toward Rhys. "You do realize, if he's a fae, he could find a way through the veil, right?"

Reko grew and deflated with a heavy sigh in my grip. "You heard her. She won't go without him. It's a risk we'll have to take."

The typical trees morphed into giant, twisty things that appeared to be homes at one time. Long ago. Overgrown shrubs and leafy vines obscured doorways, and cobwebs framed arched windows. Roofed balconies protruded higher up. Bridges crossed from tree to tree at varying heights as far as I could see. Dangling vines acted as curtains blocking the path. Taneli pushed them back for Reko and me to pass through.

Whatever this place once was, it was a ghost now. A chill swept through me. "Where are we?"

"One of the many elfin ruins." Pirkko clicked her tongue.

We continued along what seemed to be the main throughway. Iisakki bounded up the trail before us in puppy form and disappeared. One second he was there. Then he was gone. He hadn't run around a bend or anything. He just... vanished.

Nineteen

I stared down the eerie path where Iisakki had disappeared, holding my breath, waiting for my eyes to readjust and reveal him. But he didn't reappear. "Where did he go?"

Wait. Now Taneli and Pirkko vanished in the same spot as if they'd walked through an invisible wall. Reko continued with me on his back. But when we reached the place where the others had disappeared, nothing happened.

"Curses!" Reko swore as he stopped, eyeing the space between the trees as if he missed something.

"What's happening?" Rhys caught up to us.

"I was hoping we could get through." Reko removed his cap and raked a frustrated hand through his hair.

"Get through?" I tensed, perhaps tightening my hold too much on his neck. "Get through *what*?"

"To Folaím." Reko squatted to let me down, then rested against a tree.

I hobbled along the path where they'd all disappeared, searching for anything to help me understand, then gave up, and sank beside him. "What are you doing now?"

"Waiting for Taneli and Pirkko to figure out what happened and find a way to get you through."

Rhys narrowed his eyes and approached Reko with an accusing finger. "With Colleen on your back, you planned to escape with her through a portal, thus abandoning me?"

I motioned to Reko to explain.

Reko scrubbed at his face. "It's not a portal. It's a veil. Folaím exists in Betören. It's just... hidden."

"That's not the point." Rhys closed in on us and stamped a foot like an angry bull.

My stomach squeezed and my breathing hitched. Why was he acting like this?

"Settle down, runt." Reko's voice sent an icy chill coursing through me.

"Both of you calm down." I braced myself to rise—to stop them or get out of their way remained to be seen. But as much as they bothered me, Iisakki's disappearance upset me more. He was in some strange rebel fortress without me. Could he escape? "What about Iisakki? How did he get through?"

"He's a dragon. And"—Reko threw Rhys a withering stare—"I'd hoped Colleen could get through since she's bonded to him. That she was on my back hadn't occurred to me."

"So, you admit to conspiring to leave me behind." Rhys blew air out his nose.

"My apologies, was that a secret?"

Rhys threw up his hands, muttered one of his "to be sures," and slumped against a tree facing us.

They were plotting against me to leave Rhys behind? Fire burned my gut. "If your people get us through, I'm not going unless Rhys goes first."

His injured expression morphed into a smug smile.

He'd lied to me. He brought me to these people he didn't know. Neither trusted the other. Why should I want him with me? Why trust him?

As these arguments raged within me, something in his smile— that my standing up for him brought him satisfaction—was endearing. He lied because he believed me to be an elf who could save the people. Would I do the same to save my world? Probably not. I couldn't imagine deceiving anyone even if it was for the greater good. But I could understand why someone would.

But that was no longer my biggest concern. My concern now was why he wanted to bring me to these people he didn't know. Trustworthy or not, he was just a boy. A boy in over his head.

I WAS on the verge of falling asleep when a figure bounded through the air. Clomping hooves stomped before me. I jumped to my feet. Where in wherever we were did a horse come from?

Taneli. Why'd he come back with a horse?

"Thank the fates." Reko stood and dusted off his pants. "Took you long enough. Have you found a way to bring Colleen through the veil?" He caught my steely gaze and withered. "And Rhys."

"That I have." Taneli tossed something to me.

I rolled the purple thing in my fingers. A pebble? A dried berry? "What is this?"

"A blueberry spelled to allow you through the veil. Come." He reached for me. "You can ride upon my steed. We'll bring you to the healer before seeking audience with Valtteri."

He expected me to leap up onto the horse behind him? I crossed my arms. "I'm not going without Rhys."

Rhys stood with his hands clasped behind his back. With his face down, he peeked up at them.

"I thought you might say that. Here." He tossed a berry to Rhys.

I still didn't trust them. "He goes first. If he disappears through the portal, I'll follow."

"Veil," Reko corrected.

Rhys swallowed the berry. "How long does it take to work?"

"It's instant." Taneli motioned toward the place he'd come through. "Go."

Rhys cast me a tentative look, then inched to the gateway. He pushed his hand toward the invisible wall. For a moment, he appeared handless. He retrieved his hand and inspected it. Seeming satisfied, he walked through and disappeared. But had they sent him where we were going? Or someplace else? We should have gone together.

"Ready?" Taneli reached toward me once more, wagging his fingers.

No matter what they'd done, Rhys was gone. I had no other choice now.

God, please protect me.

I gulped the berry and nodded, hoping to find Rhys and Iisakki on the other side.

As if we'd been resurrected from death to life, both places looked identical. But since the one I'd left was dark and dead, this bustling life startled me. No visible cobwebs. Lights dotted the trees like stars. The dark windows and balconies glowed, warm and inviting. Chatter, footfalls, and squeaky wheels overtook the silence. People ambled past with overloaded pushcarts and braying donkeys. A flute played somewhere. The savory grilling meats caused my stomach to cry out from neglect.

"Impressive hideout."

Taneli laughed. "We'll feed you, then fetch the healer."

Was my stomach that loud? Or had he felt the vibration? I wasn't comfortable sitting sidesaddle in his lap. He smelled like sweaty dirt. Iisakki bounded toward us as a puppy, morphed into a dragon midair, then landed on me as a kitten. He made his way up to my neck and nestled in, purring. My muscles relaxed, and my heart sighed as I nuzzled his little head with my chin.

We came to a canopy of trees. Twinkling lights dangled from the branches, lighting up the tree, making it seem more magical, as if a swarm of lightning bugs had decided to stay lit and settle in for the night.

Reko guided the horse to a stop, and Taneli helped me dismount. They brought me to a chair at a table under the leafy canopy. As soon as I was seated, Iisakki hopped onto my lap. He kneaded my leg, spun in two circles, then settled down. I stroked his soft forehead, starting his engine within. His purr grew so I heard it over the chatter of those engaged in conversation at other tables.

Pirkko approached with another man. At the same height, he was hard to notice behind her, but he was stockier and walked with a slight limp. A range of light colors surrounded him. Good. Unless he was a contented murderer, I should be safe.

The man dragged out a seat for Pirkko. He looked rather... puffy. Deep slits ran between his nose and cheeks and between his eyebrows. His windblown gray hair still had streaks of red as opposed to his white-as-the-surf beard. He smiled as he sat beside Pirkko, widening his slits for eyes long enough to see the blue beyond. Something in his smile and the way he carried himself disarmed me.

He reached across the table. This time, I understood and allowed him to give my hand a firm shake. His smile expanded, revealing an uneven row of small teeth. "It is an honor to meet you. Colleen, is it?"

"Aye. I mean, yes." Did they understand my Ariboslian speech here? I'd have to be careful to stick to the strict English Fallon and Aunt Stacy had taught me.

He shifted sideways to allow room to lift a leg across the other. He clutched his knee and stretched. "My name is Valtteri." He placed a hand over his heart and looked around like a proud father. "I'm honored with the privilege of overseeing this humble village." His smile quirked to one side. "Pirkko tells me you'd like to go home. Is that what you want?"

"Oh yes. Please." Why did home seem like such an unrealistic hope?

"I can make that happen." He released his leg, scooted up to the table, and leaned closer as if to share a secret. "But first, I understand you're bonded to a dragon. May I see the mark?"

"Mark?"

"When a dragon and elf bond, it leaves a mark." He rubbed his upper arm. "Around here."

Why would he want to see the mark? I scrutinized him, but his easy smile... What harm would it do to show him? If we were to trust each other, we'd have to start somewhere. I lifted my sleeve.

He clapped his hands and pressed them to his lips. "Colleen, I'm not sure you'll want to leave right away."

I should've known they wouldn't let me go. My heart clenched, hardening to protect itself from exploding at whatever this man was about to say. "Why not?"

"Because you'll want to meet the king."

"Why would I want to do that?"

He closed his eyes and smiled a thin, nontoothy, satisfied smile. "Because he's your father."

TWENTY

I must've misheard. "He's *what?*"

"Your father." He spoke as if I was an alien who didn't understand the language. "Your mark. The dragon bond. Every elfin family has a distinctive bond mark, and that"—his elbow slammed against the table as he pointed toward mine—"be Auberon's mark. Do ya know nothing of your heritage?"

This man was off his head. I yanked my sleeve down before my tattoo betrayed me further. "You mistake me for someone else. I've never been to this realm before."

"Ah, but ya have. You were born here. That mark settles it." Valtteri waggled his fingers. "Lift your sleeve again."

I hesitated, and he raised his eyebrows, hand poised in the air, waiting. With a heavy sigh, I complied.

"See this thick line?" He traced the mark encircling my arm. "They form a leaf shape with smaller offshoots. That's your paternal lineage—Auberon's family line. The lines within the band are your maternal lineage. But, in this case, they're dots or disconnected lines —evidence your mother wasn't an elf. If you aren't Auberon and Delyth's daughter, no one is."

The air hung thick between us. Was he telling me the truth? Or was he inventing all this, knowing I was ignorant and, therefore, an easy target? He could tell me anything with a bit of conviction, and I'd believe him. His entire presence oozed confidence. Even his aura. I stared at the tattoo. If he was lying, he had a talent for making things up on the spot. I covered my arm, wishing I could scrub it away.

"When your father ordered the elves' execution, your mother sent you to another realm to protect you, being you're half-elf."

Nausea coursed through me. My father... a murderer. A genocidal murderer. Maybe my mother was a better person, and I took after her. Wait. Did he say... "She wasn't an elf?"

"Delyth? No. She was fae. Her marriage to your father was an attempt to unite the kingdoms."

"So, I'm half-elf and—"

"Half-fae." Valtteri nodded.

Seeming to gather I was sizing him up, he lifted his protruding brows as if allowing me to see his eyes and the truths held within. I turned from him to the others surrounding the table—Pirkko, Taneli, Reko, and Rhys—in turn. Each watched me as if waiting for me to implode.

"Why are you telling me all this? Why am I here?"

"Well, those are two very different questions. First, I'm telling you this because you appeared in my village unawares without any understanding of your heritage and I thought you'd like to know. For the next"—he shrugged and dipped his jowls lower—"until God Himself reveals His plans in detail, it's anyone's guess."

He squinted as he hyperfocused and pointed a thick finger at me. "But I'm betting you're here to aid us in our quest. If you're willin'."

I shivered under those eyes trained on me. "To break the curse?"

Leaning back in his chair, Valtteri jiggled the leg he'd crossed over the other. "Well, I'm glad my people shared something of value. From what we've learned, only an elf can break your father's curse."

"Sorry." I shook my head. "I know nothing of curses nor how to break them. If it's an elf you need, a full elf would be best, right? If I survived, might there be another?" I waited for nods or signs of agreement. But as their stares remained unchanged, my hope waned.

"You're the one," Valtteri said.

Now they nod? I clutched Iisakki, barely breathing.

Valtteri bowed over the table, low as if about to share a secret, tapping with a stubby finger. "You're the one person who could get close to him without question." He scooted back, perhaps giving me room to consider his words.

"Close enough to kill 'im," Taneli added with a bit too much positive energy.

Now the onlookers broke their trance with guffaws, clicking tongues, and shaking heads.

"Taneli!" Pirkko cocked her head and skewered him with a reproachful stare.

I jumped from my seat. Sharp pain surged from my toes. "Kill him?" The words emerged through gritted teeth as if I could bite back the sting. I lowered myself back down, careful not to anger my forgotten injury further. "I won't kill anyone. I don't care who they are or what they've done."

"Are you hurt?" Valtteri peered over the table at my foot. "Why didn't you bring her to the healer straightaway?"

As if he'd swallowed a mouthful of sand, Taneli ducked his head and mumbled, "We thought it best to feed her and have her meet you. She's fine if she stays off her foot."

Valtteri huffed like a bull. "Does this sit well with you?"

"Aye... yes." It was the conversation that bothered me.

Valtteri growled. "Taneli spoke out of turn. Auberon's death is the obvious solution, but there may be another way now you've arrived. According to our spies, Auberon has been searching for you."

I sucked in a breath. "Why?"

"Elves live a long while, but he's getting older. Can't be king forever. Word is he seeks an heir. Perhaps, with you next in line for the throne, we can eliminate the curse without bloodshed."

This made no sense. "Then why did he try killing me all those years ago?"

"Can't say. But he'll turn Betören inside out to win ya to his side." Valtteri scratched his beard, making a prickly sound.

"But–but—" Questions blasted through my head faster than my mind could articulate them. I needed time alone to process. To think. But what was there to think about? Even if their claims were true, I could never be queen. I knew nothing of running a kingdom. Nor did I care to. And I couldn't subject myself to the teachings of a mad king. What would happen when Auberon learned that, although he'd found me, it was all for naught? Would he kill me then? "Can't you use your spies to get close to him?"

Again, Valtteri gave me that look as if he questioned my ability to follow his language. "They're not elves." His eyes twitched as he appraised me. "We won't leave you unprotected. Our people will watch over you."

"I can't be queen." Did I just make that a shameful whine?

"Wouldn't ask it of you."

"But while Auberon attempts to connect with me in the false hope of making me queen, you want me to get close enough to betray him. That *is* what you're asking of me?"

Valtteri shrugged. "If that's the way you choose to look at it."

"How could I betray someone like that?" I asked more to myself than anyone else. And what if, after attempting to connect and reason with him, the Saors killed him anyway? I'd be an accomplice to murder.

"Betrayal of one is worth freedom for countless souls. I trust you'll come to understand." Valtteri stood as if fighting against a massive weight, using the table to push himself against gravity. "Other pressing matters require my attention." He rubbed my shoulder and gave me what he surely meant to be a reassuring smile. "Glad to have ya with us, Colleen. And get that foot looked after."

Pirkko and Reko returned to our table, arms laden with plates for everyone. As my plate clanked before me, savory steam wafted into my face. I salivated on contact, and my stomach hailed the coming food. Rib meat, roasted vegetables, leafy greens, and a roll.

Reko tossed a raw bone to Iisakki under the table. Iisakki morphed from a cat to a dog and settled in to enjoy his treat.

Pirkko seated herself across from me and picked up a rib. "Do ya believe in God?"

I chewed meat from the bone. Unfamiliar spices brought all the flavors together like a culinary masterpiece. Juicy and tender. I always thought I preferred vegetables, but then, I hadn't had much opportunity to eat protein that didn't come from the sea. I swallowed. "Of course."

"What if people weren't allowed to believe in Him?" Juice dribbled down her chin. She swiped it with the back of her hand.

I dropped the bone and wiped my fingers and mouth with a cloth napkin. "God always makes a way for people to know Him." I tore apart the flaky roll, trying to keep the crumbs from escaping onto the table.

"How do ya know?"

I stopped chewing. What made me believe that? Had I heard it from Fallon? Her Bible perhaps? I gulped my bite. "I don't know. But I can't imagine a loving God allowing so many people to die without giving them a chance." I popped another piece of bread into my mouth.

"What if you're the way?" Pirkko spoke past a wad of food tucked away in her cheek.

I nearly choked on my bite and held up a finger as I swallowed. "How would *I* be the way?" And why did that sound so very very wrong?

"Your father..." Seeming to catch my annoyance, she changed her words. "I mean... Auberon has cursed the people. They believe him to be God. Not *a* god. *The* God. How can anyone come to know the real God if they're convinced they already do?"

I shoveled a mouthful of roasted root vegetables. If what she said was true, I should care more. But they were just words about strangers from strangers. And for all I knew, they were all lies. A trick to keep me here, compliant, willing to help them kill a king. That would *never* happen. I'd never be an accomplice to murder. Even if I survived, how would I live with myself?

His back still ramrod straight, his brown eyes still hard as iron, Reko elbowed into our conversation. "Don't ya care? What if *you* were lied to, made to believe in a false god? What if *you* died, left in torment, without God, forever?"

That would be terrible. I shoved my plate away and slumped against the hard back of my wooden chair. But lies, betrayal, treason, murder... How could I justify such things? "There must be another way."

"Didn't you hear a word Valtteri said?" As her face and aura reddened, Pirkko combed her fingers through her reddish hair and yanked at it. "What if God *does* 'ave a plan to save countless lives, and you're it? You're worried about Auberon, but what of them? If you choose to disobey God, you're single-handedly condemning all those lives to hell."

"'Disobey God?'" I clutched the table's edge, my aura reddening to match hers. "What is lying and murder but disobedience? And how is the fate of all these people on me? I'm not God."

Pirkko closed her eyes and seemed to work to steady her breathing. Was she doing what I did to calm down? Whatever it was, it worked. The red lights pulsing about her faded to a dull pink. She leveled her eyes at me and folded her arms across her chest. "Valtteri will do everything possible to do what must be done without losing lives, including Auberon's. He's not asking you to murder him or help anyone else kill him."

"No, he's asking me to help your people get close enough to him to do whatever they have planned. Even if you don't kill him, you're asking me to lie to him. Last I knew, God frowned on lies."

Pirkko rolled her eyes and heaved a heavy sigh. "Forget about all that right now. Don't ya want to meet your father? Maybe you don't have to work with us. Just meet him. Maybe you can convince him to lift the curse. Maybe you can save them all."

TWENTY-ONE

Warm light filtered through fluttering white curtains covering holes in the tree. Tree? I bolted upright, unsettling Iisakki. He yawned, stretched, then readjusted his small cat body for another doze as the events of the prior days came flooding back to me. Iisakki hatching from an egg, then running through the portal. Meeting Rhys, then the others. Hopping the train. Valtteri. The evil king—my father? The last thing I remembered was the healer telling me I'd broken three toes, taking medicine to ease the pain, then hobbling back on crutches to this place, and passing out as soon as I collapsed onto the bed.

How had so much happened in two days?

What would happen today?

I sank back into the puffy ivory bedding. While Iisakki opened one eye at me, I took care not to disturb him further. If only I could wrap myself up and sleep forever. Anything to avoid whatever might happen next.

Hadn't I dreamt of such an adventure? Perhaps I preferred adventure from the safety of a book I could close at my whim.

I wanted to go to America with Stacy, not some unchartered

realm by myself. But did I really? I wasn't American. Or human. I didn't belong there.

I didn't belong anywhere.

Everywhere I've ever been, safe or unsafe, comfortable or frightened—from the home for orphans in Notirr, to the hovel where I hid from fasgadair in Bandia, to my adopted family in what others would consider paradise—all I wanted was to escape. Nothing satisfied me.

Was I always in the wrong place? Or was I broken?

I missed my family. They must be so worried. If only I could reach them to tell them I was okay... all things considered.

What if I never saw them again?

My blue aura deepened as tears slipped down my cheeks.

Was this God's punishment for my discontent? Was He taking everything from me, so I'd learn to appreciate what I had before it was gone? Pinpricks of light pierced through my aura like a thin sheet over a porcupine with razor-sharp quills, and an unfamiliar voice broke through my thoughts—

Seek Me.

Where had *that* thought come from?

And what were these lights? I scrubbed at my arm as if my aura were a tangible thing I could wipe away. I'd never seen piercing lights poke through an aura—ever. The lights dimmed, and my dark-blue aura turned purple with my confusion.

That thought. That voice. It was in my head, but it hadn't come from me.

Seek Me.

Was that God? Had God spoken to me?

It had to be.

But what did He mean? Seek Him? Wasn't He everywhere, all at once? Invisible to us? Why should I seek Him if I couldn't find Him? Were things different in Betören? Could I find Him here?

Fallon's voice sounded in my mind, *Why don't you ask Him?*

Her voice in my mind cut me to the quick. The reality of my situation, that I may never see my family again, stung my soul. I buried my face in the pillow.

But I couldn't give in to the sadness. Feeling sorry for myself wouldn't solve anything. Fallon's advice had sounded in my mind for a reason.

How, God? How do I seek You? I paused, searching the sky—or rather, the shiny tree-trunk ceiling—as if God might appear with specific instructions.

Why did You bring me here? There must be a reason? What would You have me do? Should I trust these people? Should I meet my father?

As expected, yet again, no answer came.

If Fallon were here, she'd assure me God had a plan. If only He'd let me in on His secret. But, when He didn't, I needed to trust. He brought me here. To these people. On purpose. I should learn as much as possible. When would I get an opportunity like this again?

And Pirkko was right. I *was* curious about my birth parents.

But these people must understand how much an orphan longs to know their birth parents above all else. What if they used that to get me to do their bidding?

Even if I wanted to meet my father, what if what they said about him was true? Did I want to meet an evil king? What a disappointment.

Worse, what if I was a disappointment to him?

My cyclical thoughts funneled downward, threatening to drag me into another panic attack. Iisakki breathed deep and released a loud contented purr. A soft breeze carried a light floral scent through the open window along with joyful morning greetings from early rising villagers. Birds trilled their morning songs. Tree critters chirped.

If only I could enjoy this. How often did anyone get the chance to spend the night in a veiled tree village? I sighed. Whatever lay ahead of me today, I had to rise and face it.

Three sharp knocks sounded at the door, and I bolted upright, clutching the covers to my chest, disrupting a cranky cat.

The door opened, and Pirkko peeked through the opening, her red-brown hair fisted in a ponytail at her nape. "Aces! You're awake." She dropped her hair and plopped down on the end of the bed, making me bounce. "I've some britches for ya."

She deposited a bundle of clothes, then tugged the covers. "If you're to help us, ya need to ditch that dress. But I'll have it washed. Come on then. I'll show ya where to clean up."

I was still wearing yesterday's clothes. They were filthy. And I stank. Guilt pooled in my stomach at the mess I must've made of the bedding.

"After ya've cleaned up and eaten, Valtteri wants to make plans for ya to meet your father."

Frustration simmered red as I reached for my crutches to hobble after Pirkko. What gall! How could Valtteri assume I'd follow his plan after last night's conversation? Had he heard nothing I said?

I WIGGLED and twisted my hands in my lap between Rhys and Pirkko on a cushy maroon couch in Valtteri's office. Perfectly still, Reko and Taneli sat kitty-corner in similar seats. The room looked like the one I'd slept in except the floor was bare, showing off the polished rings, exposing the tree's advanced age... or manipulated age. Gleaming and uneven grainy walls followed the tree. I hadn't the opportunity to feel the tree for the life within, but I sensed it. How in Ariboslia had the elves teased the life within to prompt it to form these homes? If only I could meet one and learn.

The reality stabbed my heart. Was my father the only one left from whom to learn?

Valtteri sat behind a massive wooden desk. He leaned back in his chair, hands folded across his chest. Lines on his scrunched face deepened as he considered the question at hand—how and when to introduce me to my father. And who should accompany me? He'd been discussing it with the others when Pirkko and I arrived.

I couldn't hold my tongue any longer. "You're making plans as if my agreement is a foregone conclusion."

Valtteri braced his elbows on the desk and clasped his hands. "What can I do to convince you?"

Taken aback by his straightforward response, I clenched fisted hands on the cushion beneath me. "You're asking me to conspire against a king. My supposed father. A man who, if all this is true, wanted me dead. I'm no criminal, and I don't want to risk my life to help anyone else commit treason. So, I'm sorry. I can't imagine anything you can do or say would convince me."

"Well, then." Valtteri pressed his lips into a thin line and, after three quick raps on the table, stood. "I suppose we're done here."

What? I jammed my hands beneath my thighs and studied the others. Rhys looked as surprised as I felt. But the others glanced at each other as if they shared inside information and concluded this wouldn't have worked all along. They followed Valtteri out the door.

I trailed. Hope dared prick my heart. "Is that it then? Can I go home?"

Pirkko wrinkled her petite nose. "You're always free to go. But without Valtteri's amulet, you can't get home. He won't force you to do anything, but no way is he going to give you a way out."

My gut clenched as my arms hung limp at my sides. Valtteri and his amulet, my only way home, slipped away.

She gripped my upper arm. "Come. Let me show you the village."

I slumped and allowed my friendly captor to drag me away.

Twenty-Two

I spent the day with Iisakki and Rhys following Pirkko on her village tour. If not for the knowledge that, as kind as they were, I *was* being held against my will, I might've enjoyed the visit. Folaím was like something from human fantasy novels. But ideas on how to get home turned over and over in my mind like meat on a spit. But all outcomes ended in my capture and inevitably meeting Auberon.

Perhaps I should just go willingly.

We rested on logs formed into smooth benches inside an elf-manipulated gazebo beside a wandering garden. Branches from several trees spaced evenly to form a circle intertwined to create railings and a leafy roof. Trickling water from babbling brooks and gentle waterfalls worked to still my restless mind. If not for my concerns, I could see myself spending my days in a place like this. If only I had a book.

I tugged at the material clinging to my legs. I'd never get used to pants. Especially these short things that stopped just below the knee. What was the purpose in that?

Iisakki chased his tail in puppy form, utterly oblivious. Further evidence of no mental connection else he'd sense my distress at the least. If only I could be so carefree.

What was the point of being bonded to a dragon? When would he grow up and be of more use?

Creeping crabs! Go easy on the poor beast, Colleen. He's only three days old!

Still, if I knew how we might communicate, then I could practice. I stared at the dragon in puppy form, now chewing on his foot. *Iisakki!* I yelled in my mind.

He switched to scratching behind his ear with a blank expression.

I conjured an image of him and tried to push it from my mind to his.

He continued to stare.

So much for that idea. Time to consider possible escape plans… again. But if I did escape, how would I get home? And how would I keep Iisakki from exposing us to the wrong people? Then again, what if he already had? Was it because he was a baby, or could he not read people at all? He seemed content here. Unconcerned about where they might lead us. Or what they might do to us if I continued to refuse.

Did he know that if I die, he'd also die?

I had to figure out where to go from here. For both our sakes.

PIRKKO LED us through the village along a stone path. The tree houses ended. Normal trees without windows or doors surrounded us now. The path narrowed and darkened with the sun incapable of filtering through the thick leafy canopy. Light blazed ahead, too bright to see anything beyond. I shielded my eyes. As they adjusted, an outline of a twisty tree with exposed roots emerged and solidified. Its arms jutted toward the heavens. Brilliant leaves seemed to produce their own light. Scattered among the greenery were tiny purple flowers. A ring of the same blossoms blanketed the ground at its base.

In cat form, Iisakki bounded to the tree and rubbed his face against an exposed root.

Pirkko approached and touched its trunk as if it were a friend. "This is the croí tree. It's the heart of Folaím. It is the power behind the spell the fae cast to hide it from the king. As long as the blossoms remain, we are safe. But once they fall…"

"The veil will collapse, to be sure."

Pirkko fisted her hair into a ponytail. "The fae who cast the spell wanted to remove Auberon from power. The powerful spell required several fae who wanted to restore Betören to its former glory. But they feared we would hide away and neglect our promise to remove the king. Therefore, the blossoms will continue to fall as long as he reigns. Should the last blossom fall whilst he rules…" She loosed her grip on her hair, and it splayed apart. "Obviously, we can't allow that to happen."

I stepped away from the tree. "I can't." Why was I in this position? It was unfair. "I can't help you commit treason."

Pirkko reached out as if she could magically pull me back. "All we ask is that ya meet him. Decide for yourself if you will help us. Once you're with him, we'll have no recourse against you. Do ya realize how much trust we're putting in *you*?"

"But what if he kills me?" I continued my retreat. "Sorry. I c– can't."

I fled.

Twenty-Three

"Have ya changed your mind about meeting your father?" Valtteri sat beside me under the canopy of magical lights as I awaited my supper. This had become a welcome routine over the past days. Though my answer hadn't changed, he'd purse his lips, sigh, then rise and say, "Maybe tomorrow," before sauntering away.

But each day his sigh and his frown deepened.

Each day, the nagging sensation in the pit of my stomach tugged harder.

The words *Seek Me* echoed in my mind, and my stomach twisted into an impossible knot. I'd spent days considering leaving. Rhys had agreed to join me. But he, too, wanted me to meet Auberon. No matter how I spun it, I couldn't conjure a plan that didn't result in me being caught and delivered to the king.

Perhaps there was no other way. Perhaps I was *supposed* to meet my father. Meeting him didn't mean I was working with the conspirators. They might be planning treason, but I wasn't. If I went, it would be to follow the path God had placed before me and meet my father with a pure, nontreasonous heart.

So, what was stopping me? What kept me from agreeing?

"Seek Me," said a small, feminine voice.

Startled, I turned toward the voice. A little brown-haired girl with frizzy curls stood behind me, tapping my shoulder so gently I could scarce feel it. "Oh, hello." I smiled, still baffled. Did she say... "Seek me?"

The little girl hunched, hiding her laugh behind cupped hands. Her sparkling green eyes shone. Her skin was darker than most, darker than the selkie even. A stunning contrast to her eyes. She uncovered her mouth, swinging her arms by her sides. "No, I said, 'scuse me.'" She let out more chuckles as her gaze roamed over Rhys and Pirkko at the table.

"Oh." Her giggles were infectious. I motioned to the seat beside me. "Would you like to sit down?"

She slid into the seat, keeping her gaze on me, then kicked her dangling feet.

"What's your name?"

"Liisi." Her face warmed, and her light aura shone about her like a golden halo.

"That's a pretty name. What can I do for you, Liisi?"

She giggled again. "I just—" She kicked with more enthusiasm and brushed her shoulder with her cheek. "Are you going to save us?"

"Save you? From what? You're not under the curse."

"No, but—" Her eyes downcast once more, her aura darkened and morphed to blue. "I'd like to go home."

"This isn't your home?"

Everything about her—from her tipped head, narrowed eyes, and oranging aura—illustrated her confusion.

Pirkko cleared her throat. "Do ya mind if I tell your story, Liisi?"

Liisi straightened and nodded as if she'd like nothing better.

"Liisi's da worked at the aether plant. He's one of the men we were able to free from the curse to have someone on the inside."

"How does one work at a plant? And what is an aether plant?"

"Not that kind of plant. Aether is a fuel that provides power. The plant is the building where aether power is harnessed and distributed, so we have lights at night and such."

"Like electricity?" I didn't know much about it other than from books I'd read and what Fallon explained. Stacy did bring us some things like lanterns that ran on batteries. But Fallon wanted to limit those things in the house in case visitors wondered about them.

"Um..." Pirkko's face twisted. "Maybe? In any case, Liisi's older brother, Luukas, was about to turn of age and refuse the curse, which meant he'd have his mind expunged and be removed from his family. So, their da escaped with them."

"What about their mother?" I barely breathed as Liisi's imploring green eyes met mine.

"She's still in Betören." Pirkko lowered her voice. "Under the curse."

"But you can save us!" Liisi reanimated, tugging at my curls. "You can remove the curse so we can go home and be a family again."

This poor child. Displaced. Separated from her mother, like I was. At least she still had her father and brother. I was alone. If I could help her and her only, I'd do anything in my power. But what could I do? "I—"

"Liisi!" a distant voice called. "Liisi!"

Liisi straightened, and her eyes opened wide as saucers. "That's my brother. I gotta go." She shook the table as she scrambled free, then waved over her shoulder. "Bye!"

"Bye," I called as a new form of helplessness settled into my soul.

Taneli appeared with plates of food. He placed one before me, the other before Pirkko while Rhys scowled beneath his cap of black hair. "Sorry, little man, ladies first."

"Hmph." Rhys crossed his arms. "And it has nothing to do with your prejudices against me, to be sure."

As Taneli returned to his kitchen for more food, my mouth watered in anticipation. Taneli must be the best cook in the realm. Nay, in all the realms. He was a wizard with spices and combinations of meats and vegetables, enhancing their natural flavors in new and magical ways. Rhys always complained about being served last, but he didn't realize how difficult it was to smell the steaming deliciousness wafting up and have to wait for the others.

Taneli returned with Reko and three more bowls, serving Rhys last.

Once everyone was seated and I silently thanked God for the meal, I sunk my fork into the colorful concoction. The sweet, peppery scent of unfamiliar spices hit my nose. Spicy goodness ignited a blissful slow burn. By the fourth bite, my entire mouth, even my lips, were on fire. I tried to keep my composure as I reached for the cool milk to quench the heat.

"Now..." Taneli chewed. The food in his bowl was redder than everyone else's. He didn't flinch and required no milk. He kept his gaze focused on his meal as if trying to avoid eye contact. "Ya hit Valtteri with the same answer again today?"

No reason to respond. He didn't appear to be asking, anyway.

"Ya seen the croí tree?" Taneli stabbed his food with more force than necessary, his gingery freckles blending into his skin as it reddened. "The blossoms be falling faster since she arrived." He pointed his forkful at me, dripping red sauce onto the table. "Bucketloads dropped last night. The veil will collapse any day now. Blast! Could be tomorrow." He slapped the table beside his bowl, his aura and expression oozing pure disgust.

"Taneli." Pirkko reached to touch his hand.

"Whist!" He yanked his hand away, then fixed his gaze on me until I shrank under those murderous greens. "There be children here. Families. What d'ya think'll 'appen to 'em when the veil collapses?" He plunged his fork back into his bowl and pushed it away with a clang that made me jump. His sneer twisted up his lips, exposing uneven teeth. "Eat without me. I've lost my appetite. Enjoy your meal."

As if I could eat now. The food lost flavor after he left. It was as difficult to finish chewing as it was to swallow. What I had already eaten hardened into an indigestible lump in my gut. I put my fork down.

Was I being selfish? I knew nothing of this realm. What should I believe? Who was telling the truth?

Taneli seemed to be telling the truth.

Liisi was telling the truth.

If I could meet Auberon and convince him to lift the curse, I could then reunite Liisi's family... spare her the destruction that happened to me. Shouldn't I try?

People milled about. Most had finished their work for the day. But a few carried loads along the main thruway. Families clustered at tables similar to mine outside their homes, eating their evening meal. Several children played a game involving hitting leather balls with thick sticks into spilled baskets.

What would happen to these people? How many of them were separated from other family members... and might be for eternity? Did their health and happiness, their very souls depend on me?

A woman and two small children sat at a table across the thruway. The boy chattered away, shoveled a bite of food into his mouth, then continued his conversation with a big ole mouthful. A wad fell out onto the table, and the woman wiped up the mess, chastising him for speaking with food in his mouth while the girl giggled.

Where was their father? Still working? In Betören?

Dead?

A galloping horse and rider came from nowhere and nearly collided with our table. I jumped from my seat as the horse reared, its front legs kicking the air mere cubits from my face. Both horse and rider seemed as frightened by their sudden appearance as the villagers who scattered like birds from a charging dog.

The spooked horse circled, nickering, fighting the reins as the bewildered rider wearing a strange uniform fought for control.

"Defender!" someone shouted.

Villagers screamed. The boy across the way stared, mouth agape, while the girl cried. The mother wrangled both from their seats and fled with the children stumbling after in her grip. Footfalls pounded the dirt path. Children cried as adults scooped them up and carried them away. Squeaky wheels quickened. Carts and tables toppled. Food and dishes skittered about.

Two men crouched, daring to close in on the intruder. Taneli approached from the opposite side. The rider pulled something long from his saddle holster.

And something ice cold pooled in my extremities, rooting me to my spot. Was that a—

"Gun!" one of the men shouted.

The rider lifted the weapon to his shoulder, aiming it at those who dared venture too close.

The shouts intensified. Reko upturned our table. Bowls of Taneli's food scattered their contents, appearing as bloody innards strewn across the road. Pirkko latched onto my arm and yanked, drawing me from my trance. We huddled behind the upturned table with Rhys.

Reko motioned to us. "Come with me."

Crutches abandoned, I ran through the mayhem. I tried to ignore the pain shooting from my toes as I hobbled after Reko in Pirkko's grip. A thunderous crack rang into the night at my back, urging me onward. Screams such as I hadn't heard since the Fasgadair Wars turned my blood to acid, threatening to melt me from the inside out. I stumbled. Pirkko yanked as I regained my footing. The shouts grew faint, and Pirkko jerked me into a doorway. Reko ushered the others inside and slammed the door shut.

Hand on my heart, I fought to calm my breathing as the ache from my toes settled into a dull throb.

Light in. Dark out.

Light in. Dark out.

Iisakki weaved about my legs in cat form.

I scooped him up and held him close. "What happened?"

Reko peeked out a window. "A defender broke through the veil."

TWENTY-FOUR

Folaím was different the next morning. The few people outside were those cleaning up the mess. No children played. No one ate outdoors. Everyone remained in hiding for fear more soldiers might arrive. I didn't see anyone, but I felt their eyes, their silent accusations, as I passed their windows.

Pirkko barely spoke. Profound blues with a depth of sadness I hadn't seen since Bandia surrounded her and the cleaners.

My fault.

This was—All. My. Fault.

I plodded along behind Pirkko to Valtteri's office. What would I say to him today?

The person behind the desk today was a different man. His disheveled gray hair was even more so. It stuck out in clumps as if he'd been pulling it in tight fists. He heaved a heavy sigh and rubbed his eyes, then widened them, rolling them around as if attempting to clear something from his vision. Dark bags and redness betrayed his lack of sleep.

I slid into my usual spot, keeping a trained eye on Valtteri, uncertain what he might do under this stress.

He scrubbed his puffy cheek. "Colleen, I've been as patient as I can. But I can no longer placate your ideals. We must act, and we must act now." With a sudden burst of energy, he pointed at nothing. "Did ya see that defender? Four men injured! Good men with families, mind you, risked their lives approaching an armed defender. Do yas think we walk around here, armed, prepared for a fight?"

"We will from now on, sir," Pirkko spoke so quietly I barely heard her.

"That we will." Valtteri then skewered me under his stare. "What if there are others? The veil is disintegrating. Before this night falls, we may find ourselves under attack—" His voice cracked, and he dragged a heavy hand down his face. "What do you expect will happen if more defenders storm this village?"

My stomach squeezed, ready to ingest another helping of guilt. But something rose from within, combating the shame I put upon myself. Not this time. Nay. I wouldn't accept the blame. This was not my fault. Like the fasgadair attacks weren't my fault. I had no part in this. I didn't cause this war.

"Please." He held up a hand as if he sensed my rebuff. "Visit the defender."

That I did not expect. "Th–the one who attacked the camp last night?"

Valtteri turned his hand palm up in entreaty. "We have him contained. He can't hurt you."

"To what end?"

"Tell him who you are. Perhaps he'll talk to the daughter of the so-called god he worships."

"Why would he tell me anything? I'm as trapped as he. I can do nothing for him."

"First"—Valtteri lifted a finger to illustrate his point—"I want you to see firsthand what's happening here. And second"—he pinned me with a hurt look—"do ya think you're a prisoner here? You've always been free to go. I made that plain."

"So I'll be captured and delivered to the king against my will?" I dared look him in the eye and share my real thoughts. "You're not willing to help me return home, not without me doing as you ask."

"Do you blame me?" He lifted his arms as if holding the world in his palms, then dropped them, smacking them against his desk. "I have a village to protect. If you go to your father, see his error, and help us get inside, I can keep them safe. I don't believe he'll kill you." He gripped the edge of his desk and stretched over it, steeling his usually not visible watery blues at me with such ferocity, I had to look away. "Truth be told, if I could sacrifice myself—one for the good of many—I would."

Ouch. I backed into the cushioned couch as if it might open and swallow me, allowing me to escape the judgment in his eyes. Was I being selfish? Visiting the defender, a captive, wouldn't be as bad as going to the king. What harm would it do to talk to him? I blew out a defeated breath. "Okay—"

The door burst open, and a man clung to the handle, fighting to catch his breath. He reached into his pocket and pulled out a pink glowing thing. "A–Annukka had a v–vial."

"Praise God!" Relief cracked the stress frozen on Valtteri's face as he held out his hand. When the man placed the glass bottle in his hand, Valtteri inspected the pink liquid segregated by purple veins that refused to mix. His aura shifted from black and blues to yellows and greens. He held the potion out to Pirkko. "You know what to do. I've no doubt Auberon's puppet will be more compliant after his dose."

"Yes, sir." She pocketed the vial.

Valtteri trained his eyes on mine, his grin and aura widening. "Thank God for His timing. Watch this potion in action. I'm betting you'll want to help once you witness this."

Pirkko escorted me to a tree house on the village outskirts. We climbed a circular staircase inside to a room with no furnishings other than a table and two chairs.

"Sit there." She pointed to the chair facing the doorway.

Two men I didn't recognize hustled the prisoner inside, one tall and lanky, the other stocky and thick-necked. The captive swayed like a rag doll in their grip. Without releasing him, the thick-necked guard kicked the chair out, sending a squeal echoing through the chamber, while the lanky guard dropped the captive onto it.

The prisoner had no aura, and his ocean eyes were cold. Still, something squeezed my heart, propelling a hot wave of unfamiliar anger through me. I fought to squash it, keeping it under the surface, but it refused to be squelched. "Is it necessary to treat him so roughly? His hands are bound, for Pete's sake."

The thick-necked guard scowled while the other feigned hurt.

"Four good men are in the infirmary right now because of this waste of flesh." Thick Neck pushed the chair in.

The prisoner lunged forward.

"C'mere," Pirkko said. "This man ain't responsible for his actions."

The guards harrumphed and crossed their arms.

What did she mean? Everyone was responsible for their actions. And this man should be punished for what he'd done. But I didn't approve of treating a bound man inhumanely. A dirty rag propped his mouth open. Sweaty hair dangled across his forehead in clumps. His oceanic eyes flashed despite his obvious exhaustion, as if some-thing within him refused to admit defeat... pride perhaps? If the eyes were a window to the soul, this one revealed nothing. An empty vessel. No remorse.

And where was his aura? Was he human? Or something else?

"How am I supposed to talk to him with this thing in his mouth?" I asked, pointing to the gag.

Thick Neck seized the cloth near his mouth and wrenched it down so it hung about his neck.

The prisoner worked his jaw. He looked young but older than me. A shadow from a missed shave darkened his face, even under the dirt and blood caking his skin.

I tried to ignore the lurking men and the prisoner's discomfort to ask what Valtteri wished to know. "How did you pass through the veil?"

The prisoner scanned my face, and something flickered. Recognition? Then he eyed the others and set his face.

"Were there others with you?"

He stared straight through me.

"Allow me." Pirkko motioned for me to give up my seat. She folded her hands across the table and peered into his eyes. "Who sent you?"

More silence.

She turned to me and whispered, "He's compelled to answer certain questions. Watch. Who is Auberon?"

"King of Talamh Sí," the captive responded.

"And what is the king to you?"

"King Auberon is my lord, my savior."

"Who does King Auberon answer to?"

"No one. There is none above him."

I gasped.

"What about God?"

"King Auberon *is* God."

I sucked in another breath. This was playing out as they'd said. Yet seeing it for myself had opened my eyes as Valtteri predicted.

Pirkko took out the vial and pinched it between her fingers. "Drink this."

"I'll not take anything without King Auberon's authorization."

"Thought ya might say that." She uncorked the bottle. Pink glittery smoke wafted out and dissipated. She poured the contents into a tapered tube with a bulb at the end. "Hold him."

Thick Neck stepped forward and yanked the prisoner's head backward. Pirkko tried to unclench the prisoner's jaw, then pinched his nose instead. But the captive continued to breathe through clenched teeth. Pirkko pinched his nose with one hand, holding the tube between two fingers, and covered his mouth with the other. The man's face turned red. Veins popped from his skin as he fought. I wanted to scream that they release him. The instant she freed him, the prisoner gulped for air. Pirkko squeezed the bulb, forcing the potion down his throat, then clamped his mouth shut once more, keeping him from spitting it out.

When she stepped away and Thick Neck released the defender's head, a thin pink dribble trailed from the corner of the prisoner's mouth. The hair that had been covering his forehead now flopped to the side, and something shifted in his eyes. They looked the same, but different. He winced and lowered his head as if fighting back a massive headache. The beginnings of an aura sparked, pulsing in varying colors before steadying and settling into deep purples and oranges.

"What's happening?" His eyes narrowed as he shrank back into his chair. "Who are you?"

"We're friends." Pirkko held out another vial. "You're coming out of an unseelie curse which is a painful process. Drink this. It will ease your discomfort." She uncorked the lid and brought it to his lips.

The prisoner turned his head, spilling medicine along his cheek.

"Unbind him," Pirkko ordered.

"Don't think so, miss." Thick Neck tightened his arms across his chest.

But she spread her hands. "Why should he trust us if we don't trust him?"

"He shot four of our men." Thick Neck's aura seethed and pulsed in reds. "Curse or no, I shan't release him. Not without Valtteri's orders."

Her shoulders deflated as she sighed. "Do ya recall last night's events?"

"I do." The prisoner squinted and clutched his head, pulling the hair away from his face. "But it doesn't seem real. What did you do to me?"

"We freed you from Auberon's curse." She pointed to the half-empty vial on the table. "If the pain gets too much, tell me."

Purples and oranges flared from him in spurts as he narrowed his gaze. "How do I know *you* didn't curse me?"

His emotions sparked back to life. He had to feel the difference. "What you're feeling right now"—I gripped the table—"that's real. They gave that to you. How did you feel before? Numb? Would you rather go back to the way you were?"

His turbulent ocean eyes cut deep into my soul. Their blues matched the glow surrounding him, overtaking all other emotions. Had I ever seen anyone so sad, even in Bandia?

Pirkko picked up the vial, but the prisoner shook his head.

The silence nearly suffocated me. I breathed in deep as if such pitiful sound could break silence's spell.

"King Auberon..." His aura intensified, purple overtaking the others. The poor guy was genuinely confused. "King Auberon. He... He..."

Pirkko threw him a sad smile. "We were all under the same curse. Well, except Colleen." She motioned toward me. "Valtteri rescued us from Auberon's lies too. What's your name?"

"Liam." His face crumpled. "He took me from my family and—"

"I know." She touched his hand briefly. "I know."

Red flashed like lightning. "He made me believe he was God!" He fought his binds as if King Auberon were in the room and he wanted nothing more than to kill him. "Do ya know what I've done in his name?"

"I can imagine." She splayed her fingers on his hand and left them there this time. "Were there others with ya yesterday? Any who might betray our location?"

"No. I patrolled alone."

"Good. We're on a mission to remove Auberon from his throne. Will ya help?"

"Help?" Liam sprang from his chair, sending it toppling behind him. "I'll do more than help. I'll peel that coward from his throne of lies and skin him myself!"

I backed toward the exit.

Pirkko chuckled. "I like your enthusiasm. But we need ya to get her into the castle." She jabbed a thumb my way. "Will ya do that for us?"

Liam squinted at me. The pulsing glow about his skin darkened. "Are you... I'd swear you're Auberon's daughter."

Black surrounded me. "Why do you say that?"

"You're an exact replica of your parents."

My heart stalled, and I understood why one might prefer to be under a spell than in the real world. It was too real. "You know them?"

"Their portraits litter the city." He jabbed an accusatory finger at me.

Did that mean... Would everyone in this realm recognize me?

"You expect me to deliver *her* to Auberon?"

I backed against the door, squirming at the way he said her.

"If she agrees, yes." Pirkko aimed a hopeful gaze my way.

I was about to agree in Valtteri's office. But now... How much damage had Auberon caused? How many families had he destroyed? Bile burned my throat. I rubbed the shivers from my unmarked arm. Valtteri was right—if I was uncertain about helping before, between Liisi and this, I harbored no doubt now. "Y–yes. I have to do *something*. What he's doing is wrong."

"That's an understatement." Liam huffed.

Pirkko quirked her lips and shimmied as if trying to contain her joy. But the alternating white and yellow glimmer dancing around her gave her away.

Liam's jawline twitched as he clenched his jaw. "Hoy, I'll do whatever ya want. I'll break into the castle and kill the king with my bare hands. But I'll *not* go anywhere with her."

Twenty-Five

Before dawn's light, we readied our horses in the stables while Iisakki groomed himself in cat form on a bale of hay. I brushed Clover, a beautiful seal-brown mare with a black mane and tail. She was groomed, packed, and ready to go, but I brushed her anyway while Pirkko finished prepping her dapple-gray gelding, Cullen.

"How did you convince Liam to go along with your plan?" I pressed lips tight against the sour thought of a journey with a hostile, ex-cursed defender who held a vendetta against my biological family.

"I didn't." She shook her mass of hair down her back, the reddish brown strands shimmering like her gelding's mane. "He may not join us. But Valtteri was speaking to him last I knew. I can't imagine it'll take much convincing. You're a necessary part of our plan. Liam must see that."

"What is the plan, exactly?" The sour flavor of bile rose in my chest until I had no choice but to swallow it—like this plan of theirs. "Liam is going to pretend to be under the curse and bring me to my father. Then what?"

"Hmph. Assuming Liam can hold his temper." She tugged the

stuffed saddlebag strap with more force than necessary, making Cullen sidestep, then fastened the latch. "Valtteri is working on a plan to free the entire city of the curse at once, but that requires people, equipment, planning... and antidote. For now, he wants ya to integrate yourself into your father's life. We have people on the inside. They'll reach out when it's time to act."

The lack of specifics made me nervous. To what was I agreeing?

But time was good. Perhaps, with enough time, I could convince Auberon to remove the curse himself.

Perhaps if I fed myself such sweet optimism, my stomach would stop churning up this bile.

We walked our horses out of the stables. Iisakki hopped from his perch and chased us. A strange tingling sensation bubbled under my skin, making me itch.

I was on my way to meet my father.

My *father*.

What would he be like? How would he respond to me? Would he try to kill me on sight? Or would paternal instinct overtake him?

But I wasn't just meeting my father. I was meeting a king. A genocidal king. And I was bringing a former loyal servant, now out for blood. And three mercenaries who wanted the same. I was fraternizing with his enemies. Nay, worse. I was *conspiring* with them. Even if I didn't understand the full extent—or even part of their plan —I *was* part of it. No king would look kindly on that... should he find out.

It was treason. I was a traitor to the crown.

And still, I marched on to face him.

We met the others on the main thruway where I'd entered Folaím. Where the defender, Liam, broke through. The road was still deserted. Other than those preparing to leave with us—Taneli, Reko, Rhys, and Liam. Valtteri must've done some heavy convincing.

Liam waited with his steed. Both cleaned up nicely aside from the scowl darkening his face. His groomed white horse with its flowing silver mane, embellished saddle pad, and ornate bridle gleamed in the morning light. Liam had combed his black hair, revealing his forehead and thick eyebrows. But he hadn't shaved. Stubble covered his face. He looked... handsome, despite the dark aura of stormy emotions and turbulent oceanic eyes.

I'd never seen anyone so bloodthirsty. Not even the fasgadair.

I swallowed. Hard. All optimism vanished like smoke in a strong wind. This was going to go very, very badly.

To ignore Liam, I focused on Taneli, Reko, and Rhys as they emerged from the stables. A broad smile crinkled up Taneli's freckled cheeks, his uneven teeth endearing, his anger at me apparently vanquished. Creeping crabs, his moods changed faster than Fallon's.

"You can ride, right?" Reko, still ramrod straight, ran his fingers through his blondish-red hair and replaced his cap.

"It's been a while." How old was I when I'd last ridden? Six? Not since we fled Notirr. None had the skill I had at such a young age, capable of latching onto and scaling a running horse onto its bare back. I doubted I could do that now. It hadn't occurred to me until now how fearless I'd been as a child... before the fasgadair.

He shrugged. Surely, he hadn't relaxed his posture a smidgen? No. Not possible. "It's like walking and talking. Once ya learn, ya never forget."

"True enough, but prepare to hurt." Taneli winked. "Your body'll hate ya for neglecting those muscles."

"If only *some* would forget how to talk." Pirkko rolled her eyes.

"What?" He raised his arms. "She'll find out after a day's ridin'. Would I 'elp her any by failing to speak?"

Her hair shimmied over her back as she shook her head. "Are ya helping her by speakin'?"

"Hoy, stop actin' the maggot." Reko smacked the back of Taneli's head. "Clover's a good horse. She'll be good to ya."

"She's a beauty." I stroked her neck.

Clover snorted her agreement, shaking her black mane.

We all laughed. Well, all but Liam. But I tried to pretend he wasn't there.

Iisakki wound his small cat body around Clover's leg. When she lowered her big horsey head to inspect the critter, he brushed his face against her cheek, then rolled on his back. She nudged his belly as he batted her nose.

"That's so adorable," Pirkko gushed.

"Watch your things around her. She's a thief disguised as a horse," Taneli said.

Holding up a hand beside his mouth, Reko leaned in to whisper. "She *is* mouthy, but she only steals from Taneli. She has something against him. Whatever her reason, I'm sure Clover's actions are justified."

He clapped and raised his voice for all to hear. "Saddle up." Then he mounted his black horse and reached for Rhys, who either didn't know how to ride or wasn't trusted to ride on his own.

I anchored myself into the saddle. Iisakki morphed into a dragon, flew up to hover over Clover, then descended onto her withers in cat form.

The horse fidgeted as I tugged the trousers Pirkko insisted I wear. They made it easier to ride a horse and run. But as the constricting things kept riding up and scratching my thighs, I missed my dress.

Iisakki stood and stared at me as if to ask if I was finished fidgeting.

"Yes, I'm done."

He gave me one last long look, then crawled into my lap and began spinning.

"Are you finished?" I asked him.

Iisakki spun once more, then settled down.

Trying to ignore my discomfort and avoid crushing Iisakki, I spoke in the mare's ear as I stroked her neck. Her ears flickered at my breath, but her body relaxed.

"Mrrreow," Iisakki complained.

I sat upright. "Are you going to be like this the entire time?"

He licked his lips, then pulled his head into his paws so he looked like a ball of fur with no beginning and no end.

A door slammed behind me, making me spin in the saddle.

A little girl ran toward us, waving. Liisi.

I waved back.

"Liisi!" a boy called with a sharp tone from the doorway in the tree house. "Get back here."

She stopped, feet spread as if in indecision between continuing her approach and obeying her brother.

I wanted to say something inspiring. But I didn't know what. So, I resorted to the Ariboslian saying that always comforted me. "You are loved, Liisi!"

She clasped her hands together and pressed them to her heart as if stuffing my words there, then darted back home.

Reko swiveled in his seat, peering around Rhys. "I'll lead ya through the veil. Follow me." He clicked his tongue and tugged the reins to get his horse moving. When they disappeared before me, I aimed for the same spot.

As if a curtain of disease swept over the village, it snuffed out all light and life. The magical disintegrated into a dead façade—an illusion of an abandoned village—sapping the joy Liisi had supplied, however brief.

TWENTY-SIX

Taneli was right. My body hated me. The ache had settled in after two hours of riding. Now, my muscles begged me to stop, find another position, leap from the horse... anything else. The others seemed fine. Their horse-riding muscles must be in better shape. Mine had atrophied.

At least I remembered how to ride.

The sun had long since reached its apex and was well into its descent. We'd only stopped once to water our horses. I'd snuck a bit of cheese then. My stomach had given up growling for attention and settled into a dull ache as if punishing me for its neglect.

I tried to shift my focus from my physical discomfort to the woods. But not much changed in the landscape... the width of the trail, the refuse littering the ground, and the branches I needed to sidestep or duck.

Clover was a good horse. She followed the others with little instruction from me. If only I had something to prop myself up, I could sleep.

The boring landscape allowed my mind to wander to places

better left unexplored, and I asked myself, once again, why I was on a suicide mission to a crazed king.

But what about God saying to seek Him? And what about Liisi and even Liam? No matter how much Liam despised me, God had brought me here. Even for snarly scunners like him.

Iisakki hopped from Clover's back and ran beside us as a puppy. I smiled as I watched him, ears flopping, tongue hanging out of the side of his mouth. He must've gotten bored too. If only I could join him. Though I ran fast, I'd never keep up with Iisakki or the horses in my present state.

The path widened, and wings sprouted from Iisakki's sides. Green scales overtook his fur from his nose to his elongating tail as he took to the sky. He finished his transformation with a barb on the end of his tail. I'd only seen glimpses of him in his dragon form. And now, his yellow underbelly hovered above my head. That might come in handy in the rain. How strange to have a dragon flying with me. A baby still, like the cat and dog versions of himself. Either that or he was a small dragon. His torso was smaller than Clover's in every way. But his wingspan was impressive. From tip to tip, they must've been wider than my height, and I was tall for a girl. He cast a shadow overhead, sending a gust of wind with each flap.

If only I could fly.

Watching Iisakki filled me with awe of the God who created such a magnificent creature.

"Can you tell your dragon to pick a shape and stick with it?" Liam's sharp voice sapped my improved mood. He directed his horse to walk alongside Clover. "Anything but the dragon." His eyes flashed with his angry aura. "We don't need one of *your* father's slaves spotting and reporting us."

I stiffened at the way he stressed your and sneered at father, but the next word was more offensive. "Slave?"

"What would you call someone whose every freedom has been stolen? Even if they enjoy their cage, they're still caged." He kicked his horse's sides and cantered out of conversation range.

Coward. Only a jellyfish would say such hateful things and saunter off without allowing a rebuttal. A scared, spineless jellyfish. My insides boiled as I twisted the reins around my hand, hoping to alter his brain composition from a mere look.

Rare red tendrils whisked from my skin. Who was he to treat me as if I were my father? A man I'd never even met. As I sat up straighter, every offended part of me pressed me to follow, to make him see I'm not my father, but I slumped back into the saddle. It would accomplish nothing. And what did I care what a reformed defender thought of me? He was a temporary companion. Nothing more. And not much of one at that.

And what did he want me to do about Iisakki? I had no control over him.

Iisakki!

Nothing.

"Iisakki!"

He dropped at my approach. Then he returned to the air, hovered overhead, and landed on my lap in his cat body. He cocked his head as if waiting for me to explain why I'd summoned him.

"You're not allowed to travel as a dragon."

Iisakki huffed. Twin puffs of smoke escaped his nose. Did he understand?

"And if we come upon strangers, stick to one form. Okay? You can't let on that you're a dragon."

He narrowed his eyes, all too defiant for a cat, then crawled over my leg to settle on his favorite spot on Clover's withers.

Why did it seem like I had a petulant child on my hands?

And was there no end to this accursed forest?

What little sunlight pushed through the leafy canopy waned as night fell. My aching muscles tightened, refusing to obey, and I lagged even further behind.

Liam glanced back at me. Again. Did he shake his head? "Whoa, Nessa." He pulled his horse to a stop. "We'll camp here tonight."

"Good." Taneli dismounted. "I'm knackered."

I struggled to peel my lame leg from the saddle. My feet buckled when I landed. Unfamiliar muscles screamed at me.

As the horses' hooves stilled, a bubbling brook rose from my left. Good. My canteen was almost empty. I led Clover to the source. She submerged her lips and slurped. A wavering image appeared beside me as I dunked my canteen. I shifted sideways, winced at Liam's scowl.

Without as much as a glance, he tended to Nessa.

He reminded me of the orphans in Notirr. When they were mad at me, they'd make a show of pretending I didn't exist. He had the darkest, most powerful aura. Almost all red. Was he just angry, or was this his natural state? Or did my presence bring it out?

Should I attempt to mend whatever was wrong between us? It would make this journey more pleasant. But did I dare? I took a deep breath.

God, help me.

Steeling myself, I wheeled around to face him. "Have I done something to offend you?"

"Your existence offends me."

What? I jerked sideways so fast my foot lost its balance and I nearly slipped into the stream. But seriously. Did he say that? Pirkko came up behind me. Had she overheard?

She wrinkled her nose. "Your stink offends me."

"Pa—" My hand flew to my mouth at her quick-witted response. But if I had any hope of getting along with this scunner, I shouldn't laugh.

Liam scoffed and coaxed his horse to follow him downstream.

Pirkko's hand hovered over her clamped mouth. Her bright brown eyes gleamed, and her shoulders quaked. When Liam walked out of sight, she burst out laughing, though he must still be within earshot.

As her infectious laughter did me in, I joined her.

Bent over with tears streaming down our faces, each time we made eye contact, we burst into a new fit. Iisakki seemed to enjoy our display. He scampered about as a puppy, bowing into play position and leaping between us.

Rhys approached with hands up. "Have you taken leave of your senses?"

I waved toward the trees where Liam had disappeared, and an undercurrent of annoyance swept away my mirth. Not even Beagan irritated me so. "Why'd he agree to come if he's just going to be unpleasant?"

"Give him time." Pirkko gathered her wild hair away from her face, twisting it together before letting it loose.

"Emotions make little sense. To be sure, to be sure." Clasping his hands, he rocked back and forth on his feet. "Anger and fear in particular. They oft go hand in hand."

Pirkko quirked her lips. "The kid has a point. It's easier to be angry than afraid... or sad."

"Aye, but why should I have to—" Ugh. Even I couldn't stand my whininess.

"He woke from under the curse only yesterday." She touched my shoulder, her hand and her brown eyes soft. "Emotions are strongest and most difficult to control the first few weeks."

"Weeks?" I snorted. *That* didn't buoy my hopes of surviving this trip.

She released my shoulder and slapped my back. "Until then— don't take his sass."

Riiiight.

Twenty-Seven

The cool night sky blotted out all but the closest trees and nipped at our exposed skin, but the warm fire soothed its bite. Crackling flames and gnawing teeth filled the dead air between conversations. Taneli handed me a stick with a charred rodent carcass, dripping with grease.

"What's this?" I pointed to a blackened thing sticking out from my food.

"The tail?" he asked.

"T–tail?" I gagged.

He rolled his eyes, gripped my meal, and tore the tail off with a sickening crack and slimy rip.

My stomach rolled. He'd cured my hunger.

Then he bit into the thing with a crunch, like a rat cracker.

"Try it." Pirkko gestured with her stick, rodent meat juice dribbling down her chin. "It tastes like chicken."

I doubted that. Besides, I didn't care much for chicken either. But, despite my revulsion, my stomach growled, not caring what it received as long as it received something. If only I could bypass my mouth. I picked up the slimy thing and took a nibble. Taneli had seasoned it with something. It wasn't terrible.

Was this what it had been like for Fallon? Setting off on a precarious journey with strange companions. Eating fresh kill roasted over a campfire. Reality wasn't as glamorous as I'd imagined. And she hadn't traveled with an incredible chef to make the local ground dwellers more palatable.

Iisakki loved his meal. Whatever these rodents were, they were plentiful. He bounded around our camp in dragon form, pouncing on vermin and gobbling them whole. Thick tails wriggled between his jaws. Disgusting.

At least I didn't need to fear them crawling on me while I slept. Not with him nearby. Not if the nasty things valued their life.

"We part ways in the morn." Liam didn't glance at any of us as he spoke.

"W—" I choked on a piece of meat and coughed it up. After more unladylike coughs, I managed the full word. "What?"

"We've neared the end of my territory. Tomorrow, we'll reach the boundary where another defender patrols." He refused to meet my gaze.

"What does that mean?" I steadied my stick before dropping the rodent on the ground.

Silence reigned until Reko sucked a bone clean. "It means it's time to enact the next phase in our plan to get you to the castle."

"And what is said plan?" Somehow, I'd managed to keep my voice level.

"It means we turn back, and you continue on with him." Reko waved the bone toward Liam. "He'll tell the other defender he's under direct orders from Auberon to bring you in. Having any others with him will confuse the issue and risk exposing us all."

I gulped. The rodent squirmed as if its pieces had reanimated and proceeded to use my stomach as a running wheel. I almost scooted closer to Pirkko. I didn't want to continue without her. Delivering myself to a genocidal king's hands was unnerving enough. But traveling with this guy who didn't bother to hide his hatred? Who would defend me if we were alone?

This was getting real. Too real.

"But you—" Reko growled, waving the vermin's skeleton at Liam like a sword. "Keep your head. Play your part and play it well."

Taneli scowled as if Reko had eaten his last ration. "That's a fret! We'll be lucky if this eejit doesn't get 'imself killed before reachin' the gate with his rippin' temper."

What a point, but while I appreciated the sentiment, Taneli wasn't one to speak of ill tempers.

"If he wants to get himself killed, I say, let him," Pirkko jammed her hands on her hips and tossed her wild hair over one shoulder. "At least a cursed defender will ensure Colleen's safe arrival to the castle gates. And in a more gentlemanly manner at that." An unspoken warning flashed in her eyes. "If any harm should come to her whilst under your care..."

Taneli tossed a clean bone at Liam's feet, the implication clear. "You'll 'ave we to contend with."

"You'll have *all* the Saoirse Trodaí to contend with." Reko loomed into the guy's space, going all protective like one of my uncles. "And you best put on a good show of being cursed. You've a better notion of what Auberon might do if he suspects you're Saor. But what do you think they'll do to her, traveling with the likes of you? They may suspect she's a traitor too."

They wouldn't be wrong.

With an eye roll, Pirkko fingered through her hair—the girl probably never needed a comb. "Let him act the maggot. All Colleen has to say is she was using him to lead her to the castle. None would dare lay a hand on her, not without Auberon's official command. She'll still find her way home, and his attitude will change like a bird in a whirlwind when they expunge his mind."

I fidgeted with my rodent stick, nearly dropping it. I couldn't lie as she suggested. But no point in saying so.

Liam balked. "Don't start me. The king—" He rolled his eyes and groaned. "I mean, *Auberon*"—he spat out his name—"isn't bothered by you or any other rebel. His worshipers won't allow his enemies within a thousand ship lengths. He's untouchable. All he'll care about is her."

Taneli toppled his plate as he jumped to his feet. Rodent bones skittered across the dirt. "If ya think using that fact might help ya in whatever ya might be scheming, have another think. Any harm comes to her, you'll have Auberon's army *and* the Saoirse Trodaí out for your blood."

"I'll accompany the princess."

I jumped at the squeaky voice by my side. In all the bluff and bluster, I'd forgotten Rhys was there.

While everyone shifted toward him, the boy's shoulders rose, and he peeped about as if expecting—yet hoping to avoid—opposition.

"With what explanation?" Reko waved his stick between us. "Who are you to her?"

Rhys seemed to shrink. "Her adopted brother?"

No. I stiffened. "I won't lie. The last thing deceived people need is more lies." And everyone needed to know I wasn't like my father.

Something prickled the back of my head. My gaze flicked to Liam, and the tingles slid down the back of my neck at him assessing me. His aura wasn't pulsing now, and orange streaks flared, breaking up the deep red. What did that mean? What was making him uncomfortable?

Rhys squared his shoulders. "No lying necessary. To be sure, to be sure. I *am* a friend, am I not? She'll not traverse these wilds alone with him. I'll not allow it."

Something within burrowed a Rhys-sized hole into my heart and tucked him away inside.

"If they turn on her, they'll turn on you too." Reko's fingers rasped against his stubbled jaw even as his stern countenance softened.

"She has Iisakki?" Why did I hear Pirkko say that as if in question, trying to convince herself Iisakki would be sufficient?

The kitten cleaning himself stopped, surveyed our sudden attention, then returned to his all-important task. Dragon or not, Iisakki wasn't real security. Not yet. Perhaps if we waited a month or a year... However long it took a dragon to mature. But we didn't have time. The veil was coming down now.

"He can come as my prisoner." Liam braced his elbows on his knees and pressed his clasped hands to his mouth.

"Catch yourself on." Taneli charged forward, leaning into Liam's face. "He'll be hanged."

"Hanged?" Everything within me constricted as my spine lengthened. "He's just a boy!"

Rhys cocked his head to one side, his face scrunched up beneath his cap of black hair. "For what crime?"

Surely, he wasn't—he *was* considering this?

"For whatever fool idea this cluster comes up with." Taneli's freckles receded into his reddened face.

Pirkko scooted closer to Reko and touched his forearm. "Auberon wouldn't hang a boy. Would he?"

"He'll have a lighter punishment as a minor." Black hair slipped onto Liam's forehead, licking along his matching brow as his ocean-blue eyes narrowed. "How old are you?"

"Twelve?" Rhys's gaze flashed my way.

Twelve? Liar! He didn't know his actual age. And didn't he say whatever he was, he was older than twelve? And he'd had the gall to seem insulted when I suggested that's how old he appeared.

"Is that a question?" Pirkko had her hair in a fist again as if it was the only thing she could fight in this moment—and fight it she would.

Why didn't I tell them? Why didn't I call him out? What held my tongue?

"He looks twelve." Reko nudged her hand loose, freeing the much-abused untamable mass. "True or not, go with it. It's under the age of the curse. Liam can claim Rhys is an orphan caught stealing food. What'll happen to an underage orphan caught stealing?"

Liam rolled his shoulders and rubbed the back of his neck. "Most likely, he'll receive the curse and be recruited into the king's service."

"What's the worst they might do?" Reko held Pirkko's hand.

"Expunge his memory first."

At the ex-defender's response, Reko eyed Rhys. "If you're willing to accept the risk, I'd rest easier if you accompanied Colleen. And if it comes to the worst for you but our plan succeeds, you won't have to live under the curse long."

"It's a chance I'm willing to take. To be sure."

I couldn't catch Rhys's eye or read his insufferable aura. This wasn't the first he'd lied. But he *was* willing to risk his safety. For me. And if lying about his age spared his life, shouldn't he? Perhaps it was best to let it go. For now. He hadn't caused me harm. And having him with us was better than being alone with a hotheaded scunner. "What is the plan?"

Taneli and Pirkko both silently questioned Reko.

He released a heavy breath. "I don't know all of it. And it's best you don't either. Liam can't fall under the curse again, and it doesn't work on elves—so you're both safe from that. But Auberon is mad. No telling what might befall you if he believes you're part of a plot to undo his curse. And we can't risk information leaking. We've only got one shot at this."

So in the morning, I'd be alone with a vendetta-driven man and a liar.

Twenty-Eight

Breakfast offered an improvement over dinner. Our combined supplies, leftover rodent, and some wild roots and mushrooms made a decent stew. After we cleaned up, we packed the horses.

Liam attached a rope from Clover to Nessa, then jerked a thumb to Rhys. "If you're to be my prisoner, you must appear the part."

"To be sure, to be sure." Rhys hopped onto Nessa's back and offered his wrists, which Liam tied tight together.

"Take care, Colleen." Pirkko settled into her saddle, twisted her hair and shoved it into her cap, and gripped the reins. "I pray we see each other again soon."

"Right, watch yourself. And that horse." Taneli removed his hat and bowed as his horse shimmied beneath him.

"Peace be with you." Reko mimicked Taneli's bow.

All three then disappeared among the trees. A hollow in my heart widened.

What did that leave me with? A seething defender-turned-traitor and a lying mystery boy. Yet he was willing to sacrifice himself —for me.

OUR HORSES TROTTED with a steady rhythm of thuds on the soft earth. The dark colors bathing Liam waned as the day wore on. He threw glances over his shoulder periodically. Each time, his aura would be at its lightest point before he looked, then would darken after he glimpsed me. Creeping crabs, the sight of me worsened his mood.

Hours later, our horses slowed, and renewed aches settled into my already impaired muscles. Still, not one of us had uttered a word. This time, when Liam looked my way, orange overtook his aura. "We should water the horses."

Was *I* causing his discomfort?

I pulled Clover beside Nessa and dismounted. My numb legs buckled, and I faltered. I tried to avoid Liam's gaze as I righted myself, but cringed instead as he stifled a snicker in my periphery. My face warmed, and I pushed my hair forward to conceal the blush. I fetched the decanter and fumbled through the saddlebag for a bowl to pour water for Iisakki. Everything was more difficult with the deep fatigue settling into my bones, but I'd not complain.

"I have some crackers to stave off our hunger until we can get to the farmhouse." Liam's lighter aura took me off guard. Riding in silence seemed to have done wonders for his mood. But his scowl remained. "Your dragon won't need as much to eat *if* he stays small."

Iisakki didn't seem concerned with conserving resources. He bounded through the trees in his true dragon frame. At about the size of a young foal, he was getting bigger. He snatched something with his teeth and threw it down his gullet.

I laughed, then caught Liam's glare. "Iisakki." I fought to find a believable admonishing tone. "Remember what I said about changing shapes? No dragons allowed."

Iisakki gulped once more, licked his lips, and shrunk into a cat.

What happened to the creature he'd eaten whole? Had that shrunk too? Certain things about this world I'd never understand. I dared a glance at Liam, who munched on a cracker. He held one out to me. I approached to snatch the food as if stealing from an uilebheist's mouth.

"I won't bite." He motioned to the grass beside him. "Sit."

You won't? I bit back the temptation to ask. And though stretching and sitting cross-legged felt good, I wiggled, self-conscious doing so wearing pants. My selkie dress was packed away, and Pirkko was right. Pants, even short pants, were far more practical.

I nibbled the cracker, hating the silence. One could ride in silence, but sit? Nope.

Wait. Hadn't he mentioned a farmhouse? I'd like to know about that, but dare I attempt conversation? I took a deep breath as if preparing to dive into a deep ocean. "We're going to a farmhouse?"

He handed me another cracker. "Yes."

"Are they cursed?" *Please don't make my attempts to talk be like attempting to swim through a jellyfish field.*

"Everyone is. On this side of The Divide, that is."

"The Divide?" Now, I sounded like a parrot. "Oh, Rut-Rot—"

"Rotko. The cursed land that divides the elfin lands from the fae."

"It's also called the Forest of Shadows?"

"Some call it that."

"How is it cursed? Aren't we in the cursed lands?"

"A different kind of curse."

Why did every question lead down another dead-end neas trail? His clear disinterest in answering didn't help. And I had no idea how long until this oyster clammed up. I should ask more pertinent questions. "Why are we going to the farm? Isn't it risky?"

"No riskier than making the trip without sufficient supplies."

I rubbed the shivers from my arms, not sure how I felt about being around a cursed family. Or taking their food. "I'm just supposed to pretend to be the princess so they'll give us food and a place to sleep?"

"You *are* the princess." He stood and brushed himself off. "It's not you who needs to worry. I'm the one they'll seek to kill if they suspect my allegiance no longer aligns with theirs."

I followed him to the horses. "Aren't you worried?"

He shrugged as we freed our horses' reins. "It's worth the risk."

I hoisted myself onto Clover as Iisakki made himself comfortable on her back.

Liam shoved Rhys into the saddle, then flung himself onto the blanket behind him. He clicked Nessa into a walk, and I followed.

If he didn't care if he died, why should I? His choices and bad decisions and terrible attitude were his own.

So why did I have a nagging feeling something was about to go terribly wrong?

TWENTY-NINE

The woods cleared, and fences lined the hillside. Black cows dotted the space within, their scattered forms reminded me of seals sunning themselves on the rocky shore. Their mooing rang from the distance. A farmhouse and barn loomed on the horizon. What would these people be like? Cursed. But how would that manifest in regular people?

A skinny boy skipping rocks in a pond outside the fence spotted us. From here, he could've been a stick figure in short pants and a flowy tunic. He waved and shouted something I couldn't comprehend, then sped off toward the house.

We made our way to the road climbing the hill to the house, and the place grew noisier—chickens clucked, sheep and goats bleated, ducks quacked, pigs grunted, and some sort of hammering rang out above it all. A foul stench of beasts and their excrement polluted the sweet air, strengthening as we neared.

The boy reappeared with a slam of the screen door. He ran toward us while the others remained behind. "I knew it!" He skipped to Liam's side, and with orange-red hair and a missing tooth, the stick figure became a jack-o'-lantern like in the American picture books. "I knew it was you."

Liam smiled and bent down to ruffle the boy's hair. "It's good to see you, Kieron."

Either he was a good actor or he loved kids enough to put aside his anger. Or perhaps he liked *this* kid. Either way, auras didn't lie. A rainbow of light colors danced about him. He looked nice bathed in brightness... and smiling.

Liam slid from the horse and walked beside Kieron.

"Have you come to sup with us? Mum says you can. I asked." Kieron bounced, and his yellow and pink glow lagged behind.

"We'd love nothing more."

Iisakki hopped from my lap, landing on all fours with ease. He switched to a puppy and pounced on the boy. I sucked in a breath. Did Kieron see Iisakki shape-shift?

Then again, would it matter? If everyone knew I was the king's daughter, wouldn't it make sense that I had a dragon? So why was Liam so surly about him changing into a dragon and attracting attention?

If the kid had noticed, he didn't seem to care. He laughed at Iisakki's antics and dodged the tongue swiping at his reachable face.

"Is this your dog?" He looked my way, then to Rhys, his eyes widening at the sight of his bound hands. His glow darkened as one brow rose to impressive heights. His eyeball dipped up and down in the corner while he lifted a hand to cover half his mouth and leaned into Liam. "Are they your prisoners?" he asked in a not-so-hushed voice, jabbing a thumb our way.

"The lad is, yes. But the girl... Can you guess who she is?" A sparkle danced in Liam's eye.

The boy pinched his bottom lip. He swiveled back to Liam. "Who is she?"

"Princess Eerika."

Eerika? It hadn't occurred to me I might have another name.

Wasn't Auberon's father's name Eerikki? They must've named me after him.

Kieron's aura changed faster than most children's. It surged from a deep purple to light yellow and pink. His eyes brightened along with his glow. He jumped up and down, pointing at me. "She's the princess? The long-lost princess? I've read about you!" He burst back inside the house, his squealing voice screaming through every open window. "Guess who's outside! Princess Eerika! The long-lost princess!"

I swallowed the lump forming in my throat. If only I could shrink away or gallop far, far away.

A young girl stepped through the front doorway. Unlike Kieron, she eased the door closed behind her. Dark curls that had escaped her braid framed her slender face. Freckles splattered her nose and upper cheeks as if someone had flicked a wet paintbrush at her. She curtsied. "May I water your horses, Highness?"

I cringed. I wanted to correct her on the title, but she was right. Though I hated the illusion in her adoring eyes, I'd rather not crush her. Or get Liam in trouble. So I smiled. "Yes, thank you."

The girl beamed as she hurried to take the reins, and I dismounted.

"Come in. Come in." Kieron motioned for us to follow into a room with a large wooden table. "Sit here." He grasped a chair taller than himself and dragged it away from the table, then worked on the next one. "Want me to sit them in the dining room, mum?"

"Goodness, yes. We can't serve royalty in the kitchen. Gracious." A woman with the same face and hair as the girl with a few wrinkles and grays burst from an adjoining room carrying a pitcher. She had no aura. "You must be parched. Have some water."

"Thank you, Mrs. O'Donal," Liam said.

"You're most welcome, Defender Liam. It's always an honor to see you." Though she smiled at him, she came to me first and filled a water goblet. "Forgive me, Your Highness. I've never so much as met a royal, never mind hosted one in my humble home." She curtsied.

"Has King Auberon had the pleasure of seeing you? Or are you going there now?"

"We're on our way." I lifted the goblet.

"Oh dear, I pray he'll forgive me for layin' eyes on you first." She clucked her tongue. "Mr. O'Donal will join us in a moment. He's out mendin' the fence."

When Mrs. O'Donal filled Rhys's cup and he reached for a sip, she gasped at his bound hands. "Kieron, run and fetch your brother and sisters."

Kieron dashed from the room.

Once he'd left, she glanced over her shoulder. "Forgive me for questioning a humble servant of our king, but have you brought a criminal into your servant's home?"

Liam swallowed his sip. "He's no threat. Merely an orphan boy. And a petty thief."

"A thief? Goodness! What'll happen to him?" More wrinkles crinkling into focus, she gazed upon Rhys as if he were already condemned.

"Since he's under the age of atonement, the king will sanctify him and put him in his service," Liam said.

Mrs. O'Donal pressed her lips into a tight line. "Of course, a just and merciful act from our just and merciful king. There's no greater blessing than to be in the king's employ." She clutched the stone pitcher in both hands and watched Rhys as if struggling with inner conflict. "Again, I beg your forgiveness, but if I'm to serve the lad, I must know King Auberon would approve."

Liam stood and bowed. "As an honored member of the king's military, I can assure you you're doing your king and country a service. He's underage, orphaned, and hungry enough to steal bread." Liam sounded so stately. "Wayward children with no guardian to speak on their behalf do sometimes surface. It's my job to deliver them to our most gracious and charitable king. He is a fair and just king and will ensure the lad is delivered to a suitable charity house."

Her shoulders relaxing, she smiled now. "Our goods go to charity houses."

"A service for which your king and country are grateful." Liam bowed once more.

Wow. He was an incredible actor. He almost convinced me he was under the curse.

Mrs. O'Donal touched Rhys's shoulder as only a mother can. "You must've gone through such an ordeal, going hungry with no guardian. And underage! King Auberon will ensure you are cared for. Until then, it's my honor to help." Then her sheepish look reemerged.

"Is there something else, Mrs. O'Donal?" Liam smoothed his uniform.

"Far be it from me to question the king's representative once more, but is it necessary to keep the binds on him whilst he remains in our home?"

"I don't think the lad is a flight risk." Liam cocked his head toward Rhys. "What say you? If we untie your binds, do we have your word as a citizen of Talamh Sí to behave honorably and remain by my side for the duration of our visit?"

Rhys nodded. His eyes widened as Liam removed the binds.

After a curt nod, Mrs. O'Donal sauntered back into the adjoining room, surely the kitchen based on the wonderful smells wafting from there. With my stomach both queasy and famished, food would either settle or aggravate it. But, although they seemed nice, I wasn't looking forward to an evening with my father's worshipers—and how it spilled over to me.

Why did I feel like I was lying?

Because I was. Liam and Rhys were lying, and I said nothing. And I pretended to be a loving daughter, seeking her long-lost father. What an impostor! My mere existence now was a lie. And I'd have to play the part the whole visit.

Thirty

Mrs. O'Donal served salad and some sort of meat and vegetables in a pie topped with creamy potatoes. The savory scents teased me, making my mouth water. Once everyone was seated, they bowed their heads.

"Lord, King Auberon..." Mr. O'Donal began.

I snapped my head up.

"... thank you for this food which you have provided...."

Everyone's eyes were closed with heads bowed, but Liam peeked at me askance and made a threatening huff.

I closed my eyes. *God, please forgive me for bowing my head and closing my eyes. I'm here, but I'm praying to You, not Auberon.*

"... and thank you for delivering the princess to our humble home, which you have so gracefully provided. I pray for her safe return to a blessed reunion with you, her father, lord and king. Amen."

Everyone raised their heads and looked at me, eyes bright and smiling—happy. Whilst I felt as if I stood up to my neck in a pool of shrimp nibbling at my skin.

Something flashed across Mr. O'Donal's face as his gaze flickered between me and Liam. But Liam smiled too as if all was right with the world. If Mr. O'Donal caught anything amiss, it was because of me.

I warned them. I told them I couldn't lie. But had they listened? And now, without having spoken a word, I'd given us away. No one needed my ability to see auras to read my thoughts. I might as well have tattooed them on my skin or stitched them on my clothes. No way could I contain my horror at that ungodly prayer.

Mr. O'Donal studied me, then said, "Eat up, everyone."

I tried to breathe and avoid his gaze... anything but act like I'd done something wrong, which probably made me look even guiltier. So I ate. With each tasty bite, I realized how hungry I was. I'd barely finished one forkful when I shoved another into my mouth, bent over my plate, and noticed everyone looking at me. My face reddened. How unroyaltylike.

"Have you been feedin' the princess?" Mrs. O'Donal scowled at Liam as if he'd confessed to conspiring to kill the king. "Here." She carried her plate to me, her fork poised to push her meager portion onto my plate. "Have some of mine."

I stayed her hand. "No thank you, Mrs. O'Donal. I have more than enough." I looked at all the other plates. How had I not noticed the discrepancy in the portions? I had the most by far. Liam next. Even Rhys's carried a heftier serving than everyone else's, but not by much. They hadn't been expecting us. Would they now go hungry because we were eating their food?

My appetite disappeared. "It seems the children don't have enough. Would you mind if I give them some of mine?"

"By no means! I shan't have the young'uns receiving more than my lord and savior's own daughter!" She returned to her seat, clicking her tongue. "We've all we need, 'aven't we?"

Her children nodded, except for Kieron who paled more than his mother had. Given his expression and orange aura, he didn't agree.

But he rebounded and prattled away about the frogs he'd found in the pond, filling the would-be awkward silence.

Thank you, Kieron.

I paid minimal attention to the boy's antics. The older children, Gilroy and Viona, and their parents had no aura. But they still had emotions. How? Wasn't the aura the visible expression of emotion?

Mr. O'Donal ate as if that were his job and he wasn't paid to talk. His children, who I had thought were replicas of their mother, looked like a complete cross between the two, with his wide-set eyes and her oval face. Everyone shared the same spattering of freckles, but Kieron received a more generous portion. And only Mr. O'Donal and Kieron had red hair, but Kieron's was super thick and wavy, probably the way Mr. O'Donal's once was.

Viona, a more mature copy of her younger sister, sneaked side-glances at me between petite bites. She seemed petrified to make eye contact or take part in any conversation.

Gilroy, a male version of his sisters, would watch me, then turn away when I caught his eye. His face flushed.

They were all lean. Were they naturally so? Was tonight a fluke and they didn't have enough to eat because Rhys, Liam, and I had taken it? Or were they accustomed to not eating enough?

Their expressions of emotions despite not having an aura perplexed me like nothing else. Liam's emotions had overwhelmed him when they returned. Was he an overly emotional person? Or perhaps his feelings hadn't left him but had been subdued. Or manipulated.

Excited pinks and happy yellows engulfed Kieron and his other sister, Neve. Though Neve was quieter, choosing to smile and stare at whoever spoke, usually Kieron.

"We never see anyone around here." Kieron's face twisted. "Just the priest to collect the offering, the merchant to deliver and collect our goods, and the king's defenders." He tilted an adoring gaze at Liam. "Someday I'm gonna be a defender, like you."

Liam's aura darkened, and his smile faltered as he tousled Kieron's hair. "The kingdom will be lucky to have you."

His act had been impressive until that last part. No one seemed to notice except Mr. O'Donal. He studied Liam, then me. I dropped my gaze to focus on capturing a scrap of lettuce with my fork.

Please, God. Don't let anyone guess we're not loyal to Auberon.

Iisakki yipped from under the table, and I leaped from my seat. Once I recovered from the fright, I pressed a hand to my heaving chest. "Iisakki, that scared me!"

"A wee bit jumpy, are we?" Mr. O'Donal skewered me with a hard stare.

My heart squeezed, and my lungs refused to take in air. Did he suspect we weren't allies?

After a pregnant pause, Kieron busted out into laughter. Neve joined in. Her uncomfortable chuckles morphed into a genuine fit of giggles. The others followed. Everyone but Mr. O'Donal, who returned to his meal.

I breathed easier, joining in their laughter. But my heart wasn't with them. My nerves wouldn't allow it. What would happen if they found us out?

"There's no luck involved in the king's choosing. Our Kieron would make a fine defender." Mrs. O'Donal removed her napkin from her lap and wiped the corners of her mouth. "Viona, dear, light the candles."

Viona jumped from her seat and lit candles in lanterns on either side of the room. I hadn't even noticed it growing dark.

"Forgive us for the dim lighting, we have limited aether this far from the city," Mrs. O'Donal said.

"Do you have aether power in your home?" Kieron tipped his head to his hero.

Liam swallowed his bite. "In my lodging, I do. The entire city is connected to an aether power plant. But I spend most of my time patrolling the woods. I've no need of it out there."

"We don't need it for modern conveniences." Mr. O'Donal shot his son a stern look. "But we need it to run the farm and supply our fair kingdom. Mr. Murphy delivered the other day, but he gave us half the supply, saying something about a shortage. Do you know anything about that?"

"No, sir. But when I return to the castle, I'll investigate the matter and ask they ensure you get what you need for the month, especially with you caring for the princess."

"Bah." Mr. O'Donal waved his forkful in the air. "No need to bother the king or his devoted servants. King Auberon will provide. He always does."

"And it's our honor to serve the princess." Mrs. O'Donal dropped her napkin onto her clean plate. "Blueberries are in season, and a fresh pie is cooling on the sill. Can I interest anyone in a slice?"

"I've heard of blueberries, but I've never had any." Other than the spelled one to get through the veil.

"Never had—? Well, I'll be. Where have you been all these years if you don't mind me asking?" Mrs. O'Donal stood and jammed her hands on her hips.

Mr. O'Donal lowered his cup as Viona's eyes peeked out over hers. All awaited my response.

I glanced at Rhys and Liam, but they only shrugged. "I grew up in Ariboslia."

"Ariboslia?" Mr. O'Donal braced his elbows on the table and rested his chin on his clasped hands. "Is that somewhere in the seelie court?"

"It's in another realm."

"When the queen kidnaped you, we thought for sure she brought you to the fae, and they were keeping you hidden somewhere." Mrs. O'Donal raised eyebrows at her husband. "No wonder King Auberon's defenders failed to find her."

"They searched other realms as well," Mr. O'Donal said.

"True. But that's like searching for a firefly in the stars." Mrs. O'Donal sauntered off into the kitchen.

"How many realms are there?" I braced my hands on the smooth wooden tabletop.

Mr. O'Donal frowned. "I'm not sure it's possible to know that."

Rhys wore a smug as-I-said expression.

"What was it like in Ariboslia?"

"Is your mother still alive?"

Kieron's and Neve's questions tripped over each other. I tried to answer both. "Not that I'm aware of. I don't remember her. I was raised as an orphan in a village called Notirr. They were good to me." No need to bring up the fasgadair or fleeing to Bandia.

"Imagine. Our Princess Eerika. An orphan." Mrs. O'Donal returned with a pie and clucked her tongue. "I'm so glad you're home to claim your rightful place beside your father."

My rightful place? Was he searching for me to make me the queen? Or was it a ruse to lure me in and kill me?

Which was worse?

THIRTY-ONE

Mr. and Mrs. O'Donal wanted to give up their bed for me and put Liam and Rhys in the barn.

"No." I planted my feet, refusing to go upstairs. "I can't take your bed."

"And I must watch over both the princess and the thief." Liam crossed his arms and widened his stance.

I tried not to laugh at Kieron behind him, mimicking his posture.

Mrs. O'Donal wrung her hands together. Her brows furrowed. "We can't have the princess in the barn. Nor can we have a defender or a thief in her room."

Liam raised a hand. "I can sleep outside in the hallway with the boy."

"No, no, no." Mrs. O'Donal's hands twisted with more anxiety as she raised imploring eyes to her husband. "We can't have the king's servant sleep on the floor. That won't do. Oh dear."

"Perhaps we can find a suitable arrangement." Mr. O'Donal motioned for us to follow.

"The barn? You can't mean to suggest the princess—our lord and savior's own daughter—should sleep in the *barn*?" His wife's face paled.

"Give me a moment, Lotta." He bent to kiss her cheek. "We'll find an agreeable solution. See to the kids, and we will work this out."

She patted a hand on her chest as if reminding her heart to beat. Then she peeled her anxious stare from her husband, to the kids. "You heard your father."

Like obedient subjects, their children rose and left the room, saying good night as they went.

"Follow me." Mr. O'Donal led us to the barn.

He delivered us to some hay bales, then strode to a side door. "Wait here."

Liam grasped my hand and pulled me toward the barn doors. "Something isn't right."

My heart hammered. "Do you think he suspects—"

"—suspects what?" Mr. O'Donal reappeared holding something propped against his shoulder.

A gun.

I gasped, and my hands flew to my chest as if they could protect me from a bullet. "Are you planning to shoot us?"

"Not you, Princess." He waved the gun barrel toward Liam. "Him." Then he jerked it toward Rhys. "And possibly him."

Hands shaking at my sides, I stepped between the weapon and Liam. "Not if I have a say in the matter."

Confusion creased Mr. O'Donal's face as the weapon wavered. He lowered it but kept it at the ready. "I can't hurt you, Princess. But this man is an impostor. His heart is against our king."

So he'd seen through Liam at dinner. How would we get out of this with our lives? And no gunshot wounds? "I'll not allow you to hurt him. If he's an impostor, as you suspect, my father will know. He will deal with him when we arrive at the castle. It's not your place." My voice wavered. How would I ever be queen if I couldn't speak with authority for two seconds?

"You're on the land my lord has seen fit to provide to me and my family. I'll protect my lord and all he has given me with my life."

"We haven't threatened you, nor will we. We can remain outside—"

The gun jerked upward. "And risk you breaking in whilst we sleep?"

"I promise you—"

"Sorry, Princess. You've been away too long. I don't know that I can trust you either. This man is an impostor. An enemy to the king, your father. And yet you travel with him."

I attempted to close the gap between us to grasp the gun. "Then let us go."

"Go?" He stepped away from me, eyes crazed. "And risk you harming my lord?"

"Why would I harm my father?"

"If you're in league with the—"

Iisakki swooped from the rafters behind Mr. O'Donal onto his back, pushing him toward me. I seized the gun as Liam grasped my shoulders and steered me away. As Mr. O'Donal righted himself, Iisakki flew into him, knocking him down again. We dashed to the barn doors and pushed them closed before Mr. O'Donal could get through. Liam slid a lock in place as Mr. O'Donal crashed against it. He pounded his fists, cursing.

We charged off into the night. It wouldn't take Mr. O'Donal long to escape through another exit and follow us.

"Psst!"

Our heads snapped toward the sound. We rounded the bushes. Liam took the lead, arms splayed behind to keep us at more of a distance, to find Neve hiding in the bushes.

"Your horses are saddled behind the house. The back gate is open. But you must hurry."

"God bless you!" I said before realizing I shouldn't say that. "How did you know?"

"There's no time." Her gaze darted behind us. "You must go. Now!"

We rushed past her and rounded the house. The horses were just as she'd said. With the swiftness I'd had as a child, I mounted Clover and waited for Liam and Rhys. Then we galloped across the field after Iisakki's flying form.

ONCE WE WERE a safe distance away in the thick woods, Liam slowed. "We should rest."

I couldn't agree more. The fear of being caught had spurred me on. But that energy wore off, replaced by deep fatigue. We watered our horses, then huddled under our blankets, afraid to start a fire.

Liam turned onto his side and propped himself so he could see me over Rhys and Iisakki's dog form. "I can't believe you did that."

"Did what?" I snuggled up to Iisakki and massaged his shoulder as he grunted, fighting sleep.

"You shielded me from the gun. Why?"

Good thing the darkness covered my blush. "I don't know. I–I couldn't let him hurt you."

Silence ticked away.

"Thank you."

I rubbed what I could of Iisakki's belly, and soft snores escaped him. What could I say? I'd made the safest choice since Mr. O'Donal wouldn't risk harming me. "I only did what seemed right at the time."

"Never do it again."

Something in his grumpy voice and the thump as he returned to lying on his back made me smile.

THIRTY-TWO

Though the summer sun beamed above us, the temperature dropped. Gray clouds swirling ahead darkened the sky, giving the illusion of riding into the night. Leaves rustled, flipping over as if to protect themselves from the increasing winds. Birds squawked as they flew overhead from where we'd come, warning anyone who would listen of the perils ahead.

Rhys's black hair danced in the wind, hardly having time to settle between gusts.

With this storm fast approaching, the cold wind filtered through my clothes, biting my skin, icing my veins, urging me to flee. "Shouldn't we take cover?"

"There's a cave up ahead. We'll shelter there." Liam's voice barely penetrated the howling winds.

We picked up our pace as the clouds rolled in, engulfing us in fog. Liam disappeared into the gloom. My heart constricted as if someone were wringing the blood from it. What if I lost them?

I stood in my stirrups and prompted Clover to pick up her speed. Nessa's white rear emerged from the fog, and my heart resumed its pumping. But I couldn't relax. I held the reins in a white-knuckled grip, keeping in close pursuit—closer than comfortable. Every limb, every muscle tensed on high alert, refusing to let me fall behind.

Iisakki changed into a dragon and flew overhead. We ran into a wall of rain as if running into a waterfall. Drenched like we'd gone for a swim, my clothes soaked through. My itchy trousers chaffed my frozen skin. Nessa splattered us with mud, but the pelting rain washed most away.

The winds strengthened, picking up debris. I ducked as low as possible, but I needed to see where I was going and cling to the reins.

How much longer could we endure?

The rain stung as it struck. Nay, not rain. The droplets bounced. Hail? I lifted my hand to protect my face, throwing me off-balance. I righted myself and clung to the leather biting into my palms and winced at the assailing hail.

Then everything—*stopped*. The winds. The hail. Everything. But it was so dark. Clover nearly collided with Liam and Rhys as they slowed. I steered her away to swoop past, then turned her back.

"What happened?" I yelled though I no longer needed to. My loud voice echoed as if enclosed in a cave. Visibility was still low, but they looked a fright, like they'd gone for a swim through stinging jellyfish. "Are you okay?"

Rhys massaged the back of his head.

Liam pointed into the sky. Was that Iisakki's scaly underbelly? Wings as big as his body flapped. Hail and flying debris pummeled an invisible wall surrounding us. Patchy fog billowed outside the bubble, but inside there was none.

"Iisakki's doing this?" Was he in a protective bubble too? Or was he taking the brunt of the storm for us? My heart slammed in my chest. "We need to get him out of here."

"Let's go." Liam coaxed Nessa forward.

Iisakki matched our speed, keeping us within the protective sphere.

I cringed over what his body must be enduring. And he was tiring. I sensed it. A renewed sense of urgency shot through my overwrought system, exciting every nerve. We had to get him somewhere safe. Now. "How much farther?"

"We're here." Liam jumped from his horse and helped Rhys down.

The cave must be nearby, but I couldn't see anything but black outside the circle. I dismounted and followed Liam into an overhang, entering a space large enough for the horses, thank God. The moment we were all safe under the shelter, a sick sound of flapping wings rang from the cave's mouth as Iisakki plummeted from the sky, thudding on his back.

I raced to his side, and hail pelted me once more. "Help me bring him inside!"

Since Liam was already on the opposite side, we grabbed hold at the base of a wing and dragged Iisakki into the cave. We'd better not be doing more damage to his back. As soon as he was safe from the hail, I snatched a towel from my satchel and rubbed the debris from his belly, then his face. No obvious damage. Nothing but tough scales. Thank God. But his stomach hadn't taken the damage. I'd have to inspect his back if I could roll him over.

But he was still. Too still. My heart stalled. Was he alive? I put my head to his chest where I assumed his heart would be.

Rhys came beside me and listened as well. "They're faint, but I hear both heartbeats." He sat back on his feet. "He'll be all right."

Two hearts?

"Dragons have two hearts, to be sure. And although they tend to fall to their backs when injured, they do not enjoy lying on their backside. Ahem." His gaze darted between me and Liam. "Help me roll him over."

When had Iisakki gotten so big? His torso was nearly as big as Clover's.

Liam tucked the wing on his side under Iisakki. Together we shoved until the dragon rolled onto his stomach. I moved his head to a more comfortable position, then inspected his back. My stuttering heartbeat lurched harder—I didn't see any injuries.

"The scales on his back are stronger than his stomach." Liam looked up at me.

I couldn't read his eyes or his aura in the dim light, but his relieved voice penetrated my soul, releasing me from the building tension, squeezing the fear from my soul. Tears sprang to my eyes, and I crumpled like a rag doll.

Liam knelt beside me. "He's okay. We're all okay."

"As am I." Rhys ran his fingers through his slick black hair. It still fell back into place, but in clumps. Rivulets of water ran down his face.

Liam stood. "As you should be. You think I didn't feel your face buried in my back?"

Rhys huffed. "I'll inspect the horses."

I swiped my eyes, embarrassed by my unexpected emotional display.

Light blazed as Rhys lit a lantern.

"Did you see what you just went through? And you're worried about a dragon with natural armor." Liam stroked Iisakki's scaly snout. "He's going to be fine."

How could he be *sure?* Iisakki's back rose and fell with his breath. What if he hurt himself in some other way? "What if he has internal injuries? What if he never wakes up?" My voice cracked. I choked back a new deluge. At what point had I grown so close to him that I couldn't bear the thought of losing him?

"Right now he's suffering from exhaustion. I have no idea how he created the wall around us, but he must've spent an enormous amount of energy. But what about you?" Liam dabbed at my face with his towel. "You look like a human pincushion."

That sounded like an apt description of his own dirty face, blotted with scrapes and bits of blood. Yet his concern was not for himself—but for me. How? Just yesterday, he despised me. Was this some kind of game? Who changed their emotions so fast? I stepped back and bumped into Clover.

Liam's hands poised in the air as if he didn't dare move. "Did I hurt you?"

"No." I couldn't understand my feelings to explain them. "But your face is a mess too. Do you have anything to disinfect the wounds?"

"I keep a bottle of whiskey in my satchel for injuries." He winced as he stood. "I have a salve too. It's nothing short of miraculous. There's nothing it won't cure."

He hobbled to his horse. As he rummaged through his saddlebag, a tear in his pants gaped below his knee. Was that blood?

"You're hurt." I peeled his pant leg and nearly vomited at the gash along his calf's outer edge. "Superficial wounds can wait. We need to attend to this first."

I tossed his rolled bedding against the stone wall. "Sit there."

"Yes, ma'am." Liam threw me an infuriatingly cute smile.

I took out my vengeance by tearing his pant leg the rest of the way through so I'd have room to work. Then I poured his whiskey over the wound, and he sucked in air through gritted teeth.

"Sorry." My gaze roamed to his face. Just long enough to catch something in his eye. Did he find this funny? "It's going to have to be stitched. Do you have a needle and thread?"

"In here." He handed me a tin box. "The salve is in there too."

I fumbled through first aid supplies. I knew how to sew, and I'd been trained in first aid. But I'd never had to stitch skin. My stomach lurched.

Light in. Dark out.

Light in. Dark out.

Okay, it's just like fabric.

I doused my hands with alcohol, then wiped the needle and thread.

God, help me.

I fought to push the needle through his flesh and gagged.

Not like fabric!

I covered a cough with the back of my hand.

Liam grasped my hand. "You don't have to do this."

"Yes, I do." I allowed myself a deep breath and imagined myself back home in my room at my desk, mending my torn skirt hem.

I tied off the thread, sank back on my knees, and released pent-up breath. It. Was. Over.

"Where'd you learn to do that?" he asked.

"When we first moved to the selkie lands, we were pretty remote. My parents made me and my brothers and sister learn. Just in case." I dabbed the salve over the stitches. "But I've never had to stitch a real wound."

"In case of what? Was it dangerous where you lived?"

"No. But we had all come through the Fasgadair Wars. No fasgadair had survived on our lands. Still, Fallon, my adopted mother, remained paranoid for a while. She made us learn everything to survive—start a fire, mend our clothes, scavenge for food, hunt, cook, dress a wound." I wrapped the bandage from his kit around his leg. "Everything she could think to teach us."

"That must've been a tough way to grow up."

I dropped the unused supplies back in his tin and sat beside him. "Aye and nay. I mean, I'd just been rescued, so I was grateful to learn anything to help me survive should something like that happen again."

"Rescued?"

"Yeah." I wrapped my arms around myself. But did I want to get into this? I'd never spoken about it. I never had to. I'd buried it so far down, my voice struggled to unearth it. "M—my brothers and sister. They were orphans too. Notirr had lots of orphans they rescued from Gnuatthara. But that's another story." I waved it off. "They were all younger than me. We had escaped Notirr before the fasgadair attacked and were hiding out in Bandia. But the fasgadair seized the city. I—"

My throat clogged as the image of me and my siblings hiding in that disgusting little house resurfaced. Somehow talking about it made it all seem so... recent.

"It's okay. You're safe."

Am I? I bit my tongue.

Rhys rounded Clover. I'd forgotten he was here. "The horses are fine, to be sure. Only scratches. Nothing rest won't cure."

"Thank you for checking the horses. I'm glad you're okay." I stood and turned to Liam. "Thank you for your help with Iisakki."

I went to retrieve my bedding from Clover's saddlebag. But Rhys had taken the liberty of freeing my horse from her adornments.

"The bags are over there." He pointed to the far wall.

The blanket had gotten damp, but it was better than nothing. I placed it over Iisakki and curled up beside him.

God, I pray Iisakki will be all right.

THIRTY-THREE

Light streamed through the wide opening. Dust particles glittered in the beams, reminding me of shiny people. The rare few whose auras sometimes turned pure white. Sully was the only one I'd spent any time with. That was before I understood the emotions associated with the colors. I'd wanted to bask in his presence. His white light must've been pure happiness. An impenetrable joy unaffected by anything around him, even in the midst of the Fasgadair Wars. His was the only aura that never wavered. But sometimes it sparkled.

I wanted to be like that. Shiny. Thinking about it filled me with warmth. But a white aura wasn't something I was ever likely to possess. Even Aunt Stacy's aura rarely turned white, and she was the happiest person alive. There must be more mysteries to auras left to explore.

Iisakki stirred beside me. A low rumble rose from deep within.

I leaned over to see his face. "How are you feeling?"

He shifted into the puppy version of himself and licked my face.

I laughed as relief washed me like his tongue. He nearly toppled me over as I got to my knees to inspect him. From his shiny eyes, butt wiggle, and tail wagging, he seemed healthy. "I'm so glad you're okay." I wrapped my arms around his squirming body. "Thank you for saving us."

My stomach grumbled. We'd been too exhausted yesterday to think about food. Good thing Mrs. O'Donal had insisted on feeding us.

Where were Liam and Rhys? Their blankets... everything. Even the horses. They wouldn't leave without me and Iisakki, would they? Liam seemed to want to exact vengeance against the king. What if he feared I might stop him?

Cold seeped through my pores into the pit of my stomach as I rose and followed Iisakki outside the cave. Liam sat beside a fire. Skewered fish lay atop some contraption over the flames. My nerves softened, and the warmth returned to my core.

He smiled—everything about him lightened at my approach. "I was about to send Rhys to wake you. Breakfast is ready." He pulled a fish stick from the rack and held it up for me.

I sat cross-legged and blew on the fish, then tested it. Careful not to burn myself, I peeled a piece off and threw it to Iisakki.

"I have enough for him. You don't have to give him yours." Liam ripped a fish from a skewer and tossed it to Iisakki.

Rhys sat and helped himself to breakfast.

The world was a mess. Downed limbs, scattered piles of debris, and pockets of unmelted hail littered the forest. "What happened last night?"

"I assume you're referring to Iisakki's shield since we clearly went through a hailstorm." Liam shrugged. "Search me. I've never seen a dragon before. I don't know much about them. Rhys seems to be the resident expert. Which I'm curious about since the dragons went extinct along with the elves before he was born." Liam scraped the last of his fish from his stick.

"He reads. He knows about dragons, fae, pookas—"

"*He* is right here, to be sure. You can cease speaking of him as if he were elsewhere."

I rolled my eyes. "Have you read anything about a dragon having a shield?"

Liam's eyes narrowed. "Such books are banned. Any copies still in existence are locked in Auberon's private library."

Rhys's atypical quiet made sense, though Liam was no longer cursed and assisted in our quest, he was bringing Rhys to the king as a prisoner. What if real accusations could be held against him with harsher penalties? "What is the punishment for reading a banned book?"

"If the king finds out, he'll force Rhys to take an elixir to erase his memories, then recruit him into his service."

"That's likely to happen anyway." That's what almost happened to Liisi's brother. "Does the king do that often?"

Liam breathed deeply. "It's effective. Keeps the would-be troublemakers in line and the rest of his subjects none the wiser, not that that would matter. Their minds would justify his actions. You'd think the curse was better than killing people, but I'm not sure."

"How does he do it?" I ripped a bite of fish from the skewer.

"Physically or morally?" Liam loosed a bitter laugh. "Physically, he has access to fae who create such potions. Morally? Your guess is as good as mine. I don't know how he lives with himself."

"You won't turn Rhys in, right? I mean... for real?" I stared into Liam's eyes—hard. "You have no reason to tell Auberon anything other than that he's an orphan who stole something to eat. Right?"

Liam held his hands up as if to ward off my attack. "Right, right. I won't say a word." He shook a finger at Rhys. "But when we're in populated areas, you may want to keep your knowledge to yourself if you care to preserve your memories."

"To be sure. To be sure." Rhys nodded emphatically, tossing his squid-ink hair.

But it didn't make sense. "What does it matter what anyone reads when they're under the curse?"

"Clearly"—Liam opened his arms wide as if putting himself on display—"people can be freed. My memories are intact so, had I read any contraband, I'd remember. Kids are freethinkers until they reach the age of atonement on their thirteenth birthday when they start thinking more critically for themselves."

Right. They believed whatever their families told them.

"So, do you remember everything from before you were cursed?" I tore off another mouthful of fish.

"I do. My family was so fanatical about the king it was infectious. I couldn't wait to join Auberon's employ. As you heard Mrs. O'Donal say, it is such an honor." He spoke in a mocking tone. "I fear for Kieron. The lad idolizes me. And he reminds me of me. He's sure to become a defender once his Atonement Ceremony ends. If only I could go back and warn him." His oceanic eyes darkened with his blue aura. "I shouldn't have lied."

My heart broke for him. "You did what you had to." I gave his arm a reassuring squeeze. The moment my hand felt the taut muscle, a warm sensation struck me. As if the life within him surged into me without my having to tease it out. And through his shirtsleeve no less. I pulled my hand away and dropped my gaze.

What was that?

I'd touched people before. Never once had I felt their life force within or attempted to manipulate it. I didn't dare. I might in an extreme emergency. But I'd prefer to allow them to heal on their own. Altering a plant's energy was one thing, but a person? That was quite another.

And never, *never* had energy come to me on its own. Even plants needed to be coaxed.

I dared look at Liam, now watching me with a curious expression and a slight smile. Yellow and purple light overwhelmed his blue aura.

Creeping crabs. My face warmed more than it already had. Orange, purple, and even black surrounded me. What was happening? Had he felt it? I needed to do something, say something... anything to get things back to normal. "So..." Ugh, my voice wavered. I cleared my throat and fought to steady it. "Is your family in Talamh Sí?"

"Yes." He maintained his inquisitive, amused expression.

"Do you plan to visit them when we arrive?" *Please, please, please get your mind off what just happened and stop looking at me like that.*

Liam released a sad sigh. "I couldn't pretend around them. I don't want to endanger them. It's best to wait until they're cured."

I winced at making him sad again, but his attention *was* off me.

He ducked his head and rubbed a hand over his face. His dark hair flopped over his eyes, and his stubble rasped beneath his palm before he raised his head. "Where's your family, Rhys? Why are you alone at such a young age?"

"I'm an orphan?"

"Is that a question or an answer?"

"An answer?"

How exasperating. Rhys had his secrets. Juggling my fish in one hand and the water bag in the other, I uncorked the water bag and took a sip. "Whenever you're ready to share your life story, we're here to listen. Until then, we need to pick your brain while we're alone." We were indeed alone, right? My bondmark itched, and I scratched it while looking about. "If you have any information about what happened with Iisakki last night, I'd like to hear it."

When Rhys threw Liam a sheepish look, Liam waved a hand. "Go ahead. If you have something to share from a smuggled book, do tell."

After one last uncertain glance, Rhys cleared his throat. Did he just get bigger? "My readings suggest a dragon can create an energy field to protect their bonded elf."

My hand on my arm slowed and dropped idle to my side. "Does it only protect the elf? Not the dragon?"

"The shield protects the elf and the dragon's more vulnerable underbelly, leaving the rest of the dragon exposed. But a dragon's back scales can withstand almost anything."

"That must be why he didn't seem hurt from falling on his back," I mused. "Does generating the shield harm the dragon?"

"It expends a tremendous amount of energy." Rhys's gaze drifted toward Iisakki.

He was hiding in the grass as a cat, shaking his butt. Then he pounced upon an unsuspecting mouse. How had he managed such a feat without sufficient energy? "What would happen if he overextended himself?"

"Methinks he answered that question last night, did he not?"

Irked whenever Rhys posed questions as a statement, I looked to the heavens for help dealing with him. "Where was all this information before?"

"What information do we need? How does one know until we've need of it? That's why one should read, so the information is here"— Rhys tapped his head—"ready to rise to the surface when needed."

"Tell me everything. All you know about dragons. You were so chatty when we met. You've been quiet since we left Folaím."

Rhys's eyes widened. Scratching at his ear, he shifted in his seat and seemed smaller as he curled his shoulders in on himself.

"Well?"

"Your observation is correct, to be sure."

"Why?"

"Why what?"

I blew out an exasperated breath. Had he always been this obtuse? "Why have you been so quiet?"

"Needless chatter makes for a lot of noise." He shrugged before chomping a bite of fish.

What was the matter with him? He'd talked incessantly, interrupting to share his vast knowledge of books. I could use some of his useless information right now. "What else do you know about dragons?"

"I'm not a walking book. I don't recall everything I read until something prompts the knowledge to resurface."

"Well, I hope you're not forgetting anything important."

"If I am, I'll remember when it's pertinent, to be sure."

"Right." I tossed my stick into the fire. "I hope we don't find ourselves in another sticky situation and your information is too little and too late."

THIRTY-FOUR

Liam dismounted Nessa. Rhys followed. The sun, still somewhat high in the sky, warmed me as I dropped from Clover's back. "Why are we stopping again so soon? Is anything wrong?"

"We've reached the edge of Talamh Sí."

"What?" I spun around. Nothing but trees. "Where?"

He wrapped the horse's reins around a limb. "I'll show you."

"I'll fetch some firewood." Rhys squared his shoulders and set off. "Should you care."

Liam and I rolled our eyes at him, shared a silent laugh, then walked through the woods. Odd noises wafted our way, low at first, then rising with each step. Chugging, whirring, banging, bleeping sounds such as I'd never heard before. I slowed my steps, falling behind Liam. The woods opened up, framing an amazing yet terrifying scene of an unnatural world. Strange buildings packed so close together there was no room for an apple to fall. Or so it seemed from afar.

Above the buildings, hot-air balloons and ships that should've been sailing in the water clogged the sky.

Beyond it all lay an ocean. From the waters rose a massive building. Spires of varying heights pierced the heavens.

I scrambled back a few steps as if the view was a giant vortex threatening to suck me into it. Whatever I'd been expecting, this wasn't it. "Creeping crabs, we're going down *there*?"

Liam cocked his head like a puppy trying to understand human speech. "That is the kingdom. *Your* kingdom. Isn't it beautiful?"

"Beautiful?" I choked. "It's terrifying." I watched the flying machines. Then dared near the edge to peer over the cliff. "And steep." I didn't think I was afraid of heights—until now. "How do we get down there?"

"There's a trail that way." He pointed to my left. He quirked his lips and studied me. "But I thought you might appreciate this view."

"So, we'll camp here one more night?"

"I thought that would be best. I don't have coin for lodging or a bus, and it will take most of the day for the horses to navigate the city. We wouldn't make it before nightfall."

I'd rather spend more time in nature. "Will people recognize me as you did?"

"A friend runs a shop on the outskirts. I'll buy some clothes, and she can arrange your hair with a hat to make you less conspicuous."

"You're not considering putting my hair up, are you?"

He gave me his confused-puppy head tilt.

"People will see my ears."

"What do you think I'm going to do, plaster your hair to your head? Have you never worn your hair up?" He studied my hair. "You have so much hair. It will conceal them just as well as wearing it down. And with it tucked under a hat, your blonde hair won't be as noticeable."

"Is blonde hair bad?"

"No, it's just uncommon. In fact, I'm not sure I know any blondes. People in Betören have red, brown, or black hair. Or gray, but everyone grays."

The only people I'd ever come across—gachen, human, and pech —all grayed. "The fasgadair don't. But they're unnatural."

"You mentioned the fasgadair before." He settled onto the ground against the tree. "I assumed that was their people group name. What are they?"

This wasn't a conversation I wanted to settle in for, but I sat beside him anyway. I waved a hand as if it was a trivial thing. "They're undead demons that feed on blood."

Liam's eyes flashed. He sucked in a breath at what was surely the last description he'd expected. "That must've been horrifying."

"It was. I was only a child when we fled to Bandia." I picked up a stick and scraped at the dirt between us.

"Good thing you had people to take care of you."

"I didn't." His aura grew as confused as his expression. "I mean, not while the fasgadair were in control of Bandia. I was responsible for caring for my brothers and sister—keeping them hidden—safe. For months."

Liam breathed deep. "How old were you?"

"About six."

"I can't imagine..." The light coming off his skin darkened to a deep blue as if my pain was his pain. My heart warmed and spread its heat throughout my being. I'd never talked about what happened in Bandia. I hadn't expected to come away more concerned about the listener than myself.

His oceanic eyes flashed. "I wonder how your father will feel about all he's put you through." He spat the word *father*, then shook his head. "Well, you've got me now. And Iisakki." He motioned to the dog rolling around on his back in the only patch of grass.

"And me." Rhys piped up behind us.

Liam huffed. "Sure. And Rhys. A kid who's about to be brain-washed and put in the king's employ."

"You don't know that will happen." Rhys grunted like an old man as he sat.

"I have a hunch." Liam ran his knuckles over the stubble shadowing his face. "Whatever happens, the Saoirse Trodaí had better get on it. The king doesn't muck about with courts and delayed systems. His actions are swift and final. None question him."

"Creeping crabs." Somehow, it hadn't occurred to me before, but — "What if he curses *me*?"

"Elves can't be cursed." Rhys scratched his head. The displaced tuft of hair returned to its rightful place.

"Why do you always say that?" Liam flashed a smile.

"Say what?"

"Creeping crabs."

"Oh. Ha. I lived near the coast where crabs would come out at night and swarm the beach. My adopted mom hated that. She'd say, 'creeping crabs.'" I mimicked Fallon's voice and screwed up my face the way she did.

Laughter jostled him. "I'd like to see that. Crabs are great... the way they walk sideways with their giant pincers making them look unbalanced, like the weight of the things should tip them over." He reached over and pinched my arm.

His touch jolted me despite his weak pinch. It was as if the life force in his fingers surged into my arm. But again, he didn't seem to notice, and I acted like nothing abnormal had happened. I wiped away the spot where he touched me. "Crabs are nasty."

"Not all crabs walk sideways, nor do they all have large pincers." Rhys picked at something from his trousers.

Liam rolled his eyes. "Thanks for sharing, Encyclopedia."

"Encyclopedia?" I chuckled and clapped.

"Yeah, it's a—"

"I know what an encyclopedia is, Encyclopedia."

"I'm not Encyclopedia." Liam pointed to Rhys. "He is."

Unimpressed, Rhys watched us through drooped lids.

I squelched my laughter. "Anyway, it became a thing. Then we came up with a few more—squirming squids, jiggling jellyfish.... Over the years they just... stuck. Especially creeping crabs. Anyway, Encyclopedia"—I turned to Rhys but caught the approval in Liam's eyes—"what makes you say elves can't be cursed?"

Rhys narrowed his eyes and paused as if searching files in his brain. Then he shrugged. "Why would Auberon kill the elves if he could have cursed them?"

"Good point." Liam quirked his lips. "Regardless, my understanding is that he plans to crown you. But whatever you do, play along. No telling what he'll do if he suspects you're not with him. And insist on keeping me on as your personal defender. He'll assure you it's not necessary, but after all you've been through, insist you'll feel better with a personal defender you trust."

"So, I have to lie?"

"Why?" He feigned a hurt look, but his aura betrayed him. "My presence wouldn't reassure you?"

"That's not what I meant." I pushed his arm with mine. The second our upper arms came in contact, even through our clothes, the same sensation surged through me. As if his life force within was eager to connect with mine.

If Liam noticed, he didn't let on. "Think of it as doing your part to free the country."

"But isn't it too dangerous? Wouldn't you be surrounded by many of Auberon's men? What if they found you out?"

"No more dangerous to me than to any of the other spies within the castle."

My stomach soured as I peered out at the looming city. He was right. I'd have to lie for the greater good.

But I was a terrible liar. The king was sure to see through me.

THIRTY-FIVE

We emerged from the wooded shelter and continued through a sleepy village into the overwhelming city. It was impossibly shiny—and brown. Reasonably sized buildings grew, blocking out the rising sun. But the place was well lit regardless. Imitation lights on posts lined the streets, and more dotted the buildings on sconces. Smoke billowed from tubes crawling up the buildings like angular caterpillars. Signs littered the landscape, some with blinking lights.

The opposing landscape and sounds overwhelmed me. The buildings seemed to close in on me, making me dizzy. I tightened my on the reins and ground my teeth against the urge to turn and race Clover back to our wooded refuge.

Something blared behind me. Clover and I jumped. Our auras blackened as I fought to remain seated, and she skipped sideways. A strange contraption of spinning circles with teeth and tubes leading to one big central one spewed smoke the color of Rhys's aura. I gripped the reins as Clover shimmied to avoid the beast. My heart stilled.

Beyond the noisy gadget sat a man in a rounded box. He smiled and waved as he sputtered past.

"Was that a car?" But Liam couldn't hear me. It wasn't like the ones I'd seen in American books—more like a cross between a car and a carriage with a who knows what in front. A motor? Behind the driver's box lay a wagon filled with wooden boxes.

Another car followed. This one had a similar noisy front gadget, but the entire carriage was enclosed. Four people sat inside. A man and a woman in front and children in the back.

After the vehicles passed and the street was clear again, the world swam, and I nearly fell from my saddle. Once I righted myself, I pulled her to a stop on the cobblestone road, not to take it all in, but to block it out—and catch my breath.

Light in. Dark out.

Light in. Dark out.

I opened my eyes and caught an eyeful of a flashing sign.

Maybe not so much light. I freed a hand to squeeze my temples.

"Are you all right?" Liam sidled Nessa up to me. "You're as white as a bleached shirt."

"It's just—" What? What *was* I feeling? I gripped Clover tight to avoid falling. "It's all so, so—disorienting. Were those cars? And what is all this stuff? These lights with no flame. These tubes, smoke, bright signs. All the circles with teeth."

"Circles with teeth?" Liam laughed. "Gears? Many motors work with gears."

"So those *were* motors on the cars? The smoking things?"

"Smoke?" He cocked his head.

Rhys gave me a strange look.

"Yes, the strange-colored smoke. What color was that?" This was my chance to name it.

Liam dismounted. "The motors emit exhaust, but it's invisible. You can see it?"

"Uh..." Creeping crabs.

Liam held out a hand.

"What are you doing? We're supposed to—"

"You need to take a break. To assimilate." He wagged his fingers. "Come on. It will only get more overwhelming from here. We don't need you falling off your horse, taking a ride in an ambulance, and meeting your father in the hospital."

He helped me down, and I swooned. Yes, *swooned.*

"Can you walk?"

"I think so." I followed him to a platform along the street, and we hitched the horses to a bench outside a door with a sign for Erno's Apothecary.

"I'll just be here," Rhys called from atop Nessa. He mumbled something else I couldn't hear.

We sat and watched more vehicles and people in the oddest clothing. Most were too preoccupied to notice us, but some threw me sidelong glances or double takes. The children tended to stare.

"What will they think of us sitting here?" My fingers twitched to check the hair covering my ears.

"They'll think we're waiting for Erno to open his shop."

"But my clothes..."

"Not to worry. The adults are too busy, and the kids are just kids. Adults tend to ignore them."

Despite his words, I squirmed with every look.

So he bent closer to me. "Just focus on them and how strange they look to you."

A man passed by in a top hat dressed like the man who left me Iisakki's egg. Had he come from here? If he had, he wasn't under the curse. He'd had a strange aura, like Rhys. But these people were all cursed, like the O'Donals. None but the children had an aura.

Why did all the adults wear hats? Top hats or flat caps like the Saoirse Trodaí for the men. Women wore similar top hats of varying sizes. Some covered their heads. Others were tiny and tipped slightly askew, defying gravity. Many partially veiled their faces while others carried fancy umbrellas though the sky—hidden as it was by the buildings—remained clear.

And their dresses! Skirts with layers and layers of material or skin-tight pants under short skirts with frilly shirts tucked under some tight vest-like thing. How very, very strange.

But strangest of all were the glasses. Big bubbly things. Everyone wore them—on their hats or their foreheads, but rarely over their eyes.

"Why does everyone have those odd glasses?"

"They're mostly worn as protection when flying in a ship or riding on a fast vehicle. But they're helpful on smoggy days."

A woman hollered from an upper window between buildings to children below. The unusual sounds grew louder, giving me a headache.

Sitting here, watching everything helped me assimilate somewhat, but it wasn't getting me any closer to the castle. As much as I didn't want to move on, deeper into this cement world of noises and gadgets, I wanted to get it over with. "We should go."

Liam gave a solemn nod. "We'll stop at my friend's shop next. It isn't far."

The break didn't seem to make Clover any less skittish. Dark colors emanated from her body. With every new sound, black surged throughout her aura, and she'd skip sideways. Her fear wasn't calming mine.

A familiar sound blared—a train whistle.

A series of beeps followed by a loud honk sounded behind me. I nearly fell off Clover as she sidestepped out of a car's way while it roared past.

Light in. Dark Out.

Light in. Dark Out.

Iisakki rubbed his face against my hand and purred.

"This way." Liam motioned me to follow down a side street.

Our horses stepped into the darkness, and a chill swept over me.

But the noises were somewhat muffled, and the visual onslaught subsided—for now.

"Stay behind me. Keep to the side," he said.

We followed him single file. Surely, one of those horseless carriages wouldn't be driving by us here. There was no room. My chest squeezed, tighter and tighter until we came through the other side to another, more open and quieter street. I breathed easier.

A horn blared behind us, and Clover jerked sideways, nearly tripping over a stoop. A man passed us on a strange contraption—much slower than the cars. He sat high above on a seat suspended by bent rods over the largest wheel I'd ever seen. Two much smaller wheels rolled beneath something full of those toothy things—gears. It clanged and hummed. The rider's thick boots moved, pushing little platforms as if propelling the mechanical beast. His long black and bronze striped legs rose and fell with the gears. He smiled at me, his eyes blocked by his buggy glasses. He looked like an insect in fancy garb. Two flaps from his coat wagged like tails behind him.

Was he pedaling? Was that thing a bicycle? From what I'd read, bicycles had only two wheels and were much lower to the ground.

Two vehicles, more like I imagined bicycles, roared our way. The riders didn't seem to be pedaling the fast contraptions. Instead, they laid on the contraption like a red panda dangling over a tree limb, holding onto bars. Their tight hats fit over their heads and glasses like another layer of skin coming down over their ears, strapped under their chin. The same colored smoke as the other vehicles poured from a pipe.

Were they motorcycles?

In stories, it all sounded fascinating but unreal. As if the things that didn't exist in Ariboslia were as made up as the stories. But I wanted nothing more than to shut this book and reopen it later when I was more prepared—if that day ever came.

Every time a vehicle passed, Clover skipped sideways, whinnying and shaking her mane in protest. Even after she calmed, the tension remained in her taut muscles. Poor girl, in a constant state of stress. If only my ability to enhance life also worked to calm them. But I couldn't help her. I couldn't even help myself, though I tried to shut out the assault by focusing on her feet clomping on the cobblestones.

Rectangular and rounded buildings made from some sort of smooth stone grew taller and more condensed. Skinny windows of varying shapes covered every wall. Triangular and conical roofs jutted from every top. The same flag waved from many peaks in varying sizes but the same proportions—bronze with something resembling a black wheel with three spokes that wound into three more wheels. The strange-colored smoke streamed from massive pipes, dissipating in wisps.

Was that invisible too?

A ship sailed overhead, casting us in its shadow.

Nessa stopped. Clover nearly ran into her, and I lurched forward.

"We're here." Liam tied Nessa to a hitching post.

When I started to dismount, everything spun. So I closed my eyes, then tried again. This time, I fell into Liam.

"I've got you." He helped me right myself. "Can you walk?"

The ground waffled. "Y—" I ran to the side of the building and retched.

Liam and Rhys both stared at me like I might implode.

"I feel a little better now." It was mostly the truth.

Liam's sidelong glance said he didn't believe me as he wrapped Clover's lead with Nessa by a door with a glass window marked Moira's Boutique.

"Can I trust you to stay here with the horses?" Liam asked Rhys.

"If the brute recalls, I'm here of my own accord. Plus—" Rhys twisted to show Liam his bound hands.

Liam gripped the bronze door handle. His aura blackened. His hand shook.

Why was he stuck there—fearful? "Is something wrong?"

He turned, his face ashen. "Don't go."

"What?" I must've misheard him. My gaze darted to Rhys, who watched us with extreme interest.

"It's not too late." Liam grasped my upper arms, his intense gaze searing my retinas, making my eyes water. "Auberon doesn't know you're here. He doesn't need to know. Come away with me. We can live off the land. Please." He pressed his imploring face inches from mine. "Don't go."

THIRTY-SIX

"Why are you saying this?" I fought myself free from his grip. "Have you changed your mind?"

"No. No. I—" He removed his cap and raked his fingers through his black hair, probably pulling some out in the process. The vein in his temples pulsed. Surges of orange and purple infiltrated the black surrounding him. "There's no telling what he might do"—he spoke under his breath, then glanced about as if to ensure he wasn't overheard—"to you... to Iisakki."

If he was trying to frighten me, it was working. My resolve faltered. I fisted my shaking hands and looked to Rhys, who appeared ready to break his binds and leap to my rescue.

"It's not—I mean—" Liam rubbed the back of his reddening neck. "I'm not saying I'm in love with you or anything."

"Of course not!" Heat rushed to my face. It must be as red as his neck.

"I'm *concerned*. I know your father. No good can come from setting foot before him."

Was he right? Should I run?

His oceanic eyes appeared haunted. "You don't know him like I do."

Iisakki wound his cat form around my legs, purring. I picked him up. As I clutched him to my chest, Liisi filled my mind, then Kieron. Children. Innocent victims of Auberon's curse. My father's curse.

A confidence I didn't know I possessed, a newfound resolve, filled me to the brim. I was too close to turn back now. All I'd been through—no, all God had brought me through—had gotten me to this point. I needed to stop running away and move ahead with purpose, face my fears.

I leveled my gaze on Liam and firmed my voice. "I have to see him."

Liam backed away with a nod. His shoulders slumped. "I was afraid you'd say that." Looking tired, he turned back to the door, then threw one last glance over his shoulder. "You sure I can't change your mind?"

"I'm sure." I punctuated my answer with a firm nod.

He heaved a heavy breath, then pushed through the door.

Tinkling bells rang overhead. A sharp smell assaulted my nose. It wasn't like anything I'd ever smelled before—floral and sweet. My aching head pulsed, and my nose twitched, threatening to remove the noxious odor. But I held back the sneeze. Like an army, shelves of faceless heads displaying hats prepared to do battle with rows of shoes on the opposing wall. Racks of clothing scuffled in the center, a melee of maroon, gold, black, or brown. Not one bright, happy color. Between the lack of space, oppressive colors, and overpowering perfume, breathing didn't come easy.

A woman in a blood-red dress with no aura burst through maroon curtains in the back of the shop. Below a tiny top hat askew upon her head, dark curls framed one side of her face, not falling past her jawline. But on the hat side, her hair spilled down to her shoulder. Her gaze landed on Liam, and her eyes lit up beneath layers of makeup, then dulled. She squared her shoulders, feigning aloofness. "Liam, darling. How wonderfully unexpected." She glided toward him. Her red-painted lips kissed the air on each side of his face. Then she turned pouty. "It has been far too long."

Darling? Who was this woman? His wife?

As he squirmed, she raised an eyebrow at me. "Introduce me, darling."

"This is my, ah, friend, Colleen. Colleen, this is Moira."

"Mistress Moira."

When she spoke with more-than-necessary force, he closed his eyes and took a deep breath. "Sure. Mistress Moira." Hands poised in the air, Mistress Moira advanced on me with a sashaying walk. She jutted a hip out and pressed her fingers to her lips as her gaze roamed the length of my body. "What peculiar clothing. Where are you from? I haven't seen you before, yet you look familiar."

I scooted behind a rack of dresses, away from her scrutinizing gaze. And why hadn't we prepared an answer for such a question? My brain scrambled for one. "I—"

"She's an orphan." Liam stepped between us. "She's just been released from the Interim Housing for Displaced Children."

Chin rising, she flattened her red lips into a thin line. "Why weren't you placed with a family?"

"None were available with sufficient space and resources."

"In all of Talamh Sí? Not one available family willing to take in a poor soul on the king's behalf?" She scoffed. "Who would be so insolent as to deny our king?"

I opened my mouth, but Liam placed a hand on my shoulder. "You can take it up with the king if you so choose, but I've orders to clothe her in suitable attire befitting His Majesty's presence and bring her to the king."

She circled me now, still sashaying, one dainty boot-clad foot tapping the ground before the other in some kind of dance. "How should an orphan be so fortunate as to obtain such an audience?"

"That"—Liam skewered Moira with a hard stare—"is between her and our esteemed king. Now are you, Mistress Moira, going to deny our king's request to update this poor orphan's attire?"

"Forgive me." She waved a hand. "I will do all the king asks and more! But this is all so strange. So unlike you to bring a stranger into my shop. Aren't you stationed in the north woods?"

"Orders change."

"Very well." She ran a finger down his arm. "Does this mean you'll be at the next gala for young eligibles?"

Ugh. I could vomit at the look she threw him.

"No." He squirmed out of her reach.

She gripped a fistful of my hair. "Blonde. Such a rare sight. Shall I put it in an updo for you? Perhaps with a top hat like mine?"

"And a veil." Liam fingered a veiled hat on a faceless head.

Moira's gaze snapped back to him.

He snatched his hand away as if the hat stung him. "It's befitting a young lady arrive in the king's presence with a veil, is it not?"

Moira tipped her head and studied me once more. "And the clothes?"

"Whatever young ladies are wearing these days fitting for the king's presence. Something modest but without too many layers." He winked at me. "Elegant, yet simple."

Did he know how much those gaudy dresses with their excessive material would bother me?

"What you describe is not fashionable. Perhaps you should try Glenna's Resale Shop."

"Surely there's something."

Moira sighed. "You're not going to a dinner party, are you?"

"No, nothing like that."

She pressed a finger to her lips. "Hmm. There might be something. Give me a moment." She darted to the back of the shop, and the curtains wagged behind her.

"Are you sure you can trust her?" I crossed my arms over my chest, my thudding heart hammering against them. If only she had an aura. Something about her bothered me—besides the lack of emotional tells.

"No. But if we're to get you through the city with me at your side, we have no choice."

Hours later, the shop's bell tingled above as we exited Moira's Boutique. I fiddled with the bulge from my updo. A cool breeze swept through the alley, filtering through the strange scarf Mistress Moira made me wear—an endless line of tied fabric she wrapped around and around my neck. I fiddled with it. More like rope than a scarf. But she insisted it would "spruce up" the black dress she claimed could be a nun's habit—whatever that was. The fluttery black veil attached to the hat tickled my nose. The excess material flowing from my sleeves brushed my skirt as I walked, making my wrists itch. Of all the uncomfortable—*and* ridiculous—costumes.

I shuddered again as the image of my face in the mirror flashed. With my skin so coated in makeup, I could've been a clown. I twisted my hands at my sides to keep them from somehow trying to hide my face before anyone could see me like this, though no one here knew me—yet. Other than Liam who seemed to suck in his lips to avoid laughing.

Then I ran into Liam at the post where we'd left the horses. They weren't there. Something cold seized my heart as I searched up and down the street. Where were the horses? Rhys? Iisakki?

Liam's neck snapped back and forth.

They couldn't be gone. They couldn't. I spun back to the post as if they might materialize. "Where are they?"

Uniformed men approached and gripped my elbows.

"Princess." An older defender with curly wisps of red and gray hair sticking out beneath his cap smiled. "Please come with us. Your father is expecting you."

"But how?" I turned to Liam, pleading as two more defenders accosted him as well.

His eyes wide with panic, he stiffened when defenders snapped metal bracelets on his wrists. His body lurched left, then right while he fought to free himself. "Who called you?"

Bells tinkled, and Mistress Moira stepped outside her shop. "Forgive me, Princess. But Liam is not to be trusted. These defenders will see you to your father."

"*You?*" Liam's voice cracked. His face blotched as though he'd received a punch to the gut.

"Of course, I called them. Did you think I could spend so much time with the princess and not recognize her? She looks exactly like her father. And your heart has turned from our lord. Why else wouldn't you entrust her to the defenders to deliver her to her father? Why come to my shop with lies and disguise attempts when her rightful place is one of honor? She should arrive at the castle in style, out in the open, with fanfare." She clicked her tongue. "Not to worry, Princess. The defenders will transport you in a way befitting royalty, isn't that right?"

The older defender whistled, and a white vehicle with strange adornments and tubes chugged toward them. Long with finlike curves, it could have been a white whale, but for the city's flag waving on either side and the symbol painted on the door. Once the thing swam up beside me, it stopped. A man stepped out and opened the door behind the one he'd left. Then he straightened and posed like a statue in a uniform similar to the defenders, but white instead of gray as if to blend in with the vehicle.

The defender led me to the door.

"Colleen!" Liam's fright chilled me. They were yanking him to a blue vehicle across the street.

Nay, this couldn't be happening. I needed him with me. But how would I get the defenders to allow it? Act like royalty, like I had authority, and hope they bought it? "Let him ride with me."

"Sorry, Your Highness." The defender's clipped speech didn't sound sorry at all. "We have our orders. Take it up with the king."

He nodded to those holding Liam, and they shoved him inside. The door slammed behind him, revealing the city's symbol beneath the words *Talamh Sí Police*. The front doors closed, and the vehicle drove away.

My stomach plummeted. This wasn't how it was supposed to go.

Like me, Liam couldn't hide anything. No way could our plan have worked. We hadn't fooled anyone.

My father would see through me too.

"Where are you taking him?" I asked.

"He's going to the station for questioning."

"Where are our horses? The boy? Or the cat we were traveling with?"

The defender stilled and cocked his head my way, one brow rising. "My apologies, Your Highness. There were no horses here when we arrived. Or anyone else waiting for you. Can you give us a description?"

I held my breath as a chill gripped my heart. Had Rhys sniffed them out and hidden with Iisakki before the defenders could apprehend them? As much as my heart hurt being separated from Iisakki, wasn't it better for him to be with Rhys—for now?

Knots twisted my stomach into an impossible puzzle as the defenders drove Liam away.

Defeated and alone, I choked on a sob and allowed the defender to stuff me into the car. The vehicle rumbled and chugged through the city. Even if I could figure out the latch to open the door, I didn't dare jump out onto the city streets. And where would I go? Nay, this was my quest. Perhaps I could appeal to my father to release Liam and give me resources to locate Iisakki. I closed my eyes. At least the enclosure softened the noises.

God, please watch over Iisakki, Liam, and Rhys. Keep us all safe.

I should've run when I had the chance.

THIRTY-SEVEN

I must've dozed. Dim light met me when I woke. Was it evening already? The sounds outside lessened, and the car angled upward, climbing a narrow, twisty path to the castle resting upon a mountain in the sea. The road leading to its main gate seemed to have been part of the mountain. But its sides were shaved, and a gash was cut between it and the castle. Crashing waves licked the sides. A drawbridge allowed passage. With no walls like those surrounding Ariboslian castles, the raging sea and the jagged, slippery foundation provided a natural barrier.

Larger than I'd imagined, the strange castle rose from the rocks like a mechanical heap with brass ornaments. From every angle, circular towers fanned out to support odd-shaped rooms with cone roofs and varying spires appearing like needles ready to sew the sky.

At the peak where the rock fell away, we crossed the drawbridge. As the tires thumped across the rough wood, I closed my eyes and tried to unsee the distance to the ocean below. A fall from this height would kill someone.

The closer and larger the building grew, the colder I became. Though the seaside might be chilly, none of the car's windows were open. Still, I shivered, feeling the cold seep into my bones, and grasped my arms to warm myself.

An iron gate lifted, and we stopped before another massive set of double doors. A sentry wearing a red uniform flipped a switch. Then the doors whirred open to reveal a great courtyard and an impeccable lawn crisscrossed with green shrubs and vibrant gardens—like the chessboard Aunt Stacy brought from America. We drove along a stone path, passing a pond with trim green grass swirling in a familiar pattern.

"That's the symbol on the flags."

I hadn't realized I'd spoken aloud until the driver responded. "Yes, the triskelion—the triple spiral."

"What does it mean?"

"It's a symbol of allegiance to the king. He likes threes."

We continued past the pond through a tunnel of red flowers, then rounded bronze walls lined with trellises of climbing vines.

"The king's quarters are this way."

"Where is everyone?" Back home, castles were always full of people.

"The castle is quiet unless the king hosts a gala. Other than that, you'll only see defenders, sentries, caretakers, or servants on errands."

"But where do the people have an audience with the king to submit their complaints?"

The driver chuckled. "The king doesn't receive complaints. But he does meet with his subjects on occasion. Just not here. He likes his privacy."

Something felt eerily off—and sad. Emptiness amongst such beauty. Like a gilded cage.

At the end of a circular path, the driver stopped the car before an ornate double-doored entryway and another sentry. I fumbled with the latch, but the driver opened the door before I figured it out. I followed him to the entrance.

"Please announce Princess Eerika's arrival," the driver said.

The sentry sucked air through his teeth, then straightened. He placed a hand on his chest. "Your Highness." He pressed a button that emitted a heinous buzzing sound, but the door didn't open.

Moments later, a woman emerged.

I gasped. She had an aura! Was she one of the Saoirse Trodaí?

Her smile faltered as dark purple and black infiltrated her otherwise bright aura. White frills lining the straps of a white apron over her long black dress matched her cap from which frizzy red hair had escaped. Face flushed, she curtsied.

"Iida, show Princess Eerika to King Auberon."

"With pleasure." She curtsied again, then widened the door for me.

A deafening ticking repelled me in the tall room. Hundreds of clocks bedecked red walls overdone in gaudy trim and molding. Who needed so many clocks in one room? An entryway, no less. How maddening.

Arched doorways opened straight ahead and to the right. A spiral staircase with a carved banister braced like an upright snail shell in the corner, rising to railed hallways above. An enormous chandelier with artificial lights drooped from the tall ceiling.

"This way." The woman led me through the leftward entryway to a room with plenty of floor space and seating for a large gathering.

I checked to ensure we were alone, then whispered, "You're one of them, aren't you?"

She wheeled around. "One of what?"

"Saoirse Trodaí."

Her aura blackened, and she stepped back, looking at me like I was a ghost. "I–I–"

"Can you help me find Iisakki? Release Liam?"

She took a deep breath and closed her eyes. Her lips moved. Was she meditating? Praying? Color pierced the black engulfing her like the sun breaking through storm clouds. She opened her eyes and smiled. "Your father will be with you in a moment. Please, have a seat."

Red padded couches and chairs with bronze pillows seemed to

take position like waltzers upon a dizzying floor of octagonal shapes. In a domed glass alcove adjoined to the far side, lampstands clustered around as if listening to the dormant white piano. Bookshelves with a staircase to their upper levels lined the right. On the left, paintings of landscapes, dragons, creatures I'd never seen before intermingled with portraits of people with unusually large eyes, like mine, all hung beneath strange lights that seemed to glow only upon the paintings. Several wore crowns. My parents?

"Are these..." I turned back to Iida, but she was gone, the closing door the only evidence she'd been here. I sighed and returned to my explorations, avoiding looking at the floor as my feet gravitated toward the books. I ran my fingers along spines of intricate lettering. English. Thank God Fallon had taught me. Books might be all I have in this place. Should I survive.

"Eerika." A man's voice spoke my name with the warmth and relief of someone reunited with a loved one—

I turned.

Thirty-Eight

I gazed upon the man and gasped. He appeared young and old all at once. Short white hair covered his head beneath his gold crown. His hairless face showed no signs of stubble—or wrinkles. But the sharp contrast obscuring his age wasn't what stole my breath. It was as if I was looking into a mirror that bent time and gender. My face—my old, yet young, male face—with the same luminescent blue eyes, straight nose, and small mouth with full lips, with more masculine thicker eyebrows and a stronger jawline.

King Auberon—my father.

No wonder I failed to conceal my identity from those who knew him. I shouldn't need to prove my identity by revealing the bond mark.

His presence took up more than his physical space. It wasn't his spastic aura cycling through a myriad of colors or his fancy attire. Not that the red cloak or his buttoned shirt were overly fancy, despite the gold stitching and embellishments. His plain taupe trousers certainly weren't. But the high neckline covering all but his Adam's apple made him appear elevated somehow. As did his ornate shoes with thick soles. He stood nearly a cubit taller than me. But that wasn't it either.

His smile widened, and he opened his arms as if he expected me to come running into them. But I didn't know this man. He lowered his arms and quirked his lips as his restless aura saddened. "It has been a great many years. Too long."

Perhaps I'd spent too many years wondering about my parents. Perhaps those imaginings were tainting this very real meeting, despite how surreal it felt. Or maybe it was the rumors that my father was a genocidal manipulator feigning God's rightful place. Half of me wanted to embrace my father and never let go whilst the other half wished to find my friends and run from the crazed king. Standing here, on the precipice of idle chitchat with the man who'd enslaved the kingdom seemed like a betrayal.

God, what would You have me do now that I'm here?

A range of different colors surged through his aura as he studied me as if his emotions were all over the place and he didn't know what to think. Like me.

Conceal the mark.

Was that God interrupting my thoughts? Again? It was the same as when He told me to seek Him. A different voice spoke in my mind.

It must be God.

But if I should hide my bond mark, should I not mention the dragon who marked me? But if I couldn't mention him, how would I find him?

Perhaps I'd try to get Iida alone again... if I survived this meeting.

"Do you not remember me, Daughter?" Orange and purples overshadowed his light aura.

The king felt uncomfortable? Because of me?

"N–no. Sorry. I don't."

He frowned, but why would he expect a three-year-old to remember anything?

"I feared this day might never come." He stepped closer, closing the gap between us. With the bookshelf at my back, I had nowhere to go but toward the glass alcove.

He stopped, deep blue wisps of light flitting about him. "What have I done that you should retreat, my daughter?"

I stopped slinking along the shelves. "I–I'm overwhelmed is all."

He nodded with a sigh. "To be expected, I suppose. You were so young when I last saw you." He waved toward a cluster of seats. "Come, sit with me."

I didn't move.

"What can I do to put you more at ease?"

"Bring me my friends."

"You have friends here?"

"I met them when I came to this realm. They helped me find you."

"Well..." He pressed his palms together and brought his fingertips to his lips. "I must honor those who assisted my daughter. What are their names? Where can I find them? I'll summon them at once." He walked toward a desk with strange gadgets and punched one of the many buttons along the wall.

"Security," came a staticky voice.

I glanced around, trying to find from where the voice had come, but it seemed as though it came from the wall.

Auberon ushered me to come near.

I trudged across the floor as if it was made of mud.

He hit the button once more. "We're in search of my daughter's friends. You are to bring them to me at once." He released the button.

"Of course, Majesty." The tiny voice indeed came from the black concave circle embedded in the bronze box above the button.

"Describe your friends." Auberon pushed the button.

I leaned in, assuming the voice would hear me as it appeared to have heard the king. "Liam is one of your defenders. He was taken away by your defenders this morning."

"Well, we must rectify that at once. And the others?" Auberon asked, keeping the button engaged.

"We were traveling by horse." When Auberon ushered me closer to the listening circle, I stretched nearer. "Rhys, a boy with black hair and blue eyes, and Iisakki, my pet..." Should I say dog or cat? He tended to prefer cat mode. "Cat. He's gray and white. They should be with the horses, Clover and Nessa. Both mares. Clover is brown with a black mane and Nessa is all white."

"Do you have all you need?" Auberon asked, then released the button.

"Yes, Majesty. We'll bring them to you."

Auberon smiled. "Does this please you, Daughter?"

"Yes, thank you." As tension left my shoulders, I breathed easier.

"Very good." He motioned to the seats. "Shall we continue our conversation?"

How did his aura seem so... so... normal? Like anyone else. Then again, what did I expect from a crazed king's aura? Despite how warm and friendly this man might seem, he dared consider himself as God. I mustn't let his kindness make me forget. I had to tread carefully. Very carefully.

Auberon reclined in his seat and crossed his legs as if settling in for a long chat. "You must have many questions, Daughter."

I did. Too many. I settled on the edge of the red cushion. There wasn't any harm in asking questions while I waited for my friends. And one question plagued me my entire life. "Why did you and my mother abandon me?"

The lights surrounding Auberon dimmed, pulsing with purples and oranges. "You think Delyth abandoned you? By no means. She loved you more than life itself."

"Maybe she died then. I–I don't know. I grew up without parents —orphaned."

The king leaped from his seat as if the cushion was stuffed with insects. He clasped his hands behind his back and hung his head. His aura darkened to a deep blue. After a few heartbeats, he turned a sad smile my way. "I'd rather hoped she lived still, and we might all be reunited."

Either he was a master manipulator, or he loved and missed my mother.

"And you, Princess Eerika, my daughter, Queen Delyth's daughter, raised as an orphan? That should never be." He pinched the bridge of his nose as if to cut off any tears at the source. "Forgive me."

In all my imaginings over the years and especially after all I'd learned upon arriving in this realm, not one scenario played out in my mind like this. My mother took me away, and he blamed himself? What was I missing? He must've done something to make her so desperate. So, why did I want nothing more than to lighten his aura and put a smile back on his face? "My adopted family was good to me."

"My men searched the realms for you. Where have you been all these years?"

"Ariboslia."

He dropped back into his seat and squeezed his nose again. "I know of it. Searching those lands was challenging. Many of my men died at the hands of blood-drinking demons."

"The fasgadair."

"You survived such creatures—alone?" The blood drained from his already white face, leaving it impossibly pale. "I shouldn't have given up. Once I learned of those beasts, I ordered my men to stop their search for fear of their lives, certain Delyth would never leave you in a place like that. But perhaps she didn't know. Or perhaps it was too late...." A sad, faraway look sheened his eyes like he was visiting the most depressing place in his mind. "What happened to you? What do you remember of Delyth?"

"I don't remember her at all. I was a baby when the Cael rescued me. I thought I was a Treasach, like the other abandoned babies. They brought me to a home for orphans in Notirr. Then, after the Fasgadair Wars, when I was about eight, I was adopted."

"Delyth would never abandon you, ever. Especially in a realm full of such hideous beasts. It can only mean... I'd hoped..." He took a deep breath and closed his eyes. The vast array of ever-changing colors surrounding him gave way to a deep blue again. "She was the finest woman to have lived, your mother. I'm sorry you didn't get to know her. That was my one solace in all this time—that she was caring for you."

A myriad of emotions like his warred within me. I wanted to leap into this man's arms and unleash pent-up sobs over my lost childhood —to mourn the mother I never knew, would never know. But I didn't know him. I couldn't trust him.

His brow furrowed. "Why do you say you were a baby when you were rescued?"

"Well, maybe not a *baby*. I was three, I think. I've no memory of it."

"You were six years old when your mother left with you."

So many shocking statements loaded that comment I wanted to unpack. My age. That had always eluded me. And he'd claimed my mother left with me.... He didn't accuse her of kidnaping? My mouth hung open as my sluggish brain attempted to process and contemplate which to address first. "Six?"

Auberon nodded.

"But if I was that old, why don't I remember anything?"

"Your mother might've given you something to forget." He spoke as if erasing one's memories was a normal thing to do.

"When is my birthday?"

"You were born on the third day of the third month. And you are the third to ascend the throne. You are very special, indeed."

I tried calculating my age with the new information, but he hadn't given me the year. And I didn't know how long I'd been in Ariboslia before being adopted by the Cael. But if what he said was true, I wasn't seventeen. "How old *am* I?"

"Twenty human years."

Three years older? "But how would the gachen think I was only three when I was six?"

"Elves take longer to age. As do the fae. Once we mature, around age twenty-five, we remain in that state much longer than gachen or humans. We don't show signs of growing old until we reach one hundred years."

I gasped. "How long do elves live?"

"About one hundred and fifty years. Give or take."

"How old are you?" I clamped a hand over my mouth, hoping I hadn't offended him. I was forgetting myself and to whom I spoke. Asking an elder their age was unacceptable even amongst the lowborn, never mind nobility. "Forgive me."

Auberon waved it off. "This is the least of all you should know to run the kingdom. I'm one hundred and twenty-three human years."

"With no wrinkles?" I slapped my mouth yet again. Why did I keep forgetting myself?

The king chuckled. Why'd he have to be so likable? "Elves don't wrinkle. Neither do fae, for that matter. But wrinkles or no, I'm well into old age with only about twenty-five more years to teach you all you need to know. But—" He eyed me. "Is it too much for one day? Should we rest and continue this tomorrow? I can have your food brought to your room."

"No. It's okay." Though the mention of rest made my muscles ache, I'd gotten a nap in the car and still had so much I wanted to know. "What happened to all the other elves?" The moment the question was out, my gut twisted. Who knew what he would do with me if I displeased him?

Auberon stared. "Good question. But it requires a bit of history to understand. Let me get you some food. You must be famished. Jaakko!"

The door opened in a rush as if the servant had been standing by, awaiting orders. A shadowy figure obscured by Auberon's massive chair strode into the room.

Its aura was the same color as Rhys's.

Thirty-Nine

I peered around the chair, hoping to find Rhys. Instead, a child-sized black rabbit walking like a human rounded the chair and bowed. "May I be of service, Your Majesty?"

The hare had perfect enunciation.

"Bring the princess a meal."

The creature nodded and ducked back out of the room. Why did he have the same, unidentifiable, never-changing aura as Rhys? I wanted to ask the king, but then he'd wonder about my ability to see emotions. It might be something all elves could do, but I didn't trust him with that yet. Not now. Perhaps not ever.

"What was that?" I asked.

"Jaakko? He's a pooka." He waved it off as if that were nothing.

Didn't Pirkko and the others mention something about a pooka?

"Where were we?" Auberon gripped the arms of his chair. "Ah yes. Your grandfather, Eerikki. He learned of the megaliths and made a living traveling between realms, collecting and selling wares. He had quite a knack for it."

"Where did he get the amulet?"

He was skimming details. I needed as many as possible to catch differences in his story from the Saoirse Trodaí. Not that I'd then know who was telling the truth... or that I'd remember all the details. But I had to try.

He blinked, appearing confused, though his face remained smooth. "What amulet?"

"The pechish inter-realm travel amulet. They're necessary to get through the megalith."

"Ah." He smiled as understanding set in. "He didn't need one. He had a pooka. Jaakko, to be precise. He's aetherian." He studied me, probably catching a blank look. "Are you not familiar with aetherian beings?"

When I shook my head, he scrutinized me further. "Are you familiar with aether?"

"No."

"It's the fifth element. Air, water, dirt, fire, and aether."

"Oh." This was beginning to feel like school. I thought my education days were over. I struggled to focus, but my exhaustion was beginning to settle in.

"As a powerful force, aether eludes many. It's otherwise known as the breath of life. It is the life force, the energy, if you will, of every living thing. We've learned to harness its power. It is difficult to extract, however, as it requires living things—plants, animals, people—to give their lives."

That woke me up. "Were the elves killed for their life force?"

"By no means. But you are a thinker." Auberon tapped his head. "That is good."

"What does all this have to do with the pooka and the megalith?"

"Aetherian creatures—those created by fae using pure aether—can travel through the megalith without an amulet."

"What kind of creatures are those?"

"Pookas, unicorns, phoenixes, griffins, fauns, centaurs... those sorts of beings."

I nodded, but I'd never seen any such creatures. Other than the pooka I'd only seen now for mere seconds. Unicorns existed in

Ariboslia, but I never saw one. And I'd never even heard of the rest. But Iisakki didn't need an amulet, either. "What about dragons? Are they aetherian too?"

He gave me a sidelong glance. "You know of dragons?"

Creeping crabs. "I, uh..." I pointed to a wall. "You have paintings."

"Ah, yes." He stood, hands clasped behind his back. His aura darkened to the saddest blue as he gazed at one of the dragons. "They were supernatural creatures with unusual abilities, so it's possible they could have traveled through the megalith."

"What happened to them?"

He frowned. "The bonded dragons died with their elves. The females lay but one egg in their lifetime. There were no eggs in existence nor any males to fertilize them."

Now I was *really* curious as to how I received one. And how it hatched. "Okay. So, the pooka got my grandfather through the megalith without an amulet. Then what?"

"He visited Ireland in the human realm in their mid-1800s during an extreme famine. People dying of starvation fled their homeland or died trying. My father was a compassionate elf and had to help."

"He brought them here."

He moved to another painting—a man with similar features to Auberon. "He promised to find a way to provide for them, certain the peaceful elves would assist him. But he was mistaken. Many elves wanted the humans returned to their realm and the natural order restored. But the humans made my father their king, which outraged the elves. The nation became divided between the elves and the humans. And the elves became divided between those who wanted to help the humans versus those who wanted to drive them out."

I stood beside him. "Is this your father?"

He nodded. "They spent an entire elfin lifetime in conflict." He passed me to another picture, a woman who looked just like—me.

I gasped. "Is that—?"

"Your mother, yes. When she fled with you, the humans rose up against the elves with their human weaponry and wiped them out."

"At your command?" I barely registered the words as they escaped of their own accord. In my trance, I was only vaguely aware that my question might get me killed.

The king's face fell. "You, too, believe I would order the extinction of my race?"

I winced, wishing I could retract the comment.

"They tried to kill me too," he said. "Would they do that if they were following my command?"

I had no answer. "What did you do?"

"I fled to the one place they wouldn't come looking for me, Rotko, the Forest of Shadows. A terrible place."

"How'd you get your kingdom back?"

He heaved a heavy sigh. "If you're to understand all you need to know, you must understand the alliance between my kingdom and the seelie court. I told you about aether and how it costs lives to extract. The seelie fae created a synthetic version called keino. It's the reason I married your mother, Princess Delyth, sister to Queen Rhiannon of the seelie court. Our marriage was arranged to unite our kingdoms and ensure a continual supply of keino for Talamh Sí. It's necessary for just about everything... transportation, goods production, even agriculture. If you're to be queen, you must understand how imperative it is that we maintain good relations with the seelie fae to ensure we have a sufficient supply to power the kingdom."

"You want me to be queen?" I'd hoped Liam was wrong about that. But then, he had suggested I would be the third to ascend the throne. My intestines jellified.

"Correct. Queen Rhiannon wanted a blood member of her family on the throne to unite us. Part elf, part fae. She was on the verge of renouncing our alliance. You arrived just in time."

Was *that* the reason he searched for me? To avoid losing his power supply? "Why would my mother kidnap me and risk destroying the alliance?" I was derailing the conversation by going down this rabbit trail, but more was going on than I was led to believe.

Another frown creased his otherwise wrinkle-free face. "When the humans rose against us, she disappeared with you—to protect you —from the humans."

Forty

I moved back to my seat and rubbed my temples as if a massage could straighten out everything everyone had ever said. According to the humans, Auberon was trying to kill me. It shouldn't surprise me that he would blame it on the humans. But who was telling the truth? And why did sorting out their stories hurt my head so? "Why would the humans want me dead?"

"You're half-elf. They killed all the elves."

I groaned. Both the Saors and Auberon seemed to believe their stories. And both made sense.

"Your mother got you out just in time." He grasped the lapels of his cloak as he gazed upon her portrait. "The humans had already stormed the castle. I'd hoped to bring you both with me to another realm. Someplace safe. But she was gone. Whilst I wished she'd waited for me, I was glad you'd both escaped with your lives."

"And that's when you fled to Rotko?"

"Yes. I expected you and your mother to return when order was restored. But—" That faraway look captured him again.

Either he was a spectacular actor with an incredible ability to manipulate his aura, or he spoke the truth.

But then why did my mother leave him? Why didn't she flee *with* him? Unless she believed the humans. Which I wasn't sold weren't telling the truth. How would an entire group of people all believe the same lie?

Then again, they believed my father was God, so... There was that.

But all this made him sound so, so... innocent. A little too innocent. He wasn't. "But you c–cursed the people, didn't you? To believe you were God?"

His face darkened. At least, his expression *looked* real. "I confess to consulting with those with abilities beyond mine to assist me—though I didn't foresee the outcome."

"Who? The fae?"

"Of the worst kind."

"What happened?"

"After the humans massacred the elves, insisting I'd compelled them to commit such a heinous act, and your mother was nowhere to be found, I traveled to Pohjola in Rotko. There I met Noita."

"Who's Noita?"

"A powerful sorceress."

"She gave you the curse?"

"You keep calling it a curse!" He pounded the arm of his chair. His fingers curved around the edge of the armchair, squeezing it tight. "It was no curse. It was the solution. I saved them!"

Startled by his sudden outburst, I shimmied away as far as my seat would allow. Had I done it? Would he kill me now?

He spread his arms out as if to steady himself. "It solved all our social and economic problems. There is no more strife. No hunger or poverty. Everyone is content and provided for. At last, the peace my father dreamt of was realized. Nothing in this realm or any other I've searched can compare to the paradise I've created here."

"But it's fake!" I forgot myself and stood. "It's all a ruse. They don't know what's real and what isn't. Worse, they think you're God! As long as they believe that, they'll never know the real God."

The clocks grew louder as the seconds ticked by. His gaze held mine captive like quicksand, sucking me in, refusing to let go as the incessant tick tick ticking thrummed away. "Why are there so many clocks in here?"

"To remind me of my limited time. And I fear I may not have enough." He pinched the bridge of his nose. "You believe there is a God? A real, knowable God?"

"I have no doubt."

"That does complicate matters. Perhaps you can help me come up with a solution."

A knock sounded at the door.

"Enter!" King Auberon rubbed his hands together as Jaakko entered. "Ah, your food has arrived."

Jaakko crossed over to me and placed a domed platter on the table beside me. And I almost shivered. Something about his eyes... Not only the way they simultaneously watched and avoided me, but something within them seemed... familiar. He removed the lid, revealing an aromatic and appealing dish in a rainbow of colors. My stomach got the message and grumbled, reminding me I hadn't eaten since breakfast and food was long overdue.

"Have you ever feasted like an elf? This is ateria—a traditional elfin dish. Meatless. Humans plan everything around their meat when there is a bounty of flavorful fruits, vegetables, and spices. Ah, spices. Those are what make the dish."

Was that why I didn't tend to care for meat? Was it the elf side of me? Whatever scent wafted my way from the platter right now was unfamiliar—a unique mixture of spices. My stomach rumbled again. I reached for the fork, but something made me hesitate to eat, despite my hunger.

"Jaakko, where's the princess's wine?"

"Wine, sire?"

"Yes. We should celebrate should we not? Bring out the special wine for her homecoming."

"*Special* wine, sire?" Jaakko's questioning tone came out flat.

"Yes, Jaakko." King Auberon pinned the squirming pooka under his gaze. "The special reserve for such a celebration as this."

Jaakko nodded and bumped into a table, pausing to right the lamp sitting atop it before continuing his hasty retreat.

"Eat, eat. I can still answer your questions."

I scooped a forkful of the colorful mixture but didn't bring it to my mouth. What if it was poisoned? But then, why would Auberon give me all this backstory, trying to teach me if he was just going to kill me? And God brought me here for a reason. He couldn't have brought me here to die.

My stomach grew impatient, and I slipped the food into my mouth. Then my taste buds exploded with a sensation no food had ever created before. I had my favorite foods, especially Aunt Stacy's monkey bread. But this. What even was it? Sweet with a bit of heat. A spicy, flavorful heat that made me want to savor the food. Similar to Tenali's cooking, but better. "You suggested coming up with a solution for the curse."

"Why do you refer to it as a curse?"

"Isn't that what it is?"

"It's a fae spell. An unseelie one at that. But I'd hardly refer to a solution to our great kingdom's problems a curse."

I took another bite.

He drummed his fingers on his armrests. "What do you expect will happen if I reverse the spell?"

"The people will be free to think for themselves again—free to worship the real God."

"How many of them do you think will choose the real God... if there is one? The people will have different beliefs—different ideas of what is right and wrong. Some will want to serve me still. Others will want to stone me. Some will turn to other gods. Others will reject them all. Others still will make themselves as god. The kingdom will be thrown into chaos. What would you suggest we do to temper that?"

The pooka returned with a goblet. He hesitated, avoiding my eyes as he placed it on the table beside my plate. Was he afraid of the king?

"Have a drink, Daughter. The wine will soothe your nerves."

I eyed the cup. I'd never had wine before. Perhaps just a sip. I raised the goblet. A sour, earthy scent filled my nose before the liquid hit my lips. Bitter yet sweet, with a hint of berries, it warmed my throat.

I'd have preferred water. But Auberon seemed satisfied. The warming sensation fanned out from my throat, tingling my extremities. Was that the "soothing" Auberon spoke of? It was more unnerving than soothing. I shoved more food in my mouth to counteract whatever the wine was doing. Suddenly ravenous, I readied my next bite, then the next before dropping the fork. I was eating like a pig. He might as well throw the food into a trough and shove my face inside. I had to pace myself. I was nobility now.

Wait. Where did that thought come from? I wasn't nobility. Not until something was done about the curse.

A knock sounded at the door.

"Enter," my father said.

A defender entered and moved to the side. Liam appeared behind him.

FORTY-ONE

"Liam!" I ran to him and threw my arms around him. As he stood stiff in my embrace, without returning the hug, I realized my error. Despite our travels together, we hardly knew each other. And we were in the king's presence. My face warmed, and I backed away and cleared my throat. "How are you? Are you okay?"

"I'm sure I'm fine, Princess."

What was wrong with him? Did he feel awkward being normal around me in the king's presence? Or was he pretending to be under the curse? He still had his aura, though it was rather—flat. I'd have expected him to be fearful or angry, anything. Something.

"Please, come sit with us," Auberon said.

Liam sat on the edge of the couch farthest from me. His back was straight, ready to jump to my father's command.

I sipped my drink and watched my father and Liam over the rim.

"Liam, you're a defender. What do you think of my kingdom?"

"It's a beautiful city, Your Majesty."

"I understand you know my daughter." Auberon motioned toward me.

Liam looked at me, his expression blank. "Not personally, your majesty."

"What are you saying? You helped bring me to the city. To my father. Tell him."

Liam raised an eyebrow.

He must be acting. But why pretend not to know me? "Tell him!"

"My apologies, Princess. If I've met you, I don't remember. The last thing I remember was patrolling the woods. I'm not sure how I got back to the city."

"No." Cold dread poured over me, sending a shock like a bucket of ice water. "You rode Nessa... with me."

"You know Nessa? Do you know where she might be? I'd like to find her."

I jumped from my seat to stand before Auberon. "Did you erase his memories?"

"If something happened to his memories, I've nothing to do with it." Auberon turned to Liam. "Were you in an accident?"

"I'm not sure, Your Majesty. I don't think so."

My heart felt as though it had been squeezed in the winepress along with my drink. One of the few friends in this realm, the only one I was beginning to trust... My father's men had erased his memories.

"You look distraught, Daughter. Have more wine."

I didn't want to do anything this man asked. Even so, I took a long drink, emptying the glass.

"Liam, my daughter and I were discussing the people and how best to rule them. Do you think it's more important for people to have free will or safety and peace?"

"I would think safety and peace would be best, Your Majesty."

"How could—" A sharp pain stabbed my temples, sending searing white flashes across my vision. I squeezed my eyes shut while stars popped behind my lids. The tiny explosions subsided into pinpricks, then fanned out from my eyes, settling into a dull throb in the center of my head. I peered through slits, but everything was blurry. I could barely make out the figures who seemed to be talking. All I heard sounded like ocean waves from beneath the surface.

The seat cushion dipped beside me, and a warped version of the king swam in my vision. Something touched my shoulder. Words spilled from his twisting lips, but they came out in incomprehensible slurs.

Was I drunk? Was this what being drunk felt like? If so, I'd never touch another drop.

I rubbed my temples. My mind was a storm cloud, rendering thought impossible. "Wha ap ee?"

What was happening!

Why couldn't I speak? Was I losing my mind?

Another sharp pang shot from the center of my head, threatening to split my head in two. I bent over, gripped my head, and squeezed my eyes shut.

Light—

Dark—

In. Out.

A comforting hand stroked my back.

After several deep breaths, the pain in my head eased somewhat. I dared open my eyes. The blurry scene sharpened, but a dull ache remained behind my eyes, shooting sharp pulses to the center of my brain.

Ticking clocks and rushing voices filtered through the ocean waves. Sharp images appeared in my periphery, but everything I tried to look at was blurred. I blinked, hoping my lids might remove whatever obscured my sight. But my vision continued to toy with me.

"Daughter?" Genuine concern laced my father's voice.

The pain ebbed away as the cloud lifted. My father now sitting beside me came into focus, as did the guard kneeling on the floor before me. My face warmed under the defender's intense gaze. Why'd he have to be here now, witnessing my fit?

And why'd he have to be so good-looking?

"I've sent for the physician," Father said.

"I–I'm all right." I could speak. Relief flooded me. My mind felt sluggish, but I was regaining control. "That's not necessary."

"Regardless, I'll feel more at ease once the physician confirms it."

Despite a dull, lingering headache, my mind cleared. And I felt —peace.

The guard breathed deeply, then rocked back onto his feet. He brushed off his trousers. "I'm glad you're well, Princess." He turned to Father as if awaiting his command.

Father's face darkened as he studied the man. If only they had auras to give me some idea of what they were thinking.

I looked beyond the men to my strange surroundings. Renewed panic welled within. "Where am I? How'd I get here?"

FORTY-TWO

I dreamed I was flying low to the ground, weaving through trees.

Colleen, came a voice not my own from within my mind.

A cottage came into view with a barn behind it.

Colleen.

What was that voice? Calling me. Inside my head.

I flew along a path through overgrown grasses and wildflowers to a worn picket fence. Just as I feared I might fly into the cottage, I swooped up over its steep mossy roof. Birds twittered around me as I glided to the barn. I was about to swoop into the dark entrance when the voice came again, sharper, *Colleen!*

I woke with a jolt. My body bounced on soft bedding, and my eyes snapped open.

Where was I? And who was calling my name? I searched the giant room but found no one. I was alone, lying in the biggest bed I'd ever seen. A caged tree grew through the center of the room. Twisty branches jutted out from its windy trunk, climbing up to the domed glass ceiling in search of the sun. Shards of light streamed through its leafy canopy. Birds flitted from branch to branch, twittering as they went.

I stared. I'd seen this tree before. But it was different. Smaller, perhaps. And in my memory, I saw it through white slits.

An inexplicable need to touch the tree came over me. I peeled away the covers. Where did this nightgown come from? Please tell me I put it on myself and I'd just forgotten. Try as I might, I couldn't remember what happened the night before. Nothing since crawling through the megalith.

I tested the soft cream carpet with my toes. An intricate gold pattern swirled throughout the rug. Everything here was so grand. So... strange. I wrapped my fingers around the cold brass caging the tree. Was that a door? I lifted a latch, and it swung open with a squeal. Soft dirt met my toes as I crossed to the tree. I placed a hand on its rough bark. The energy within surged and met my hand. "I missed you too."

A tiny bluebird landed on my shoulder, sang a little song, then flew back into the foliage.

Whatever this place was, it was magical.

But where was I? How did I get here? Why did I know this place?

Think, think, think. What had happened yesterday?

Flashes of strange images flooded my mind. The megalith. A glowing orb. A cat.

Wait. I followed a cat through the megalith.

A knock came from the door, and I jumped. The door cracked open. Something black and fuzzy pushed through the opening, and I darted behind the tree, then peeked around the trunk.

Was that? Nay. I rubbed my eyes and looked again. A giant black rabbit? Walking like a human?

What kind of place had the megalith brought me to? A world full of hybrid human-animal creatures?

"Princess?"

The thing talks too? Its gaze roamed my way, and I sucked in a breath as I ducked back behind the trunk.

"King Auberon requests your presence at the breakfast table."

King Auberon. Warmth spread over my heart. I stepped out from behind the tree. "My father?"

"Yes, Princess." The thing looked rather relieved to find me. If a bunny can look relieved.

"Why do you look like a rabbit?"

"I'm a pooka."

"Is this my room?"

"Yes, Princess."

"Why is there a tree in my room?"

"Because elves love nature, Princess. Your father wanted you to always be close to it, even amongst all the modern human advancements."

I heaved a contented sigh. How kind of Father to do such a thing for me. In my confusion, I'd nearly forgotten he'd summoned me. I mustn't make him wait. I looked down at my nightgown. "Is there anything else I can wear?"

"To be sure. To be sure. Your wardrobe is full of suitable clothing." He pointed toward a carved wardrobe taking up one flat section of the octagonal room. "I'll wait just outside."

"Thank you."

The door closed, and I clicked the lock, then padded across the floor to the wardrobe. Dozens of elegant gowns glistened inside. As I rummaged through them, the strange creature's words and the way he said them rattled me—"To be sure. To be sure."

THE POOKA LED me to the dining hall, then disappeared. My father sat at one end of the table. The sight of him eased all my tension. A maid and a guard stood at attention against the far wall, opposite the windows.

Father folded some papers, set them aside, and beamed. "How are you feeling this fine morning, Daughter?"

Much better now, in Father's presence. "I'm well. Though I've a bit of a headache." What I wouldn't give for some feamainn. Did they have that in this realm?

"Ah, Iida. Please fetch the princess a soothing tablet."

The maid nodded and darted away as if she were on a mission to save the world.

"Please sit. Your breakfast awaits." He motioned to a place setting kitty-corner from his. "I see the gowns I had brought for you are a good fit. Stunning. Simply stunning. That blue suits your eyes."

I gathered the many layers of shimmering fabric to sit. It was beautiful, but it would take some getting used to after years of thin selkie dresses. I removed the dome from my plate to reveal a bowl of what looked like porridge and an array of fruits—most recognizable. I picked a grape and popped it in my mouth.

"I trust you slept well."

"I think so. My head is still fuzzy. But I think I remember something."

"Oh?" He straightened and put down his fork.

"I remember the tree in my room. But in my memory, white slits obscured it."

"Oh!" His laugh sounded relieved. "That has been your room since you were born. You must be remembering seeing the tree through the slats in your crib. You were very young. It's impressive you remember something so far back." Then his smile faded as his face grew serious. "Do let me know if any other memories surface, will you?"

"Of course, Father." I scooped some kind of porridge, then dropped my spoon back into the bowl. "Speaking of memories, try as I might, I can't remember anything after arriving in Betören until this morning."

"Traveling through realms can put quite a toll on one's mind. Perhaps it was all too overwhelming."

"Is that why I can't remember living here before?"

"Possibly."

"Then why do I remember you?" Not that I had any specific memories, but he was familiar.

"I'm your father."

Though it was no answer at all, somehow it settled the idea in my spotty, disoriented mind.

"Why would I suddenly have a memory of being a baby?"

"Good question. But do try to put it out of your mind. For now. It wouldn't do to overwhelm you after all you've been through."

Iida returned with two white things in a cup.

"Take those," Father said. "They will make your head feel better."

I popped them in my mouth and chewed, then shuddered at the chalky, bitter flavor coating my tongue. I took a drink to wash away the nasty taste.

"You have much to learn, Daughter." His amused eyes peered at me over his mug as he sipped. "Next time, try swallowing them whole." He wiped his mouth and discarded his napkin on his plate. "I've meetings to attend to in the city today. And I've consulted with Queen Rhiannon. She plans to send you a lady-in-waiting, but she won't arrive for two weeks to a month's time. Until then, Iida is at your service." He gazed at the maid until she returned to her post, then scowled at the guard beside her. "And Liam. He will be your personal defender."

"What's a lady-in-waiting?"

"A friend of nobility to stay by your side and attend to your needs. Queen Rhiannon insists upon sending the daughter of a member of the seelie court."

"So, you're buying me a friend?"

His deep, hearty laugh lit up everything within me. "Ladies-in-waiting aren't paid. The accommodations we provide and the relationship she is blessed to have with you is payment enough."

That didn't sound right. But Father said it, so it must be so.

"Tomorrow we'll begin your training. But for today, rest. You're free to explore anything that isn't locked. And don't leave the castle grounds. Understood?"

"Understood."

"Good. Stay out of trouble."

FORTY-THREE

By noon, we'd only toured half the castle, and I was tiring. Not one person I'd seen since arriving in Betören had an aura. It never occurred to me there might be people without auras. Or perhaps something in the atmosphere here stifled it or made it invisible. That would explain why I couldn't see mine either.

I'd always seen my ability as a problem to hide. But now, without it, I felt not only disadvantaged but also disabled. Part of me was missing.

Everywhere we went, a continual tick-tick-ticking sound followed or met me. Clocks along with gears and gadgets for who knew what clogged up every room. All the rooms, well lit now with large windows and sheer curtains, were probably just as bright at night with all the electric lanterns on tabletops or the floor or stuck to wall sconces or dangling from cords and pulleys or hanging in chandeliers.

Lights and clocks everywhere.

And though it was perfectly warm without additional heat now, all the rooms had either a fireplace or what Iida called a radiator.

"It gets rather chilly in winter and when strong winds blow

across the ocean... your bedroom especially. Only the west side offers any protection," Iida explained. "But there is a fireplace *and* radiators to compensate. It's the price to pay for having the best ocean view."

"I haven't had time to look around. Not that I could see much past the tree. How kind of Father to do something so considerate for me. And to keep it ready and waiting all these years." Complete comfort washed over me—like a soft breeze swirling around me in a gentle embrace.

"Yes, well. He is a wonderful king." Iida smiled and continued the tour.

Something bothered me. Her speech? Her mannerisms? Something didn't ring true. If only I could see her aura.

"When are you going to explain the—what's it called—intercom?" I pointed to the button over the desk in yet another guest room. "Why do some rooms have more than one button? And what do the different symbols mean?"

"Every room has an intercom to reach the security office. But others have intercoms to other places such as the kitchens, the physician's office, the apothecary.... The symbols specify the location. Until you learn them, use the button on the left. That one is always security. Press and hold the button, identify yourself, state your need, then release."

"How will they know where I am?" I rubbed my forehead as if to stimulate my brain into understanding these foreign contraptions.

"Each office has an indicator map with all the rooms and floors. Wherever you call, they will know your location." She then turned to Liam. "If you're to be the princess's defender, you must familiarize yourself with the grounds and the castle staff. Know it as well as you know your face in a mirror. And ensure she is always attended. Do not leave her alone... even for a minute."

He nodded.

I rubbed at the back of my neck, a sudden tension pinching it as I envisioned Liam atop a white horse. Then in a barn with a weapon trained on him. Then a bloody ankle. I shook off the images. My mind must be playing tricks on me.

"Once her lady-in-waiting arrives, she'll alleviate much of the burden." Iida smoothed her gleaming white apron.

"It's no burden to safeguard the princess." My defender stood taller, hands clasped behind his back.

Was that the first I'd heard him speak? He had a nice voice. Deep and rich.

We stopped for lunch and took our meals out in the gardens. Walls of green shrubs and ivy climbed the iron fence surrounding us on all but the ocean side. There the fence was tall enough to protect anyone from falling over the cliffs below but low enough not to obscure the view. Our table nestled beside a decorative pond with a trickling waterfall. Iisakki would have had so much fun here.

Wait. Where did that thought come from? "Do you know someone named Iisakki?"

Iida choked on her salad. Her gaze darted in every direction as she sipped her water and got her cough under control. Once she collected herself, she leaned in low and whispered. "How do you know that name?"

"I don't know." I looked to my defender who continued eating his meal, his movements as rigid as his starched uniform.

He looked everywhere but at me, eyeing the hot-air balloons decorating the skies, even the sea birds, as if they were a potential threat. Every sound vied for his extreme attention. I'd never seen anyone with such focus. He pushed his plate away. "Excuse me while I search the perimeter."

I turned to my maid. "Is Iisakki a real person then?"

"I don't know him, but I've heard the name. I can look into it if you like." She fidgeted with her fork, turning it around and around in her fingers. Why did she seem so nervous?

"Aye. Please do."

She set down her fork, glanced over her shoulder, then leaned in closer, gripping the table edge with whitening fingertips. "Might you permit me to ask you a few questions, Princess?"

"What would you like to know?" I scooped a bite of salad.

"What do you remember?" Why did she look like she might be sick? Was the food bad?

"I remember everything except whatever happened after I went through the megalith to this realm until this morning. What realm is this?" I tested my bite. The sweet cheese mixed with cooked root vegetables dressed in something spicy was like heaven on my tongue. No. The food wasn't the problem.

She pursed her lips. "Betören. How do you remember your father?"

"I don't—I—" But I did, didn't I? I knew him. Somehow, I just knew him. "Did I just meet him for the first time this morning? I've no memories of him before that. And yet, it feels like I've known him all along."

I cuddled into the warm, fuzzy feelings before I shivered as if that blanket were a trap. "But I keep seeing things that might be memories."

"Such as?" Iida swiped a red wisp of hair from her face and tucked it back into her cap.

"Well... one was a dream, but it seemed real, like a memory maybe. I was flying through the woods to a cottage and a barn."

"Oh?" She straightened in her seat, her face pinched.

"It was overgrown with a path and an old picket fence. Is there a cottage like that? Perhaps I've been there."

"I can look into that too." She picked at something on her apron, then brushed it away.

"Please do. Although I don't know how I'd have a memory of it from the sky. I was flying too low to have been on one of those flying ships." I pointed to one flying along the horizon. "And someone was with me. He kept calling my name."

"Which name?" Iida tugged her lower lip as her eyebrows twitched.

"Colleen." I studied my maid. Was she always this nervous? She was like a seal resting on a rock surrounded by shark-infested waters. "I also had a memory from when I was a baby. Father confirmed it. I saw the tree in my room through the slats of my crib." I studied Iida's nervous, yet rapt gaze.

Liam returned to his seat and resumed eating his meal.

"I also saw Liam."

That got his attention. His eyebrows quirked.

My flowy sleeves caught on the rough edges as I bent closer to him and braced my elbows on the natural-cut wooden tabletop. "Do you own a white horse?"

Liam grasped the back of his head and furrowed his brow as if thinking hurt. "Nessa. But that doesn't mean anything. Many defenders have white horses."

"Has anyone ever threatened you with a weapon?"

"I'm a defender."

I stared at him.

"So, yes."

"Do you have stitches on your right calf?"

"No."

"Can you show me?"

Liam scowled, then pushed away from the table to pull up his pant leg. There, just where I'd imagined, jagged black stitching gripped his flesh. He sucked in a breath and snapped his head up to me. "How did you know that?"

Iida watched us with extreme interest—or was it dread?

"I–I don't know. I think I stitched it." Moving my elbows from the table, I scooted further from him. "You don't remember?"

He shook his head. "I remember everything up until about two weeks ago. I was patrolling the woods. But I don't recall returning to the city or how I got here." His scowl deepened, pressing his lips white and narrowing his dark brows. "Or what became of my horse."

I dared look into his eyes, a most amazing blue, like the ocean. I'd never seen such color—or had I? "Is it possible we know each other? How is it we both seem to be missing similar times in our memory?"

"Actually..." He pawed the back of his neck again. "When I arrived at the castle, you seemed to know me. But before we retired for the night, you'd... forgotten."

Iida paled. "Keep this information to yourselves. Say nothing to anyone."

"Not even Father?" How could I keep anything from him? And how could she ask it of me? I glared at her, awaiting a reasonable explanation for her treasonous request.

Her gaze darted about like before, and she leaned in. "There are things you don't understand yet, but please... I beg of you to trust me and say nothing of this... to *anyone*. For now."

Why would I trust her, a maid, over Father? If he asked me a pointed question, I would answer. And my father's subjects shouldn't ask me to lie to anyone—least of all him. I should report her as soon as we returned.

But what had happened in the missing days between when I came through the megalith and today? And Liam and I must know each other. But how? Why were we both suffering memory loss? And why would my father entrust my safety to a guard with spotty memories?

FORTY-FOUR

I tossed around and around, twisting my nightgown and blankets around my legs. After giving one final irritated flop, I sat up. For whatever reason, though I was exhausted, sleep eluded me.

If only I could flip a switch and shut off my mind as easily as the lights around here. What had happened to me before arriving at the castle? I didn't have any injuries. People didn't lose their memories for no reason. And what about Liam? How was he missing his memories too? We knew each other. We had to. His stitches proved it.

But how did we both lose our memories without hurting our heads? Did we pass through a storm cloud with the power to steal memories, then got separated? A ludicrous thought, but then, no sane explanations offered reason for this happening to us.

I was never going to sleep.

I stole away from my bed and rounded the tree to the little alcove where Iida slept. Soft puffs came from her sleeping form. Though I wanted to talk, I shouldn't wake her. Perhaps some fresh air would help. I eased the glass doors open, and cool air swirled around me, ruffling my nightgown. I smoothed the goose bumps roughening my arms.

Letting the breathtaking view calm me, I breathed in the salty air and remembered home. A brilliant moon hung over the ocean. Its rippling replica shone on the water's surface. Waves crashed against the stone beneath me, but when I stood at the rail and spread my arms, I could imagine myself soaring above the sea.

My family must be worried to death. How long have I been gone?

I should ask Father if I could visit them. Or have them come to visit me. There was no reason I couldn't do that. Was there?

I couldn't bother him by asking now. It would have to wait until morning. Which would be a long while from now if I never slept. Better try again.

I closed the doors behind me with a soft click.

Screee bzzzzt.

I snapped my head toward the sound. What unholy noise was that? I searched the darkness but found nothing. Iida was still asleep in the alcove. Whatever it was hadn't disturbed her. I held my breath and listened. All I heard was my heartbeat thudding in time to the rhythmic tick, tick, tick of the clock on the far wall. No strange screech.

It must've been my imagination.

I crawled back into bed.

Screee bzzzzt.

I leaped from my bed as though it had zapped me. In a crouch, I moved toward the sound.

Screee-EEE bzzzzt.

It was coming from outside my room. I unclicked the lock, opened the door, and peeked my head out. Nothing moved in the hallway. I climbed the short staircase and padded down the hall to Father's quarters.

Screee bzzz bzzzzt.

The sound was growing louder. A strip of light illuminated under his bedroom door. Did I dare open it? What if he was in danger? When I put my ear to his door, his muffled voice filtered through.

I tried the handle. It wasn't locked. I inched the door wide enough to peek through, but I didn't see anything.

Screee-EEE bzzz bzzzzt.

"My apologies once again for the bad connection, Your Majesty," said a staticky voice.

"Not to worry, Alpertti. You can't be held responsible for a hailstorm causing interference."

Who was he talking to?

I poked my head inside. My father sat at his desk in front of a strange-looking cube. A tiny man peered back at my father from inside the cube.

What strange magic was this?

"As I was saying, Ruuta's family requires two more weeks to prepare her for the trip."

"What should I do in the meantime? My daughter can't be left unattended."

"She has a maid, does she not?" The tiny man appeared to be sitting at a table. Or a desk, like Father. Only his chest and face appeared in the box with something hanging behind his back. Curtains?

"She does, but—"

Screee bzzzzt.

The tiny man morphed into wavy lines, then reappeared whole again.

"Has the maid proven untrustworthy?"

"Well, no. She's been in my employ several seasons now. But—"

"As long as the princess is safe, what you do while you await Ruuta's arrival is none of Queen Rhiannon's concern. Her only request is to have a trusted ally by the princess's side to help her learn her roots and to aid her in her transition to power."

"I understand," Father said. "And what of the defender, Liam? As an unspelled, he's a danger to my daughter. Why does Queen Rhiannon insist I employ him as her defender?"

"It seems they made a connection in their travels, did they not?" the man in the box asked.

"Several witnesses were given that impression."

"Then he must remain close, should the queen have need of him."

"But for what purp—"

Screee bzzz bzzzzt.

"—beron." Box Man's image reformed and enlarged as he leaned forward. "You do wish to maintain our alliance, do you not? Free trade. Passage through Rotko. Keino. Aivopestä..."

"Of course. Of course." My father shifted in his seat.

"Then don't concern yourself with Queen Rhiannon's reasonings. Simply concede to her request. Unless there is some reason you cannot?"

"No, no."

"Very good, Your Majesty. As discussed, the keino supplies to cover the next month and to compensate for the hijacked supplies will be shipped over the next several days. I will send you the manifest in advance, but until we know how the thieves are pilfering our supplies, we will vary our air routes and keep them confidential. Queen Rhiannon apologizes for the difficulty this will cause in your warehouses and with air traffic control. We will stagger the shipments so as not to overwhelm them and do our best to ensure safety in the air and along our border."

"And, just to confirm, those shipments will include aivopestä and unohtaa, correct?"

"Correct. Are there any other seelie potions you require?"

"Only what my physician requested. And please ask Queen Rhiannon if there's anything aivopestä might do in the wrong hands. They might be after the keino only, but the shipments they're targeting include aivopestä. It can't be a coincidence. I must know why my supplies are being stolen."

"Of course, Your Majesty."

Father scribbled a note on paper. "Thank you."

The tiny man backed away and reached for something. A feather appeared before his face. A quill? He seemed to be writing. After a moment, he replaced the quill and returned his attention to my father. "Will that be all for today, Your Majesty?"

"Yes. Thank you, Alpertti."

The man in the box nodded. He morphed into wavy lines that merged into the center of the box and blinked out. Nothing but black remained.

"Keep Liam as Eerika's defender? Rhiannon must be out of her mind." Father leaned back in his chair.

By the time it occurred to me I should back away and leave, it was too late. My father spotted me. He was up and standing at the door before I could think what to do.

"Daughter?" He pulled the door open, and I fell inside. "Were you eavesdropping?"

"What's eavesdropping?"

"When you listen in on a private conversation, usually from outside, close enough for the water to drip from the eaves onto the listener."

"I–I didn't know it was private." My fingers twitched to check that my hair covered my ears—a silly reaction. He knew I was an elf, but somehow, I felt as if I needed to hide something. "I couldn't sleep. I heard noises."

"And you saw me using the teleview?" He pointed to the box as he moved toward it.

"Is that what that box is?" I followed him for a closer look.

"Yes, it allows me to converse with others over long distances."

"Like the intercom?" It had knobs with strange markings and a similar screenlike thing where the sound came out.

"Yes." He clasped his hands behind his back. "But with a much wider range. This allows me to converse with those across the Divide —Rotko—all the way to Seelie Clós."

"Like a phone?"

"A telephone?" His eyebrows pinched together. "They had those in Ariboslia?"

"No, but I read about them in books."

"That makes even less sense, Daughter."

"I, uh, my adopted mom. Her friend brought things from America... like books."

"America?" He rubbed his hairless chin. "That's in the same realm as Ireland, is it not? In which language were these books written?"

"English."

His eyes widened. "Well, that will be helpful. Quite helpful, indeed. More evidence of your rightfulness for the throne."

"What's eye-vo... whatever it is." I waved a hand as if my frantic stirring motion might be able to conjure the strange word out of the air.

"Aivopestä?" He sat at the edge of his canopy bed and motioned for me to sit at his desk. "It's the serum the seelie fae provide to keep our people... content."

The hard uncushioned chair creaked under my weight. "Does it take their memories away?"

"By no means. What would make you think that?"

"Did you take away Liam's memories?"

"What would make you think such a thing?"

I shrugged. "It's just strange.... We're both missing similar time frames from our memories."

Father let out a long sigh. He stood and jutted out his elbow. "If we're both up and ready for a conversation, let's take it to my office, shall we?"

I took his proffered arm. Just outside our private quarters stood a defender who bowed as we passed. Father rapped on the first door to the right. Fumbling and a crash sounded from within. Then the pooka opened the door wide enough to peer through. With recognition in his sleepy eyes, he straightened. "Your Majesty. How can I be of service?"

"Fetch the princess a drink and bring it to my office."

The rabbit flinched like he'd been struck. "The wine, Your Majesty?"

"Yes, Jaakko. The wine."

FORTY-FIVE

After breakfast, as soon as we entered the gardens and no others were in sight, I wheeled around on Iida and Liam, my skirt and oversized sleeves billowing. "What were those looks you kept giving each other whilst Father was speaking?" I narrowed my eyes and pointed an accusatory finger at each of them in turn. "I demand you let me in on your little secret, or I will tell Father you're conspiring against him."

Iida wrinkled her nose as if she'd caught a whiff of something foul.

Liam rolled his eyes. "Look who's taking on her role as princess rather quickly this time 'round."

I must've misheard him. "What did you say?"

Iida scowled.

"What?" He stepped out of her arm's reach as if she might hit him. "What difference does it make if I tell her? She'll soon forget again anyway."

Her scowl deepened. "One of these days, she might stop forgetting. So be careful what you say."

Their banter irked me. "What are you two blathering on about? If you know something, tell me."

"My apologies, Princess." Iida curtsied, then shot him another warning glare. "It's just that, in truth, these conversations are growing tiresome."

"What does that mean?" I breathed in the salty air carrying an unrecognizable floral bouquet as I moved through a vast array of colored blooms to a bench beside a small pond. Fish gurgled beneath the surface. A lizard scrambled across the rocks into the water, his tail swishing from side to side as he swam. A niggling feeling, a memory of... *something*, pricked the back of my mind as I watched him.

Liam grasped the back of his neck, annoyingly adorable with his head bent, dark hair falling into his ocean eyes. "This isn't your first day at the castle. You've been here for three weeks as of yesterday."

That news hit me like a tree branch across the face, smacking away any rational thought as I attempted to wrap my mind around such a preposterous idea. My servants couldn't be toying with me. Nay, not if they valued their positions in the castle. "Three weeks?"

Iida and Liam shared a sidelong glance that communicated far more than I could comprehend. If only they had auras.

A ship crossed the rising sun's path, bathing us in its shadow. The breeze quickened, and I shivered. The floral scent seemed stronger now. Overwhelming. "But j–just yesterday I followed a cat through the megalith. What happened to me?"

"What happened, indeed." Liam scoffed. "Each time you lose your memory you act more—how's a nice way to put it?—royal."

Now perturbed, I nearly stamped my foot. "What's *that* supposed to mean?"

"It means you're a royal—"

Iida smacked him. Hard. Liam's face twisted as he soothed his arm.

Whatever he was about to say, it wasn't kind. Better to ignore the miscreant... and his ocean eyes. "Was I in an accident?"

That might explain the lack of auras too. Perhaps it wasn't that they didn't have them, but that I could no longer see them. I looked down at myself, prodding my arms, then legs for other evidence of injury.

"No, you weren't in an accident." Iida sat beside me. Her arm twitched as if resisting the urge to reach out to me.

The shadow moved on, warm sunlight again illuminating me. So why did everything still feel—dark? Obscured? Why was I so chilled? "I didn't hit my head?"

They both shook their heads, their lips set in a grim line.

"Then what happened?" Alarms sounded within me. Blaring. Setting off every nerve. "People don't lose memories for no reason."

"I wish I knew." She swiped at her forehead where her red curls quivered in the breeze fighting for freedom from her white cap. "Perhaps it's a strange illness from wherever it is you were—Ariboslia, was it?"

"No." She was wrong. If anything, I'd caught a sickness here where nothing made sense. Ariboslia was safe. Who knew what foreign diseases attacked unsuspecting victims here. I wrung my hands together as the alarms heightened. My stomach twisted and squeezed, threatening to reject my breakfast. "There's no such sickness."

She lowered her hand, her shoulders slumping. "Perhaps it's an effect of passing through the realms."

"I've never heard of that happening."

"Well." Liam crossed his arms. "*Something* is wrong with you. You lose your memory every day or two."

"What?" Had some memory-stealing illness infected me already? "That's not possible."

"Apparently, it is." He motioned toward me as though I contained all the evidence needed.

A purple flower swayed in the breeze within reach. I touched the smooth petal as if it might comfort me. I sensed its hearty energy within. So calm. At peace. Doing what it was made to do—use its beauty and invigorating scent to attract. It had no worries. How I envied the plant for that. I wanted what it had. The petal in my fingers stiffened and browned. I released the plant as if I'd killed it and been caught with the murder weapon in hand.

Had I done that? I'd never taken life before. I'd only given it.

I looked to my servants. Had they seen what I'd done? Liam scanned our surroundings as Iida looked to the sky.

Good. They hadn't noticed. I plucked the evidence and tossed it beneath the bench. The rest of the plant looked healthy. The rest of the flower too. Just the one petal.

Iida threw her arms up. "I don't know what to make of this. And I don't know how to handle it any longer. Your father must be out of his mind."

"My father?" A warm feeling came over me. "Is he here? I'd like to meet him."

Liam groaned.

"He had to attend to some shipments at the docks early this morning. He'll be back this afternoon. You can see him then."

Her words struck my chest, forcing my breath from me. "He didn't want to see me? But I've just arrived."

"No, you haven't." Liam dragged a hand down his face. "Didn't you hear a word we just said?"

Iida planted her hands on her hips. "If you value your place here, you'll mind your words, defender."

"Please, make him fire me. Return me to patrolling the woods. I'd give anything for the peace and quiet over catching the princess up every other day and watching her grow more and more... *royal.*" His ocean eyes flared.

I didn't know this man. He was merely a servant. Still, his attitude stung.

"I swear I don't know why King Auberon keeps you around." She gave him yet another scathing look. "I know you want answers, Princess. But we can't continue to risk having conversations you're likely to forget. In a day or two, if you remember this conversation, perhaps we'll talk."

THAT AFTERNOON, while I waited for my father in his office, I rummaged through his library. Being in the presence of so many books soothed my soul. Most were old and written in a language I couldn't understand. Still, something was beautiful about them despite their nicks, creases, yellowing pages, and cracked spines. Lovingly read books. Thoughts written on pages by authors likely long since deceased. Yet their words carried on, traveling through time to the minds that absorbed them.

I studied the foreign gold lettering on a spine. It was like a code, and I itched to decipher it. I pulled out several books, caressing their covers, fingering the print on the yellowed pages as though I could siphon their meaning as I could the life force from a plant. Too bad it didn't work that way. I replaced each book before retrieving another, but the next one I came to was stuck. When I tugged harder, the entire bookcase shifted. I grasped the wooden lip and dragged it out.

Something was back there.

What could it be? My breath hitched as I peered into the darkness. I probed the inside edge until I found what I was looking for. I flicked the switch, illuminating the cramped room, every wall lined floor to ceiling with bookshelves. I sucked in my breath—a secret library.

But why were these books hidden?

I perused the titles, running my fingers over the spines. Most of the books were written in that same, unfamiliar lettering. Then I came to those I recognized. They all had the same title *The Holy Bible*. God's word? We had one of these at home. A wave of homesickness washed over me, souring my stomach and making every muscle ache.

But why hide God's word?

Colleen!

An image of a field of tall grass overtook my vision. Though I was aware of my body standing still, holding a book in the library, I also felt as though I was running and leaping through the grass. It was disorienting, like my spirit had split and taken up residence in two places at once.

Colleen!

"Who's there?" I asked. The voice sounded like it came from my head.

A cottage overrun with wildflowers and weeds came into view with a massive barn behind it.

Come to me.

"Who are you?" I asked. "Where can I find you?" I searched, but all I could see was the barn closing in through a haze of shelved books.

"Can I help you, Daughter?"

I whirled around, and my vision snapped back to the library. A shadow of a man wearing a crown stood in the entryway. My heart thumped like a rabbit with an itch. The king. Why did my first meeting with my father have to be like this?

"I see you've found my secret library."

Shame washed over me as he stepped into the light, and I gazed up at his face for the first time. A black bunny peeked over his shoulder.

"Jaakko, fetch the wine."

The bunny slumped. "Yes, Your Majesty."

FORTY-SIX

Ruuta, my lady-in-waiting, disembarked from the ship. A parasol obscured most of her face. Though she wore heels, her steps were steady despite the plank's steep incline and sway. She moved as if she were in control of the universe and feared nothing. She spotted Father and me and waved.

With her parasol and shimmering blue gown, she stood out among all the browns, reds, and black that seemed so fashionable here. I peered down at my blue dress. I must stick out too. But unlike mine with a tight bodice, which I'd never get used to, hers was loose—flowy, with a draped neck. Her slitted sleeves dangled by her side, freeing her lower arms. It was closer to a selkie dress than what I wore. I missed selkie dresses.

When I pushed through the crowd to greet her, she folded the parasol, draped it over her arm, and hurried to us. Her luminescent blue eyes shimmered as she grasped my hands. Blue face markings framing her eyes like butterfly wings gave her an uncarthly appearance.

"Eerika, forgive me for taking so long to come to you." She gathered me into a hug, bathing me in whatever sweet scent clung to her.

"I would've dashed away in an instant to be with you, but Mother and Father refused to release me until all the arrangements were made to their satisfaction. Several ships have been hijacked as of late."

"Oh?" I looked to my father who avoided my eye. "I wasn't aware."

She squeezed my hands, then released them, and curtsied to Father. "Forgive me, My King. I trust the princess wasn't too burdensome without me."

Father patted my hand and brought it to his lips for a quick kiss. "This dear child? Of course not. But I'll rest comfortably knowing she's in your good hands."

"Well, then. Let's start now, shall we? Perhaps you'd like to show me this lovely city. I can scarcely remember the last time I was here." She tipped her head to Father. Her wavy blond hair was pulled up like many of the women here. Twisted ringlets spilled over her shoulder from the back. But she wore no hat, which I appreciated. Though she looked as though she would wear a hat well. "I trust your men will see to my things?"

"Of course, of course. Enjoy getting acquainted. Liam will be near should you need anything."

Liam acknowledged Father's command with a nod.

Ruuta's gaze followed Father's to where Liam stood. She gave him an appraising look, then leaned in, giving me a knowing one. What she knew though, I wasn't sure. She let out a laugh and tugged me through the crowd. "Afternoon, gentlemen." She nodded to the men collecting her things, then steered me toward the park.

I don't know what I was expecting from my lady-in-waiting or a fae, but this wasn't it. I'd never met anyone so full of life and so... so... bold. Even Father didn't ooze this much confidence, and he was king.

Ruuta tugged me closer as we walked along the sidewalk away from the docks. "Thank goodness we've a moment to ourselves." She glanced at Liam trailing us. "Well, other than that fine specimen of a human. His eyes are—"

"Like the ocean."

"Oh." She pulled me close with a devious smile. "I see you've noticed."

Something in her manner toward him bothered me. Time to change the subject. "You've been to Talamh Sí before?"

"Once or twice as a child. It's nothing like home. Seelie Clós is much brighter. And not so loud. There's so much clunky machinery here. And clocks. They're everywhere... especially in your palace. Ticking, ticking, everywhere... I remember scarcely sleeping with all that racket."

I laughed. "You get used to it."

"If memory serves, there's a park this way." She steered me away from the heavy traffic on Eastport Street down Killarney Road.

"How long has it been since you've been here?" She must know her way around quite well if she was taking me to the park from the back entrance.

"I believe I was seven human years? Fae don't keep track as humans do. But I've an impeccable memory and sense of direction."

We strolled down the sidewalk beside the quiet cobblestone street. Rows of identical rectangular residences with arched windows and doorways lined the walkways on either side.

"You won't find rows of bland buildings in Seelie Clós either."

"They are rather dull, aren't they?" Nothing dressed up this street. Was the park created to make up for that?

"Speaking of dull and things we don't have, there are very few humans in Seelie Clós. Does make life dull, if you ask me." She eyed Liam again.

I positioned myself to obscure her view. "No elves either?"

She stopped. Still in her grip, I stopped too. "You are aware there are no elves left."

"Yes, I just... hoped." My hopes of learning more about elves from someone who wasn't Father dwindled. Not that I minded learning from him. But he seemed to be holding back. Or perhaps I'd forgotten what he'd shared before one of my episodes.

"Well, hope no more. They're gone. But enough of sad tales." She smiled and resumed her stroll, propelling me along to the dirt path leading to the park. As we passed through the trellis, it was as if we'd walked through a megalith to another world. The traffic's normal buzzing, chugging, and whirring sounds filtered through the trees, creating a monotonous hum with occasional squeals in the background. Twittering birds and chattering tree dwellers sounded louder here. Cherry blossoms glided on the breeze like pink sweet-smelling snow.

We followed the windy gravel path beside a groomed stream.

Ruuta fingered a cherry blossom dangling overhead as we passed. "What do you know of the fae?"

"Nothing, really. Only that my mother was one. So, I'm half-fae, half-elf."

"Oh dear, you're so much more than that. You've been here a month already. Has your father taught you nothing?"

"Has it been a month? My memory hasn't been reliable since I arrived in Betören. But it seems to be getting better. I haven't had an episode in a week."

"An episode?" She brought me to a bench, her dainty heels trampling a dandelion as if she didn't see it there.

"Aye." As I sat, I focused on the dandelion. It puffed back up, undisturbed by her carelessness, even as I shrank into myself over what I must admit. "I keep losing my memory. So, I may have been here for a month, but all I remember of being in this realm is from the past week."

Ruuta snapped her fingers over her head at Liam. "Guard!"

Frowning, Liam marched over.

"You're the princess's personal guard, are you not?"

"I am."

"What can you tell me of these 'episodes' in which the princess loses her memory?"

He shrugged, his at-attention stance loosening. "When she first arrived, she seemed to lose her memory every day or two. But she's been improving. She hasn't lost her memory since last week."

"Have you noticed anything about these episodes? Does anything occur before she loses her memory?"

Liam grasped the back of his neck as if searching for a switch that activated his brain.

"Let me guess." Ruuta pressed a finger to her lips. "The princess's memory loss tends to follow a visit with her father. Am I right?"

I sat upright, ready to stand and defend my father. Just what was she insinuating? And who was she, just arrived from Seelie Clós, to make such accusations?

Liam winced as he massaged the back of his neck. Was he concerned about speaking out against Father?

Did Ruuta make him nervous? He wasn't acting himself. I motioned for him to speak. "If you know something, please tell us."

She folded her hands in her lap. "We'll not hold it against you."

He trained his ocean eyes on me and quirked his lips. "I, uh, I've suspected there might be something in the wine he gives you."

Every muscle within me clenched. He, my *defender*, actually believed my father might purposefully be doing something to me? And he never said anything? "What wine?"

"Then my parents were correct. Your father has been erasing your memories."

I scooted away from her, my dress snagging along the triskelion carved into the wooden bench. My fingers shook as I freed my skirt and traced the carving's rough-hewn edges. "My father is a wonderful man. He would never harm me."

Ruuta touched his arm. "Do be a dear and give us a moment."

He gazed at me, awaiting my response.

I pressed my stomach as if I might be able to push away the sick feeling and keep myself from vomiting. "Thank you, Liam."

He studied me as if giving me time to change my mind. "I'll be close."

"Good," Ruuta said. "Scan the perimeter. Ensure we're not overheard."

Who was she to be giving commands? She was starting to make my blood boil. And yet, I couldn't stop her.

Liam threw Ruuta a sidelong glance, then stalked away.

Silence reigned between us as we waited for him to duck out of hearing.

"My sincere apologies, Princess. But you and your guard have confirmed our suspicions."

"What suspicions? Who is 'our'?"

"My family. Queen Rhiannon. After the humans rose up against your father, he cursed them. Were you not aware?"

"No." I sucked in a breath, aghast. Though that somehow sounded familiar. "Cursed them how?"

"They revere him as God."

"G–God? As in... *the* God?"

"Do you not find it strange that all of Talamh Sí so willingly follows your father? There are no disputes. None question a word from his lips. Does that strike you as natural?"

"He's a good king. He provides for his people." But with my throat oddly tight, my words came out weak.

Ruuta tipped her head, giving me an are-you-daft? look. "In no place in all the realms does every subject worship their ruler and serve him or her without question. None."

What she said made sense, but it gave me an icky feeling like I'd swallowed poisonous bugs that swarmed my stomach, spreading a vile sickness. If what she was saying was true, then my father...

"How else could he keep the throne after what he did to the elves?"

"He didn't kill them." I don't know how I knew that, but I knew. Deep in my soul.

"I'm not here to debate history with you. Whatever your father has done and whatever his reasons, he's cursed the humans. And he's harming you too. I trust he may not be able to curse you, but he's manipulating you. The potion he's using, unohtaa, can only affect memories in the faerie realm. That is why you still have memories of wherever you came from. You do have those memories, do you not?"

"I do, but—"

"Do you feel a strong loyalty to your father, whom you scarcely know? And what of auras? Do you see them anymore?"

The breath whooshed from me as if I'd been punched in the stomach. "You see auras?"

"All fae can see auras. Well"—she loosed a shaky laugh—"all but those who've had their minds scrambled by their self-proclaimed deity of a father. Despite your elfin side, I assume then that you can see them too? Or could. Under normal conditions."

"Aye, I mean—I could before I arrived in Betören."

"Not anymore? You don't see mine?"

Something heavy pressing in on me, I shook my head.

"And you're loyal to him, though you've only known him a month." She huffed a graceful, closemouthed laugh. "Well, only a week that you recall."

With my mind reeling, I needed a moment to collect my thoughts. A splinter pricked my fingertip when I pressed it too hard against the carving on the bench.

"So, it's as we suspected. Queen Rhiannon was right to send me. Your father has been ordering large quantities of aivopestä and unohtaa. Aivopestä is the potion that makes the humans think he's God. It won't work on elves. Or fae. But I'm guessing it makes you more... compliant, loyal, amiable. I suspect this information would normally heat your emotions to boiling, yet your aura is dull... subdued."

"You can see my aura?"

"Yes. You still have one. You're not cursed, but you're under a powerful spell."

I swept the shivers from my arms, not wanting to believe her, but... She was telling the truth, wasn't she? "Why would he do such a thing?"

"He wants to see you ascend the throne. What do you think will happen if you don't follow his ways by keeping the people under the spell?"

"They'll think for themselves?"

"Right. They'll no longer blindly follow whoever is on the throne. In fact, once they're free and realize your father has been manipulating them, they're likely to rise against you."

This was bad. Very bad.

She quirked her lips as she appraised me, then patted my hand. "I came here hoping none of these suspicions were true, but I mean it when I say I'm here to help you. I would be negligent to allow your father to continue with his misguided attempts to keep you safe. He doesn't realize there's another way. A better way. And all of Seelie Clós is behind you, supporting you. Queen Rhiannon will do whatever it takes to see you crowned."

"What other way?"

Ruuta reached into the folds of her skirt and pulled out a vial.

"What's that?" I arched away from her.

She pinched the glass between her thumb and pointer finger, swirling the liquid inside. That color. The man in the woods back in Ariboslia... with the top hat. His aura was the same color. I hadn't thought of him in some time. Did he have anything to do with all that happened to me?

"You don't need to follow everything your father says. You're not under the spell. You're free to make your own choices. So is he." She pointed to Liam who ducked his head into an alley.

"How do you know that? What if everyone *wants* to follow him, like me? He's a good man." Why did I keep saying that? And why was my voice even weaker than before? One conversation with Ruuta was making me question everything.

"I know for many reasons, but namely because you have an aura. So does he." She pushed the vial into my hand. "Take this."

I gripped the vial, studying the strange-colored liquid. "What is that?"

"Vastalääke. It will reverse any fae magic. All the memories that were suppressed by fae magic will resurface, and your emotions will normalize. Well, to whatever your emotional state of being was before your father began dosing you."

"Why should I believe you?" I didn't know her from Queen Rhiannon. Did the queen even send her? She could be an impostor sent to throw the kingdom into chaos. "What if you're the one manipulating me?"

She gave me that are-you-daft? look again. "Think it over. You know what I'm saying is true."

How could I protect myself from dueling powers? How could I know who was telling the truth?

Nay. She'd done nothing for me to trust her. I pressed the vial back into her gloved hand. "My apologies, but I just met you. I won't be ingesting anything a stranger gives me."

She appraised me, then gave me an appreciative nod. "As much as I'd like to free you from the spell and help you see clearly, I respect your choice." She returned the vial to her pocket and patted it. "But it will be right here when you're ready. Somehow, I think you'll want to take it sooner rather than later."

FORTY-SEVEN

Ruuta and I stood in the stunning library—my favorite building in all of Talamh Sí. I'd just finished reading to the fourth group of students. Only one more reading to go. Alone with Ruuta, the room was quieter than ever as I admired the intricate yet elegant architecture. Everything in this room revealed people's creativity, from the complex interconnected bronze octagonal and diamond shapes jutting out from the ceiling, giving it more depth, to the domed gables offering more intimate workstations. The tinted windows and dangling lanterns gave off the perfect amount of light for study. And despite the bustling city outside, it was quiet.

It was easier to pretend I didn't have a habit of losing my memory here. Liam was kind enough to remind me of the school administrator's name, Martta, and escort me inside to her every time I came for a reading, so it didn't matter if I'd had an episode or not. Though I hated not asking the children their names for fear of forgetting again.

Martta returned from assisting the teacher in escorting the last group of students back to their classroom. "Princess, thank you for taking time out of your day to read to the students." She folded her hands before her brown pantsuit. With her hair drawn back into a slick bun and no accessories to speak of, she looked bland, especially standing beside Ruuta with her glamor face markings accentuating her beauty.

"It's my pleasure, truly. I get to share stories with adoring children once a week. You have the difficult job of overseeing the school."

Martta waved off the compliment. "You have a short break before the next class. Let me know which book you'd like to read next time, and we'll set it aside. Highness." She bowed before retreating. Her shoes, muffled by the carpet, clacked when they reached the tiled floor and echoed in the large space before fading out into the hallway.

"What do you think?" I asked Ruuta.

"The windows are nice." Her critical gaze scanned the area. "But the story was rather... uninspiring."

"What's wrong with it?"

She narrowed her eyes at me as if, for the first time since arriving, reconsidering her new position. She picked up *Raakel, the King's Faithful Dog* between pinched fingers and dropped it in my hands. "Read it again."

This time, I tried to ignore the cute illustrations and focus on the story rather than speaking aloud in a singsong way to amuse the kids. The message to follow the king without question, as told from the ignorant perspective of the king's mutt, smacked me in the face. Even the title reeked of propaganda. How had I not noticed that before? Why, of all the books in the library, did I have to read this one when Ruuta accompanied me? There had to be something more interesting, especially for the older students who would be in next. "Let's see if we can find something better."

I riffled through the books: *A for Atonement, Aether Makes the World Go, All Things Run on Aether, Antonni's Day of Atonement, Atonement Equals Peace....*

Why were these all about atonement and aether? Didn't anything else begin with A?

Ruuta pulled two books from the shelf, and her face scrunched, making the butterfly markings around her eyes fold their wings.

"Would you care to read *Talamh Sí: The Greatest Kingdom in Betören* or *Tomi and Tuomas Visit the King?*"

My face warmed. I'd done nothing to prove her wrong about my father.

Martta opened the door wide, and chatter filtered through. The teacher led the students past the wooden tables that had been pushed aside to make room on the carpet for them to sit. I made my way to greet them, forcing myself to smile, wishing my heart was still in this. The children always made a fuss over having me in their presence, but today Ruuta got most of their attention. Nothing intelligible stuck out from their murmurings, but their whispers and sidelong stares her way left little doubt as to what had caught their interest.

After I introduced Ruuta and squelched some of their curiosity, they settled down. I moved to my chair and picked up *Raakel, the King's Faithful Dog* for a fifth reading. My cheeks warmed, and my voice refused to cooperate. I drank some water and tried again.

My voice worked again, but I couldn't bring myself to read with the same enthusiasm. I sputtered, tripped on the words, and struggled to turn the pages. I think I skipped one. The children gave each other quizzical looks, but I didn't go back to correct my mistake.

The painful reading came to a merciful end. I placed the book beside me, wanting to purge my soul of whatever damage I contributed to in these impressionable youths.

"Well..." Martta pressed her hands together. "Thank you for that interesting reading, Princess. Does anyone have any questions for the princess?"

Please, please, please don't have questions.

A hand shot up.

"Yes." I pointed to the boy with an aviator hat and goggles. "I love your hat. Do you hope to become a pilot?"

The boy brightened. "I do. I applied for the aeronautics program."

"That is one benefit of reaching the age of atonement, exploring different opportunities before choosing your profession." I gave myself a mental pat on the back for keeping the conversation positive, despite my strange mood.

"I'm very excited about that." The boy's face grew somber. "But I'm worried about the Atonement ceremony."

I gripped the book tighter as I willed myself to be encouraging. "Have you spoken with your parents about it?"

"I—" The boy ducked his head from his classmates. "My parents are dead—an accident at the aether plant."

"Oh." I frowned. "I grew up as an orphan too." I wanted to know if it had been recent, but I couldn't bring myself to ask. "What about the family you live with now?"

The boy shook his head, jostling the straps of his aviator cap. "I haven't been placed yet. I'm still staying at the Interim Housing for Displaced Children."

So, his parents had died recently. Or there was a delay in placing him with a family. Either way, my heart broke for him. "I see." Although he could ask others, I opted not to continue pushing his question aside. "What is it you want to know?"

"Before my parents died"—he threw his teacher and Martta a wary glance, then swallowed before focusing on me—"they told me not to be atoned."

Martta clapped her hands, loudly. The kids snapped their attention to her as she waded through the students toward the boy. "Pauli, please come with me."

Pauli grasped her extended hand and allowed her to help him up, but he set his bewildered gaze upon me, his panic palpable. "But—"

"Come." Martta tugged him to follow. "You have some personal questions the princess should address in private. We'll wait in my office."

He stopped short, making Martta lunge backward before righting herself. His pleading eyes trained on me. "You will come see me?"

"Of course, I will." I tried to sound confident, but why was Martta tearing him away? Couldn't we go together after the clock chimed the end of class?

I didn't want to look at Ruuta, certain of her smug expression. But morbid curiosity turned my head her way. Her expression mimicked the children's shock.

The class turned, murmuring among themselves as Martta dragged their classmate from the library.

FORTY-EIGHT

Ruuta whispered in my ear. "We need to find out where they're taking that boy. Now."

I agreed, but many eyes watched me. "I'm sure he's in Martta's office. We can talk to him after class."

"I don't think so." Ruuta tugged me from my chair.

"My apologies." I waved to the baffled teacher as Ruuta dragged me out of the room. "I'll answer your questions next week." I'd barely gotten the full sentence out before reaching the hallway.

"Where's Martta's office?" Ruuta asked.

"This way."

Staccato clicks echoed in the hallway as we raced to the office.

"Your Highness." Martta's secretary jumped up with wild eyes before curtsying. "How may I assist you?"

"I'd like to see Martta. And Pauli."

Her already wide eyes stretched further. "I beg your pardon, Highness. But Martta already left with the boy."

My gut clenched. "She said they'd be here." Why would Martta leave without giving me the opportunity to speak to him? She heard my promise. Was she making me a liar?

Ruuta smacked the desk. "Where did they take him?"

The secretary burst into tears. "I'm sorry, Your Highness. I don't know. I never know."

Ruuta and I stormed out of the school, searching the street for any sign of them. How did they disappear? We dashed to where Liam propped against the car.

He straightened, eyes wide at our hurried approach. His hand drifted toward his weapon. "What happened?"

"Did you see Martta leave here with a boy?" I asked.

"No one has come or gone since I arrived." He checked his time-piece. "About an hour ago."

Creeping crabs, they must've gone out the back. "Where would they take a child who refuses atonement?"

Liam's thick eyebrows pinched together as he drew his head back. "Has that ever happened?"

"It's happening now." I jumped into the back seat and scooted over for Ruuta. Liam sat in front beside the driver, Vilppu.

I bent to speak to Vilppu. "Where is my father?"

Vilppu revved the engine to life. "Tied up in court."

I huffed. This had to be yet another unpleasant result of the aether shortage. What an inconvenient time for this to happen. I needed to find the boy. How could I do that without my father's help?

What made me so certain the boy needed help? Martta cared for the children. I had no reason to believe anything bad would become of him. Was this Ruuta's influence? I eyed her, but I only found genuine concern. A nagging feeling insisted I must find him straight-away. "Take me to the Interim Housing for Displaced Children."

"As you wish, Princess." Vilppu put the vehicle in gear and drove into the afternoon traffic.

I'd grown to appreciate the continuous hum of vehicles bustling through the streets. But I'd barely had a minute to think before we arrived at our destination. What was my plan? Who would I talk to?

Vilppu parked before a row of townhouses. Each structure was identical but for the differing neutral-colored brick with one flat wall with arched windows beside a rounded tower. The words *Interim Housing for Displaced Children Office* arched in black over a brass sign. I made my way up the steps, trancelike, gripping the wrought-iron railing with Ruuta and Liam in tow.

I turned the buzzer key. Once I released it, a grating ring squealed inside until the key returned to its original position. Heels clicking on hardwood approached, and the door slid open.

A woman with tinted glasses and gray curls peeking beneath her top hat beamed. "Princess!" She curtsied. "So good of you to visit us again."

Again? Nothing about this place seemed familiar.

The woman stumbled out of Ruuta's path as she barged inside. "And you've brought a visitor."

I forced a smile and stepped into a sitting room.

"You don't have to ring the buzzer during office hours. You're welcome to come right in. Have a seat." The woman gestured to a seating area. "Can I get you anything? Tea? A biscuit?"

A maid curtsied and awaited our request.

"Nothing, thank you," I said.

Liam stood at attention as Ruuta and I took up seats. I wanted to ask her name, but if I'd been here before, that would be insulting.

The woman waved the servant off and smoothed her dress as she sat. "Does this have anything to do with Kaarle? Your father showed him great kindness by giving him a place in his royal defense."

The maid brandished her feather duster and dusted a lantern behind the woman.

"N–No." Kaarle? Who in Betören was she talking about? Had I met him before one of my episodes? "I'm looking for a boy named Pauli. I understand he lives here."

The woman straightened. "I was on the phone with Martta's assistant. She informed me that Pauli, too, will take a position on your father's royal defense. Are you helping your father recruit? Pauli was applying to the aeronautics program. But your father wouldn't withhold a child's opportunity if he didn't have something better planned."

"Of course not." But my conviction wavered. Had whatever happened to Pauli happened to another boy in the past? "Do you know where Martta took him?"

I caught the maid's gaze, and she snapped her attention back toward the lampstand. She hyperfocused on one spot, licked her thumb, and rubbed the blemish... if there was one.

The woman narrowed her eyes as though she suspected I was an impostor. "You would know better than I. Whenever your father recruits one of my wards, they don't return from school for their belongings. Not that they own much. But I assume your father ensures they receive all they need." She stared at me in such a way that I wanted to shrink. Then she stood, smoothing her dress once more. "If that's all, I have much business to attend to."

"Of course." I followed her, eyeing the maid watching us.

The woman held the door for us. She curtsied as we passed. "Good day."

Defeated and confused, I tromped down the steps to the awaiting car. Ruuta grasped my arm, keeping me from entering.

"What is it?" I asked.

"Give it a wink. I believe the maid—"

"Your Highness, Your Highness!" The maid hurried down the steps, her long skirts gathered in one hand, her duster waving in the other.

Her uncertain gaze bounced from the others to me.

Taking the hint, I held a hand up to keep them at bay as I approached her. "Aye?"

Her gaze darted up and down the street before her words rushed out in a hushed tone. "Check the processing center."

"Where's the processing center?"

"In the Atonement building. The basement. That's where they brought the boy. That's where they bring all the children who refuse to atone."

"Oh, bless you!" I dashed back to the car, hurrying to my seat beside Ruuta. "To the Atonement building."

Vilppu swung into traffic.

I laid a hand on Ruuta's. "How did you know the maid would come out?"

She shrugged. "She had an aura, and I had a hunch."

FORTY-NINE

The Atonement building lay at the northernmost point of
Talamh Sí. Giving us plenty of time to think and overthink,
Vilppu navigated the city and backcountry roads where
civilization disappeared. Nothing but trees and farmland met us out
here.

Aside from the library, this was one of the most beautiful places
in all of Talamh Sí. The atonement building rose from the trees'
midst. Three conical roofs with spires pierced the sky. The center
towered several feet above the others flanking its sides.

We drove up the smooth drive lined with a well-manicured lawn
cut to resemble a green chessboard to an iron gate. A sentry vacated
the gatehouse and opened the gate as we approached.

"Why is there so much iron?" Ruuta asked, but judging from her
tone, she wasn't looking for an answer.

"Do you dislike iron?" I asked.

"Fae are allergic." She squinted at me. "Has it never burned
you?"

"No. It *burns*?"

"And never completely heals. Fae can hide the injuries with

enchantments and take potions for the pain, but it's best avoided." She wiggled her gloved fingers. "That's why I wear gloves. I remember the humans' infatuation with all things iron." She returned her gaze to her window. "Your elf half must render you immune."

A burn that never healed. I shuddered. Thank God I hadn't inherited that quality. That would have been terrible to learn the hard way. Already I'd learned more from Ruuta in one day than I'd learned in the week I remembered with my father. And the day wasn't over yet.

The first time I saw the wrought-iron gate, I thought it was beautiful. Now I wondered—Why was a place where adolescents and their loved ones expressed and celebrated their decision to follow their king so guarded?

The opulent architecture sprawled out before us. Its circular center housed the massive auditorium. Stairs rising to imposing pillars lined the magnificent entryway protruding from the center. Twin wings jutted out from both sides, beginning with two towers surrounding the spiral staircases leading to the upper levels. The rest of the wings were shorter, rectangular offshoots with ornate windows.

How many times had I been here? I only remembered two visits —once for a tour with my father and another for an atonement ceremony. Both times, the building had taken my breath away, but there was something about the ceremony. Everyone dressed in their finest clothes. Not a digit of space existed between them as they filed up the stairway into the grand foyer to the auditorium. Some entered the main doors on the floor level, while others climbed one of two staircases skirting the foyer to the upper level. Those with seats either on the third or fourth level took a spiral staircase. The joyful chatter, shuffling feet, wisps of varying perfumes... all brought the building to life.

I appreciated watching all that from the balcony above, not in their midst. My chest compressed as I shivered over all those bodies so tightly packed together.

We exited the car. The main entryway only opened during ceremonies, so we followed the pristine stone path to the entrance on the left wing. I pressed the buzzer.

Bzzzzzzt.

The sound echoed in the empty hall.

"Good afternoon, Your Highness." An usher bowed, gripping his red cap to his chest. He replaced his hat and smoothed his red jacket.

Now what? I didn't know the way to the processing center. But what if I'd visited before and didn't remember? It shouldn't cause too much alarm to ask to be escorted. "Please take us to the processing center."

"Of course." The attendant turned down the hall toward the auditorium. "King Auberon hasn't arrived yet." He checked the time-piece dangling from his pocket. "There's still an hour before the proceedings. Would you care to wait?"

"Aye." Perhaps he wouldn't see through me.

"Very well." The usher swiveled on his feet. "Follow me."

Ruuta ungloved her hands and circled the usher to face him. She reached under her neckline and freed something attached to a chain. A stone. Black with purple sparkles. She gripped it tight in one hand and the usher's shoulder in the other. Her already brilliant eyes blazed as she stared into his. Neither blinked.

"You will lead us to the processing center, then return to your post, and forget we were here."

The usher's irises widened.

"You will say nothing of our visit to the king." Ruuta released him and replaced her gloves.

"I will say nothing...." The way his body moved reminded me of a robot the engineers were working on. "I will say nothing...."

"What did you do to him?" I avoided his eyes. That vacant gaze was the stuff of nightmares.

"A compulsion enchantment. He'll return to himself with scant more than a niggling headache."

Liam leaned in and whispered loudly, "Still think she's harmless, Princess?"

She replaced an errant blonde hair to her updo. "You allow a servant—a mere *human*—to speak to you that way?"

"I'm sure I've got some iron on me." He patted down his pockets.

"Careful, human." She clutched her stone. "Unless you want me to scramble your brain like an egg."

"Stop!" Would this be my life now—in the constant company of two boorish servants determined to argue?

"Good thing he's cute." Ruuta smoothed her hair should any others have deviated from their proper place as we followed the mindless automaton down the corridor.

We passed unoccupied offices and meeting rooms. After I'd seen the place so full of life, it seemed... dead. A body without a soul. The usher led us to a room resembling a birdcage, surrounded by iron bars leading to a peaked ceiling. The bronze floor wobbled when we crowded inside.

"Lovely. More iron," she mumbled.

"I will say nothing...." The attendant closed the outer door. We shuffled aside to allow him to close an interior barred gate, sealing us inside the cage. He reached through the bars and yanked a lever.

Grinding gears whirred as the floor seemed to fall out from beneath me, knocking me off-balance. I grasped the bar. "What's happening?"

Liam gripped my arm, steadying me. "Still not used to lifts, Princess?"

"A lift?" The walls moved as we descended. "Is that what this contraption is? A room that goes up and down rather than stairs? Seems rather extravagant when simple stairs would do. And why call it a lift when it's *lowering* us down?"

Liam huffed, shaking his head at me. "It will make more sense on the return trip."

"I suppose, but why not call it a lift and drop? Or an up and down? Or a vertical transport?"

A number above the gears flipped from *1* to *0* while the platform lined up with another door. I swayed despite Liam's grip as it jerked to a stop.

The usher slid the doors open with a squeal. "I will say nothing...."

We followed him along the dark corridor. Dim light bulbs in cages dangled overhead every few cubits. Why were they enclosed in cages? Did they have a light bulb thief in their midst? Such "shades" did nothing to dim or direct the light. And there was no threat of a burn from such weak bulbs. They created odd shadows, making the entire hall feel ominously like a cage.

The attendant pressed a button beside double doors, and they swung open to the back of an auditorium. But, unlike the lofty auditorium upstairs lined with balconies, dressed in red velvet, and decorated with gold embellishments, this dingy space offered no decoration, no cushions covering the folding chairs... nothing to warm the sad replica. I ran a finger along the back of a chair. It came up grimy.

The usher turned to leave, but Ruuta gripped him and her stone and stared her magic into him again. "Is there a place we can hide?"

"I will say nothing...." The empty-headed usher moved down the steps past the rows of seats to the bottom of the stage. He skirted the front row to the paneled wall and shoved. Part of the wall opened. I stuck my head into the dark space to find two seats and some standing room.

"Thank you for your assistance." Ruuta locked eyes with him again. "You may go and forget you saw us now."

"I will say nothing...." The usher swiveled and wandered back the way we'd come.

"What if another usher or a defender finds him in that state?" I fidgeted.

"Never fret." She waved it off. "They'll follow him to his post—and he 'will say nothing.'"

I sat in a seat. An iron grate obscured the hideout but offered a perfect view of the stage.

"Oh joy, more iron."

"Why is there a hiding place with seats?" Someone put this here.

Liam and Ruuta offered nothing but shrugs.

"We have time." Mischievousness crinkled up Ruuta's gossamer butterfly marks. "Let's investigate."

FIFTY

Unlike upstairs, no curtain covered the stage. We crossed the platform to a rusty door and peeked through the grimy window. Another dimly lit corridor. I stepped aside to allow Liam and Ruuta to see.

"It's empty." Liam's hand hovered by his holster.

She pushed the door, but I gripped the handle, keeping it closed.

Everything within me itched. Maybe this was a bad idea. "I don't like this. What if we stumble upon something we shouldn't?"

"That's why we must investigate." Ruuta attempted to push the door again, but I held on. She steepled her fingers to her lips. "I understand your concern. You've investigated missing children before, but each time, your father found out and—" She made a slashing movement as people often do at the neck to illustrate death, but she did it at her head. "But not to worry. I'm here now. No one will alter your memories."

"If what you're saying is true, what makes you think you can stand up to my father?"

"Powerful allies."

I rolled my eyes. "Without your memory, you wouldn't know to ask your 'allies' for help."

Her tinkly laughter somehow desecrated the dismal place. "Do you think I wouldn't come prepared? Nothing Auberon has at his disposal can penetrate the fae magic protecting me. I can do the same for you, the minute you decide to trust me."

"Take nothing from her." Liam stepped between us.

I groaned at them and thrust the door open with more confidence than I should've had.

Claaang! SCREEeeeeee!

I froze with a cringe, my curled fingers hovering midair. My courage ebbed as I held my breath, listening for an onslaught of tromping feet.

Liam elbowed past me on the right, shaking his head. Ruuta and I followed. Unlike the prior hallway, iron doors lined this one's sides. They had slits below what appeared to be a sliding mechanism.

Liam and I crowded around the first door we came to. Ruuta hung back. Probably because... iron. He put a finger to his lips, then eased the slider aside, revealing a slim barred window. Our heads pressed together as we peered inside.

A room with rough-cut rock walls. Was this a cell? It looked comfortable with two lamps giving off a soft light, a cushioned chair, a wooden secretary's desk with a matching armoire, a plant on a stand, and a red bed covering. A changing screen doubled as a headboard.

Leave it to my father to cozy up the jail cells. He was always thinking of others' comfort—even prisoners. He probably considered them guests, not captives.

"No one's here."

"Why are the lights on?" Liam gave the room one last look before sliding the window panel closed.

We moved across the hall to the next room. Identical to the first, this one wasn't empty. A man in an ivory robe and leggings sat in the comfy armchair beneath a lamp, reading.

An icky feeling swept over me since he might catch us watching him. I ducked.

"Who's there?" The voice came from inside the cell.

Liam slammed the cover shut and whispered, "He saw me."

Bang! Bang! Bang!

"Who's out there?" The voice filtered through the feeding tray slit where eyes peered out at us.

We all backed away. I moved to the next cell.

"Are you insane? We're going to get caught." He consulted his timepiece. "We'd better get back."

"But what about Pauli? I came here for the boy. He must be here somewhere. I have to find him."

"We'll come back when the proceedings are over, and the defenders have left." He didn't hide his impatience as he motioned for me to follow him.

Slam! Slam! Bang!

"I hear you out there. Let me go! You've no right to keep me in here. Let me out. Let me out!"

Voices and clattering sounded at the opposite end of the corridor. My head snapped in that direction. People were coming. Probably defenders. Ruuta, Liam, and I exchanged horrified glances. My body struggled to keep up with my feet as we dashed back the way we'd come, past the man watching us through the opening.

Liam flung the door open, ushered us inside, then pulled it shut, silencing the anxiety-inducing sounds. Panting, I dared to peek through the window to find two defenders inspecting the man's room. One fumbled with a key in the lock.

I shot back down. We huddled together below the window, catching our breath, before sneaking back to the hole in the wall.

It felt like mere seconds had passed when the lights snapped on, brightening the dingy auditorium. Disturbed dust particles danced in its glow. Two ushers entered with my father. Their marching footfalls echoed in the chamber. They led him to his throne to the left of the stage. I pushed back into the shadow, hoping he couldn't see us.

The ushers departed. Doors slammed. Two more defenders appeared, dragging a prisoner between them. They attached his cuffed hands to a table and sat him in a chair. Once they stepped aside, the prisoner's face came into view—the man who'd screamed at us in the hallway.

A defender handed my father a file.

Sitting tall on his throne, the lights highlighting the golden glints in his short white hair and the flawless skin on his face—*my* face—my father leafed through the papers. "Are you Floyd O'Malley?"

The man fought the restraints. "Release me! I've done nothing wrong."

"Leave us." My father waved, and the defenders vacated. Slamming doors followed their departure. Only my father and the prisoner remained. "You are part of the rebel group known as the Saoirse Trodaí, are you not?"

"I don't know what you're talking about."

"Your denial is unnecessary. I'm not here to torture the information out of you. But I must act to protect my peaceful city."

The prison's face mottled a blotchy red. "You have no right to do anything to me."

"Am I not king of Talamh Sí?" Father's full lips thinned out, his small mouth pinching tight. "Have I not the right to do as I deem fit for the benefit of my people?"

"You're lying to them." The man rattled his cuffed hands against the metal table. "Do you think they'd act as they do if they knew you aren't God?"

"Certainly not." Father settled back in his throne, head cocked to one side, one thick white brow rising. "But history has shown us what happens when people think and act freely. The things they do to one another—and even themselves—are horrific. By following me, they have what they need. They have peace. They are content."

"Not once they're free of you and realize what you've done to them."

"What harm have I done to you, Floyd?" Father tugged a piece of paper from the file and placed it on top. "It states here you're employed in the aether power plant. You live in a modest unit on Alvar Rivitalot with your wife and two children. You receive a monthly allotment of food and clothing. Your son receives sugar-balancing injections, and your daughter has teeth alignments. Is that correct?"

The man glared but said nothing.

"Is anything about your living arrangements unsatisfactory?" Father waited but received no response. "Is your house in disrepair? Are your children in need of medical care or education? Do I not provide all these things for you?"

Still nothing.

"What, pray tell, is your grievance against me?"

"Y–y–you've taken away our right to think for ourselves, our freedom."

Father smoothed his white buttoned shirt, the gold stitching and embellishments winking in the dim light. His Adam's apple bobbed above his high neckline. "Don't you think that's a rather small price to pay for comfort and security for you and your family?"

The man's jaw hardened. "You're no god."

"If there is a God, do you think He would care for you as I have?"

My heart pounded as I clenched my fists at my sides. I wanted to shout—to stand up for the real God. To tell my father it didn't work that way. But I had to remain hidden. Silent.

"That you work in the power plant and someone within my city nullified you from my cure for humanity has me curious. Thieves have grown bolder as of late, stealing my supply from the aether plant and my shipments from Seelie Clós. It must stop. If you give me a name, I shall be lenient."

Floyd's red face darkened.

Father rested idle hands on his armrests, crossing one leg over the other. So calm and relaxed. "Your wife and children are good citizens. I'd hate to bring them into this."

Floyd blanched. "You monster!"

"It's not something I want to do, trust me. But that's one difficulty of being king. I must do what is necessary for the good of the majority. There is a threat against them, so I ask you—Who is stealing aether from the good citizens of Talamh Sí?" Father clasped his hands together in his lap. "Is it so important to you to protect thieves? Over your family?"

"What will happen to them?"

"To whom? The thieves? Or your family?"

"Any of them."

"Well, that depends on what I find. I despise killing. Nasty, gruesome business. Expunging memories is much cleaner."

"What will become of me?"

"I'll expunge your memories. You'll never see your family again."

"Can't you put me back under the curse?"

"Why does everyone keep calling it a c—" Father's voice rose in speed and pitch until he cut himself off and pinched the bridge of his nose. "No one who would dare consider my grace a curse is deserving of such a gift. But regardless, my cure for humanity's ills cannot be administered twice. All attempts to do so have failed. The only options are to expunge your memory or kill you. As much as I despise the latter, I will do so. If that is your wish."

"If I have no memory, where will I go? What will I do?"

"What I do with all my nullified citizens—your family will receive news of your death in an aether plant accident that will render your body unfit for viewing. I will employ you in my royal defense. You will patrol the remote edges of the kingdom to ensure our borders remain safe or scout the unseelie lands for growing threats."

The man blinked, his jaw and shoulders going slack, his eyes dull. "You'd send me to the Forest of Shadows?"

"Not without proper equipment, but yes. It's a possibility. Whatever happens, I'll ensure you're far from any who might recognize you. It's a merciful punishment."

"Punishment." Floyd slapped the table with his manacled hand. "I've done no wrong."

"You committed treason by consorting with my enemies."

"If I give up a name, what will become of my wife and children?"

"They will mourn their spouse and father, but their lives will continue as they have. Your children will be atoned when they come of age, as is customary. They will receive occupations, homes, spouses. They will be well provided for, as you were."

"And if I don't give up the name?"

"I will have their memories expunged as well. Since I can't expunge the memories of every acquaintance, they will be subject to the same fate as you. Their unfortunate deaths will be publicized, and they will become members of my defense in remote areas or servants in a remote village."

"Even my daughter?" Floyd choked.

"If your children grow to be unrecognizable and are atoned, I may allow them to reassimilate into society. But I can't make any promises."

Floyd slumped in his seat. "Taneli. Taneli O'Rourke."

FIFTY-ONE

Taneli. Why did that name sound familiar? My intestines twisted like a clump of intertwined slithering snakes fighting to disentangle themselves as defenders ushered Floyd off the stage. How could my father speak of erasing memories as if it was inconsequential?

Everything Ruuta had said made sense. It was the only logical explanation for what was happening to me. The moment we had an opportunity, I'd drink her antidote. I needed a clear mind with all my memories intact for whatever was to come.

Defenders returned. The same ones or different, I couldn't tell. They all looked alike in their uniforms. But this time they carried a boy in their grip—Pauli. Tears streamed down his face.

I sucked in a breath, then clamped my hand over my mouth. My heart writhed as the defenders sat Pauli down, clasping his wrists to the table. My fists shook. I fought the urge to storm the place, to free him from this injustice.

Father grasped the file from the defender and riffled through it. "Are you Pauli Sullivan?"

Pauli nodded.

"Were you aware your parents were traitors to the crown?"

Pauli shook his head.

"Is that why you don't want to become atoned? Your parents forbade you?"

"I–I—" Pauli burst into audible sobs.

Father plucked something from inside his coat and flicked it free. A handkerchief. "There, there, son. There's no need to cry." He rose and dabbed the boy's eyes. "Free the boy's hands. He's no threat."

His kindness calmed my shaking somewhat, but still livid, I wanted to scoop up the boy and run off with him.

Pauli's sobs subsided as the defender freed his hands.

"There." Father returned to his seat. "Is that better?"

Pauli smashed his fists into his eyes.

"You're a smart boy. Good grades." Father flipped through the papers. "I see you're interested in the aeronautics program, is that right?"

"Y–yes, Ma–Majesty."

"I can make that happen for you. Would you like that?"

"Y–yes." He smiled through his tears.

"You need to be atoned to be admitted into that program."

Pauli hugged himself. "I w–wanted to ask the princess if it would hurt."

My writhing heart stilled and split in two. Why oh why, didn't they let the boy ask and avoid all this?

Father's frown twisted up his small mouth. "You planned to pledge yourself to my service, despite your parents' wishes?"

Pauli bowed his head. "I–I never understood why they didn't want me to be atoned. They wouldn't tell me. I–I thought it might hurt."

Father returned to Pauli and drew him into a hug. "My boy, I assure you it doesn't hurt. And I will accept you into the program. How would you feel about being atoned early and going straight into the program instead of returning to school and the Interim Housing?"

"Where would I stay?"

"You'll need to stay here until you're atoned, but after that, I'll send you to live with the other aeronautics students."

"How long is that?"

"I can arrange for someone to come out to you this evening for your atonement."

"Don't I have to wait for a ceremony?"

Father waved the thought away. "That's merely a public profession for something that is already done."

"Oh."

"Come." Father took his hand. "I'll bring you back to your room. But it's only until tonight. Can you stay here that long?"

"I think so."

Father turned to the defenders. "That was all for today. Send defenders to search for Taneli O'Rourke, a physician to expunge Floyd O'Malley, and a priest to atone Pauli Sullivan, then deliver him to the aeronautics dormitory."

We waited in our hiding spot, silent, until all footsteps and door slams ceased.

"We need to free them," Ruuta spoke my mind.

"But how?" I asked. "We don't have a key."

"I can get one." She clutched the stone from under her neckline. "Wait here." She stormed off.

"Wait." I rose to follow her, but Liam grabbed my arm, rooting me.

"Let her go. I can't risk your father erasing your memories again... or mine. We need to remember what we've seen here today."

"So, you believe Ruuta? You'll let me take the antidote?"

"If she helps us free them, yes. But I'm taking it first, understood?"

"But if something happ—"

"If something happens to me, don't drink it. Tell your father. Make sure she's exposed."

"I don't like this plan."

The door to our hideaway opened, and Liam smacked his head on the low ceiling.

"Got it." Ruuta held up a key on a giant ring.

"Isn't that iron?" I asked.

"I'm wearing gloves." She shrugged and handed Liam the key. A wicked smile spread up her cheeks rounding out those gossamer wings as if this was the most exciting thing she imagined doing today. "Let's go free them."

We peeked through the window, sneaked through the door, and tiptoed down the hall to Floyd's cell. Liam jiggled the lock.

Floyd's face appeared in the tray slot. "Let me ou—"

"Shhh!" Ruuta and I hushed him.

"If you want to save your family, shut it." Liam pushed the door. "Come with us... and be quiet or so help me...."

Floyd followed. "Are you with the Saoirse Trodaí?"

"Something like that." Liam guided Floyd into the hall.

We checked several cells before finding Pauli.

"Pauli," I whispered through the slot.

"Princess?" He rose from the bed and neared.

"Yes. We're going to get you out of here, but you must be quiet. Okay?"

Liam unlocked the door.

Pauli returned to the bed. He picked up his legs and clutched them to his chest, shaking his head. "No, no. King Auberon is going to let me into his aeronautics program. I'm going to atone today."

I sat on the bed beside him. "Pauli, do you know what it means to atone?"

"It means I pledge my service to the king."

"There's more to it than that." Ruuta wiggled a gloved hand, the motion almost hypnotic. "It's an unseelie curse that will make you think King Auberon is God. You won't be able to think for yourself anymore. He will take away your freedom."

On the bed beside him, I jostled his shoulder with mine. "That's why your parents didn't want you to do it."

Pauli buried his face in his knees and rocked.

What have I done? Did I break the boy? I looked to the others for advice. "What should I do?"

Ruuta sat on Pauli's other side. "We're planning to free everyone from the curse."

My head snapped up.

She rubbed the boy's back. "You can stay here and wait until we free everyone or come with us now. Either way, we'll help you."

His wet lashes clumped together. "Where will you take me?"

"There's a hideout. I'll make sure you get there safely."

The boy picked at his pant leg. "What if you're wrong?"

"I'm not wrong, but unlike the king, I won't steal your freedom to choose. If you want to stay, stay. Otherwise, come with us." She got up and met Liam and Floyd in the hallway.

I followed, monitoring Pauli, staring into his wide, teary eyes. The crack in my heart widened with each step I took away from him. I began to pull the door shut.

"Wait!" He hopped off the bed and launched himself into me.

I hugged him tight and fled with him down the hall after the others.

FIFTY-TWO

We made it to the lift. Liam operated the rickety thing, bringing us back up to the main level.

"Can you hide them?" Ruuta asked me, pointing to Floyd and Pauli.

"Hide them? How?"

"Can you not create a veil? Most fae can. I can't, but"—she tapped the stone under her neckline—"I can compel the defenders to forget us if necessary."

"I think you'll have to." My heart was thudding hard. "If I can create a veil, I don't know how."

"Very well. Follow my lead."

We rounded the corner, and the sentry on duty saw us coming. "Good evening, Your High—" His eyes flicked from me to the others. "You're taking the prisoners?"

Ruuta grasped her stone. Her eyes blazed as she connected with the man's arm. "Defenders have taken the prisoners per Auberon's command. Two unfamiliar defenders. You will not remember seeing us. Once we are out of your sight, you will return to your senses, but you will only remember seeing the defenders leaving with the prisoners."

"Two unfamiliar defenders," the sentry muttered.

She smiled and released her grip. Her eyes returned to normal. "Very good."

We walked outside, the door closing between us.

"Two unfamiliar—"

"Now what? Vilppu is waiting for us, but only us." I motioned between me, Ruuta, and Liam. "Not them."

"There's a break in the fence in the northeast corner." Floyd placed a hand on Pauli's shoulder. "I can take the boy to the hideout."

This was all too much. I rubbed at my throbbing temples. "What hideout?"

"It's a cottage in the woods. He'll be safe there. And I can warn Taneli." A green hue shadowed Floyd's face. "Please, find my family. My address is Alvar Rivitalot Unit 4. Tie a red ribbon around the exhaust pipe. That's the signal for my family to meet me at the hideout should it come to the worst."

I nodded. "We'll make sure they get the message."

AFTER WE RETURNED to the castle, we sent Iida to Floyd's house to warn his family. It seemed everyone around me knew much more than I did. How much had I forgotten? Was any of it necessary to rid this realm of Auberon's Curse? If Ruuta was right and could restore my memories, I had to know. Once we entered my private quarters, I whirled on her and Liam. "Time to take the antidote."

"Uh-uh, Princess." Liam pushed me aside. "Auberon hasn't been around with his wine, so you must remember our deal—I'm first."

Ruuta found her things in the alcove where Iida used to sleep. She pulled two vials from one of her bags, uncorked one, and gave it to Liam.

"How much am I supposed to drink?"

"The whole thing."

"No." He thrust it back into her hand. "I'm drinking the same thing as the princess."

Ruuta sighed but gave him an appreciative look. She retrieved two vials, mixed them in a larger bottle, then poured them back into the vials in even doses. She handed the vials to Liam and me. "Better?"

"Yes." He saluted me with the vial. "Don't let her switch that potion for another." He lifted it to his lips.

"You might want to—"

He tipped the contents into his mouth.

"—sit."

His eyes rolled back in his head, and he slumped to the floor.

She rolled her eyes. "Help me move him to the couch."

We each seized an upper arm and dragged him, then attempted to pick him up onto the couch before deciding to leave him leaning against it on the floor.

"How long will he be out?" I asked.

"For a fae, ten minutes at most. But I haven't had many interactions with humans in Seelie Clós so..." She shrugged, throwing me an almost apologetic smile. "As I understand it, humans are more susceptible to fae magic, so he might be out longer."

The clocks ticked the minutes by as I paced, wringing my hands together, staring at Liam's lolled head resting on the cream seat cushion, awaiting any movement. An eye to open. A finger to twitch. Anything.

Please, God. Make him wake. Let nothing bad happen to him.

After fifteen minutes, almost on the dot, he groaned.

I dropped to his side. "Are you all right?"

"Princess?" His eyebrows raised, but his eyelids didn't care to follow. Then he jerked as if poked with a needle. "Colleen?" His neck jerked every which way as he got his bearings and scrambled off the floor.

"A little informal with the princess, are we?" Ruuta arched a brow.

"Easy, easy." I helped him to the couch.

"You—" He pointed at me, then to Ruuta. "She—"

She flickered her gloved fingers. "What do you remember?"

He clutched his head and groaned. "Everything."

"Anything specific?"

He squeezed his eyes shut as if he needed to block his senses to focus on his memories. "Patrolling an abandoned elfin village. A veiled Saoirse Trodaí village. They surrounded me. I fired my weapon. They forced me to drink something. A cure. My life was a lie. Auberon, he—"

"Yes, we're well aware of what Auberon has done. But what do you remember since being freed from the curse?" Ruuta flounced onto the couch beside him. "What brought you back into the city?"

"The Saors convinced me to bring Colleen to her father."

The way he looked at me—like he was remembering many things I'd forgotten—made me feel naked. "My turn."

Springing to her feet, my flighty lady-in-waiting flung out an arm at Liam as if he were a successful project. I sat first, getting myself into a position where I wouldn't go far when I passed out, uncorked my vial, and drank. The bitter liquid warmed my tongue and throat in its descent. A bright flash of light crossed my vision, and all went black.

FIFTY-THREE

I woke in Liam's arms. His dark hair spilled into his turbulent ocean eyes. I raised a hand to touch his face, then reality set in. Why was my head in his lap? My face warmed, and I jerked upward, my head catching his chin. A sharp jolt shot through me, and I recoiled.

"Ow!" We both winced. I clutched the sore spot as he rubbed his chin.

"Sorry!" My hand vacillated between reaching out to his chin and feeling for a lump on my forehead. "What happened? Did I fall asleep?"

"You took the antidote, remember?" He worked his jaw.

Ruuta moved to sit on the couch, but Liam pushed us both over so I was up against the arm, leaving only the space beside him. Was he trying to protect me from her? My heart warmed, misguided though his loyalty may be.

"How do you feel?" Head tipped to one side, blue eyes as alight as the corresponding glamor on her face, she watched me with extreme interest.

The low-grade headache I thought was my new normal was gone. Other than that, I didn't feel much different. But... "I can see your auras."

"Huh?" Liam cocked his head like a confused pup.

Creeping crabs, I'd only been thinking about what I could share with Ruuta, not Liam. I wasn't built for keeping secrets.

She clapped her gloved hands, then pressed them to her lips as if watching an infant take their first steps. Glee lit her luminescent blue eyes as her aura surged and brightened. "What do you remember?"

I shuddered at everything that had happened to me since following the cat through the megalith. Nay, not a cat. A *dragon*. I gasped. "I'm—" I almost said I was bonded to a dragon, but I couldn't trust Ruuta. Still, something in me broke. All this time I'd wasted... and Iisakki was out there somewhere. Was he safe? Was he alone? I had to find him.

"Yes? You're what?" She leaned in close.

"I—" I had to give her a reason for my sadness. She could see my blue aura. "I miss my family." Not a lie. I did miss my family. And Iisakki was my family now too.

She quirked her lips and gave me a sympathetic nod. "That's understandable. But what do you remember?"

I thought back to Rhys. Then Pirkko, Reko, and Taneli. Illegally boarding a train. The elfin village beyond the veil. The Saoirse Trodaí. Liam.

Liam! "You tried to convince me to stay behind. You feared me going to my father. You were right." Something stirred in the pit of my stomach as I stared into his eyes' watery depths. More memories swept over me. "The hail storm. I stitched your leg—"

"And stepped in front of a gun." His eyes flashed unspoken threats. "Never do that again."

"My father took you away. He erased your memories." Fire burned in my heart at the damage my father had done. But flashes of carriage rides through the city, arms linked as we waved to our subjects, sprang to mind. I'd never felt so comfortable, so protected, so loved with anyone as I had with my father. Was that the curse? Or was the real curse knowing I'd experienced it once and would likely never experience such freedom to love and be loved again?

My father was good. Yet he wasn't. I loved him. Yet I needed to stop him. There was no way things wouldn't end badly for him. But I couldn't allow my feelings for him to stand in the way of doing what was right. Of freeing the people.

"What do you remember since arriving at the castle?"

"My father, Auberon, kept trying to convince me what he was doing is right. He denies it's a curse, instead referring to it as a spell as if that were somehow better. He thinks he's doing the right thing, helping them. Us." My heart thudding, I twisted my hands in my lap.

"When did you lose your memories, after drinking the wine he gave you?"

"Aye. He'd give it to me when I disagreed with him cursing the people. And once after I overheard a conversation with a man in a box."

"The teleview?" One delicate golden brow winging up, she edged her face around Liam.

"Yes, that's what he called it. And another time after I'd found his hidden library. The boys!" A jolt shot through me as memories of the boys came to me—Simo, Juhani, Kaarle, Pauli…. I jumped to my feet, ready to hunt them down. "The processing center. I have to go to the processing center."

"We just came from there, remember?"

Liam touched my arm. "We freed Pauli."

"But the others. What happened to the others?" I dropped back down, burying my face in my hands as hot tears seeped through my fingers. There was no hope for my father. Kind and loving as he was to me, as he seemed to be, he wasn't. He hurt people who didn't do what he wanted. Children… He tore families apart.

Liam rubbed my back as Ruuta crouched before me.

"There were others you weren't able to rescue?"

"I—" My voice refused to cooperate. I swiped at fresh tears.

Breathe, Colleen. Just breathe.

Light in. Dark out.

Light in. Dark out.

Ruuta coaxed along, acting like a breathing coach.

When my breath steadied enough, I let out one more deep breath and tried again. "There were three others that I'm aware of."

She heaved a heavy sigh and floated to her feet, backing away from me. "There won't be any more, I assure you. We'll restore as many families as we can."

"What of those whose memories have been erased? Will the cure help them too?"

"The cure is the same as I have given you. It will undo any and all fae magic—glamors, luck, clairvoyance, banishing, binding, protection, compulsion, healing... everything. And if there are any fae living among you as spies, they will be revealed."

I didn't know what all those things were, but I remembered Liam's anger. I studied him, expecting fiery red to erupt around him. Though his aura had little red flashes, probably as he recalled things that angered him, it remained mostly stable. "Aren't you angry?"

"I–I—" he stuttered. "Of course, I'm angry. But I'm also relieved. And we're well on our way to removing the curse."

"So you won't give us away?"

His lips formed a lopsided grimace. "I hope not."

Ruuta winked. "He knows what's at stake. If he hopes to aid in our quest and not tempt your father to resort to killing those who defy him, he'll play along."

He glared at her, his aura darkening.

She flounced to me, slid her gloved fingers under my chin, and tipped my face to her. "You must act the doting daughter whilst we enact our plan to remove the curse and ensure you're given credit so your people will consider you a hero who saved them. It's imperative that you ascend the throne."

I didn't want the throne, but I didn't want to get into that. And I still valued my life. "I'm not a good liar."

"No fae are. We can twist the truth, but we can't lie outright. But don't you fret. I'm here now, and I'm capable of handling your father." She patted my chin. "Just leave it to me. There's much planning to do. It won't be long now before this kingdom is free."

FIFTY-FOUR

I was flying again. But this time, I flew over the ocean. Thick salt air clung to me as I glided over the dark sea. The large moon cast a shadow beneath me over the water's surface. Was that my shadow? Though it moved with me, it couldn't be mine. Rather, it belonged to some kind of a giant bird. Its wingspan was longer than its body, which narrowed to a never-ending tail cutting through the air behind me. No birds had tails like that. Was it... a dragon?

Colleen.

The voice I'd heard in my dreams called to me.

Wake up, Colleen. Come outside.

Come outside? Wasn't I already outside, flying over the ocean? My vision shifted from the shadow beneath me to something dark protruding from the sea along the horizon. We flew nearer. Was that... a castle? *My* castle?

I was flying in fast. I tried to slow, but I couldn't. I was going to crash... into my balcony.

Wake up!

My body jerked in bed as something crashed outside. My heart raced like a hummingbird's. I scanned the room. A shadow crossed the moonlight streaming in from the balcony. A cat rubbed against the edge of the open door.

"Iisakki!" I cradled him as he nuzzled my chin. After scanning the room for Ruuta, I tiptoed outside and shut the door behind me. I still wasn't ready to trust her with him.

He leapt from my arms, morphing into a dog.

"You've gotten so big!" Had I missed his entire youth? He might not be fully grown yet. Still, my heart ached. I grasped his blocky head behind the ears and kissed his snout.

Iisakki grew into his dragon form and pranced around me, crashing into the railing. He let out a series of grunts. Was that supposed to be laughter? *Colleen got small.*

"You can talk!"

Not out loud. In Colleen's and Sakki's minds. Try it. Try it. Try it.

He hopped about, keeping me spinning to watch him. *Like this? Can you hear me?*

Yes! Yes! Yes! His hops grew more theatrical. Then he stopped and morphed into a dog. He aimed half-moon eyes at me. *Sakki called Colleen. Colleen didn't listen.*

I'm so sorry I didn't search for you. My father stole my memories. I wrapped myself around him and dampened his fur with my tears. How could I explain that, even once my memories were returned, I had to keep him safe?

Sakki tried helping Colleen remember. He licked my face, then resumed bouncing.

"You knew I'd lost my memories?"

Sakki could see what Colleen saw. Colleen couldn't see Sakki? He stopped and cocked his doggy head, training those inquisitive eyes on me.

I saw you flying in the woods to a field with a cottage and a barn.

Yes! Yes! Yes! The hideout. He sat back, wriggling back and forth on his paws, then stilled. *Colleen didn't respond.*

I didn't know it was you. I thought it was a dream.

Sakki is better at mindspeak than Colleen. He resumed prancing around me.

I laughed. *You may not look like a puppy anymore, but you still act like one. Since when are you called Sakki?*

Since friends shortened Sakki's name. He looked to the balcony. *Sakki must return to the hideout.*

Who are your friends? Is Rhys with you?

Sakki planted his feet and gave me his questioning face again. *Rhys is not with Colleen?*

I haven't seen him since that day we were all separated.

Sakki hasn't either. He looked like I'd taken away his favorite toy.

Then who's with you?

Friends—Pirkko, Taneli, and Reko.

What? How? Didn't they return to Folaim?

Friends planned to return. But fae said friends were needed in Talamh Sí. Rhys brought Sakki to friends' hideout, then left, and never returned.

Fae? Are they in on the Saoirse Trodaí's plans to remove the curse?

Yes. Fae have helped all along. Does Colleen remember the croi tree?

That's right. The fae were helping hide Folaim. I'd forgotten. Does that mean it's safe for me to tell Ruuta about you?

Ruuta? He froze, then broke out into a toothy doggy grin. *Oh yes! Yes! Yes! Ruuta is helping too. And your maid, Iida told Sakki when to visit safely so no defenders would see Sakki approach.*

All these plans were happening without me? Didn't they trust me? What am I to do?

Find Rhys.

How? He left us. What if he doesn't want to be found?

Colleen can find Rhys.

How do you know?

Sakki knows many things. God tells Sakki.

He speaks to you?

Yes, yes, yes! There's no barrier between God and Sakki like with people or fae.

Did God tell you to have me find Rhys?

Sakki nodded his canine snout. *That's why Sakki thought Rhys was here.*

Did He say anything else? Did He give any clues as to where to look?

No, but God asked so Colleen can do it. He sat and trained his doggy eyes on me. *God wants Colleen to pay more attention to God. Colleen doesn't listen well.*

What? He told me to seek Him, and I have. I—

Sakki wrinkled his nose. *When does Colleen talk to God? Sakki doesn't hear Colleen.*

Can you hear me... all the time? Even my thoughts? I swallowed, though my throat was dry. I didn't like the idea of a voyeur in my mind. Even my bonded dragon.

No, no, no. Sakki hears when Colleen speaks—to God, Sakki, Colleen. Colleen talks to Colleen a lot. But Colleen rarely talks to God.

Whew. At least my private thoughts were safe, well, from Sakki... not God. But he was right. I rarely spoke to God. When I was little, I talked to Him all the time. What had happened? When did I stop? Once I was rescued—safe—and no longer needed Him?

But I still needed Him even after I was rescued. And now more than ever.

Sakki must go. He morphed into his dragon form, taking up much of the large balcony. He turned, flapped his wings, and leaped into the night sky. *Colleen must find Rhys, then come to the hideout. Sakki and friends will be waiting.*

FIFTY-FIVE

Ruuta, Liam, Iida, and I sat in the courtyard, eating our breakfast. Auberon was preparing for the next Atonement ceremony, so we were safe—for now. I dared entrust the truth about Sakki with Ruuta. Iida and Liam already knew. I told them about our reunion.

"But I don't know how I'm supposed to find Rhys." I turned to Liam. "Is there any way to track him? I already asked my father to find him when I first arrived. He never did. Then again, he thinks I've forgotten. Maybe he never even looked for him. But, if he was just going to erase my memories anyway, why'd he bring you?"

Liam shrugged.

"Queen Rhiannon demanded it." Ruuta skewered her last bites of sweet potato so they barely fit on her fork and popped the whole thing in her mouth. Only she could do that and make it look appealing.

I rubbed my temple as lost memories came to the surface. "I remember overhearing my father speak with a man on the teleview. He said Queen Rhiannon wanted Liam to stay close? But why?"

"Good question. I overheard my parents meeting with her. She mentioned his name and said something about a connection between you—"

My eyes locked with Liam's, and he grasped the back of his reddening neck and looked away.

"—and insisted he remain as your defender."

I rubbed my face as if I could wipe away the redness. "I still don't understand."

"Queen Rhiannon has eyes and ears everywhere on this side of The Divide. She knows Liam was freed from the curse and would help you. She is for you and against Auberon. She will do all she can to stack events in your favor. But we must lay all this aside and focus —on finding Rhys." Ruuta wiped the corners of her mouth and dropped her napkin on her plate. "Do you know anything about his family, where he's from, his interests?"

I sighed. "In all the time I spent with him, I don't think I knew him at all, not even his real age. He never said anything about his family. But he had traveled through the megalith too many times to count."

She perked up. "He did? Does he have an amulet? Perhaps we could track it."

"He said the amulet he had was spelled to take him to an elf."

One arm braced on the table, she leaned in closer, eyes wide. "What was his aura like?"

"It was a color I'd never seen before coming to this realm. Like the color of aether smoke."

"Aether smoke?" Iida and Liam spoke simultaneously, then looked at each other with confused expressions and auras. Then Iida added, "If aether has any emissions, they're invisible."

"It's a color only the fae can see—värikäs." Ruuta pushed her plate away.

"That's the name of the color?" I ate my last bite of perfectly seasoned cinnamon-pepper sweet potato. Why was it such a relief to have a name for it?

She dusted something I couldn't see from her purple sleeve. Did she always match her face makeup with her dress? And were her eyes purple today too? "If his aura was *värikäs*, then I trust Rhys wasn't human or fae. He's aetherian."

In one conversation with my father, he'd explained aetherian beings. "So Rhys was created by a fae?"

"Yes, and if he appeared as a boy, he was a shape-shifter, which means—he was probably a pooka."

The blood drained from my face.

"Jaakko," Liam and Iida said.

"Nay." My stomach curled in on itself. "That's not possible. Rhys was my friend. But Jaakko? Jaakko is my father's loyal servant. He... He brought me the wine each time Auberon erased my memory! He must've known what he was doing. Rhys wouldn't betray me like that."

"Unless he was biding his time until he could take action against your father." Ruuta stood and smoothed her skirt. "If it is him, he's brilliant. My parents and Queen Rhiannon knew Saors were in the palace. We placed some of them here. But we never once suspected the pooka."

"It might not be him." I voiced the feeble hope aloud, but a memory of both Rhys and Jaakko echoed in my mind—*to be sure, to be sure.*

Little use denying it—Rhys was Jaakko.

THE FOUR OF us were anything but the picture of royal grace as we dashed through the maze of hallways and stairwells to Jaakko's room outside the royal quarters. When we arrived, I took a deep breath. *God, help us.*

Liam pounded on the door. "Jaakko!" Each knock opened the door a little wider until there was room to poke his head inside. "Jaakko?"

No answer.

Liam looked back at us.

"Go in, go in." Ruuta waved her gloved fingers at him, ushering him forward.

He shoved his way inside, and we all crowded in behind him. Thick curtains blocked the sunlight. He flicked the switch on the inside wall.

Light flooded a tiny—*disastrous*—room. An unmade bed, a side table, a dresser, and a desk with a chair, all littered with clothes and books. Socks and trousers dangled over the bed. Shirts draped the back of the chair. Laundry piled up in one corner. Books towered everywhere as if creating the layout of a miniature city.

"Clearly, the maids don't frequent this place." Ruuta crinkled her nose and waved a gloved hand before her face.

"Certainly not." Iida bristled, lifting the hem of her long black dress further from the floor as frizzy wisps of hair shook about her face. "Servants are responsible for their own spaces."

"Hmm... What need has a rabbit of so many clothes?" I asked in a salty tone, my mood souring with the dirty laundry.

Ruuta picked up a shirt between pinched fingers, holding it away from her. She dropped the shirt onto the bed and scrubbed her gloved fingers together. "Our suspicions have been confirmed."

"Rhys claimed to read a lot." I riffled through an open book with a folded page, fixed the page, and placed the book back down properly. I didn't care if I'd lost his place. Books shouldn't be treated like that.

As we were about to leave, Jaakko rounded the corner with a book under his nose. We stepped aside while he approached. He reached for the door handle. His gaze darted around as the book fell from his hands. "T–to what honor do I owe the p–princess for a personal visit to my private room?"

"We know... Rhys." I sneered at him.

The pooka worked his jaw before finding words. "I recall the name of this Rhys you speak of. 'Tis the friend you asked His Majesty to seek, is it not?"

"God told me to find you." I crossed my arms over my chest. "Don't make your betrayal worse by denying it."

"Betrayal! Is that what you call all I've done for you?"

"Aha! It is you."

His shoulders sagged. "What does God want with a lowly creature like me?"

"I don't know, but I'm to find you and meet Iisakki and the others at the hideout."

Rhys's pooka eyes widened far more than humanly possible. "You know of it?"

"Aye. Iisakki came to see me."

"And what do you think your father will do should he return to an empty castle? He'll turn this kingdom upside down to find you."

"I only know what God told me to do." Which already wasn't easy—forcing me to work with a traitor.

"If that is God's will, I'll go with you. But wait until tonight after your father is asleep."

God may want me to do work with Rhys—and I'd do my best—but I still wanted answers. "How can I trust you after all you've done to me?"

"Just what have I done, pray tell?" He tapped an impatient rabbit foot.

My blood steamed, making me quake like the lid on Fallon's teakettle. "You lied to me! From the very beginning. Tell me, *rabbit*, why didn't you take me to my father straightaway?"

He scoffed. "I only knew we needed you to free the kingdom. I brought you to the Saoirse Trodaí because they gave me the amulet spelled to find you."

"To find *me?*" I pointed to my chest. "I thought it was spelled to find an elf."

Jaakko/Rhys/the betrayer jabbed a paw my way. "You."

He might as well have skewered that word on a spear and stabbed my heart. "If you were looking for me, if you needed me so badly, why'd you *poison* me!"

"I never poisoned you. And giving you that tonic to expunge your memories and keep you content ensured your safety."

"How?" I hugged my crossed arms around myself, waiting for his feeble excuse.

"What do you think Auberon would do to you if he believed there was no way to get you on his side? He has much darker fae magic at his disposal even he hesitates to use."

That made me shudder and tighten my grip on my arms. "You're as bad as my father. You think you can do anything to a person in the name of safety." The vehemence in my voice had lost its strength. "*You* are a liar. You've always been a liar."

"To be sure, to be sure. Yet I brought Iisakki to the hideout and kept him safe. And I've been monitoring King Auberon and his loyal subjects to ensure you and your careless entourage don't get caught. A task you have *not* made easy, to be sure."

My heart softened—slightly. I couldn't trust him, but he was a pooka. An aetherian creature. Lower than animals created by God. Was it right for me to expect more from him than any other animal, just because he could speak and appear human? Did he even know right from wrong? Or was he like a dog attacking a rodent, an animal acting out of instinct? Perhaps he couldn't be held responsible for his actions. Perhaps I was being too harsh, just because I felt betrayed.

All things to explore later, when I had more time. But he was right. We'd been careless with our conversation on Auberon's grounds, and we were being careless now. Thank God we'd had him covering for us.

"Why do you help us?" My grip on myself loosened. "What do you hope to gain?"

"When your grandfather rescued me, the fae magic that created me indebted me to him for ten years. He was a kind man who wanted nothing more than to see the elves and humans live in harmony with one another and with God. So, when my ten years ended, I pledged the remainder of my life to his service. When he died, I chose to remain with his son. Though he had good intentions, Auberon made several errors. Choices that would have angered Eerikki. Elves are good beings. There is nothing—no sin—separating them from the God I wish would turn an eye my way. But I am a lowly creature. And Auberon threw away his connection with God when he purchased the curse. Now he is forever lost. Eternally separated from God. But you are different. You will rightly rule the people your grandfather loved. At least, I want to help give you the opportunity to do better. And I want to restore the people Eerikki loved to the God he loved. Since you are in Eerikki's line, I've chosen to transfer my loyalties to you." He bowed. "I am in your service."

I didn't expect that response. It made me feel so small—unworthy of his allegiance. "Thank you."

The pooka flinched. "Plus, you *did* rescue me from a train. If I hadn't already chosen to serve you, I'd be compelled to do so." He cleared his throat. "If your God wants us to go to the hideout, we will. Prepare to leave tonight. I will see what I can do to ensure we don't rouse Auberon's suspicions."

"Very well." What a difference one conversation can make. I had felt so hurt—so betrayed. Now I felt honored the pooka was involved at all. And somehow, a creature who readily confessed to being a liar had become one of my greatest confidants. Hopefully, he could find a way to cover for us. If we were all caught conspiring against my father, having our memories erased might seem like a flick on the nose in comparison to what he could do.

Fifty-Six

Ruuta and I sat at the dinner table with my father whilst Liam stood at his post. Each time Liam's aura flared red, he closed his eyes. His chest rose and fell as his aura calmed. It was good he was doing what he could to remain calm, but defenders were always to be alert. I prayed Auberon wouldn't see him close his eyes— or worse, see Liam's temper flare.

The clocks ticked away as my father read his newspaper, awaiting our meal. I studied him and his steady, neutral aura, so unaware of all the conspiring around him. And I was part of it. That truth carved its way into my heart, branding me a traitor, making my soul cry out in agony. What kind of person betrayed her father as I was about to betray mine? I chastised the rabbit for lying, for his betrayals. But I was worse—much worse.

Was it possible to do the right thing without hurting anyone? And why, of all people, did it have to be someone who I truly loved and who truly loved me back? That wasn't a lie. My father's affection was genuine. And though I wanted to be in control of my thoughts and emotions, I enjoyed the freedom of being, without all the anxiety, without whatever it was that always held me back, rendering me incapable of loving and being loved.

Whatever my father had done to me broke through those barriers. I'd give anything to have them destroyed—forever. Anything but have my free will stolen.

With no alternative, I had to set my personal feelings aside and do what was right. And somehow, keep the truth from my father until our job was done.

"Eerika."

My name from Ruuta snapped me out of my gloomy thoughts.

"Wouldn't it be lovely to take the train and travel the countryside? I'd love to see more of this beautiful kingdom." Her eyes danced with what might appear to be excitement to my father, but I knew her better. I saw the devious joy within.

But what if the pooka came up with another plan and her last-minute idea got in the way? "I don't know. I—"

My father snapped his paper and folded it in half. "That's a wonderful idea. You should see the rest of this kingdom if you're to rule it. Perhaps I could excuse myself from my duties to join you. I am king after all."

"Your company would make the trip most enjoyable, Your Majesty." She batted gossamer eyelashes, each flick sending sparkly things aflutter in the air around her face. Wasn't she concerned? She shouldn't be making up her own plans without consulting anyone. And I thought fae couldn't lie. She must be twisting the truth somehow.

Iida emerged from the servants' entrance. Another servant behind her carried platters with lidded plates and beverages. She placed the food before us.

My father lifted the lid and sniffed. "Ah, smells wonderful."

Vilppu, my father's driver, darted into the dining hall out of breath. "A letter just arrived for you, Your Majesty. From Queen Rhiannon."

"Oh?" Father tugged against the wax seal to unfold the parchment. His eyes roamed back and forth, narrowing as they went. He refolded the letter, tucking it into his jacket as he stood. "My apologies, Daughter. I shan't dine with you this evening. Queen Rhiannon has summoned me. I shall depart tonight."

"How long will you be gone?" I leaped to my feet, and my napkin slid off my dress.

"That's difficult to say. I might be gone for several weeks." He pressed a hand to my shoulder. "Sit. Enjoy your meal."

"How disappointing for our trip." Ruuta pouted in a graceful way only she could manage.

As if on cue, Auberon's personal servant appeared with his traveling cloak.

"You should go." He slipped his arms through the awaiting coat. "Bring your defender and maid and any other servants you deem necessary. With any luck, I'll be home before you. Defender, alert the staff that Eerika and Ruuta will be taking a trip."

"Thank you, Father." I dared a glance at Ruuta, amazed by our stroke of luck.

No, not luck. God.

Thank You, God.

"Perhaps the pooka should accompany us as well?" She dabbed at her mouth, then moved her fork to spear an olive, seeming disinterested in her suggestion as she focused on the food. "He seems rather helpful."

"Well, I had planned to have him accompany me. But you're quite right. He knows this kingdom like no one else. He would make an excellent guide." Auberon gazed into nothingness as he considered the request, then nodded as if he'd concluded the debate in his mind. "That's a wonderful idea. I would feel more at ease with my most trusted servant by your side. And I shall have plenty of defenders with me. There's no reason I can't spare Jaakko." My father kissed the side of my head. "Forgive me for the hasty retreat, but I must pack my things and leave this evening. May your travels be blessed."

"Thank you, Father." His kiss lingered, searing me with the stings of betrayal. But just who did he suggest would bless us. Himself? Nay, I refused to feel guilty. Images of all the boys he'd taken sprang to mind. I was doing the right thing.

Once my father was gone, Ruuta leaned in beside me. "We should still leave before first light and travel by horseback so none know the direction we take. No drivers and no servants other than Rhys, Liam, and Iida."

"Agreed."

"Eat up, Princess." She patted my hand with gloved fingers. "For tomorrow, our adventure begins."

WE PREPARED the horses by the light of dim lanterns, then stole outside into the gray morning. The pooka arrived in Rhys's shape. Seeing him stole my breath.

"I thought you might be most comfortable with this shape." He dipped his head in a bow, his hair spilling like black ink before returning to its proper place. "Or does it offend you?"

"This is fine. What should I call you? Rhys? Jaakko?"

Blue eyes, darker than the deepest water, peered up at me. Something in them—a desire for approval, perhaps—drew me in. "What makes you most comfortable?"

"If you're in this form—Rhys."

"Very well, Rhys it is."

I hiked myself up into Clover's saddle.

"One more thing, Princess." Rhys shuffled his feet, almost hopping from one to the other. "You seem to appreciate honesty, so I want to indulge you."

"Aye?" I braced myself.

"I'm also Balder."

"Balder?" That name sounded familiar. "Who's Bald—" Wait. "The strange man with the top hat? The one who gave me Iisakki's egg?"

"Yes, that Balder."

Something within me squeezed, preparing a verbal attack. But I clamped my mouth shut and breathed to calm the rising fury. He didn't have to share that. I would never have known. He was attempting to show his loyalty. "Why did you change shapes?"

"Balder... frightened you. I thought a boy might invoke less fear than a man."

"That's true. But where did you get the egg? My father thinks none exist."

"That's a story for another time. But I promise to be honest with you going forward." He held his hand out. "Agreed?"

I laughed and shook his hand. "Agreed."

He smiled and mounted his steed. Apparently, he could ride. Iida and Rhys took the lead since they knew the way. We followed from the stables through the trails beside the castle to the main gate—the only way out of the castle grounds.

The sentry bowed as I approached. "Good morning, Princess. Starting your trip straightaway, I see."

His demeanor was friendly enough, and yet, I was on edge. Sinking back in my saddle and unclenching my fisted hands from the reins, I tried to relax. "We wanted to get an early start."

The sentry didn't seem to notice how forced my words sounded. "Good choice. Stay ahead of the traffic." He pushed the levers to raise the gate and lower the bridge. "Enjoy your trip, Princess."

Rather than take the king's road through the city, we turned down a side street. I grimaced with each of the horse's footfalls on the cobblestones. They echoed off the buildings far louder than normal in the morning quiet. But we turned off the rocky streets to a sandy path sandwiched between two buildings, leading to the beach.

Once we were free of the buildings and out of earshot, Iida sidled up to me. "We'll ride the horses nearer to the shore. It will be easier for them to run on packed sand. Thankfully, it's low tide. We should be able to take the beach much of the way. Just follow me." She wrenched her goggles from her riding helmet, then made a clicking sound as she urged her horse forward. The rest of us followed. Once we reached the harder dirt, we sped up, kicking up clumps of wet sand and water.

Racing through the salty air, focusing on my body and breathing, getting out of my head, was what I needed. All my troubles faded as I enjoyed God's creation.

Extravagant homes rose above the sand dunes and beach grass. Massive windows with incredible ocean views lined each building. Who lived in them? Were they awake? Hopefully, they wouldn't recognize us.

The beach disappeared, and we followed a thin trail single file away from the rocky coast. The trail split, and Iida veered to the left toward the tree line rather than continue to follow the coast. The sounds of gulls and the scent of salty air followed us until the trees filtered them out. Multiple paths broke off and the lefts, rights, and center changes confused me until I'd never find my way back.

Iida whistled. A reply came from the trees up ahead.

A man tumbled from a tree and dangled from a branch, blocking our path. He dropped, then tugged his barn coat straight and brushed his sleeves. He took the cap from his head and bowed with flair. "Welcome, Your Highness."

"Reko!"

"It's good to see you again. And a certain creature who can't seem to decide if he prefers to be a dog or a cat is eager to see you." He reached into his pocket, retrieved a coin purse, then deposited the contents into his palm. Pebbles? He handed one to me, Liam, and Ruuta.

Then I remembered seeing these things before. "To get through the veil?"

Reko tipped his head back as if swallowing a pill. "Down the hatch." He gave a quick salute, then returned to his tree.

"The cottage is a little further." Iida motioned for us to follow as we ate our spelled berries.

The thin trail widened. Worn bricks and overgrown shrubs lined the dirt walkway. We rounded a corner to an open field, but as we pressed forward, the foreground shifted. The field was gone. Instead, the trail continued, lined with a knee-high wooden fence holding back more overgrowth. The path wound through a gap in the fence to a cottage. The cottage I'd seen in my dream—well, in Sakki's head. Arched wooden posts marked the entryway. Steep rooflines jutted out from all angles. Moss covered the shingles. The lack of smoke from the chimney and shuttered windows gave it an abandoned feel.

"I will never get used to that." I shivered.

"What? Traveling through a veil?" Ruuta asked.

"Aye."

We followed Iida past the cottage, through matted grass toward a barn that dwarfed the cottage, even from a considerable distance. The double doors burst open, and a massive creature charged me.

Fifty-Seven

"Sakki!" I slid from Clover's back and ran to meet him.

The yellow-and-green scaly beast charging at me morphed into a dog as it ran, then sprang into my arms as a cat. The moment his fuzzy head brushed against my cheek, a blue light engulfed me and, with it, a flood of memories—of Reko, Taneli, and Pirkko. All from varying views depending on Sakki's size and location, this barn, a cozy nest inside, the cottage, a fire pit in the field, flying through the woods, catching and guzzling rodents... Then Pauli and Floyd. Sakki wiggled from my grasp back into dog form, and the connection broke.

What was that? You can share memories?

Yes, yes, yes! His tongue lolled to one side. *Colleen can too. Now Colleen and Sakki know all that's happened since parting.*

Wait. I shared memories with you too?

Yes! Yes! Yes! He hopped from side to side. *Colleen rescued Pauli and Floyd, and Colleen found Rhys!* Sakki rammed Rhys, nearly toppling him.

"I'm happy to see you again too, old friend." Rhys squirmed as Sakki bathed his reachable face with his tongue.

Sakki charged Liam with the same enthusiasm, then greeted Iida with less force.

"Sakki"—I motioned toward Ruuta—"this is my-lady-in-waiting, Ruuta."

He approached Ruuta in a crouch. She put out a hand for him to sniff, so he obliged.

Ruuta smells like grapefruit and flowers. He sniffed again. *Ruuta is good for Colleen.* He licked her hand.

"He likes you," I said. "He says you smell like grapefruit and flowers."

"Geranium." She petted his head. "It's so strange to watch you speaking telepathically."

"It's strange to speak that way. But I'm getting used to it. I love it, actually."

If Colleen loves mindspeak so much, Colleen should try it with God.

"Why you little..." I lunged at him, and he darted out of reach.

He stood with his feet planted, tail wagging, tongue lolled to the side... far too amused.

"Well, if it isn't the long-awaited princess."

I spun around at the familiar voice. "Pirkko!"

She slammed into me, wrapping her arms around me. "It's good to have you back."

Taneli waved to us, then zeroed in on Liam. "Thanks for not making me come after you with an angry mob."

Liam huffed.

"Come, let's go inside." Taneli motioned for us to follow him to the cottage.

We all walked through the overgrown grass from the barn to the cottage. Though it looked abandoned on the outside, a warm and cozy interior greeted me, despite all the clunky elements that seemed to infiltrate Talamh Sí. There were no ticking clocks. Only the sound of the wind blowing through the grass and rustling the leaves. The smell of freshly baked bread wafted my way.

"Anyone hungry?" Taneli crossed the brick floors to a loaf cooling on the counter beside the oven. "I've just baked some bread, and we've a bit of cheese left to go with it."

My stomach answered loud enough for everyone to hear.

"Sounds like a yes to me." Taneli's voice was muffled as his head disappeared into a cupboard.

"How about some tea?" Pirkko pumped water into a kettle.

"Ah." Iida sat in a wooden chair at the table. "It's nice to be served for once."

"For once?" Taneli scoffed as he placed a cutting board with the steaming loaf and a chunk of cheese on the table. "Try every time you visit."

She leveled her eyes at him. "And how often is that?"

"Admittedly, not often enough." He sat across from her.

Pirkko dragged more chairs so we could crowd the table. I took a corner beside Iida with Ruuta beside me and Sakki sprawled under my chair, resting his chin on the back rung.

A rough-cut beam crossed the interior, supporting a railed loft above. Electric bulbs suspended by pulleys dangled above us.

Pirkko opened the icebox and pulled out a bone, which she brought to Sakki. He leaped up, sniffed the gift, then caught it in his jaw. He lay beside my chair and chewed his treat.

Good bone. He stopped and stared at me. *Colleen want some?*

No thanks, Sakki. I petted his head, ruffling his droopy ears.

He resumed gnawing.

The door burst open, and everyone's attention snapped that way. Reko entered. "It's just us."

A boy darted out behind him.

"Pauli!"

I sprang to my feet and hugged the boy. "Are they taking good care of you here?"

He nodded, took a seat at the table, and glanced around, seeming proud to be among adults. "I've been helping keep watch."

Reko tugged on Taneli's chair. "Your turn. Floyd is still at his post."

"I'll relieve him soon." Pirkko ripped a piece of bread with her teeth.

I checked to ensure Pauli was distracted. He was busy scratching Sakki's ear, so I bent across the table and asked in a near-silent voice while motioning to Pauli under the table. "Did his family make it here?"

"Not yet," she mouthed back.

Taneli carved a slice of bread, slathered it with cheese, then stood. "Good to see you. And I look forward to seeing you again in a free country." He shoved his bread into his mouth as he grabbed a rifle, then his hat from the coatrack. Clutching his hat, he bowed, then unstuffed his mouth and left.

Reko took Taneli's spot at the table. "I wish we had more time to catch up." He held Pirkko's hand and they shared a smile, softening the hard edges of iron in his rusty-brown eyes. He stiffened, setting his stubble-covered jaw as he turned to me. "But we need to fill you in on your part in the plan and get you back to the castle as soon as possible."

"We have plenty of time. Queen Rhiannon has summoned my father to Seelie Clós. And thanks to Ruuta's quick thinking, everyone in the castle thinks we're touring the countryside. We've got a month, at least."

"No, we don't." Ruuta held up a hand. "I had that letter on me since I arrived, awaiting the Saors' word to deliver it when the time was right."

My jaw dropped. "Just how much haven't you been telling me?"

"Don't blame her. We couldn't risk you going under Auberon's spell again and divulging our plans." Reko cut off a chunk of bread and covered it in cheese. "Queen Rhiannon's summons was a ruse to get Auberon and you out of the castle. If anything goes wrong, we want all the castle staff to believe you're not there. We're hopeful Auberon won't figure it out and thwart our plans."

"But on a more positive note." Pirkko flipped her wild reddish hair back from her shoulders. As if as adverse to mindlessly following directions as she was, it tumbled forward again. "We've finally stolen enough keino and vastalääke to see our plan through."

My stomach writhed as if full of wriggling maggots. So this was it. I'd somehow thought I'd have more time. "What's my part?"

Reko stuffed his bite into his cheek to talk, the stubble spreading out above it. "Return to the castle. Keep everyone but Rhys hidden— yourself included. He will shift into a defender to get you through the gate. After night falls, Iisakki will fly to your room with a diffuser. Hide him so he can fly into your bedroom undetected."

"How am I supposed to hide everyone?"

"With that veil thing you do." He wagged his fingers. "All fae can."

"Not *all*." Ruuta slumped back in her seat, her butterfly markings sagging. "Only the more powerful fae."

"But I'm not powerful. And I'm only part fae. What makes you think I can do this?"

"You have—" She closed her eyes and breathed deeply as if holding something back.

Reko narrowed his iron-brown eyes at Ruuta, then me. "You've done it before. Remember when we hid from the sentries on the train? You shielded us. There's no way they didn't see us. One of them looked right at me."

Why was he looking at me as if he knew something about me, my abilities, that I didn't? I pointed to myself. "You think *I* did that?"

"Yes." Reko raised a brow at Rhys. "Unless *you* have the ability to create veils."

"I've spun many tales, to be sure, to be sure. But pooka *cannot* create veils." He punctuated his statement by crossing his arms.

I threw my hands up. "If it was me, I don't know how. I—"

Colleen also made a veil when Colleen hid children from fasgadair.

"How do you know about that?"

Colleen showed Sakki Colleen's memories. Has Colleen already forgotten? Colleen's memory is very bad.

"Only when it's messed with!"

"What's he saying?" His back ramrod straight, Reko scooted his chair closer.

"He says I made a veil when I was a child. Apparently, that's how I was able to hide from the fasgadair." That explained so much. "But I have no idea what I did. And even if I could, I was always among those hiding. How would I project it to a moving target over the ocean? Or isolate one person—or pooka—to be visible?"

"Ships don't fly at night, and they rarely head out to sea. The trouble will be when he arrives at the castle. We need to ensure the defenders don't see him enter the castle, or worse, shoot him down."

I shuddered, and protective anger heated me. God help whoever harmed my dragon. I would not let it slide.

Everyone seemed to know more about myself than I did. How long did it take me to accept that I was an elf? Perhaps they were right about this too. And if I was going to protect Iisakki, I'd have to practice. "Let me try. Tell me if he disappears."

I tried to focus on the pup at my feet, but I could feel everyone's eyes on me. Doubts invaded my mind, but I tried to push them away and concentrate. I stared at him, feeling like I was about to pop a blood vessel in my brain. *Hide, hide, hide.*

Don't tell Sakki to hide. Hide Sakki.

I stopped and caught my breath. *Not helpful, Sakki.* "I can't do it."

"Perhaps it's because we've already seen him and know where he is?" Pirkko asked.

"Why do I need to hide him at all? He came to my window once before without being caught."

"Because Iida knew the defenders' schedule, but she can't always access that information or get it to us in time. We need to know Iisakki can fly in safely, no matter what."

"I can try." My words were as weak as my faith in my ability.

"That's all we ask." Pirkko leaned past Ruuta to catch my eye. "We need you to bring the diffuser to the tallest westernmost tower, aim it out the window, and turn it on at midnight."

That was nothing but attic space. Setting up their contraption there wouldn't be a problem. And it wouldn't be difficult to sneak it past my father's room with him gone. "Is it heavy?"

"It will take two people to carry, but it's more bulky than heavy." Reko stood and moved to a clunky machine in the corner. "It's this." He patted the cone-shaped part. "This is the nozzle. Aim it out the window, then pull this pin." To demonstrate, he gripped a metal ring and tugged, slightly withdrawing a narrow rod. "But pull it all the way out. Also, two people will need to hold it in place until it's empty."

"What does it do?"

He returned to the table. "We've discovered that vastalääke, the cure for any fae magic, is even more potent diffused into the air and inhaled than ingested. Less is needed, and it goes straight into the bloodstream. If we diffuse it from several locations simultaneously, we can cure everyone in the city who breathes the air."

Why didn't I find that comforting? What would happen when everyone received the cure at once? But then, did it matter? Everyone must be freed. If this was the only way... "But what of those outside the city?"

"We can cure them later." He waved my comment away. "Once the majority of the people are no longer under Auberon's control, we'll have more freedom to take whatever action necessary to cure everyone."

My head pounded as I tried to think this through. "But how many people will be outside at midnight? Shouldn't you do this during the day?"

He kicked back his chair, lifting the front two legs off the ground as he folded his hands in his lap. I'd never seen him so relaxed or was it confident? "Too many defenders are out during the day. And we need the cover of night."

"You said several locations. What others?"

"Other ships in the air will emit vastalääke to cure as much of the city as possible."

"But..." I pressed cold fingers to my temples. "You said ships don't fly at night?"

"These will, but you don't need to concern yourself with that. The less you know, the better. All you need to know is to get the machine into the tower and turn it on at midnight. It's imperative to our plan that all diffusers fire at the same time."

My heart was pounding now. "Tonight?"

"Yes." Pirkko moved to a cabinet and unearthed several glass vials. "If you run into anyone under your father's curse, spray them with this." She deposited little spray bottles. "It works like the diffuser. Spray their face. After inhaling it, they'll be cured. It acts faster than the ingestible version, and it's much easier to administer."

I picked up my bottle and studied the pink purple-veined liquid just like the stuff Pirkko gave Liam, but lighter and thinner. Somehow, holding a sprayable version made this feel much more real. This was happening. After today, the city would be mostly cured.

But what would happen to my father?

FIFTY-EIGHT

As we rode back toward the castle, I practiced shielding myself and Clover from the others. But each attempt failed.

Despite the harm my father had caused me and others, my heart hurt thinking about whatever was about to befall him. Countless memories of him whirled through my mind—taking rides through town to wave to our subjects, visiting the ill in recovery centers, the displaced in interim homes, and the widows in elderly care residences.... I ground my teeth. He was kind. A loving father. A caring king.

But how many of those displaced children were there because he'd taken their parents?

Once my father was removed, what would my role be? I couldn't be queen over a healthy country, never mind a divided one. How could anyone unite them once we lifted the curse? Any changes would serve some of the population to the detriment of others. No way could we satisfy everyone. Not without doing what my father had done.

But there was no justifying the way he achieved his goals.

Wanting to protect the people was noble, but not when it required deceiving them—enslaving them. And at what cost? Their souls?

What if this was all for naught? Once the people were freed, what guaranteed they'd follow God? Nothing, of course. They might reject Him despite my efforts.

But that was their right, wasn't it?

Where was God in all this? How could He allow people to die with no chance to know Him—to be saved?

Didn't I believe God was in control of everything? If so, wasn't He in control of all this too? Everything I'd experienced—bonding to a dragon, coming to Betören, meeting Rhys, living in the castle... Didn't He send me here, put me in this position, to free the people, whether they chose Him or not?

Wasn't I here, *now*, by design?

Perhaps I couldn't trust Rhys. Or the Saoirse Trodaí. Or myself. But I trusted God. He sent me. He wouldn't fail me. If things didn't go as we wanted them to go tonight, it would still go according to His plan.

My tense muscles loosened, my breath coming evenly again. I was responsible for my part. No more. No less.

God, this is Your plan. Use me as You will.

Twenty minutes to midnight, Ruuta and I sat on the balcony facing the east, studying the sky over the ocean. Liam was keeping watch in the hallway while Iida stayed in my room. I had extinguished my lights to help me see Sakki when he arrived, hoping any defenders would believe I hadn't returned or had already gone to sleep. I'd been studying the defenders long enough to determine that, once I saw their portable torchlight, I wouldn't see another for at least thirty minutes.

A defender and his light rounded the corner from the south. Heart pumping, I ducked behind the rail. Ruuta and I stared at each other while I counted along with the ticking coming from inside my room.

After thirty seconds had passed, I peeked over the rail. The beam from the Defender's electric torch swept along the castle grounds, then disappeared to the north.

My heart tightened into a rock. "That was no thirty minutes."

"They're varying their schedule. They must suspect something."

I searched for signs of Sakki. The moon hung high in the sky, but nothing Sakki-shaped emerged in its light. *Sakki, it's almost midnight. Where are you?*

Sakki is close.

My held breath whooshed out. *Good.* "He's almost here."

The defender circled back from the north, shouting something. What was happening? Ruuta and I ducked again. My gaze darted to the sky. Please oh please, don't let them have spotted Sakki. I peered through the railing. First at the defender below, then into the sky above. Something darker than the surrounding night sky moved this way. Were my eyes playing tricks on me?

Nay. It was Sakki.

There are defenders! Go back!

Sakki must deliver the diffuser. No time to waste. Colleen hide Sakki.

I wanted to throw something at the defenders, jump over the edge, anything to get attention off Sakki. *God, please don't let him get shot down. Hide him. Hide him. Please hide him!*

A surge of energy ran through. Where had that come from? I squeezed my eyes shut and reached out for Sakki as if he were a plant to heal. But rather than summon the life force within me, I conjured my fear. I prayed and willed him to be hidden, safe. When I sensed his presence closing in, I pulled the air around him like a blanket and guided him to me. Powerful gusts of wind blasted my face.

The tips of his massive wings beat the walls on either side of the door as his clawed hind feet came to a rest. He folded his wings and dropped forward with a thump.

I peered over the railing.

"You did well, Eerika," Ruuta whispered from inside my room. She rubbed her arm. "Now can you allow me to see him, so I don't get hit again?"

"It worked?" I slumped as the tension that had held me rigid left.

"Yes, he's safe. For now. But something is happening inside the castle. Several defenders entered as he landed. We'd better move."

I struggled to sense the air—or whatever I'd wrapped Sakki up in —unravel it. "Can you see him now?"

"Yes." She moved to free Iisakki from the contraption on his back.

My fingers shook as I fumbled with the straps. Sakki shifted into dog form, and the machine crashed onto the floor, missing his tail by a sliver. I cringed and remained motionless, sure I'd hear defenders any second now. But no shouts, flashlight beams, or footfalls came.

I released a pent-up breath. *You need to be more careful! We can't draw attention to ourselves.*

I inspected the machine to ensure it hadn't broken. Not that I would have any way of knowing.

Ruuta moved to the other side to help me pick it up. Reko was right. The contraption was more bulky and awkward than heavy. We carried it into my room.

Iida jumped when she saw us, then rapped on the door.

Liam opened it from the other side. "Ready?"

She held the door for us. Rhys led the way with Liam in tow, walking backward. We almost toppled into Rhys when he stopped short.

My father stood in the hallway.

FIFTY-NINE

"F‑F‑Father." My heart seized. I imagined how Beagan felt, standing beside sleeping Nialla's painted face whilst paint's exact match dripped from the brush behind his back.

Nay. This was worse. Much worse. Like a kid caught dosing her father's wine with a deadly poison.

What could I possibly say or do in this situation?

Two defenders flanked his sides. Hands clasped behind his back, my father looked over Rhys at me, then the machine and the others. While confusion tightened his ageless face, he also looked as though he suspected my attempt to poison him. "What are you doing, Daughter?"

"I—We're... What are you doing home? I thought you were on your way to Seelie Clós."

He stepped closer. "And you're supposed to be touring the countryside."

"She's not ready, Your Majesty." Ruuta curtsied, and the machine dipped. "She didn't make it one night."

"I see." But his tone made it clear he did not. "And what is this contraption?"

"It's a–a—"

Liam stepped between us. "A diffuser, Your Majesty."

"What is it for, and why are you sneaking about my private quarters with it at this unholy hour?"

The floor and walls around me pulsed, making me sway. I felt far away—removed—and someone else spoke through me, ready to take my punishment for me. "We're bringing it up to the west tower."

"This doesn't make me feel better, Daughter. My defenders informed me of a threat. I returned to investigate." He pinched the bridge of his nose and squeezed his eyes shut. "Please tell me they're misinformed. Please give me a logical explanation for whatever is happening here." When he opened his eyes, the pain glistening in their luminescent depths skewered my heart. "Please tell me you're not part of a treasonous plot against your father, your own blood."

"I–I—" It was as if I had stabbed us both in the heart. The knives twisted, working their way deeper. I choked on a sob, wanting to run away. But we had minutes to get the diffuser in the window and activate it. The ticking clocks, constant reminders of the time slipping past, agitated me. "We're not trying to harm you, Father."

"All of you? All of you are against me?" His voice cracked. "Jaak—?" Rhys must've used the boy's shape in front of my father before. But his voice broke at Jaakko's name. "You've been with me my whole life. I trusted you more than anyone."

Rhys shook his head. "I loved you, Auberon. I love you still. But you're not your father. I'd give anything for a soul. Yet you sold yours to keep your kingdom."

"The people turned on me, Jaakko! What should I have done, O Wise One?"

Rhys didn't react to my father's biting tone. "Do as your father did and trust God. Perhaps you wouldn't have lost your wife and child. Eerikki did what God told him to do—no matter what. Even when it was unpopular. His faithfulness saved countless lives. He never wanted to be king. But he was a fine one... even amongst races who despised each other. He did his best to be fair, just."

"No." My father poked Rhys's chest, pushing him back. "I'm an *excellent* king. Much better than my father. The people are content. United." He stepped toward me, jabbing an accusatory finger. "What do you think will happen should you free the people? Will their lives be better, easier?"

The anger and betrayal in his eyes and his voice, his red and blue aura, because of me....

"Nay." I blinked back tears. "Not this life."

"Not this life?" He jabbed his finger, the tendons bulging in his neck. Red light engulfed him. "This is the only life there is!"

I backed away, hiding behind Liam, clinging to his shoulder. My heart split in two—writhing under Father's intense anger and bleeding at his pride and ignorance. The overload of conflicting emotions demolished the dam holding back my tears. A torrent burst forth. "Nay! It isn't!"

"Seize them!" my father yelled.

Ruuta and I stood by, holding the diffuser while Liam and Iida jumped to action, each blasting a defender in the face before they apprehended us. The defenders dropped to the ground, coughing.

My father wasn't watching his fallen defenders, but his eyes were wide, spooked. His aura flared with purple and orange.

What was he seeing? I pivoted. And gasped.

"Sakki!" Why oh why, did he have to reveal himself?

"You have a *dragon*?"

Sakki's dragon form barely fit in the ample hallway. He morphed into his cat self, dashed between our legs, then reappeared as a dragon on my father's other side. His head touched the ceiling.

What was he planning to do? Burn my father? "Sakki, nay! Don't kill him!"

My father's gaze climbed from Sakki's chest, up his long neck, to his head.

Sakki shrank—his neck, snout, and tail retracted into a human form. A man. My father blocked his body from view.

"Father?" Auberon stepped back, bumping into the machine,

then removed his cloak and threw it over the naked lookalike. "You know my father's image?"

"Sakki carries the memories of Sakki's ancestors. Sakki has seen King Eerikki through them."

A collective gasp echoed in the hall.

Was that Sakki's voice? Or Eerikki's? Whosever it was, the throaty sound and commanding tone weakened my knees.

"Why appear before me in this way?"

"To get King Auberon's attention. God has sent Sakki with this message—you will die tomorrow before the clock strikes midnight by the hands of your people."

Tears streamed down my face.

"But why? I've been a good king! I've taken care of the people!"

"You made yourself an idol, preventing My people from knowing Me. You took the honor and glory that belongs to Me alone!" Red blazed around Sakki, and fire shot from his human mouth toward the ceiling without setting it ablaze. "You who were free from the sin that too oft comes between Me and My creation—you gave that gift away to fulfill your selfish desires. Sin didn't blind you. You knew the truth! Nevertheless, you brought sin upon yourself when you failed to entrust your life to Me and elevated yourself above Me."

Tears obscured my vision as Sakki spoke the grave message. It broke my heart, but it was the truth. God's rightful judgment had come.

Liam grabbed my father's hand and clasped something shiny around one wrist, then the other. I hadn't even noticed him pass us to close in on my father.

"What?" My father glanced at his bound wrists. "Am I a prisoner now? My people will not stand for this. Defenders!"

The door to our private quarters at the end of the hall burst open, and the sentry on duty came running our way. Iida stepped in front of him and sprayed his face. The sentry's face turned red, and he coughed, then bent over, seeming to gasp for air as he fell beside his comrades.

"They'll be all right," Iida said. "Go! Get the diffuser in place. There's no time to spare."

WE MADE it to the tower and climbed the circular stairs. There wasn't enough room to walk side by side, so it was slow going. The clocks struck midnight as we arrived at the landing.

Shouts came from outside. We raced to the window before the final gong and lowered the diffuser. I yanked on the rusty latch and pushed the window open. Auberon's staff poured from the castle through the main gate. A strange light, flickering flames, hovered in the sky over the city. An airship was on fire. It would crash and set the city ablaze. I had to get down there.

Sakki! There's a ship on fire. We need to help!

Machine first.

Right. Now was our chance. No one looked our way. Nor would they. We hoisted it onto the sill with the nozzle aiming toward the city. Ruuta pulled the pin, and the machine kicked back, nearly toppling us as a pink fog burst forth. The cloudy stream dissipated, making it impossible to tell how far it went. Would it be enough? Would the wind carry it and drop it on the gathering crowd outside?

A dreadful thought formed in my mind—

They did this on purpose.

What is Colleen saying?

The Saors. They set that ship on fire to cause a distraction and draw a crowd to cure as many people as possible at this hour.

Ruuta and I held on as the machine continued to shoot out the cure. Pinkish clouds streamed and dissipated from ships flying in the north, west, and south—all aimed toward the blazing ship in the center.

This was part of their plan. Had the people on board consented? And how many more causalities before this nightmare ended?

We need to save that ship.

SIXTY

The diffuser sputtered and coughed, spitting out clouds of antidote in spurts until nothing but air hissed out, other than the pink liquid dripping from the nozzle. We gave the contraption a shake, then laid it inside the window.

"I'm going with Sakki to that ship," I said.

Ruuta sighed. "I trust I cannot convince you to reconsider."

If Colleen wants to save those people, Colleen must follow Sakki—now.

Sakki bolted out the door in cat form. I chased him back to my room to the nearest balcony, Ruuta close behind. The halls were empty, but I couldn't concern myself with where the others were. The people on the fiery ship didn't have long.

We hopped onto the balcony where Sakki shifted into his dragon form. I grasped one of the spines on his back to pull myself up, but it was soft and folded under my grip. I shifted my grip to the base of the spine and pulled myself up that way.

This was crazy. I was going to die.

"Here!" Ruuta ran from my room with a sheet. She wound it around to form a crude rope. "Use this to tie yourself to Sakki."

"Thank you!" I wrapped the sheet around myself, forming a pouch to hold me, then tossed the ends to Ruuta who tied them around Sakki's neck. I tugged. *How's that? Is it choking you?*

No. Sakki is good.

I situated myself between two perfectly spaced spines. They seemed to help keep me in place without poking me. Still, Sakki shimmied to keep me from slipping.

I hugged his neck. *I'm ready.*

He leaped into the sky and rounded the castle to the west side. What would the defenders do now? Would they shoot us down? The memory of him falling to the ground when he sheltered us from the storm shivered through me. But this time, I envisioned both of us falling into the crowd, peppered with arrows. I shuddered.

Please, keep us hidden.

We flew toward the burning ship. It looked similar to our sea ships in Ariboslia—a great wooden thing with many masts and large copper globes. Unlike balloons, the globes seemed solid, attached to the ship's rail from below by a long copper tube. The stern was aflame.

The crew paid no attention to us as we landed near the bow. They scurried along the rigging like spiders in a web, tying and untying ropes. A team on the deck held a hose and sprayed the flames, keeping them from spreading. For now.

I stepped in front of a crewman to ask how we might help. But he ran straight into me without slowing, knocking me backward. I fell onto my rear, catching my fall on my right hand. Something pinched. Probably a splinter.

The crewman did a double take at me on the floor. "What in Betören?" Rather than stop to speak to us, he shook his head and continued on his hurried way.

Apparently, my shield worked.

The hose blasting the flames stuttered until only a drip escaped the nozzle.

"Attach the hoses to the auxiliary tank!" a man shouted. Probably the captain based on his attire and commanding shouts.

I raced over to him. "Turn the ship out to the sea!"

"Princess?" He barked more orders to his crew before returning part of his attention to me. "Not possible. There's no wind, and our navigation system is out."

"Then I'll have my dragon turn it around. Get me some rope."

He flinched and sidestepped as if just noticing the giant beast on his ship. "We have to put this fire out, or people will die."

"We can save everyone."

"With all respect, Princess, if we don't extinguish this fire before it reaches the levitation system, we and everyone beneath us will die."

"Can you spare one man to gather rope and tie up my dragon? We'll turn the ship while you fight the fire."

He stared at me and grasped the collar of a young crew member as he darted past, yanking him off his feet. "Gather enough spare rope to tie the dragon to the bow."

The boy's eyes narrowed like he wanted to question the captain, then thought better of it. He saluted and dashed off in the opposite direction.

"Now, if you'll excuse me." The captain shouted more orders as his men connected a hose to the reserve tank and a fresh stream of water pushed back the flames.

The boy returned with a thick rope in tow, scanning the area. "Where's the dragon?"

"You don't see him? He's standing right in front of you." Now that I wanted people to see him, he was still hidden? How did I turn this thing off?

The boy fell backward and crab-walked away. His gaze climbed from Sakki's chest up to his head as his Adam's apple made an exaggerated bob.

"Guess you see him now. Help me tie him to the bow."

The boy scurried to his feet.

We lassoed the ropes around Sakki's neck and to each side of the bow. The boy tied expert knots in record time.

"Ready!" he yelled.

Sakki took to the sky, sending great gusts of wind as he flapped. He flew out to the front of the ship, pulling the rope taut. Nothing seemed to happen as he strained against the ropes. But staring at the distant castle, I could see we were inching out over the sea.

Several whoops sounded as crew members realized it too.

A deafening crack like thunder shot from the stern, and the ship jerked, angling down toward the stern. I slid and reached for the rope along the rail as gravity carried me along. When I snagged the rope, it burned as my hand slipped. I fought the urge to let it go, worsening the burn before getting a firm grip. Others slipped along the deck and flailed for anything to stop their descent.

"Aft levitation is out!" someone yelled.

"We're dragging!"

A chunk of the stern's portside was gone. The copper sphere on that side had broken and dangled at a precarious angle. With a loud groan, the sphere disconnected and tumbled to earth. From this high up, I couldn't tell where it might land or hear any screams from below.

God, please don't let it hurt anyone.

Sakki kept the ship on course out to sea, but I sensed his struggle. He was tiring. The ship weighed too much. We lurched, and my stomach flipped. Sakki couldn't fly fast enough or pull hard enough to level the ship. He fought, but the ship was too big.

We were falling.

SIXTY-ONE

"Is anyone near the thrusters?" the captain yelled as he dangled from a rope attached to the bow opposite me.

Shouts ran along the crew clinging in various spots down to the stern. A response made its way back up to the captain. "Soini is within reach, sir!"

"Fire them up!"

"But, sir. Soini—"

"Is about to save our hides. Guide him. Someone close should surely be able to do that!"

"Yes, sir! Fire the thrusters!" he yelled.

More shouts traveled the line again.

Thrusters? Would that do what it sounded like? "What about my dragon?" I shouted across the way.

"Tell him to board the ship. Now!"

Sakki! Get on the ship!

My stomach caught in my throat as we plunged. Sakki flailed on his back, his wings rippling in the wind at his sides as the ropes dragged him down with us.

God, please help him!

An engine revving to life and air blasting rang out in the night. The ship surged forward. A mast caught Sakki and pinned him there as the ship rocketed into the sky toward the ocean.

Sakki had set the ship on the right course. The thrusters could buy us time and push us over the ocean. But they soon sputtered and coughed. The ship leveled. There were moments of feeling weightless between surges. Sakki flailed to free himself from the net and take to the sky again, towing the ship with the little power still sputtering from the thrusters.

He flapped with renewed strength. The ship waffled, tipping forward, then back, forward, then back as the thrusters vacillated between life and death. I hefted myself up to peer over the rail. Nothing but darkness. Then I found the castle to the right and behind us.

"We made it!" I whooped. "We're over the sea!"

"We're not out of the woods yet," the captain said. "Tell your dragon to lower us. With any luck, we can land on the sea before we fall into it."

I relayed the message. Sakki didn't respond, but the bow dipped down.

"Not too fast!" the captain yelled.

Sakki was tiring. Memories of his strength failing when he saved us from the hailstorm resurfaced, and my stomach threatened to spit itself out. He had been younger, smaller. But this was a much bigger task.

Please, God. Give him strength.

The thrusters stammered and let out a final cough. The ship lurched, then plummeted. My stomach heaved. The boat slammed into the ocean, sending spray in every direction, soaking everything, and dousing the fire. The shock from the icy water slapping me stole my breath. We bobbed about on the surface before coming to a more stable teeter.

Cheers erupted along the deck as I vomited over the side. Then a different sick feeling overwhelmed me.

Sakki? Sakki! "Sakki!"

A man heard me over the ruckus and got the other's attention. They aimed a searchlight and swept it over the sea.

"Portside!" someone called. "Toward the bow!"

I ran to where the man pointed and crowded the railing with the crew members. Wings splayed out, Sakki floated, belly up. My heart lodged in my throat. *Please, God. Let him be alive.*

The crew worked together, shouting commands that meant little to me, and cast a net. They caught Sakki, then formed a line to tug the rope through the massive pulley system overhead. Every crew member grasped the rope and heaved it over their shoulders to pull Sakki over the rail. I found a spot I fit and helped.

"This dragon saved our hides!" the captain yelled. "Put your muscles into it!"

I could've kissed him.

The ropes burned my already sore hands. Sweat dripped from my brow and down my back as I heaved with the others. Before long, my dragon dangled in the air above the railing. They swung him over the deck.

"Gently now!" the captain shouted.

The rope slipped through my palms in a controlled slide to keep Sakki from falling to the floor. Blisters on my hand tore open, staining the rope red. I gritted my teeth against the pain. I would not let go. I would not let him fall.

When he hovered a cubit or so over the deck, the captain yelled, "Release!"

Sakki thudded from the short distance. I raced to help peel the netting from him. It was a tangled mess. Several men retrieved their knives and cut away the ropes. I elbowed past them, avoiding the blades, to listen to his chest.

Please be alive. Please be alive. Please be alive.

I strained to hear anything through his thick scales. The crew seemed to understand and hushed. Was that a thump? Sure enough. A faint rhythmic thump sounded, then another joined in. His two heartbeats. But was he breathing? I laid my bloodied hands on him, pushing the life within me through my arms, sending tendrils out in search of the life within him. It was there. Weak, but still there. It wasn't too late.

I summoned more of my life force into him and met a feeble wall of resistance. Why would he fight my help? He didn't have the strength to fight me, so I forced my way through. As if a levee broke, the force within me gushed in an uncontrollable torrent. I grew faint.

Sakki's chest made slight movements, and soft puffs of air escaped his snout. His wall of resistance returned, cutting off my energy, sending it recoiling up my arms to where it belonged.

"He's alive!" I gasped, pressing my hands together. I realized my error too late, but the expected sting never came. I inspected my palms. They were still stained red, but my injuries were gone. Had Sakki healed me?

SIXTY-TWO

"We're taking on water!" someone shouted.

More shouts rang back and forth, aviation jargon I couldn't understand. The crew scrambled to plug the hole with sandbags and hoist the sails the fire hadn't destroyed. The ship made horrid groaning sounds as if it couldn't take much more.

I helped carry buckets of water to the edge, slipping in my haste, spilling more than I removed. My clothes, soaked through, weighed me down. I kept stopping to check in on Sakki. As I knelt beside him for the hundredth time, the captain approached.

"How is he?"

My heart softened for this man who'd take time away from saving the ship to check on my dragon. "He seems okay. I just wish he'd wake." The ship lurched, and I caught myself on Sakki. But he didn't stir. "Are we going to sink?"

"The water pressure from the damage aft is pulling us down. But the levitation system is fighting to keep us afloat toward the bow. The opposing forces will tear this ship apart if we don't beach it first. But without your dragon to pull us toward shore, I'm not sure we'll make it in time."

"You want to beach the ship? Isn't that bad?"

"Better to salvage what I can on the beach than lose everything on the bottom of the sea."

"How much time do we have?"

"An hour. Two at most."

I glanced at Sakki sleeping amongst the chaos. How long would it take for him to recover?

I'd already given Sakki some of my energy to restore him. He'd shut me off. Should I fight harder to get past his walls? Would it wake him? There was only one way to know.... I sucked in a breath and summoned my life force once more. Someone gasped over my shoulder as my hands illuminated. I tried to block out everything else to focus on my task. Prickles ran up and down my arms as my energy surged from me through Sakki's scales. He was stronger now—his energy easier to find but more difficult to manipulate. Still, there wasn't enough, even after all his rest. No wonder he still slept.

I reached the wall of resistance. What was causing that? Was part of him awake, aware of what I was doing, and concerned for me? *Let me help you, Sakki. I'll be okay.*

I readjusted myself on my knees and took three deep breaths to prepare to push. Water traveled down my spine as I strained. His barrier broke, and my life force surged forward with frightening speed. The tingling in my arms heightened as Sakki fed. I grew dizzy, and my strength waned.

"Princess!" came a dull voice as if filtered through the ocean.

I slumped beside Sakki, and all went dark.

I LICKED MY LIPS. Salty grit filled my mouth. I spat it out onto the beach. The beach! We'd made it ashore? I jerked my head, searching. Sakki lay mere cubits from me, just out of reach. "Sakki!"

I crawled to him, wet sand grinding into my palms. His eye opened, and he lifted his head. A relieving tide washed through me as

I scratched the scales behind his ear. They felt softer there. "You're awake!"

A rumble rose from deep within. *That feels good.*

What is that? A purr? Dragons purr?

Colleen sighs. Sakki sighs... a long, rumbly sigh.

I gazed at the ship on the beach several cubits away. *What happened?*

Sakki stretched his back legs out behind him. *Captain asked Sakki to beach the ship to save the crew—and Colleen.*

Did I sleep through the whole thing?

Colleen gave Sakki too much energy. Colleen should never do that again.

And Sakki used too much energy guiding the ship. Sakki should never do that again. I huffed, mocking his speech.

He groaned like a teenager tiring of a conversation. *Sakki and Colleen succeeded.*

We did.

We crossed the beach to the ship still surrounded by sea. Crew members littered the shoreline. But not as if they'd washed ashore. It looked as if they'd fallen where they stood. *Did the cure reach them?*

Sakki doesn't know.

We walked amongst them. They were all breathing—alive. They must've inhaled the cure. What else could explain this?

One by one, they woke. Purple auras sparked like an engine attempting to ignite.

What would happen when they woke with their right minds? *Should I run?*

Sakki retreated. *Maybe step back. Behind Sakki.*

The captain stood before me. He removed his hat, clutched it to his chest, then dropped to his knees in the sand. "Your Highness, I'm in your debt."

"My son." An older man glanced about, wincing. He rose to his feet and pointed at me. Reds infiltrated his purple aura as his confusion shifted to anger. "Your father. He took my son. Where's my son?"

Sakki and I took several more retreating steps.

Mumbling arose from the other crew members. So far, they were still confused.

Sakki shoulder-checked me. *Get on Sakki's back.*

Wait. I held out a hand, staying him, and faced the crew. "I know what's happening to you. You're coming out from under Auberon's curse. He made you all believe he was God. I aided in the plot to free you."

Some of the crew resumed murmuring. Others remained silent. Each one was still confused, yet growing angrier and angrier.

The older man continued to move in on me. "How could you allow—"

"Fall in line, mate!" The captain jumped between us. "She is still the princess, next in line for the throne. She and her dragon risked their lives to save your sorry hide. Have some respect."

The man took another step closer. "But her father—"

"As you said, her *father*." The captain waved me toward Sakki. "Go. I'll—"

"Princess!" Iida yelled from atop her horse, galloping across the beach, her steed's hooves spraying sand behind them. "Don't... go... city." She lurched forward at the sudden stop and fought to catch her breath. "Not safe."

"What's not safe?" I asked.

Her horse danced, and the beast's nostrils flared as if all the excitement was too much for her to contain.

"The people. Too much unrest. We must isolate you... until they return to their senses."

That news hit like a punch to my stomach. "The people... want to hurt *me*?" A sob rose in my chest at the injustice. "But I helped restore them. I betrayed my father to help them."

Iida looked at me as if I should know better. She was right. I shouldn't be surprised. We expected the people to be thrown into disarray. They would want someone to blame. And they wouldn't stop at my father. "What if they don't return to their senses?"

"Don't worry about that now. Just fly back. Keep yourselves hidden."

I climbed onto Sakki's back, and we took off for whatever strange new world met us at the castle.

Sixty-Three

All was eerily silent as we flew over the ocean. The skies were typically full of ships and balloons, but not today, even the birds stayed away. I wanted to fly over the city to see what was happening, but I couldn't risk it. Not yet. We needed rest.

How are you holding up?

Sakki's wings catch air. Fly.

Nay, not how—I mean, how are you feeling. Are you tired?

Sakki has rested. Castle is close.

It wasn't until I lay, clutching Sakki, spending energy to keep us hidden, that I realized how exhausted *I* was even after I'd passed out.

Sakki landed on the balcony. My foot caught in the rope, and I slid upside down, dangling a hair above the ground.

Clapping sounded from within my room. "What a graceful dismount."

Liam. My face warmed. Thank goodness I was wearing riding clothes. He helped me to my feet.

"How long have you been waiting for me?" I tugged my jacket into place.

Sakki morphed into cat form and crawled inside.

Liam shrugged. "A few hours? Not too long. Gave me a chance to rest."

"What's happening in the city? Iida said it wasn't safe."

"She's right. I haven't been out there, but I've heard reports of citizens storming government offices and interim housing in search of loved ones who have gone missing or been reported dead with no body. Many are looking to overthrow the government. Others are angry at being 'woken' and want to return to the way things were. Others still are taking advantage of the chaos and looting."

My chest squeezed. It was worse than I could've imagined. "Shouldn't you be out there?" Not that I wanted him risking his life.

Sakki leaped onto the bed, found a suitable spot, and plopped without his usual fanfare of kneading the blanket or spinning in circles.

"Others are handling it. I'm *your* defender. I'm here to protect *you*, and I've been doing a sorry job of it."

"Are we safe here?"

"For now. The Saoirse Trodaí have taken over the castle. Citizens are crying out for your father's blood. And yours. As long as your life is under threat, I'll not leave your side—again."

"Don't make promises you can't keep." I flopped onto the bed. "I knew this wouldn't be good. But I didn't expect it to be this bad. Why do the people want me dead too? I had no part in my father's plans. I helped free them. Aren't the Saors out there telling them that?"

"I've been there, remember? It took you stepping in front of a gun for me and stitching my wound before I realized you're not like your father. And they"—he pointed in a random direction as if all the citizens were clumped together there—"watched you parade about arm-in-arm with your father. They haven't had the opportunity to get to know you as I have." He blew out a frustrated breath. "What's worse are the rumors of a rebel plot within the Saors."

"What kind of plot?"

He clutched his neck. "They want to overthrow the monarchical government."

"Let them. I don't care if I'm queen."

His intense gaze pinned me. "Even if they succeeded, as long as you live, some will consider you a threat."

I shivered. "Will they kill me?"

He lifted my chin to force me to look deep into his ocean eyes. "Not on my watch."

His face was so close. Did he intend to kiss me?

The door burst open, and we jumped apart.

"Oh, thank Zorac, you've returned." Ruuta didn't seem to notice how close Liam and I were as she crossed the room and hugged me. She latched onto my shoulders and shook me as she spoke. "A rebel group of Saors schemes to overthrow the government."

I peeled myself from her grip and backed away as if her presence clouded my mind. I needed to think. I pressed my fingers to my temples. "Will they succeed?"

A storm cloud darkened her face. "That would be a grave mistake. If they value this city and their lives, they'll seek to appease Queen Rhiannon. Only she can provide the keino this city requires. And if any harm should come to you at their hands..." She clicked her tongue. "Queen Rhiannon will not only cease all trade but also be out for blood."

She squeezed my hand and gave me a reassuring smile. "I've arranged for a call with Queen Rhiannon. Rest for now. We may need to flee yet."

Liam moved toward the door. "I'll be just outside. Shout if you need me."

I dropped onto the bed beside Sakki and fell into a merciful sleep.

I DREAMT I was hiding under the table in the small house in Bandia. My brothers and sisters weren't with me, but I wasn't worried. They were safe. Somehow, I knew. Instead, Sakki's cat form curled up in my lap. My hand rested on his back, but I kept it still, fighting the urge to pet him for fear he'd purr and give us away. We had to stay hidden. I couldn't let the fasgadair get him. But nay, it wasn't the fasgadair we hid from but angry, mindless humans. They ran through the town with wireless electric torches, hunting us. They were nearly upon us....

A knock sounded at the door.

They found us. I hugged Sakki close.

Knock. Knock.

Why were they knocking? Why not break the door down?

Bam! Bam! Bam!

Reality settled in as I woke. Someone was banging on my door. That wasn't my dream? "Who is it?" My voice squeaked out as Sakki squirmed from my grip.

The door opened, and Iida peeked inside. "It's me, Princess. May I enter?"

"Of course." I sat up and rubbed my eyes.

Sakki's grumpy face looked at me through squinted eyes. He readjusted himself away from me and went back to sleep.

"Where's Liam?" So much for not leaving my side.

"He's guarding the hall. He's locked all your doors and windows."

"And Ruuta?"

"She's meeting with Queen Rhiannon on the teleview in your father's quarters. She'll return soon." Iida riffled through my clothes.

"What is the appropriate attire for the fall of a kingdom?" I asked.

She groaned and pulled out my riding gear. "Best to be ready to fly." Yellow flashes intermixed her otherwise solemn glow.

I took the bundle and ducked behind the screen to change from my soiled clothes. Riding gear would become my regular attire.

"What happened while I slept? Did I miss anything?"

She sighed. "Your father—he's in a holding cell awaiting execution."

I flopped on the bench, and my breath left me in a whoosh. My empty stomach squeezed as a wave of nausea passed through me.

God had judged him. I knew he was going to die before midnight tonight. He deserved to die for his crimes. And yet... "They're going to kill him without a trial?"

"The Saoirse Trodaí have determined there is enough evidence to convict him, and execution is the only fitting punishment for such crimes against the entire population. They're blaming him for the genocide of the elves as well."

"How can they do that?"

"What difference does it make? He'll die either way."

"What difference—" I took a deep breath. "*Someone* killed the elves and blamed it on my father. It wasn't him. If they blame it on him without trial, no one will ever look for the actual murderer."

"There will be no trial, Princess. You heard God's message through Sakki."

I plunked on the bench and tugged on my boots. "What's to become of me?"

"That will take more deliberation." She was straightening my bedding when I emerged. She grasped a pillow and fluffed it before putting it in place. "There is an outcry from many of the citizens for your blood. The sins of the father and all... They don't trust you."

"But he manipulated me too!"

She splayed a hand as if to stay me from losing control. "Not everyone sees it that way. And those who do are being unreasonable. They're emotional. Which is why the Saoirse Trodaí refuse to visit the issue at this time. They know you're on their side and helped their cause. And others, such as the captain from the ship you rescued, insist we should crown you queen."

"Queen?" I wanted to go home now more than ever. I slumped onto the bed, one hand wrinkling the bedcover she'd just smoothed. "You should find someone else to lead. Why not Valtteri?"

"Not everyone trusts the Saoirse Trodaí. Many are angry over being freed and the destruction of their city. They want their lives back."

"Creeping crabs, they *prefer* to be under mind control?" I clutched my head in my hands. "What have I done?"

"You did what God called you to do. No one said it would be easy. Or pretty." Iida sat and placed a hand on mine.

The weight of all that had happened and was happening still took me aback. I flopped and stared at the tree my father had planted in my room. This was real. He had mere hours left before they snuffed out his life and he suffered without God for all eternity.

A sudden desire—nay, a *need*—gripped me. I had to get to my father before he died. He'd die for his crimes, but a chance remained to save his soul. "Can I see him?"

She looked at me as if I'd asked her to steal a child's lollipop. "How can you ask such a thing? Do you understand how risky that would be?"

"Can't the Saoirse Trodaí accompany me? Or what if I fly there with Sakki?"

"No. Promise me you won't take off with Iisakki. There's no sneaking past the Saors guarding him. Some believe in you as the future queen. Many don't. But all agree Auberon must die. If you even *appear* to be on your father's side, there's no telling what they might do. Even those on your side might turn against you."

Okay. Good arguments. "How then? I have to see him."

"Our only hope is that people will come to their senses. We need to keep this city running. That requires keino and fae magic. Like it or not, we need the fae. So, right now, Queen Rhiannon is our only hope. Let's wait to hear what Ruuta says. Okay?"

I nodded, but my hands fisted. Regardless of what Ruuta or Rhiannon said, I *would* find a way to my father. The people wouldn't see reason before his death sentence. His current life didn't depend on it, but his eternity did. He might have a chance.

Sixty-Four

I was eating breakfast in my birdcage when Ruuta returned. My meal nearly toppled in my haste to get to her. "What's happened? What did Rhiannon say?"

Ruuta forced a smile, but her dull aura and the bags under her eyes betrayed her. She joined me in my cage and patted the seat beside her.

Too fidgety to sit, I perched on the edge of the seat, wringing my hands.

"This was nothing Queen Rhiannon didn't expect. The people will come to understand the reality of their situation and make you their queen. She's threatened to withhold their goods to force their hand. Her only concern is the rebel group plotting to overthrow the existing monarchy to form a democracy."

"They should," I said.

Ruuta gaped in a rare loss of words.

"Why shouldn't they form a democracy? I never wanted to be queen. Why does Rhiannon care? She doesn't know me. She didn't consult with me. She consulted with you. Maybe she should make *you* queen."

"That's absurd. I've no royal blood."

"Royal blood." I scoffed. "How does my lineage qualify me to rule humans in a foreign world? And why does Queen Rhiannon care? What's her part in all this?"

"She's your aunt. A descendant of Zorac. She seeks to unite the kingdoms without Rotko—the Divide—separating them."

"How will making me queen help?"

"Do you not know?" Her gaze darted back and forth, trying to look at both of my eyes at once.

"Nay."

"It is said that once descendants of Zorac occupy the thrones of both kingdoms, the cursed land that divides them will fall."

Why hadn't she told me this before? "Who is Zorac?"

"He's—"

But I held up my hand. "Are you with me to see some prophecy fulfilled?"

Ruuta turned, her knee bumping into mine as she grasped my hands in hers, gripping them tight. She leaned close, her wide eyes imploring. "I'm here for many reasons. But as I'd hoped, I see in you a true friend—a ruler worthy of any sacrifice I might make. I am here for *you*. Do I want to watch Rotko fall? Of course. I want our kingdoms united. Seelie Clós is my first home, but Talamh Sí is my new home. And I care for you, Eerika. I will do whatever it takes to prove that to you."

A dull ache settled in my head as I tried to consider all she'd ever done. Ever said. How much I could trust her? Those were strong words from someone I'd only just met. She worked for Queen Rhiannon, a stranger. And she admitted ulterior motives for helping me. Something that shouldn't surprise me given the nature of our relationship. She wasn't a friend for any reason I could understand. And somehow, I doubted she'd help me get to my father. She never professed faith in God, so she'd never understand my reasons for wanting to visit him. If I told her, she might try to stop me.

But she was a fae. Fae can't lie.

Unless *that* was a lie.

But, if I trusted her with this, I'd find out if she was trustworthy or not. What did I have to lose? "Help me break into the Atonement Center."

She discarded my hands as if noticing a contagious infection. "Why would you do that?"

"My father is about to die. He will be forever separated from God if I can't get him to see the truth and return to Him before it's too late."

"You realize how that will appear? That you sided with your father all the while and make troublesome work of securing the throne."

"If God wants me to be queen, I will be. Nothing even I can do could thwart it."

"I don't believe in this God you speak of."

"That's why I didn't want to tell you."

She steepled her fingers, pressed them to her lips, and closed her eyes. If I hadn't known better, I'd think she was praying. She moved in close, her eyes flicking back and forth, then looked into mine. "If I help you with this, will you trust me?"

I nodded. "Aye."

"Very well." She stood and stretched. "I'll see who we can gather for our cause."

I PACED my room between the birdcage and the balcony. Shouts rang from outside. *What's happening out there?*

Does Colleen want Sakki to investigate?

Nay, I don't want you to get hurt. Let's wait. I resumed pacing. *What is taking them so long?*

The door barged open, and Liam jumped inside, pushing me across the room to the balcony doors. "You need to leave!"

An old man appeared in the doorway.

"Valtteri?" I latched onto the doorjamb, preventing Liam from shoving me through.

Valtteri looked behind him down the hall. "Take your dragon and fly away from here."

"I don't understand. What's happened?"

"A rebel group has turned on us. We'll cover you, but you must go!"

"Where are the others? I can't leave without them!"

Sakki leaped off the bed and morphed into dragon form.

Liam pried my fingers loose. "They're using the intercom system to divert the defenders. They'll sneak out to meet you at the hideout. But you must leave now."

Footsteps sounded in the hall. Valtteri whirled. A shot rang out. He went limp and slumped to the ground.

Did they—? "N–n–n–n—" I stared at Valtteri's fallen, unmoving body. Something in my spirit broke. "Nay!"

"Get her out of here!" Liam pushed me through the door.

Sakki pulled at my collar, lifting me. My mind snapped to reality as he lowered me onto the balcony. I spun around to Liam. "Nay! Not without you!"

Liam glanced at the closed door as if trying to determine whether he should stay and help. Then he slammed the doors shut as I climbed onto Sakki. I gripped a spine as Liam climbed up behind me and hugged my waist. The footfalls and shouts grew closer.

Please hide us. Please hide us. Please hide us.

I sensed the energy in the air and wrapped it around us. I'd found the way to construct a veil, but much of it was still a mystery. And it seemed like something that required God's help. I couldn't do it alone. So, I continued to pray as Sakki took to the sky. Armed men who looked like the Saoirse Trodaí funneled from my room onto the balcony, searching high and low.

They don't see us. It worked!

Good. Sakki is taking Colleen and Liam to the hideout?

"Is the hideout safe?" I asked Liam, but he didn't respond. The wind was too loud. I tried turning to speak to him, but we both shifted. The ground was so, so far down. My heart leaped into my throat, and my feet tingled as every overexcited molecule in my body beheld the reality of a fall from such a height. This was the first time flying without a rope... and with another passenger. Liam's arms comforted me as if they somehow secured me to Sakki. But they didn't. Nothing was holding us to him. I clutched Sakki's spine in my hands and squeezed my legs to grip his back with everything that I had.

I can't talk to Liam. I don't know if the hideout is safe, but Liam said the others plan to meet us there. I can only hope there isn't an ambush awaiting us.

Sixty-Five

Sakki landed in the field between the cottage and the barn. Something seemed... off. It might've been in my head, but I kept us hidden as we dismounted. Liam released me, and we slid down Sakki's back. My legs wobbled when I landed. My hands were cramped from my precarious grip. Before we took to the skies again, we needed some kind of saddle. And reins. Something to secure us to him. Even the sheet was better than nothing.

"I hoped you'd come here," Reko said.

I jumped and spun. Where'd he come from? Was I no longer hiding us?

"I can't see you." His gaze came close but never landed on us as if to prove his point. "But I know you're there. If you want to hide, don't land in tall grass."

I looked about at the trampled grass at our feet. Creeping crabs, why hadn't I thought of that?

Liam sidled up to Reko as I released the energy surrounding us. "I thought you were at the castle."

He startled at the sight of Liam. "The Petturi have taken it over.

Once we learned of the rebel group among us, we feared you were in danger and hoped you'd escape. We're here to help."

My gaze darted past him toward the barn, then the cottage, expecting someone to attack as Valtteri's falling form invaded my mind. My heart jammed in my throat. "Is anyone else here?"

Reko motioned to the cottage. "Taneli and Pirkko are inside."

"Good." My tense shoulders inched down from around my neck. What a relief to have them on my side. "Ruuta and Rhys will be here soon, I hope. I'd hate to go to the Atonement building without them."

Reko gripped my arm as I turned back to Sakki. "What did you say?"

Oops. Had I said that last part about the Atonement Center aloud? "I need to see my father."

He pulled me closer. Something dangerous flashed in his hard brown eyes. "Have you lost all sense?"

Liam seized Reko's wrist to make him unhand me.

Reko's head jerked back and forth between us, staring at us as if we'd both sprouted antlers. "This isn't a game. They will *kill* you, Colleen."

"Why wait. Let's kill her now."

I jolted toward the familiar voice.

Taneli stood with a pistol in hand, aimed at a frightened Pirkko in his grip. Nay. This couldn't be happening. He was a friend.

Liam yanked me back and placed himself between me and the lunatic holding his friend at gunpoint.

"Taneli?" Reko spoke and stared as if he didn't recognize his friend.

Liam's hand snuck toward the holster beneath his coat.

"Don't think so, Defender. If you don't want anyone to get hurt, throw your weapon."

Liam reached into his coat.

"Slowly." Taneli adjusted his grip on Pirkko and his gun.

Liam retrieved the weapon, letting it dangle between pinched fingers to show Taneli how useless it was before flinging it to the ground.

"You're one of *them*?" Reko asked.

"The Petturi? Yes."

"Why?" Reko held one hand up as if in surrender while the other, shielded from Taneli's view by Liam, groped about his waistline under the back of his jacket.

"Because they're the only ones with any sense. What do you expect to happen if we hand the kingdom over to another self-centered monarchist?"

"She helped us remove the curse." Reko's fingers sought what he was after. His hand rested there, ready to wield his weapon.

"She's not her father," Pirkko said.

Taneli pressed the gun into Pirkko's side, and she winced. "She will crush us as her father did. As every dictator does."

I rounded Liam. "Let her go."

"Okay." Taneli shoved Pirkko into Liam and trained the gun on me. "You're the only one who needs to die."

Pirkko dove between us, her hand lifted as if it could stop a bullet. "How can you say that? We're friends." Her voice cracked. "We're *all* friends."

"I don't want to kill you, Pirkko." The nose of his pistol waffled. "I only want to end Auberon's line."

A presence rose behind me, bathing me in its shadow—Sakki in all his dragon glory. Taneli's gaze rose to Sakki's head in the sky. A blast of fire shot over our heads, ruffling my hair with warm air, singeing the top of Taneli's cap.

Taneli's eyes stretched to impossible lengths as he touched his hair. Once he realized he wasn't on fire, his black aura blazed red along with his face. His green eyes erupted into fierce flames. "You've seen her. She's only wanted to go home since she arrived. She has no interest in us or in improving the kingdom. She only cares about herself. She's selfish. Like her father."

"Then let her go home!" Pirkko cried. "Don't kill her!"

"Would you like that, Princess?" Taneli sneered. "Would you like to go home?"

"I c–can't. Not yet."

"Oh?" He scoffed. "And why not?"

If I told him, he'd kill me.

"Well? Why do you want to stay?"

Tell him.

That wasn't Sakki. Or me. God?

You want me to tell him?

No.

That was Sakki, not God this time. *Not you, Sakki. God.*

If Colleen speaks to God, Colleen should address God so Sakki knows.

Taneli stepped forward, waving the gun. "Do you want to die? Answer me!"

It must've been God. And He knew best. I took a deep breath. "I–I need to see my father before he dies."

"Pah!" Taneli waggled his head at the others. "What did I tell ya? He got to her." His face grew stern, and he shouldered Pirkko out of his way to train the gun at my head. "She needs to die. Auberon's line ends now."

"No!" Pirkko sprinted into Taneli, pushing him aside.

Reko drew his weapon.

Two deafening shots rang out, and I froze. A loud buzz filled my left ear, muffling all other sounds. Was I hit? Where? I felt nothing. Was this what it was like to be shot? Had my entire body gone numb? I looked for the bloody wound but found nothing.

Shouts and cries rose above the muffled buzzing.

Liam had Taneli pinned to the ground as Reko ran to Pirkko's fallen body.

Nay. Nay, nay, nay... Not Pirkko. Not another. I walked toward them like a mindless automaton. Reko's crimson hands pressed on a bubbling wound in Pirkko's chest as she blubbered incomprehensible words. I fell to my knees at their side as the life left Pirkko's eyes. A sob lodged in my throat.

Liam dropped beside us. "Taneli's dead."

I draped my arm over Reko's shoulder. The second I made contact, the tears loosened. I pulled him away from Pirkko's body, and we wept into one another's shoulders.

Liam enveloped both of us as Sakki weaved his little cat body between us. I wiped my eyes and picked him up, snuggling him into my wet shoulder.

Sakki, why didn't you do something?

God told Sakki to stay still.

How can you hear me talk to God, but I can't hear you?

Colleen should. Past elves could hear dragons.

Is it because I'm not a full elf? Does the fae part inhibit me somehow?

There's something in Colleen that shouldn't be there. Sakki can feel it. Whatever that thing is, it must be blocking Colleen from God and Sakki's connection to God. Colleen's fae blood is the most likely explanation. No fae has bonded with a dragon before Colleen.

My wounded heart couldn't handle this. I looked at Pirkko, smoothed her wild hair back from her face, and closed her eyes.

Did Pirkko know God?

Sakki doesn't know.

Then there was Taneli. He might've turned on us, but he was still a friend. I cared about him too. The invisible shard in my heart went deeper and twisted. It was so unfair. Pirkko stayed loyal to the end. Taneli didn't. But their opinions and actions didn't matter in the end. Only their belief—or lack of belief—in God. What had they believed? Where were they? In heaven? Or would they be separated from God for eternity?

"If only I'd known..." My tears started afresh.

"Known what?" Liam asked.

"That this day would be their last." My heart couldn't take this. "Valtteri too."

"Valtteri's dead?" Reko choked.

I buried my face in my hands. So much death... "I need to get to my father."

"Wait for the others." Liam focused all the power his ocean eyes held on me. "There's no talking you out of going, but please wait. Don't try to get in that place on your own. They will catch you and execute you with your father."

"Fine. But I'm leaving when the sun sets no matter what."

"Don't be like your father who cut his own time short by failing to trust God. God said he would die before the clock struck midnight. I'm betting that means he'll die within seconds before that."

I studied him. If only I could see a person's heart, to know if they believed or had the capacity to believe in God. "From the way you talk, one might think you were a believer."

He massaged his neck. "Yeah, well. After watching Sakki turn into King Eerikki and you relaying that message... if Auberon dies before midnight, it'll be tough not to believe."

Somehow, after everything I'd been through and all I was about to face, that was what I needed to hear... the only thing that could put a smile on my face... almost.

God, help me do what my father failed to do. Help me wait for Your timing. You're the one who seems to want me to go, so help me trust You to get me there in time.

SIXTY-SIX

By the time we finished burying Pirkko and Taneli, the sun hovered below the western tree line, taunting me.

Sakki craned his neck. *I hear horses.*

"Sakki hears horses." I brushed the dirt from my hands.

Liam snagged his gun. "Stay behind me."

Reko readied his weapon too. I barely breathed as I followed them along the barn. Is this how it would be now? Would everyone we came upon be a potential threat from now on? My circle of friends was dwindling.

Liam peered around the corner to the field between the barn and the cottage. He visibly relaxed and holstered his weapon, then smiled and waved us out into the open as Rhys, Ruuta, and Iida rounded the corner of the cottage.

I staggered to them. "You made it."

"We could use a little watering." Ruuta dismounted, slid her hooded cloak from her head, fluffed her hair, and smoothed her gloves.

"Of course." Reko headed to the well with more life in his step.

Having someone else to help probably eased some of his sorrow, but Ruuta must've sensed our grief. Her fingers stilled in rearranging herself. "What have I missed?"

"Pirkko and Taneli are... dead." I shivered at the finality of that last word.

The glamor marking her face shifted, then returned to its proper place. "How?"

"Taneli was a rebel"—Liam waved toward the graves—"a Petturi."

Black infiltrated Ruuta's aura. "I was afraid of this. I must insist you escape this place to Seelie Clós. I can't risk anything happening to you before order is restored."

Of all the auras I'd ever seen, all had some level of black much of the time. Though my time with Ruuta had been short, we'd been through a lot. I'd been afraid through most of it. But not her. Her lack of fear both awed me and bolstered me. But to see black there now... things must be dire.

"Who is going to restore Talamh Sí if she leaves?" Reko widened his stance and crossed his arms.

"Order will be restored once the humans realize they can't survive without the fae... however long it takes." The black in her aura faded.

But I raised my chin, took a step forward. "The only place I'm going right now is to my father."

She eyed me, then Liam, jabbing a thumb my way. "She's a stubborn one."

"On that, we can agree." He dragged a hand down his face.

Her face turned serious. "Before we storm Auberon's cell, we need a plan. Let's eat and allow the horses to rest a spell. If we're to travel to Seelie Clós, it might be the last meal we eat for a while."

We sat at the kitchen table, still teary-eyed after swapping stories about Valtteri, Pirkko, and Taneli before our talk turned to plans to get to my father.

"We've gotten in and out of there before," I reminded them.

Reko straightened in his chair, his stern countenance pinching tighter. "Do you have any idea how many Saors are guarding that place?"

Rhys morphed into a defender form. How did his clothes change too? "Hide behind the veil. I'll get you inside, to be sure. With no suspicious doors seeming to open of their own will."

Reko scoffed and waved the suggestion away as Rhys returned to his boy shape. "It's not that simple. The Saoirse Trodaí have taken over. They won't allow just any defender inside. Some will be Petturi. As we learned with Taneli, we don't know which ones they are. They will shoot without questioning you."

Ruuta grasped her stone pendant. "I'll compel them."

"All of them?" Liam arched a dark brow. "At the same time?"

"One at a time."

"This is foolish." He rubbed between his eyes. "We should flee while we have the chance."

"I agree." Reko slapped the table.

Iida nodded.

Their lack of faith frustrated me. "Am I the only one in this entire realm who believes in God?"

"I am another." Rhys straightened and inclined his head to me. "I will help you, to be sure."

"Thank you, Rhys." I squeezed his shoulder and threw him an appreciative smile before turning to Liam.

"Oh, stop looking at me with those pitiful eyes." Liam waved me away. "You're going through with your ludicrous plan regardless of reason."

"And you're *not* going alone." Ruuta jabbed a gloved finger my way.

"Let's be away then." Rhys hopped from his chair. "The Atonement Center isn't far off in the north woods."

I stood as well, though my aching muscles protested any movement. "Will it take long?"

"About an hour on horseback." Reko leaned back in his chair, lifting the front legs and folding his hands across his stomach again. "I'll stay behind and cover for you should any Saors come looking for you."

"What about Taneli and Pirkko?" I waved toward the graves outside. "How will ye explain what happened to them?"

The chair legs slammed the floor as Reko grimaced. "Don't you worry about that. Leave it to me."

"What time is it?" The ticking clocks that permeated the air in the castle seemed to fill the air here, though there were no clocks to be found. The windows were all covered.

Liam pulled up his sleeve to check his watch. "A little after eight. We have time."

I strode for the door. "We can't foresee what will delay us or when he will die. No more delays. We need to go. Now."

We hurried to saddle our horses and ride out. Only three and a half hours before midnight. Fire ants tunneled through my veins, biting as they scampered along, urging me to move faster.

We moved slowly. Too slowly. Rhys led us through dense trees with little moonlight filtering in to guide us. Twigs poked and prodded us as we pushed passed the thick brush single file with me sandwiched between Liam and Ruuta and Iida trailing behind. I kept creeping up too close to Liam's horse. As much as I wanted to dart through the woods, I didn't know the way, and I didn't want Clover to get smacked with branches. So I forced myself to back away as Sakki snoozed behind me on Clover's rear. Must be nice to morph into a cat, curl up, and sleep your cares away.

Time dragged on as we trudged forth. I was tired, and my head drooped. Clover shimmied beneath me, and I snapped to attention. I tightened my grip on the reins and rolled my aching shoulders. How much time had passed? Was it past midnight already? Were we too late?

A dark tower with a needlelike spire pierced the moonlit sky like a lighthouse from the sea on a stormy night. The Atonement building. At last. The anxious fire within me subsided as if slathered with a healing balm. But a new flame ignited.

"What time is it?"

Liam retrieved his flameless torch and checked his timepiece. "Quarter of ten."

We still had time.... I hoped.

Our caravan turned, and we traveled along an iron fence.

"What do we do now? Fly over it?"

"There are breaks in the fence." Rhys led us a short distance along the fence, stopping at a broken section. "Tie the horses. We'll go on foot from here."

"Someone should stay with the horses." Liam slid from Nessa's back.

"Iida and Sakki can stay." I wrapped Clover's reins to the iron grate.

Sakki is staying with Colleen. He huffed, and twin swirls of smoke curled from his nostrils in the moonlight.

Why? Does God want you to?

God doesn't tell Sakki everything. But Sakki must stay with Colleen.

Fine. "Sakki's coming too."

Rhys led us along the fence to a spot where rusted spires dangled from the rail. Others had fallen, leaving wide enough gaps to push through. Ruuta lifted her cloak over her head to protect herself from the iron as she squeezed past the break.

Once we were all inside, we dashed like gazelles along the woods, stopping behind the trees at the edge to inspect the building. Sakki morphed into his cat form.

God, hide us.

"Are we hidden?" Rhys asked.

"Aye, I think so." I wished I could better understand my ability. The more I used it, the more I sensed the invisible blanket of energy surrounding us. But I struggled to control it, especially when there was distance between everyone. And what would happen if someone stepped between me and those I tried to hide?

"Why can I see you?"

I shrugged. "Because we're all hidden together?"

He twisted his lips and scrunched his nose.

Liam pointed at each of us. "No talking from here on out, understood?"

We agreed and followed Rhys across the well-manicured lawn. I kept praying as we neared the door.

Two men stood outside the building beside the door. Saors. Lacking uniforms, they dressed like Taneli and Reko. Anxious auras surrounded them. Ruuta fiddled with her stone as she approached. She grasped one and stared into his eyes. "You will allow me passage and forget I was here."

The Saor in her clutches leaped, yanked his arm free, and slapped at it as if she still held on.

The second Saor watched his mate. From his perspective, his friend must've appeared to be suffering from a crazed fit. His hand fumbled with the holster inside his coat. "What's happening?"

"They can't see me," she spoke in a hushed, urgent voice. "They need to see me."

The first Saor groped about, closing in on her. "Who's there?"

She jumped out of his reach.

God, let them see Ruuta and Ruuta alone. I tore at the air surrounding her and restitched it behind her.

"Ha!" The man snatched Ruuta's shoulder.

She latched onto his arm while holding her stone. "Unhand me."

The first Saor released his grip, but the other raised his weapon— a pistol.

"Watch out!" I yelled.

The man with the gun flinched, snapping his attention my way as

Liam smacked the weapon away. As the gun skittered along the paved path, the Soar gripped his hand. His aura blazed, and his expression twisted to match as he searched for his invisible attacker.

Ruuta grabbed him as Liam retrieved the discarded weapon. "You will allow me to pass, now and when I return, and forget I was here."

"Forget you were here..."

The first guard reached for her. "What are you—?"

She locked onto him and said the same thing.

We left the Saors in their trance and entered the building, but more Saors moved about inside.

One drew a weapon and aimed it at Ruuta. "State your purpose."

She walked with confidence straight at him. The others drew their weapons too, wide-eyed at her bold approach.

"Don't come any closer!" His hand holding the weapon shook.

The others circled her, wagging their guns, shouting. My heart thundered. If she could only compel one at a time, how was she going to stand up to three? She was going to get shot. *Please, God, keep her safe.*

Liam lunged forward, stretching the veil without realizing it, and kicked the weapon from one Saor, then leaped and tackled another. They tumbled to the ground. Black surrounded the untouched Soar as he retreated, shaking. Rhys dove from behind, sweeping his legs out from underneath him. The Saor went airborne, firing wild shots as he fell onto his back. His breath escaped in a whoosh when he landed and smacked his head on the tile.

I cringed—both at the painful landing and the gunshots. More defenders were sure to respond. I yelled to Ruuta. "We need to hide!"

The Saor beneath Liam flailed on the ground, shouting. "Something's got me pinned!"

"What kind of witchcraft is this?" The sole Saor still standing thrust the gun barrel at Ruuta.

She grasped his arm. "You will not harm me. You will let me come and go, each time forgetting I was here."

She compelled the other two guards the same way. Somehow, my veil bent and stretched, keeping my friends inside, never breaking, never allowing the Saors to enter.

How had I never sensed it before? It was strong now. Tangible.

Running footsteps approached.

I swallowed Ruuta in my veil and pressed a finger to my lips.

"Against the wall." Liam spoke in a hushed voice, and we all hurried on tiptoes to line up beside him.

Defenders raced past us and spread out—some questioning those Ruuta just compelled and others spilling out the door to inspect the grounds.

We crept along the wall past the auditorium, and I cringed. How many children had I witnessed offer their lives to my father and drink a potion that took away their free will in that place?

We closed in on a Saor standing outside the lift. The man fumbled to retrieve his weapon as Ruuta increased her speed. He freed his gun from his holster. She grabbed his arm and shook it from his grip. "You will not harm us. You will bring us down to the basement and wait for us to return. If anyone questions you, you received orders to keep the elevator on the ground floor. You will forget you saw us."

"I received orders...."

We arrived at the basement and hurried through the dreary auditorium where my father ran private trials. It was empty and dark.

Liam peeked through the window into the hallway with the cells. He bent and held a finger to his lips. With his other hand, he held up two fingers and motioned for us to follow as he opened the door and ran straight into the Saors guarding my father's cell.

SIXTY-SEVEN

Ruuta compelled these Saors as she had the others. Under her spell, one Saor unlocked my father's cell while the other kept watch for us. I pushed past him and rushed to my father sitting on the stuffed chair, looking regal as ever despite the lack of a crown.

He bolted from his chair. "Who's there?"

Oops. I lowered the veil around me. "It's me."

"Eerika?" His eyes so like mine widened, then narrowed. "What. Are *you*. Doing here?"

"I had to see you."

When I stepped closer, he backed away, then sat on the edge of his chair. "Why? You betrayed me. You conspired with my enemy. Whatever happens to me now is all on you."

He might as well have stabbed me in the heart. I wavered on my feet as the room began to spin. How could he blame me for everything he'd done? Would he never see his error? Was there no hope for his soul? Had I made a huge mistake? "I had to t–try."

"Try what?" He snorted, pursing his lips as if preparing to spit.

"To rescue me? You have a change of heart after having me locked up?"

Ouch. That stung. But he couldn't understand the rescue I had in mind and how it was so much more important than anything else I could do for him. "I'm not—I—"

"Why are you here?"

"I did... come to save you. But not in the way you think."

"You mean in a reconciled-with-the-real-God way?"

"You already know?"

He shook his head as if wondering how he'd gone so wrong with me. "Do you know how many times you gave me that speech?"

I searched my aching head. Snippets of conversation came to mind. Where were those before I came all this way to save him, risking my friends' lives?

Nay, I would not let doubt enter my mind. I needed to be here, even if I'd tried to talk to him about God hundreds or millions of times before. He was about to die. I had to try one last time. How could I live with myself if I didn't try?

As if he could read my thoughts, he held up a hand. "You should have saved yourself. There's no redemption for me. My crimes against God are unforgivable."

I opened and closed my mouth. I must look like a fish out of water. So he knew? *God, is he beyond saving? Are his crimes unforgivable? Nay, You wouldn't have brought me here if he was beyond hope. Would You? How can I convince him?*

Rhys entered the cell. "Your Majesty..."

"Jaakko?" My father glanced about.

I'd dropped the veil from only me? I felt for the energy still blanketing him and the others and removed it all.

"Your Majesty, you are an elf. Before you sold your soul to Noita, you knew what it was to be close to God. Yes, you've committed terrible crimes. God has judged you for those crimes. But there's still a chance. You can still be redeemed."

My father rushed to Rhys and lifted him by his neck. "I trusted you. You and my daughter, the two closest to me, conspired against me."

"And yet..." Rhys coughed and tried to peel my father's fingers from his neck. His face reddened.

"And yet—What? You're here to *save* me? Do you think that will ease your conscience? What do you know of salvation, Witch's Spawn?" He shook Rhys. "Why should I grovel to God after what He's done? If He was such a good God, why'd He allow the elves to be killed? Why'd He make the people think they died at my command? Why did He take my wife and daughter from me?" Father tossed Rhys onto the ground where he scrambled away, coughing and sputtering. "God turned away from me long ago. He pushed me into making a deal with Noita. He gave me no choice."

Spreading my hands, palms up, I stepped closer. "You always have a choice."

"Is that so?" Father straightened to new heights. His luminescent eyes turned to steel, staring down at me. "You spend a month here, two at most, without your memories intact, and you think you understand more than me?"

"God never left you." Rhys, still sprawled on the floor, hacked, massaging his neck.

Liam entered the cell with Sakki at his heels in cat form. My father watched Sakki.

Tell Auberon God is here. If Auberon repents... if Auberon seeks forgiveness, Auberon will receive it.

I relayed the message.

My father huffed and sputtered in a most unkingly way as his gaze roamed each of us before falling on me. "There's no forgiveness for what I've done."

"You're an elf." I kept my hands spread wide. "You understand the bond a dragon has with God. It's the next best thing to speaking with God directly. Why do you doubt him?"

His face cracked, and he slid from his seat onto the floor. "I'm worse than the devil! Lucifer betrayed God by wanting to be as God. *I made it happen!*"

Liam scoffed. "You're right. You're terrible. You took *everything* from me." His voice shook as he wrung his hands as if preparing for a fight. "I wanted to kill you. But you've done more harm to your daughter than to me. If she can forgive you..." He blew out a breath. "Then I can too. And if I can, I'd think the actual Creator of the universe can too."

Auberon's crimes aren't the same as the devil's. Auberon's crimes are failing to trust God.

I told my father what Sakki said. "He will forgive you *if* you repent."

"Even after all I've done—the deal with Noita, cursing the people, expunging memories, breaking up families, keeping people from heaven—God would forgive me?"

The people are being freed from Auberon's curse. But Auberon is still under Auberon's curse. If Auberon wants to be freed, Auberon must seek God's forgiveness.

"But I'm not. I'm an elf. I can't be cursed."

You are. The moment you made the trade with Noita, you were the first to be cursed.

My father looked at each of us. Then his stoic, unlined face crumpled in a way I wouldn't have thought possible. I dropped to the floor beside him and gathered him into myself as if I might hold him together. "I don't deserve to be forgiven."

As his tears wetted my shoulder, my throat squeezed, and tears sprang to my eyes. "None of us does," I choked.

He pressed his face to the floor and wept. "Forgive me, God. Though I don't deserve Your forgiveness, please, forgive me."

Something heavy lifted. Whatever it was, it had been pressing upon me for so long, I hadn't even realized it was there until it was gone. My father was safe. When he died, he would be reunited with God. I would see him again one day. Hopefully with my mother.

He retrieved a handkerchief from his pocket and dabbed at his eyes, then reached under his collar and tugged a chain free. A ring dangled from it. He slid it over his head and held it out to me. "Take this."

"What it is?" I bowed forward so he could place it over my head.

"It belonged to your mother. I won't need it where I'm going, but you've a long road ahead of you. It's been of great comfort to me. I hope it brings you comfort as well."

I fingered the ring. "My mother wore this?"

He cupped my fingers around it, closing the ring securely in my grasp. "It was too small for my fingers. I always liked having it close to my heart, but you probably don't need the chain."

I liked the idea of wearing it as he did and having something of my mother's close to my heart too—as if the ring somehow connected me to both of them. "I'll wear it like you did."

Smiling, he gathered me into a hug and pressed moist words against the pointy tip of my ear. "Thank you for not giving up on me."

Sixty-Eight

We escaped the Atonement Center and rendezvoused through the break in the fence by the horses.

"You made it!" I couldn't see Iida, but relief laced her voice. "What happened?"

"My father will be in heaven. The king's curse ends now—for all, including Auberon himself." I smiled, patting the ring beneath my neckline, more confident than ever. Never had I felt such... joy. All those years I thought what I wanted was an adventure. But nay. I wanted more than that. Much more. I wanted *purpose*. And not for personal gain. I wanted God to use me for His purpose for His kingdom. Nothing gave me such a lift, as if I were floating. I never imagined God would use someone like me.

But our seeming success was bittersweet. "We removed the curse. The people are now free to choose God, but what of all those who already died under the curse? What about the chaos we've caused?" I deflated somewhat. My feet connected with the earth once again.

If God can use Colleen to bring about God's plans, God can handle the rest too. Colleen mustn't be like Auberon. Colleen must trust God.

Ruuta clamped a gloved hand to my shoulder. "Queen Rhiannon will know what to do."

God knows what to do, Sakki corrected Ruuta. Too bad Ruuta couldn't hear him.

"What's next?" Iida asked.

We travel through the Divide to Queen Rhiannon in Seelie Clós.

"I thought you said God knows what to do, not Queen Rhiannon." I laughed.

Sakki spoke rightly. God knows what to do, not Rhiannon. However, God wants Colleen and friends to go through the Divide to Queen Rhiannon.

I shuddered at the memory of the dismal place. "He *wants* us to go through there, on purpose?" Where was that confidence I'd had moments ago?

Colleen and friends won this battle, but this is just the first of many. Colleen must follow God's plans through to the end to restore peace in Betören.

I relayed Sakki's message, nearly gagging on their bitter aftertaste.

"We've no wards against unseelie magic." Ruuta rubbed her arms as if chasing away shivers. "We never travel through the Divide without proper protection."

I gazed up at the dark sky. "Can we fly above it?"

She shook her head. "No one knows the boundary, neither skyward nor below. Airships are affected too. All bodies on board and the ship itself require wards against whatever magic possesses that dreadful place."

Fear niggled the back of my neck, trying to worm into my mind. But I flicked it away. I needed to savor this win if I had any hopes of surviving the coming trials. As Sakki said, I must trust God. "If God has called us to do it, it can be done."

Ruuta huffed. "Not without great difficulty."

I thought about all I'd been through—traveling to another world, not knowing who to trust, losing my memories... friends. "I imagine it won't be easy. But God has gotten us this far, He will see us through."

A deafening sound blared into the night. I covered my ears and ducked, searching the skies as if they might collapse in on us. "What is that sound?" I yelled, not sure anyone could hear me. I could barely hear myself over the blast.

"The alarm," Liam shouted. "They must realize we were here. We need to move—now!"

We mounted our steeds and dashed through the woods as ships flew overhead, their searchlights sweeping the trees around us.

God, please keep us hidden. Please keep us hidden. Please keep us hidden.

Shameless Request for Reviews

Authors need reviews! They help books get noticed, and I love to know what my readers think of my stories. So, if you enjoyed this book, please consider leaving a review on Amazon, <u>Goodreads</u>, <u>BookBub</u>... anywhere you think a review might be helpful. I'm forever grateful!

You are loved,
J F Rogers

ABOUT THE AUTHOR

J. F. Rogers lives in Southern Maine with her husband, daughter, pets... and an imaginary friend or two. She has a degree in Behavioral Science and teaches a 5th and 6th grade Sunday School class. When she's not entertaining Tuki the Mega Mutt, her constant companion and greatest distraction, she's likely tap, tap, tapping away at her keyboard, praying the words will miraculously align just so. Above all, she's a believer in the One True God and can say with certainty—you are loved.

Connect with J F Rogers

jfrogers.com

amazon.com/J-F-Rogers/e/B01G7N0KSK

bookbub.com/authors/j-f-rogers

facebook.com/jfrogerswrites

goodreads.com/jfrogers

instagram.com/jfrogers925

pinterest.com/jfrogers925

The Darkening Divide is the action-packed prequel
to *The Cursed Lands* Christian fantasy adventure. If you
enjoy mixing up genres with elves and dragons in a
steampunk world infested with humans, download *The
Darkening Divide* today! You'll love this intro to J F Rogers's
exciting new series.

http://jfrogers.com/free-book/

THE CURSED LANDS TRILOGY CONTINUES...

COMING IN SUMMER/FALL 2023!

Aloft

Fallon and Morrigan face off for the ultimate battle ... in their minds.

Alight

Three friends. Evil seeks to corrupt them. If they survive... what will it cost?

Pepin's Tale

Can one small peach make an eternal difference?

STANDALONE NOVELETTE

The Smeraldo Flower

Beauty and the Beast meets the Phantom of the Opera in the Secret

Garden in this standalone novelette. A retelling of the Italian folktale, La Citta di Smeraldo, inspired by BTS's song *The Truth Untold*.

Still looking for more?

Be among the first to know when new books are released.

Join her clan at jfrogers.com/join/

Join the conversation at discord

Acknowledgments

God always comes first. He is the reason I'm here, and the reason I do anything. He inspires and motivates me to good works. Therefore, I must thank Him first and foremost.

My family is always next. My husband and my daughter inspire and encourage me like no one else.

Special thanks to:

- My Realmie critique partners, Damascus Blades - C W Briar, Gina Detwiler, L G McCary, Katherine Massengill, A K Preston, and Tracy Sassaman. I miss you all terribly!
- Dierdre Lockhart with Brilliant Cut Editing. You are amazing, as always. So glad God sent me to you!
- 100 Covers and the infinitely patient Phyllis Ngo.
- My local writer friends who support me in so many ways —Sharon Gamble, Amanda Ovington, and Marlene McKenna. Thanks for keeping me on track.
- Julie Bernier and Sarah Daniels. Thanks for being such amazing friends.
- My beta readers - Angel Cross, Vickie Grider, Carla Great-house, Debbie Harris, Laura Johnson, Brigitte Lehmann, William Long, and Pamela Anne Reinert.

- My street team - Nicole Burns, Dani Coquat, Angel Cross, Sarah Daniels, Steph & Claire Gagne, Angela Grimes, Debbie Harris, Barbara Harrison, Maureen Henn, Bill Long, Pamela Anne Reinert, Mariel Renaud, Sharon Selig, Deb Shaw, Monique Summers, and Lena Karynn Tesla.
- My ARC readers, clan members, family, and friends.
- I have to give a special shout out to my youngest clan member and ARC reader who wants to be a writer one day. She remembers everything! Thank you, Claire Gagne.
- And to my readers. I pray my stories encourage you, strengthen your faith, and remind you that you're not alone and you are loved.

So many people showed up to encourage me along the way in God's perfect timing. I am beyond blessed. Thank you! I love you all!

You are loved,
J F Rogers

www.ingramcontent.com/pod-product-compliance
Lightning Source LLC
Chambersburg PA
CBHW061616210726
48287CB00001B/152